KU-606-630

DEAR AMY

As 'Dear Amy', agony aunt for a local newspaper, Margot Lewis has dealt with all sorts of letters – but never one like this...

Dear Amy,

I've been kidnapped by a strange man. I don't know where I am. Please help me,
Bethan Avery

This must be a cruel hoax. Because Bethan Avery has been missing for nearly two decades. As the present-day search intensifies for another missing schoolgirl, Margot takes the letter to the police. They let Margot in on a little secret that confirms her darkest fears and tangles her up in the search for the sender. It could save one young girl's life and cost Margot her own...

DEAR AMY

by

Helen Callaghan

Magna Large Print Books
Long Preston, North Yorkshire,
BD23 4ND, England.

British Library Cataloguing in Publication Data.

A catalogue record of this book is
available from the British Library

ISBN   978-0-7505-4491-7

First published in Great Britain 2016 by Michael Joseph,
part of the Penguin Random House group of companies.

Copyright © Helen Callaghan, 2016

Cover illustration © Caesart by arrangement with
Shutterstock

The moral right of the author has been asserted

Published in Large Print 2017 by arrangement with
Penguin Random House UK

All rights reserved. No part of this publication may be reproduced,
stored in a retrieval system, or transmitted in any form or by any
means, electronic, mechanical, photocopying, recording or otherwise
without the prior permission of the Copyright owner.

Magna Large Print is an imprint of Library Magna Books Ltd.

Printed and bound in Great Britain by
T.J. (International) Ltd., Cornwall, PL28 8RW

Prologue

Katie Browne is packing.

She gropes under her bed, seizing her blue backpack with the faux leather trim and begins stuffing clothes and toiletries into it with frantic energy, her eyes blinded by tears.

There is very little sense or order in this packing, but that's all right, because it is the act of packing and not the objects themselves – the grey and green leggings, the Union Jack make-up bag puffed up to bursting with all her lip colours, the maroon jersey top with gold stitching that makes her feel so mature and sophisticated – that makes the difference.

Katie is leaving for good this time. She is never coming back. She has had *enough*. She flounces down on the bed, pulling on the pair of shiny red-brown ankle boots that her dad bought her a month ago.

On the window of her little room, the rain taps with increasing insistence, as though urging her to think again.

Nearly tripping over her discarded gym bag with her still-damp swimming kit nestling inside, Katie swings the blue backpack over her shoulder, all the while aware of the hateful murmur of the television downstairs in the living room and its chorus of canned laughter. They've turned the volume up but she is sure she can hear hidden whispering, her mum talking about her to that useless lump Brian. As though he has any right to an opinion.

As though *he* was her dad.

She is not staying here. That's for definite. She's not going to be treated like this in her own house, which has now become Brian's house.

Brian, the big lazy sod, sitting there on the couch with his tattooed guns and loose jeans, like a low-rent Essex Buddha, one arm casually slung around her mother; always hogging the remote for the TV. Brian who thinks he can have an opinion on what she wears, where she goes, how late she stays out.

And her mum just sits there, letting him have his way. 'He works so hard, love. Can you not be a little more respectful?'

Brian can *fuck right off*.

She'll go to her dad. Her *real* dad.

Katie stomps down the stairs while popping her headphones in her ears, but not fast enough to tune out her mother's sharp, 'Where do you think *you* are going?' from behind the closed door of the living room, just before she slams out of the house and walks with brisk purpose down the street.

It's horrible outside. October now, and Cambridge's slow, hazy summer has given way to jet-black nights and sheets of stinging rain, blown at her by a cold wind that whips through her hair and bites the tips of her fingers. Katie pulls up her hood and taps through her phone and Taylor Swift starts singing into her ears; a tiny bright noise.

She strides, nearly running, up the road with its leafy canopy of dark trees, and turns the corner on to Elizabeth Way and its constant roaring traffic.

In her pocket Taylor Swift is displaced by a comedy ringtone – a man declaring, DANGER, DANGER, IT'S YOUR MOTHER CALLING!'

With a deft gesture, Katie swipes *Decline* and speeds up. The road is rising as it bridges the dark waters of the winding Cam below. Katie shivers, imagining swimming in it, with its fish and tangling weeds and muddy depths littered with broken bottles and rusted bicycles. She torments herself with the image of her white foot caught in sharp spokes, thin wisps of blood drifting out of her wounds up to the surface, where she cannot follow them.

With a snap she shakes her head, dropping the horrid daydream, returning to the real world of her own clicking heels on the drenched pavement and the approaching and retreating lights of the cars on her right as they roar past her with a hiss of crested water. She gets such morbid, mortifying thoughts sometimes, and she doesn't understand where they come from.

Things were never like this when I was a kid, she thinks. She didn't mind when Brian told her to do things; she never fought with her mum the way she does now. Back then she was just Katie, who liked to swim and liked to race and liked to win.

It had been enough then. But somehow it wasn't enough any more. Now everything was confusing, and it seemed she was always angry, always stressing out over every little thing...

'It's your age, love,' Brian had said once, when she'd made the mistake of mentioning it to him.

'There's nothing you can do. The only way out is forward.'

The phone buzzes once more against her curled fingers in her pocket, and as she takes it out and swipes *Decline* again, she becomes aware of a car pulling up beside her, its red brake lights glowing like hot coals through the rain.

The door swings open, and inside is an older man, with a baseball cap crushed down on his head. He cranes towards her, one muscled, knotty forearm holding the door handle. He is smiling at her, showing all of his teeth, almost as though he's in pain.

She has never seen this person before and she offers him an indignant stare, steps back and moves to walk on.

'Katie Browne? Is that you?' He has to raise his voice as the rain is getting harder.

Her gaze narrows as she pulls out her headphones, which tangle in her damp hair. 'Yeah. How do you know me?'

It's an unfriendly answer, and she can see him flinch a little, as though offended.

'You used to go to the youth club in Hartington Grove. I drove the bus there, don't you remember?'

She doesn't. Furthermore, she hasn't been to that youth club for about two years, since she started at St Hilda's and began swimming properly, as she no longer has the time.

She shakes her head.

'No? Well, I remember you.' He chuckles, and it's high, almost wheezy. 'Look, you're soaked through – can I give you a lift?'

There's a long moment then as Katie considers. The man clearly knows who she is, and he must be a responsible person if he's connected to the youth club. It is absolutely pouring now, each new raindrop raising its own tiny corona of water as it hits his car, the asphalt and the railings on the bridge. The sound of it fills everything. His car looks warm and dry.

But what she also considers is that this man could not possibly have spotted who she was with her hood pulled forward as she walked along – he must have passed her in his car and circled back. She considers the fact that his face sparks not the slightest twinge of recognition, and yet he can identify her, deeply hooded, in the midst of a rainstorm at night.

The disconnect between their acquaintances is too much, too alarming, and Katie realizes that however bad it looks or makes him feel, there is no way in the world she is getting in that car with him.

'Thanks a lot,' she says, being polite, thinking fast, 'but I'm only going to the steps. They're two seconds away.' She gestures to the other end of the bridge, towards the roundabout. 'My dad's waiting for me,' she adds, and this qualifying tit-bit, walking out of her mouth, surprises her – not just the words, but the little quaver of fear that enters her voice on the word 'waiting', an un-welcome note they can both hear. 'I'd only get your car wet.'

Something twitches in his face again, but then his smile is back. 'All right, if you're sure, love. Get out of the rain soon!'

He proffers her a friendly wave with his free hand and the car door slams shut. Within seconds he has pulled smoothly away, without looking back.

Her sense of relief is extraordinary, and she considers for a second abandoning her escape, returning home, slipping up the stairs to her bedroom and facing the storm when it comes.

She calls her dad, wanting him to come and get her. After two rings she is switched to voicemail, his recorded greeting chirpy yet impersonal.

Her coat and hood are now sopping with rain.

She tries to shake the feeling that he's deliberately side-lining her call, in the same way that she is snubbing her mother's calls. She would admit to herself, if pushed, that the reason she never phoned him before setting out is that he would almost certainly have tried to persuade her not to come over.

Her dad is always telling her that he will 'be there for her, no matter what', and yet whenever she actually *needs* something, like for him to turn up and watch her swim in a gala, or stand up to Brian, or, say, pick her up in the pouring rain after she's had an encounter with some creepy man, the call goes straight to voicemail.

Her cheeks burn and she ignores them.

Now that she's reached the bottom of the steps of the pedestrian exit, she starts to consider her situation more calmly. She is in a warren of residential streets near the river, outside a closed beauty shop.

Katie pauses under the awning, wondering whether to try again or simply abandon the whole venture, when she hears steps: someone is walking along Abbey Road, with heavy boots and a brisk, rolling gait, a person hidden by the intervening wall.

She thrusts the phone back in her pocket and waits for whoever it is to pass by her, but the steps just stop – there is no sign of anyone when she finally abandons the shelter of the beauty shop's porch and returns to the street, and she guesses that they must have turned into one of the houses nearby.

Well, whoever they were, they aren't there now, and she needs to get a move on. She has a plan.

Just beneath Elizabeth Way and along the riverbank there is a footbridge – just a few minutes' walk from here. She can re-cross the river there and make her way along the well-known streets back home. No car can follow her over it, and anything would be better than waiting here.

Young as she is, Katie knows that the suggestion of decamping to her dad's house when there's a crisis is like throwing a match on to the petrol of her mum's insecurity. That's why it was a great plan when Katie was furious and wanted to hurt her mother, but not so good when, as now, she's exhausted, a little scared and soaked to the bone.

If she can sneak up to her room before they see the backpack she can just say she went out for a walk to clear her head. There would still be a bloody awful row, but not as bad as it could be.

She heaves her wet rucksack over her shoulder; everything in it must be damp. What a stupid night this has been, she thinks. That bloody Brian, he lives to wind me up – and sets off under

11

the overpass, the river gurgling and pattering placidly on her right, the huge concrete pillars on her left. Above her head, cars roar.

The well-lit tracery of the footbridge is visible just ahead and she smiles slightly to herself. She will go home and get dry and, once they've stopped shouting at her, she'll get into bed and stream some rubbish TV to her laptop. In fact, her mother might even decide not to continue their fight, but instead take pity on her bedraggled state and make her a mug of hot chocolate and some toast to enjoy in front of the telly – it's been known to happen before. Katie knows that their rows make her mum feel horribly guilty, but she never understands why.

This fantasy pleases her as she trudges along the rails on the side of the river, so it takes her a second or two to work out that someone is walking up behind her – someone in heavy boots walking quickly, too quickly.

She jerks around, but not fast enough, and there is the shocking intimacy of arms – strong, knotty arms – snaking around her waist, her neck, forcing her head back, a big rough hand covering her mouth.

'Ah, Katie,' he whispers, and his breath is hot against her chilled cheek as she tries to scream, to struggle. 'I think we got off on the wrong foot there.'

1

I've always had this thing about magpies. They're meant to be unlucky if you see one on its own, but they always give me this sudden burst of optimism whenever I catch sight of one perched on grass or rusted railings, in its tuxedo of feathers and cocking its head at all corners. I admire self-possession in the animal kingdom.

One of them was watching me from the chestnut branches as I left my own portion of the animal kingdom, namely St Hilda's Academy, where self-possession isn't as highly a sought virtue as self-restraint. I was in the school car park under its leafy canopy of trees, loading my bulky bag into my little red Audi A3 convertible. I was highly strung and restless, or at least more so than usual, casting my glance at the bag containing all of the day's collected essays, which were threatening to spill out of the top.

So much for my weekend.

I got into the car alongside the offending bag and shut the door.

On the dashboard lay a copy of the *Cambridge Examiner*, which I hadn't had time to read yet. I thumbed idly through it. PUBLIC ENQUIRY ENDS IN SEMI-RIOT shared the front page with RESIDENTS PROTEST ONE WAY SCHEME. Within were the little boxes of print naming the damned souls caught trying to pilfer tinned veg and pairs of tights from the local super-market, or breathlessly describing acts of low-impact, mundane vandalism, alongside a photo of a gloomy pensioner shaking his head at youth's folly and the world's wickedness.

There was nothing in there about Katie Browne. There had been nothing for a week.

I was starting to get a very bad feeling about this.

Somewhere between the letters complaining about the failure of parents to control their children in restaurants, and the feature on Cambridge fifty years ago (it appeared to be the same seething, overheated one-horse town as now – the horse in question was posed in the photo on Magdalene Bridge sporting a floral collar and looking glum and disappointed with its lot), was 'Dear Amy', the column I write. In it I presume to advise the lovelorn and wits-ended.

I met the *Examiner's* editor through his fifteen-year-old son Conor. Conor was in my English class, but having trouble concentrating on my lessons – on everyone's lessons, to be honest. He was acting up and distracting the others, and starting to display an uncharacteristic but growing anger. The editor, Iain, was constantly being summoned to speak to the Head of Year about this, with his new wife in tow; a pale brunette with a triangular face who was about ten years his junior. Whenever I ran into her she clearly, judging from her expression, thought she might have bitten off more than she could chew in terms of the whole blended family thing, and the received wisdom, even amongst the kids, was that this was the root of Conor's defiant truculence.

But for some reason, I had a funny feeling about Conor.

After a disastrous double lesson during which he threw a pen at me and kicked over his chair (in the genteel atmosphere of St Hilda's, this latter act was received like the burning of the Reichstag – the kids were literally paralysed with shock), I finally tackled him in my tiny office – not about his new stepmother, but about his best friend Sammy, who sat beside him and had giggled surreptitiously throughout his antics.

And after some prodding it all came out, like uncorked champagne – he had feelings for Sammy, feelings he couldn't explain, not ever, and he didn't know what to do, and I must understand, no one could know. Sammy would never speak to him again. He would be destroyed.

I could have wept at his confusion and panic.

'I'll never tell a soul,' I said. 'But if you aren't going to talk to Sammy about your feelings...'

'Never.'

'...and I can see why you wouldn't, you're going to have to come up with some way of living through this. You can't get yourself expelled just because of unresolved sexual tension.'

He regarded me mournfully, rubbing his hands through his untidy red hair, a caricature of worry, while I sorted him out with some counselling switchboards outside of school.

'Ring them. They understand how you feel. You're still very young and these things are confusing, but the more you talk, the less scary it will all become. In the meantime, I'll thank you

15

to attend to your lessons and we'll overlook the thrown pen for now. And we'll say nothing to your parents. Understood?'

'Yes.'

The editor, Iain, was soon amazed at the change in him. He rang me up late at night, having got my number from school, and pitched the idea of giving me a trial writing an advice column for the newspaper. That was last year, and 'Dear Amy' is still going strong.

As for Conor, he doesn't hang around with Sammy as much any more, and when we meet in corridors or pass in the grounds, his eyes always light up and he gives me a cheerful, approving little nod, as though I passed the trial, and not he. Whatever is going on in his life, I am no longer worried for him.

I had deliberately put the paper there to remind me that I needed to call by the offices and pick up the rest of the 'Dear Amy' caseload for the week. There's an email address for 'Dear Amy', but many people still believe the anonymity of the Internet is little better than a ruse and opt for snail mail. I might pull a face sometimes, but in truth I enjoy the work – it feels useful and does a good job of challenging all my assumptions on a weekly basis.

I nearly ran over a few of my pupils on the way to the *Examiner* offices as they stepped off the kerb during a spot of horseplay on the Fen Causeway, not one of them paying attention to the traffic. I swerved hard and my brakes squealed. Three boys with identical artfully messy hairstyles turned, startled, to offer me obscene gestures before recognizing me and then lapsing into comical shock. I swept past them, honking, aware I should be pulling over, giving them a piece of my mind, but also aware that no one in the crushed traffic behind would thank me. Justice would have to wait to be served.

'You daft muppets,' I muttered to myself, reaching over the passenger seat to adjust my bag, which had nearly spilled its contents into the footwell during these death-defying manoeuvres. I glared into my rear-view mirror. 'You were nearly roadkill, Mr Aaron Jones.'

My hand on the steering wheel was trembling. I stared at it in surprise, as though it belonged to somebody else. The almost-accident must have shaken me more than I realized.

I have an ambivalent attitude to children. They drive me mad, but I can't stay away from them and miss them horribly when they're not in my life. Some time after we got married I learned that I couldn't have children myself, and my husband Eddy suggested that I quit teaching and perhaps take private adult students for Greek and Latin. I tried it. Two months later I went for the job at St Hilda's, as an alternative to smashing all of our crockery and jumping off the nearest railway bridge.

It's the only job I do well.

And as Eddy has since run off with his boss, it's just as well I have something to occupy me full time and put food on the table.

When I reached the *Examiner* offices the staff

17

were just leaving. This is always the case, even if I arrive early, or at eight o'clock at night. Wendy was clearing her expensive little phone and a just-washed mug bearing a screenprint of her three children off her desk and packing them into her handbag. She gave me a brisk smile.

'Hallo, Margot.' She reached into one of the pigeonholes behind her desk. 'Not so many this week.' She handed me a little bundle of letters tied together with a blue rubber band.

She always says this. I can never quite shake the feeling that she's waiting for me to say, 'No, there isn't, is there? I should just give up,' before leaving and never coming back.

Somehow, and without understanding why, I sense that this would please her.

I pulled the band off the letters and glanced idly through them. One in particular caught my attention. It was addressed simply in capital letters: 'DEAR AMY, THE CAMBRIDGE EXAMINER, CAMBRIDGE'.

A strong but childish hand had written the address. The 'o's were very round and the loops regular, almost fussily so.

On an impulse I tore it open. Tucked inside was a piece of crumpled, sweaty paper. Wendy put her coat on, pretending to be oblivious. She was waiting, not very patiently, for me to give some clue as to what I'd been sent. I didn't, of course. I never do.

I had a cold presentiment as I unfolded the letter. Before I'd even read them the words screamed 'Haste!' and 'Panic!' at me. Wendy came to my side, ready to leave, and I quickly folded it up, having only got as far as 'Dear Amy', and shoved it into the pocket of my jacket.

'Anything interesting?' she asked.

'No, no – can barely read it, to be honest,' I lied. I decided to head the enquiry off by changing the subject. 'I see there's been nothing in the paper about Katie for a while.'

'Who?' She clearly had no idea who I was talking about.

'Katie Browne,' I said, trying to keep my voice even. 'The missing girl.'

Her mouth opened wide in exaggerated apology. 'Oh, of course, yes, sorry. She was one of yours, wasn't she?'

'She was in my class two years ago.'

Wendy sighed. 'It's a worry, isn't it? When they run off like that.'

'*If* she ran off. That remains to be proven.'

'Well,' said Wendy, her eyes sliding sideways to the door, 'the police have been talking to Iain – they seem to think she's run off. They've talked to her family and friends, and I'm sure they'd know best.' She patted my arm gingerly. I suspect I appeared a little intense to her. 'I mean, you get your letters. You must know that not everything is how it seems in people's lives.'

I didn't reply to this rather obvious statement. I was well aware of what the police thought, and what Wendy thought.

One of the investigative team had visited the school the day before yesterday and told us that Katie had been unhappy at home for a while – something I had suspected.

But I couldn't shake the feeling that whether

19

she'd been unhappy or not, something about her disappearance felt wrong.

I had a memory of arrogant yet guarded dark eyes raking me from the back of the class; long brown hair drawn up into a ponytail.

'I'm locking up now.' Wendy jangled the keys.

'I'm ready.' I felt a bit light-headed. Perhaps almost mowing down those three delinquents was still bothering me. An evening spent worrying about having their names called out at tomorrow's assembly would do them all good.

We walked in silence to the car park. My feet were numb with cold inside the thin leather of my boots. There was an icy wind blowing, tingling like needles thrown against my exposed cheek. It was winter again, but funnily enough, I don't mind. I prefer it to summer.

We said our goodbyes and parted. Wendy and I must make an effort to be civil to one another, as we are mutually aware that without it our lack of affinity would quickly blossom into dislike. Wendy is fussy, smug and nosy, and I ... well, I'm how I am. I don't envy her children once they get a little older. I was glad to see her go.

The evening was already drawing in, amazing me by how dark it had grown so early. It always catches me off guard at this time of year, a constant revisiting of annual surprise. Sometimes I feel like a goldfish, with the glass walls of my bowl providing a continuous source of novel amazement each time I swim around them.

Once safe in the car I drew the letter out of my pocket and leaned back.

Dear Amy,

Please please PLEASE help me! I have been kidnapped by a strange man and he's holding me prisoner in this cellar. He says I can never go home. I don't know where I am or what to do and nobody knows I'm here.

I don't even know how long I've been gone, but it seems like for ever. I'm afraid that people will stop looking for me. I'm afraid he'll kill me.

Please help me soon,
Bethan Avery

There was nothing else except for the panicked, childish handwriting. No return address or clue as to where it had come from. There was a postmark on the envelope declaring it was mailed in Cambridge yesterday, but that was all the help I was getting.

'This is a prank,' I said aloud, but my voice quavered, and I didn't really believe it. Occasionally I get some very shocking letters, nothing more than extremely nasty sexual fantasies seeking some kind of release from the subconscious void their creators imprison them in. I'd rather they were released via the post than any other way, but there was something about this letter that got to me.

Other thoughts were brewing in my mind too. Thoughts about Katie Browne, the girl who went missing, who vanished with nothing but a small bag of clothes. She was a scholarship girl, a county-level swimmer from one of the council es-

21

tates in Cambridge, and had never been genuinely happy in the rarefied atmosphere of St Hilda's. I could sympathize.

Frankly, I was very worried for Katie Browne.

As for my letter, it was easy enough to sort out. I started up my car and headed for the police station. If there's no Bethan Avery reported missing, then I hope the sod that wrote this is enjoying the belly laugh they've had at my expense.

'What are you doing here?' I demanded, surprised.

My not-quite-ex-husband was standing on the front doorstep, leaning against the door when I arrived home with the early darkness and mist. In his slim-fitting dark suit and neat small collar he looked like a particularly stylish missionary, or perhaps an urban vampire summoned out of the fog. Something about his posture appeared studied, composed for my benefit.

I narrowed my eyes at him.

Eddy's full lips compressed. 'You said you wanted to talk about the settlement.'

I sighed, exhausted, as I walked past him to the front door and turned the key. 'Haven't you heard of calling first?'

'Your phone was off.'

I had been telling Eddy for weeks now that we needed to talk about the division of the household, of our shared lives. I had noted each morning as I came down the stairs that he had not yet made any moves to redirect his post. That he'd shown up at all to discuss the mediation was an excellent sign, though of course he hadn't bothered to ask first. It was still a point of principle for him that this was his house too.

I see it all rather differently. I came into this marriage with this house, which I had bought as little more than a run-down shell when I first moved to Cambridge, and thriftily renovated over the course of seven years; each improvement, each upgrade, was a reflection of my own internal home improvement, my recovery. I sat in its dusty, bare living room on the threadbare sofa the owners bequeathed with it, and dreamed of the house's better days. I chose each of the paints – striking violets, subtle lemons, warm greys – and applied them to the walls and trimmings with the sort of passionate focus usually associated with Great Masters in their ateliers, each night looking over my shoulder at the clock and realizing with a little patter of shock that it was three, four in the morning, and my arms ached and I had to go to work in five hours' time. I chose the unfussy dull pewter of the fittings in the bath that I sit in for hours, the spiky light fixtures, the contrasting rugs (the stains seem to choose themselves). I scoured and treated the reclaimed furniture myself, sitting in my varnish-spattered dungarees on the grass in the tiny garden with my cup of tea, admiring the deconstructed pieces drying on their sheets of newspaper – a wooden picnic spread out on my lawn.

It was partly my determined independence in this, and in other things, that attracted Eddy to me in the first place. Not that he is big on DIY. He uses his hands for other things, as it turns out.

'Come in,' I called over my shoulder, just to establish who was in whose territory, though as I did, I felt a little shiver of superstition – vampires must be invited over the threshold, after all.

I shook it away. Yes, we were strangers now, perhaps we always had been, despite our best efforts, and it felt very painful, as though emotions, like body parts, could be sprained or dislocated. On the other hand, we should at least be able to have a civil discussion about practical matters without mauling one another any further.

We went into the kitchen, and within seconds were blinking in the glare of the overhead fluorescents. Outside, the wind was drumming impatiently on the windows. I rubbed my eyes and stretched, hearing my bones click.

'Coffee?' I asked.

He nodded and I switched on the kettle, throwing my coat over the back of a chair.

'Bad day?' he asked.

'Huh?' I asked, fishing two mugs out of the cupboard.

'Did you have a bad day?'

'School was the same. I almost ran down some of the kids on the way to the *Examiner*.'

'Hit any?'

'Um, no.'

'Just kidding.' He shot me a look. 'You're well?'

'I'm fine.'

'I mean, in yourself.'

'I know perfectly well what you mean,' I replied precisely, closing the topic off.

I spooned ground coffee into the scratched cafetière, aware that of the two of us, I was being the difficult one. I hadn't even returned his query and asked about his day at work, nor would I, considering the reasons we were getting divorced.

But I could concede something; make conversation.

'I made a big prat of myself at the police station, though,' I muttered.

'You went to the police station over it? Did their parents...'

'No, not about the kids,' I said. 'I got a letter today at the *Examiner.*' Suddenly I didn't want to tell Eddy about this – I was asking to be patronized – but it was too late now. I stood up and walked over to the window.

'What kind of letter?'

Behind me, I could hear him foraging through the fridge for milk – he took his coffee white. Outside, the fog drifted over the hedges, veiling the surrounding houses.

'I wouldn't like to get caught out on a night like this,' I said to myself after a moment.

'Are you going to tell me what kind of letter it was?'

'A crank letter,' I said. 'Somebody claiming to be Bethan Avery.'

'Who?'

'Bethan Avery. She was a teenager who was kidnapped and presumed murdered in the nineties.'

Eddy blinked and squinted, as though consulting some lost vault of memory. 'Bethan Avery ... I know that name. She was from around here.' There was a pause. 'I remember it being in the local papers. So you thought this letter was real, did you?'

I offered an acceding shrug. 'I thought it might be.'

25

'Huh. That's pretty sick. Why did you take it to the police? I wouldn't have thought there was anything they could do.'

I stood by the kettle, which was now happily gouting steam into the air. 'I wanted to check it against the missing persons,' I said, and immediately regretted it.

Eddy laughed. 'Bet they found that pretty funny.'

'They did,' I said coldly. Eddy's laughter hitched, paused. 'Personally, I don't understand the cause for hilarity.'

'Oh come off it, Margot.'

'I just don't. If this kind of thing was less amusing to them, perhaps they'd have found out what happened to Katie Browne.'

In the interests of prudence, Eddy didn't reply. Privately, I knew that he too thought that Katie had fled her humdrum life for the bright lights of the M25.

'You wouldn't remember it being on the news anyway,' he said after a few moments, trying to be diplomatic. 'You would have been living in London then.'

But still, for a sudden freezing moment, I felt like I hated him. In the drawing darkness I had turned the letter over and over, long after I knew its cry by heart. I'd imagined being torn away from your friends and home, shoved into a dark little prison, raped, battered, murdered, your dismembered limbs cast into the dark depths of a swiftly moving river – first the splash, then the ripple, then nothing, ever again. Or perhaps, by the light of the moon, your murderer had stood over the pit containing your poor, pale remains, shovelling wet worm-infested earth over them. Months, maybe years, later, the bones might be found, to be held, worn and weathered, in plastic-gloved hands; to be pieced together like a jigsaw, with scientists breathing through masks as they wash the mud out of crevices in shins and skull, before wrapping them in rubber sheets and labelling them with numbers.

Heaven save us all from rape and murder and the anonymity of ignominious unmarked graves, which the weather beats uncaringly.

Though all of that was hardly Eddy's fault.

I set the mug in front of him on the table with a wry smile of concession. I had a sudden memory of him pushing me up against this table. There had been no words, just fumbling and heavy breathing and damp hot skin and nothing else but us in the world. Afterwards we'd realized we'd left the blinds open. Anyone could have seen us, we giggled to one another, thrilled at our own reckless daring.

'And you a convent girl,' he had murmured into my hair. 'You wicked minx.'

Of course, there's a hedge and a low wall separating the house from the street, so no one could have seen us, unless they'd been lurking on our front lawn, actively looking through the windows. You'd be lucky to get a mobile signal in this part of the village, never mind an audience. But it had pleased us both to think of ourselves as flagrant strutting libertines. At least at the time.

'One of your magpies was in the front yard when I got here,' he grunted after a while. 'It must have been waiting for you.'

27

I softened slightly, spared him a smile. 'Yeah. It's there a lot.'

Somehow we moved into the living room, which was not part of my plan – the living room, with its squashy, overstuffed sofa and multitudinous brightly coloured cushions, was a place where he had always made me feel happy, safe and comforted. Many were the times I had curled up against his chest here, as we watched absurd TV together. Remembering this made my throat swell unhappily and my heart ache with cold. It was no place for this new Eddy who was now comforting somebody else. But somehow, as he accepted the mug and moved off towards the hall as we had done so many times before, I couldn't find a way to prevent it, as though habit were a riptide, pulling us both along, and to object now would seem ill-humoured, a little mean.

I was trying to be civilized, after all.

The couch sank to accept us. Eddy drank his coffee, made expert small talk that didn't touch on the subject of his new *inamorata*, his job, or the mediation arrangements. It was as though nothing remotely strange or strained was happening. I could not have done better in his shoes. It was like a dance, and he led. I had no idea how to steer matters back on course, so decided to wait for an opening, my back against the armrest, between a rock and a hard place. Who knew when I would get him back here again, and in such a good mood?

I hugged my empty mug to my chest.

'Have you eaten?' he asked.

'Who, me? No.'

'We could call for a takeaway,' he said, kicking off his shoes, and for an instant it was like it had always been, me sitting on the couch, watching him perform this ritual every time he came in from work. 'The Mai Thai delivers on a Friday. Are you in the mood for steamed sea bass?'

And yet not how it had always been.

'Won't Arabella be missing you?' I asked.

He shrugged, as if this was of no matter. 'Well, as you say, we need to talk.'

I glanced at the antique wall clock, a wedding present from my friend Lily. It was nearly quarter to eight.

Lily had never liked him.

'Sure,' I said.

'Good girl,' he said complacently, flashing me that full-lipped grin, those brilliant teeth. 'And I've got a bottle of Sancerre in my case to go with it.'

So sea bass with lemongrass and Sancerre followed, and Eddy and I did indeed manage to talk about the financial settlement, though I was left with the disquieting impression that he didn't actually say all that much. Clearly the fair thing to do was for each of us to keep what we had owned before we met – me the house; he his po-faced 'loft apartment' in Hills Road, where he had held court in bachelor princedom before our marriage. Each to our own – our own cars, our own furniture. We could come to some arrangement about the things we had bought together – which over a little less than three years did not amount to very much.

He regarded me with those wide grey eyes,

nodding, and I was encouraged by the lack of opposition (then again, why should he object?) but now that I thought about it, I could not recall any actual agreement.

'So what do you think about that?' I asked him. I felt flushed and oddly relaxed – we are going to get through this, I thought. We are going to negotiate this like grown-ups, and maybe, perhaps in time...

'I think we need more wine.'

'That's a given,' I said wryly. 'But what do you think about the plan for mediation?'

He glanced into his glass, offered it a tiny smile and put it on the table.

'I think, why are we talking about this now?' he said, turning that smile on me. 'I thought the rule was that after ten we didn't discuss business.'

Lily's wall clock said it was ten o'clock exactly.

'That rule was for work, not business,' I murmured, unaccountably blushing. 'And it applied when we were still married.' I drew back into my corner of the couch.

But he was leaning forward, his arm snaking up the sofa towards me.

'Margot,' he said, in that sultry golden voice of his, 'we *are* still married.'

I opened my mouth to object, to draw away, but his lips were on mine, and he tasted so good, so sweet, and I'd been so lonely. I was opening up to him, letting his arms meet around my back, feeling his hard chest and tight belly against me, and I was shaking, I wanted him so badly, I...

I...

What the hell was I doing?

30

I pushed him away. 'No.'

He rocked back, clearly surprised, as I ducked out from under him and rolled straight to my stockinged feet.

'I think you need to leave.' I folded my arms tightly across my chest.

'Margot,' he pushed his blond hair out of his eyes, as though stunned at my changeability. 'What's the matter?'

I was trembling, the floor shaking beneath my feet.

'You left me for another woman and now you're here on a booty call, that's what the matter is.' I rubbed at my face, which now felt cold and damp, like the rest of me – drained and humiliated. 'How dare you? How fucking dare you?'

'I didn't see you objecting...'

'Pay attention, Eddy. This is me objecting. This is me objecting *right now.*' I flung out my arm and pointed to the door. 'You sleazy bastard. Put your shoes on and get the fuck out.'

Something flashed in his face then, a series of emotions at war with desire. Should he be conciliatory, apologetic? Should he feign ignorance of what had offended me? Should he be cheeky, seductive? But mostly he wanted to be angry that I had exposed him, and that was what won out.

'You're mental, Margot. You're crazy.'

'Get out!' I bellowed. My own shame was vanishing now, consumed by a very real anger, a furious rage. 'Get out of my house and don't come back!'

2

'I don't know why you make me do these things,' Chris says. His voice is broken, as though he's on the brink of tears. 'Why can't we just be happy? Why can't you just be grateful?'

Katie does not reply, does not seem to be expected to, even though he has removed the gag. He's not even looking at her, in any case. Her chest hurts and her right side, from shoulder to hip, aches as she huddles on the dirty tartan blanket.

She had tried to hit him with the mug and its scalding contents and run for the door, but she gained only a few seconds before he caught up with her, and his fury had been terrifying, unlike anything she could have imagined. She'd been sure that she would die, and was surprised to find, in the aftermath, as she wheezed through bruised ribs, that she hadn't.

He threw her down the steps, back into her cellar prison, and left her there without food and water for a long time.

This is his first reappearance.

'I have tried and tried my best for you.' He rubs at his sallow face with a kind of frantic energy, which she knows bodes ill. 'You girls, you're all the same.'

Katie remains silent. She has been a prisoner in the cellar for … four, no, maybe five weeks. She would strike off the days on the stone as a calendar, except that she has no way of telling when one day has ended and another begun. Anyway, marking the stone might make her captor angry, and Katie will do anything, anything at all, to prevent that from happening again – though whatever she does, it's never quite enough.

'What do you think would happen if I turned you over, eh? If the others got wind of you, got their hands on you? You can't imagine the things they'd do to you.' His eyes are huge, almost comical, though she knows better than to laugh. 'They're ruthless. They know no mercy, I tell you. There'd be nothing left of you but a red wet stain on the floor.'

She has heard this story many, many times before. He tells it again and again, almost word for word, as though it is a script, an oath, a prayer. He is part of a gang, which seizes and holds young girls for sex. She is constantly being told how fortunate she is that Chris has protected her so far from their more violent demands. He could revoke this protection at any moment.

All Katie knows is that she has to hang on until somebody finds her, or Chris makes a mistake. She imagines rescuing avengers charging in here, sweeping her up in their arms. To her surprise, it is not her dad she dreams of coming down here and beating Chris to within an inch of his life while her mum carries her to safety, but Brian; his huge beefy arms, his soft blue eyes that can go very hard indeed if, as he often says, someone 'is taking the piss'.

Chris swipes at his own eyes with his fingers.

'Why do you do this, Katie? Why?'

Now he does seem to want an answer.

She thinks for a moment, and because she is young and convinced that evil is not a universal condition, because the longing to be back with her mum and Brian is a physical ache as terrible as her crushed ribs, she tells the truth:

'I just want to go home.'

She bursts into tears.

Her voice is tiny, quavering in the dark space, but still he flinches, as though she has slapped him, and his little red eyes swivel down to her, with their ever-present rage and a tinge of fear.

'What are you on about? I already told you. You can't go home. You're dead if you go home.'

'I know, you said, but...'

His fist hits her hard in the temple, and her teeth clack together, stamping her tongue with cuts. Her mouth fills with blood.

'Do you think I'm lying? Is that it? DO YOU, YOU UNGRATEFUL LITTLE SOW?!'

He launches himself at her.

And as the terrible evening wears on, she finds at one point she is lying on her belly, her cheek crushed into the stone floor. On the wall opposite, under the swaying light of the bulb, she can see thin words etched on to the bricks nearest the floor, like hen scratchings. From here she can read them: '12/1/1998 BETHAN AVERY'.

3

It was Saturday morning, and only just dawn. The rehearsals for the school play over at St Hilda's started at ten – we were putting on *The Duchess of Malfi* for Christmas, and we'd all taken to calling it, behind the head's back, 'The Anti-Nativity'. Estella, the drama teacher, managed our teenage actors and Lily, the art teacher and my comrade-in-arms during the interminable staff meetings the head held, was leading the costume and set design side of things. I was there more in the capacity of a runner than anything, but it was all good fun, and later Lily and I would have a late lunch and a gossip in town.

At the moment, it was a good thing to keep busy.

I was faintly hung-over – feeling seedy but not sufficiently so to justify any more time spent in bed. I threw the covers off, willing myself to get up, finding I didn't quite have it in me.

Eddy, I thought to myself, with a sick lurch of guilt and regret.

I forced myself on to my feet anyway. I felt worn out. I had dreamed of Bethan Avery. Before climbing into bed, I had Googled her, and spent hours on a Wikipedia trail full of stolen children and their murderers, each link leading to a new page, before I had dropped the whole thing in disgust and headed for bed.

But the damage had been done, and I had tossed and turned all night long, rebuilding the dead girl in my dreams. All I remembered now was someone offering me a thighbone wrapped in silk. 'Oh God,' I'd replied, paralysed with dread. 'Is that Katie's? No, no, it's Bethan's. Definitely Bethan's.'

I also remembered Eddy was crying on the couch but wouldn't tell me why, keeping his face covered with his hands. It had shocked me. I found it nearly impossible to imagine Eddy crying over anything.

I shuffled downstairs to make a cup of tea. I shoved our wine glasses into the dishwasher, deliberately forcing myself not to remember the humiliating events of the previous evening. I sat down in my nightshirt at the kitchen table and shivered – the kitchen has always been a cold room.

Through the window I could see the violent rose-gold of a brilliant dawn. It was going to be a pretty day.

I forced myself into my run, driving out my ghosts with each step, and when I got back I made sourdough toast and tea while I considered the early papers. After an hour or so of letting my tea grow cold, I decided that I wouldn't entirely fritter the morning away. I had the other 'Dear Amy' letters to answer. I emptied out the contents of my bag and immediately put the essays back inside it. No thank you.

The letters lay tumbled out in front of me. I picked up one with an expensive-looking water-marked envelope, directed in a light, sloping hand.

It contained a short missive admonishing me for mentioning that adoption or abortion was a possibility for the fifteen-year-old in last week's issue, who had grown great with child after a night of passion with a member of the local rugby club.

The next was from a woman who I was sure had written before about the same thing: a husband who beat her up for her child benefit, after pissing his own allowance away down the village pub – a woman who needed a dialogue, not the occasional one-off. I read it again, rubbing my temples, and once more considered tracking her down before dismissing the idea. It would be a gross breach of faith and confidentiality. Instead I listed the women's organizations I knew, with a note that I used to volunteer for the nuns in a women's refuge and could vouch for the work they carried out.

The third was the killer. A lonely old man wrote an heroic elegy to his dead wife, describing wandering through his Edithless house; touching her things, arranging her photographs, passing the flowers she had planted, dead in their boxes and tubs. His children were trying to persuade him to go into a home, and though he couldn't blame them, he wasn't going to move away from Edith's house. He could never have borne it. Still, it was terribly lonely, all the same.

I wrote the standard reply, listing all the local help groups and social clubs, but it was plain to see that he didn't want social clubs. He wanted Edith.

After that I packed it in for the day.

After rehearsals, Lily treated me to lunch at the Oak Bistro, and despite the oncoming winter the day was bright and crisp and even a little warm, as though it had wandered in lost from another season. Boldly, we decided to eat in the walled garden, in splendid isolation. I ordered the tiger prawn linguine; Lily, raging carnivore that she is, went for the char-grilled rib eye without comment or apology.

It's one of the things I really love about her.

'You should ask them for a sabbatical at that paper,' said Lily as we waited for our food, crossing her legs before her and making her elaborate patent-leather high-heeled boots creak.

'*The Examiner?* What? Why?'

'Don't you have enough on your plate?'

I shrugged and regarded the contents of my glass of Prosecco. 'Doesn't everyone?'

'It's a divorce, Margot, not a particularly large gas bill.'

'Both are common.'

'Oh, don't do this,' she said, tossing her long hair over her shoulder. This month, it was white-blonde with lavender streaks and mint-green tips.

'Do what?'

'Minimize everything. It's nothing, it's nothing, it's nothing. All it does is piss people off because they know it's not true and then it will make you sick again ... don't look at me like that.'

I kept looking at her, in that way I was not supposed to be looking at her.

'Margot, I'm warning you...'

'I'm still not seeing what good whining about my woes to the world will do.' I put the glass down. 'Besides, he dumped me for someone richer and prettier...'

'And older.'

I managed a rueful smile. 'It's just too embarrassing to discuss in public. Better educated, too, which is the thing that stings most.'

'Better educated.' Lily snorted, her red lips contorted into a scowl. 'She's a professor in *metallurgy*. How's that meant to make you a better person? How do you hold together a truly riveting dinner party with your anecdotes about smelting and mass-scale lead production?'

I burst out laughing.

'It's indium tin production,' I corrected her. 'They use it for touch-screens.'

'There, see? It was so utterly fascinating the first time you told me that it stuck in my memory.' She topped up her glass and mine. 'Honestly, Margot, you're worth ten of her. Ten of him, if we're getting down to brass tacks. Greedy fucking chancer that he is.'

'Lily...'

'Well ... it's true.' She reached into her bag, her heavy bangles clattering against one another. 'Never mind him now. I've something to show you, I finished it this morning in rehearsals.'

She pulled out her sketchpad and handed it to me. It was a picture of our latest staff meeting, in two panels. The first was entitled 'How We See Him', and it was a caricature of Ben, the headmaster, leaning over his desk, shouting at us. His face was dark with rage. He sported a judge's wig and full academic gown, and was carrying a huge paddle. The three of us – Lily, Estella and I, sat in chairs opposite, only we were tiny little girls in pigtails and school uniforms, clearly terrified.

The next panel was called 'How He Sees Us', and this time, Ben was the tiny boy in school uniform, cowering in front of us. The three of us relaxed before him on what looked like thrones carved out of bones – she'd drawn us all as female monsters out of antiquity. Estella the harpy flexed a pair of wings and her birds' talons crossed over each other at the ankles; Lily's long hair was a cloud of hissing, multi-coloured snakes, and I sat on the end, leathery bat wings sprouting from my back, curved fangs gnashing against my bottom lip as I leaned forward, glaring at Ben, caressing the razor-wire whip in my clawed hands.

She had, in her light quick pencil strokes, captured me as one of the *Erinyes:* a Fury, an ancient Greek goddess tasked with hounding sinners to madness and death.

I laughed out loud.

'I love it!' I said. 'It's my new favourite portrait of me. Makes me look so much more approachable than the picture on the school website.'

She smiled, proud and pleased.

'I thought you'd like it,' she said. 'And that whole chaotic...'

'Chthonic...'

'...Underworld goddess of vengeance and rage thing suits you.' She took the pad off me and peeled the sheet off. 'If you'd kept up that look at home, Eddy would never have dared to go elsewhere.'

I snorted out another horrified laugh. 'You're such a cow!'

40

'I know,' she replied with a kind of smug pride. 'And it's nice to be appreciated. Here,' she was writing something along the bottom of the picture. 'Take this. I drew it for you.'

Along the bottom she had penned, 'Stay mad! Love, Lily.'

I was touched, suddenly terribly moved, and I realized I was in danger of bursting into tears. Because she was right – it had been tough, horribly tough, and humiliating and isolating and all the rest.

'I don't know what to say.' I wiped at my eyes. 'Thank you.'

She grinned. 'Don't say anything. Look, the food's here. Let's eat.'

Lily had to get back to her kids, and rather than return to my empty home I took the long route through Coe Fen, alongside the river, to get back to the Corn Exchange.

I struck off along the path through the marshes. I love it around here, especially in the autumn, when the tourists have eased off and the mist and the bowing shapes of the willows are at their most magical. I crunched through the wet, dead leaves. The path turned towards the Mill pub, and I followed it, enjoying the way the rain had made the place smell, while the river lapped softly beside me with its flotillas of parked punts, and the ducks struggled and bickered with one another. Somewhere a long way off a bonfire was burning, and the scent whipped briefly past my nose. It would be Bonfire Night soon, which pleased me, since I love fireworks. This year we

41

would invite ... but of course, I recalled, with a bewildered and sinking disappointment, we wouldn't invite anyone over for Bonfire Night because Eddy didn't live in the house any more and we were getting divorced.

I would have to get some treacle toffee together before then, I told myself. I'm a dab hand at the treacle toffee, me. In fact, I quite fancied some right now.

I had to pass by the *Examiner* offices to get to the sweet shop, and after briefly weighing up my alternatives, I went in.

There was a letter for me.

Dear Amy,

No one has come. I know it's not your fault and that you are doing your best. It's just that I didn't tell you enough about how to find me. It's hard, though, because I don't know very much. Not only that but the things he told me might be wrong, or lies. I'm frightened that if tell you something that's wrong then you'll never find me. That's the thing that scares me most.

I don't know much about where I am except that it is a cellar in a big old house. There is this kind of foam stuff attached to the walls so no one can hear me, but if I put my ear to the pipes I can hear things. Like, there are dogs that bark at night sometimes, though they sound far away.

I tried to peel a corner of the foam up, just a little, hoping he wouldn't see, but he spotted it and went absolutely mental. He nailed it back down and said that if I did it again he'd hammer the nails into me next.

I believe him.

42

I can't tell you anything else about which house I'm in, because he put a bag over my head while I was still in the car and I've never seen the outside of it. I don't know anything else about it.

There are so many things I don't know. I don't even know what will happen to these letters, or if you are even reading them.

All I want is to get out of here and go home. Please, please tell the police or my nanna about this, because if they keep looking they are bound to find me.

Love,
Bethan Avery

P. S. Please help me soon.

I stood outside the offices, taking deep breaths. I felt cold and sick. I looked down at the smudged paper and the big, childish handwriting – so like the kind of handwriting I saw in class every day – and said, 'This is a hoax, remember?'

It didn't have the calming effect it was supposed to.

I examined the letter once more, minutely. It, like its predecessor, had been posted the day before I received it. It was written on plain white paper, which was certainly not seventeen years old.

It could not be from Bethan Avery.

And yet it was from someone.

I had an idea. I thrust the letter deep into my bulky bag and hefted it over my shoulder.

It was no use dwelling on these letters unless I had some grasp of who Bethan Avery was, and of

43

what had happened to her – this dead girl who was now writing to me. I patted the bag paternally, feeling more in control.

I'd already done the Wikipedia Trail in search of information on Bethan Avery, and found only bits and pieces, hoarded in the corners of some very obscure websites. If I wanted to learn more, I'd need to up my game.

I walked to the Central Library in town, nestled in its sprawling complex of shops. I paused before the lifts for a moment, looking around for anyone who might know me, but I saw only strangers.

I couldn't breathe, suddenly, and leaned my hand against the wall, trying to master myself.

No. I refuse to have another panic attack. I refuse.

As the lift inched down my heart was chilled and marble-heavy, and there was some sort of conspiracy afoot with my nerves, which didn't want me to look into this any further. Determined to show them who was boss, I took a few deep breaths. I looked up, remembering what my therapist had told me – baby steps.

Just breathe.

The lift doors opened wide.

I balled my hands into fists, put one foot deliberately in front of the other, entered the lift and pressed the button.

These things will not conquer me.

The librarian, a tiny blonde twenty-something in a Riot grrrl T-shirt, looked up from her desk and smiled.

Don't let anyone tell you that the gold standard of feeling old is when the police and doctors seem

44

younger than you. It's the librarians that will get you every time.

'I'm looking for a book on Bethan Avery,' I volunteered after a moment.

'Who?'

'She was a girl who went missing around here in the nineties. It was presumed she was murdered, but I don't think they ever found a body. I had a look on the Internet, but couldn't see any way to find out more.'

The girl frowned, a single line bisecting her white brow, and consulted her monitor, tapping the keyboard rapidly. 'I've never heard of her. Hmm. She's not coming up on the system. Would it be Local History, maybe?'

I shook my head. 'I don't think so.' This librarian would have been in primary school when it happened, no wonder she'd never heard of the affair. 'I'd try True Crime.'

'I'm not seeing anything,' she said, 'but we do have some true crime compendiums, maybe she's mentioned in one of those ... oh wait, I've got two copies of *Snatched in Plain Sight: True Stories of Missing Children* by Moore, Linda coming up here. And...' She grinned in minor triumph. 'You're in luck. One of them's in this branch and not on loan. You could try there.'

'Thanks.' I gazed about me. 'Sorry, but where is True Crime? It's not my usual sort of thing.'

'Tucked away at the back on this floor. Follow me.'

She led me through the stacks towering over me on either side, redolent of paper and dust, but emptier than I remembered them being. From the opposite side of the shelf came the artificial cherry smell of cough sweets, and someone was murmuring into a mobile phone ('tell him she's just winding him up').

'I don't want anything too sensational,' I explained earnestly, my errand making me feel self-conscious and more than a little ghoulish. 'I just want something with the facts.'

She made a rueful face, pulling out a large mouldy-looking hardback. 'I think you might be out of luck there. This is it,' she said. The book had a nasty, dated picture on the front, showing a doll leaking blood and a grainy black and white snapshot of a young dark-haired girl in a school uniform. Above this the title loomed threateningly, dripping Kensington Gore over the author's name.

The librarian must have seen my scowl. 'Yes, it's a horrid cover, isn't it?'

I thanked her and took the book with me to one of the study desks. My hands were trembling again. I had a doctor's appointment on Monday night, where we would once again to-and-fro over blood tests and my paralysing fear of needles, and maybe when he made his ubiquitous offer of tranquillizers I'd take him up on it. He'd be thrilled.

I flicked through it, looking for an index. There wasn't one, but there were plenty of badly reproduced photographs of smiling children, heartbreakingly oblivious to their coming fates; of the doors to red brick houses rendered sinister by their sheer innocuousness; of shifty men and gaunt women wearing the fashions of yesteryear; some in handcuffs and bracketed by policemen.

46

I opened the front of the book, thinking about abandoning the project, when suddenly something in the list of contents caught my eye: 'Peggy's Darling: the Tragic Case of Bethan Avery'.

The next time I looked up it was hours later and they were closing the library. I'd been reading, true, but mostly I'd been squinting, with increasing disbelief, at the photographs of Bethan's diary included alongside the text.

4

I was still peering at some of those photographs during lunch on Monday, curled into one of the big leather armchairs in St Hilda's wood-panelled staff room. I'd made photocopies of Bethan's letters on Saturday – something I could write my own notes on – and these were tucked into *Snatched in Plain Sight*. A couple of the other teachers gave its cover curious glances.

'Doesn't look like your usual fare, Margot.'

I looked up from the last page and saw the headmaster, Ben, who'd stalked into the staff room without me noticing. He had paused to tower over my chair. His mouth, with its little grey square of surrounding beard, was a set grimace of disapproval; his pale eyes flicking down to the lurid cover and then back to me.

'No,' I stammered, realizing what I was doing. 'It was recommended to me. By a friend.'

'I see.'

I could feel my age slipping away. At that moment I was about seven years old.

But then I had a sudden flash of Lily's drawing, from Saturday – of me as a cowering little girl in pigtails when really I was a Fury.

I coolly let my eyes fall back to the book.

He was about to add something else when the bell saved me.

Ryan Sipley, the chief wag of Year Eight, was stuttering and sweating. He was engaged in a fierce war with the English language, and today's battlefield was *Jane Eyre*.

'"This is my wife," said he.' Ryan looked imploringly at me, begging me to pass the bitter cup of reading aloud to some other unfortunate.

'Go on,' I said.

I felt terrible. He hated it, I knew. On the other hand, there's plenty of evidence that reading aloud is good for kids. They have to engage with the text; even what appears to be the most colourless and stammering rendition implies choices in what to emphasize and what to play down – what to show and what to hide. It requires you to structure your language, to be fluent, to wrestle with what you are saying, to face the crowd. I could only hope that at some point in the future, in some social situation that presumably didn't involve reading aloud from *Jane Eyre*, this practice would bear fruit for Ryan.

It still made me feel like a heel.

Three girls in the last row were passing texts amongst themselves and giggling at the back of Sorcha Malone, who usually sat with them but must have offended them in some way, as she was now parked three rows in front. Her face was stony pale and her eyes pink with unshed tears.

The girls' ringleader was Amber McGowan, known bully and scoundrel. I eyed her keenly, having now chosen the next candidate for this literary trial by ordeal.

'"Such is the sole ... co-juggle..."'

'Conjugal,' I supplied gently. 'Take it to mean married.'

His face went scarlet. I decided to have mercy.

'Thank you, Ryan. Amber, can you go on please?'

Ryan sighed audibly in relief. Amber McGowan's head started guiltily at the mention of her name. It had been bent over her iPhone; her book lay under her arm, forgotten.

'What, Miss?'

'The book,' I said coldly. 'Do you know where we're up to? And there are no phones in my class, Miss McGowan, as I believe you already know. If I see it again it's going in my desk until the end of term, do you understand?'

She half-covered her smiling mouth with a mock embarrassed hand. 'I don't know where we are, Miss,' she lisped self-consciously.

One of her toadies had been following the text on her behalf, and with the place pointed out to her, she adroitly picked it up.

'"Looking collectedly at the gambols of a demon..."' She pushed a lock of her long hair out of the way of the page.

Amber read on, by rote, imbibing none of the sense of the book, only repeating the words. What a waste of time. I glanced at my watch. Another

49

twenty minutes to go...

If I didn't do this, I reminded myself, there was a good chance that at least 50 per cent of them would never ever read *Jane Eyre*, picking up the answers to essay questions from friends and parents, or even just guessing. I'd asked Ben if I could show them a DVD of it, and he'd stuffily replied that we didn't possess one. I'd asked if I could buy one out of school funds, and this proposal would now be hummed and haa'd over in every Tuesday lunchtime staff meeting until kingdom come. I could buy one out of my own money, but I'd probably have to fight to show it – the headmaster took a very dim view of the 'pornographizing' of modern popular culture, and would use the platform at the meeting to explain why he would not be 'actioning' this without more thought.

I would usually say something inadvisable in response, such as observing, in my capacity as an English and Classics teacher, that 'pornographizing', like 'actioning', is not and never has been a real word, and even if it was, it made no sense in the context of any recent film adaptation of *Jane Eyre*.

And then the others I work with would start to cough and look at their watches and make excuses to leave. And so everything stays the same; always the same.

I wondered if Bethan Avery had ever read *Jane Eyre*. I wondered whether she would just have repeated the words, or whether she would have understood the sense...

I ran a finger over the white pieces of paper I keep on my desk to make notes. The paper felt warmer than I did. The top of the book was visible from where I was sitting, poking out of my bag. I could see its bloodstained title.

It was a horrid story.

Bethan Avery was fourteen years old, the child of Melissa, a career drug addict, and fathered by some unknown quantity during a sojourn in the bright lights of the capital. Bethan slipped straight out of the womb and into care. Her mother fought intermittently to get her back, with frequent tragic bouts of determination to 'turn her life around', which could last as long as nine months; but her demons, though they could be persuaded to give her a long leash from time to time, never truly let her go. In the main the baby stayed with her grandmother, Peggy, a cheerful, gruff soul who did her best.

Eventually Melissa vanished – went abroad to pursue a 'modelling contract' in Amsterdam and was never heard from again. Meanwhile, life in the end cottage on Parkhurst Lane continued as normal. But one icy January in 1998, there was a terrified phone call from one of the neighbours – Peggy had slipped and smashed her skull on her frozen doorstep. Bethan was fetched from her first day back at school and brought to Peggy's bedside. Peggy had been prepped for surgery and was wheeled in.

At some point somebody noticed that Bethan had gone missing.

I sharply recalled myself – I was once again in my class, watching the white scalp of Amber McGowan through her pale hair as she bent over the book. It might be her that had written the letters.

It might be anyone.

I gazed over the bowed heads of my class, silent while Amber read, restless and aware that she was being singled out, and increasingly bold about showing her displeasure. I knew the kids sometimes wrote fake letters to the column, trying to get one over on me. In fact, only a few months ago, two idiots in Year Twelve had attempted such a thing over email, but had forgotten that the school's IP address was visible.

Nevertheless, they had not yet ever pretended to be a murdered schoolgirl – and considering how subdued, even shocked, they had all been since Katie's disappearance, it seemed unlikely they'd try now.

The sad fact, though, was that as tasteless as such a fraud would be, especially considering Katie's disappearance, it was still well within the bounds of possibility.

There are reasons children are not allowed to vote or be left unsupervised for long.

It took hours for anyone to realize that Bethan had not just nipped out for a moment alone – something had gone horribly wrong. She had vanished from the hospital, and nobody knew where to or how.

In the midst of this, within an hour of Bethan's last sighting, Peggy died on the operating table. While she was under the knife, it became clear that there had been nothing accidental about her death – her skull bore clear, sharp little hammer marks, and bloodstains later confirmed that she'd been killed in her home and dragged to the doorstop after she had been seen waving Bethan off at the door.

The police visited the school, to nod sagely over tearful testimonies and the wringing hands of the headmistress. Flyers of Bethan's face appeared in the local shops, were nailed to telephone poles and taped to streetlamps. The papers cried for public inquiries, for people to be sacked, for safer streets, for a return of the death penalty. The Fens and the river were all searched.

There was nothing.

But life continues for all the living, and Bethan was slowly forgotten. Two months after her disappearance, a stout middle-aged woman called Angie Holloway was walking her dog at nine in the morning along a public bridleway that tracks out west to the Fen edge. I know it well – Eddy and I had taken long summer walks along it in our early courtship, as it passed a rather marvellous country pub called the Black Swan, which served an exemplary steak pie. The pub, like our marriage, changed hands and has closed down now.

The gravel track crossed a stream called Bin Brook, and it was there that Angie spotted a white rag, stained with maroon-brown, flying like a banner from one of the posts lining the bridge, caught up in the chicken-wire fencing. There was something about the stains that drew Angie's attention; that and the fragile white fabric. It was a nylon nightdress with lacy edges, of the type not currently fashionable, and liberally drenched in blood.

Angie was able to testify that this garment had

not been on the bridge post the previous day. The hunt began again in earnest, and the forests and hills were scoured once more, the locals questioned, and all the houses, great and small, searched to no effect. The inquiry had become, through a process of slow degrees, a murder investigation.

A team of frogmen arrived to dredge the brook. At the end of three weeks, they had found a vertebra, which later turned out to belong to a sheep. They never found anything else, ever, though they dug all around the surrounding parkland. The bloodstained nightdress was, to all intents and purposes, the entire estate of Bethan Avery. Little enough to have, and anyone could have disputed her possession of it.

For instance, me. I dispute it. I've read the letters sent to me from someone who says she's Bethan Avery. What if she had escaped her captor in some way; injured, yes, but not killed? Who knows, or could dream, what terrors or pressures controlled her? What sort of woman would she be, seventeen years on? She would be utterly different from the girl who'd been lured away and seized. And she'd also be the same girl, trapped and terrified, living an ancient lie. Somewhere out there a child cried out within the woman for comfort, for rescue, for escape...

The thought chilled me.

Then again, conceivably some pervert, hunched over a Formica table long after his wife and children had gone to bed, with palms sweating and brow contorting, had penned these letters to me, dwelling lovingly on his fictional heroine's helplessness.

Perhaps it was even someone who knew what had happened to Katie Browne.

I didn't get around to mentioning any of this to anyone. I tried the police with the second letter, urging them to consider both in the light of Katie's disappearance. They were polite and attentive, they offered me institution-grade instant coffee in a tiny paper cup while I talked, but they were absolutely not convinced. I was being indulged, and I knew it. It felt worse than the first time, when they had actually laughed at me. That at least had been an honest response.

I tried to get them to take the letters, which they reluctantly agreed to do, but there was something about their attitude that made me think they considered me a crazy person and that the letters were likely to go straight in the bin the minute I was out of the building. I suspect that I was being paranoid and that they would have done nothing so rankly unprofessional, but I couldn't shake the idea once it had entered my head. In the end, they took the photocopies, and I left with the letters still in their brown paper envelope, tucked in my bag.

I had taken to calling by the *Examiner* every other day, though Bethan, or whoever it was, had fallen silent.

But on 14 November, I received an email.

Dear Mrs Lewis,

Forgive me for contacting you like this. I obtained

55

your details from the Cambridgeshire police.

I understand that a couple of weeks ago you received some disturbing letters, and that copies of these were handed into the station in Cambridge. I am writing to tell you that after some tedious detours these copies have found their way to my office.

My name is Martin Forrester, and I am the senior criminologist in the Multi-Disciplinary Historical Analysis Team. At this point you're probably wondering what we do, a question I frequently wrestle with myself. In simple terms, we work in partnership with various public bodies and police forces to analyse crime data.

I don't know who is writing you these letters. I do know that we compared the handwriting in them to copies we have of Bethan Avery's diaries – excerpts from these diaries are reproduced in Moore's book. As you observed to the police yourself, the handwriting in the letters is similar.

However, there are other reasons why the letters are interesting. To that end, and with your permission, we want to show the original letters to the forensics expert that worked on the case at the time.

If you can assist us in this, please contact me at my email address – mdf17@crim.cam.ac.uk – or call me at the Institute. I look forward to discussing this with you in person soon.

Yours sincerely,

Martin

P. S. I'm a big fan of your column.

Dr Martin Forrester
Head of Multi-Disciplinary Historical Analysis Team
Institute of Criminology
Cambridge University
Cambridge
01223 335360 (ext. 9873)

5

I wrote an answer to Martin Forrester that evening on my MacBook Air while I was meant to be writing my column. I had already Googled the Institute, and though I found the MHAT web page and his biography, there was maddeningly little information. I intended to dig a little further, perhaps find a picture of him, but within minutes of clicking *Send,* there was a reply.

'You're at St Hilda's, right? Off Trumpington Road? M'

How had he known that? At the police station I had appeared in the character of Dear Amy, or rather the Margot Lewis who worked under that name. I hadn't mentioned my day job.

How curious.

'I am,' I replied, since it was pointless denying it. 'Well guessed.'

It was designed as an opening, one where he could volunteer how he'd learned this about me, but he wasn't drawn. It was impossible to tell whether this was subtlety or social denseness at this point. He was a Cambridge academic, I thought ruefully, and after marrying one I knew it could be either.

'Could you meet me for coffee on Monday or Wednesday, depending on your schedule? M'

He was keen, I'll give him that, and clearly quite direct. I typed a quick answer: 'I have a free period between 11 and 1 on Monday, if that works. I'll bring the letters with me.'

Within thirty seconds, my email pinged in reply.

'Excellent. I'm in college Monday morning, so how about 11:15 in the Copper Kettle. I'll get us a table. Any problems, my mobile is 08978 3455 43. M'

I sent a cheery acknowledgment, but did not reciprocate with my own mobile number.

He had one last thing to add.

'Oh, and our forensic expert says that from now on, please try not to touch the letters any more than you have to. Till then. M'

After that, I had no further interest in working on the Dear Amy column, or the essays, and certainly not the legal forms for the arbitration for the end of my marriage. Instead, I sat up and drank a bottle of wine in the growing darkness, wondering what I had got myself into, and whether I was prepared to cope with the places it would lead.

I missed Eddy hard, like toothache.

At some point during the night I had researched Martin Forrester. A man with long dark wavy hair tied back out of his face, and sporting intense deep-set eyes, was gazing out of my computer at me when I woke.

I rubbed my eyes, squinting at him as he leaned

forward, frozen in the moment he bent to shake hands and accept some manner of Perspex award from the University's Vice-Chancellor. Forrester's smile was unassuming though slightly practised, in the manner of men who did this sort of thing a lot. He had a rough-hewn, dark-complected look, like a turbulent druid, and could have been any age between thirty and fifty. He was in full gown and that most rare of male formal dress codes, white tie, which made his thick unruly hair appear even more arresting. Behind him I recognized the ornate wood panelling of St John's College Hall.

I sat up, hung-over and flustered in the dark dawn, as I had no memory of ever seeing this image before that moment. I really needed to cut down on the drinking, though part of me secretly and rebelliously maintains that if a girl can't drink through her divorce, then when can she?

I checked my phone – no drunken calls to Eddy's number. Well, that was something. I tried to shrug it all off, but I was troubled nevertheless, and even more so when I shuffled down the stairs looking for strong coffee and toast and found a large white envelope lying on my doormat.

'Hmm,' I said to myself, considering it. It had come from Calwhit, Blank, Mettle LLC. It has been something of an abiding mystery to me why lawyers always seem to have such odd Dickensian last names, which they insist upon gathering into absurd lists. Perhaps they are obliged to change their names when they qualify for the Bar, like nuns taking their vows. Nothing of their old human frailty will remain. They will become dead to the world.

There was nothing Dickensian about the envelope – it sported a squat corporate font in embossed silver that meant business. I tore open the heavy paper envelope with a funny, sick feeling.

Inside was a single piece of paper – heavy, embossed like the envelope. They were acting under instructions from their client, Dr Edward Lewis, in the matter of his divorce and the subsequent financial settlement. Could all further correspondence with their client please be directed through them. They thanked me for my attention in this matter.

I read it through carefully, at least three times, while waves of hot and cold washed over me – a volcanic ocean.

You knew he would do this you knew you knew you *knew*...

I stood a long time, considering my response, which, since it involved running through the streets of Cambridge and banging on the door of his love nest like a deranged person, was probably not going to fly, strategically speaking.

He wants the house he wants your house...

It was not yet a declaration of war, but the ambassadors were being expelled and worried motions tabled at the UN. Preparations for battle were clearly underway.

Calm down, I thought to myself. It was something I said to the children in class every day, and it seemed to work on them.

I needed to get a grip. Eddy had moved in with his boss now. He had a second property he rented out. No judge was going to give him my house, too, that was just madness. We were only married for three years. And he made a lot more money than me, anyway.

But they might make me sell the house. It's worth more than the flat now – a lot more. If you were to split our assets down the middle... Oh God, he wants my house.

I wrapped my hands around my head, futilely trying to contain my racing thoughts.

Oh fuck fuck fuck...

One thing at least was clear. I would need to find myself a lawyer.

In the end I went with my first impulse, and drove round to Professor Arabella Morino's Georgian terrace in its short, frilly skirt of garden in De Freville Avenue to find him. I had not gone the whole hog and turned up on her doorstep with tousled streaming dark hair in a wine-spotted nightshirt, like a furious hung-over Bacchante; instead opting for a wash and a cup of black coffee first.

Those were all the concessions I would be making today however.

When I rat-a-tatted on her imposing bronze knocker I expected to be kept waiting as the guilty lovers procrastinated on the other side, so when the door opened immediately I was thrown, my prepared, angry statement forgotten. In any case it would have been wasted on Evan, for it was he that answered my knock.

I reined myself in, and we regarded one another in silence with the wary respect borne of mutual sympathy. Evan, impeccably barbered and heavily jowled, rested one hand on the doorframe. I caught a glimpse of the pale skin of his wrist, with its light covering of black hair, as it poked out of the cuff of his dressing gown.

Oh curiouser and curiouser. Evan moved out of this house six weeks ago, in disgusted rage, and Eddy moved in. Evan is, or rather was, Ara's partner. Her once and future partner, judging by his casual attire.

I'm too amazed to speak, so he has to.

'Margot,' he said, polite but formal. 'This is early.'

It is, isn't it? I thought. It must have been about eight fifteen. A mortified heat was rising in my cheeks. I was not being very well mannered, but then, this wasn't a social call.

'I know, I'm sorry. I wanted to call by before work. Is Eddy in?' I asked this for form's sake, I realized. There was no way on earth that Eddy was in at that moment.

Evan's face did a funny little thing where it froze, and I suspected it was because he was being assailed by a variety of competing emotions, none of which were fit for public consumption. There was the memory of humiliation; the discomfort and alarm of being confronted by a spurned and potentially volatile woman; but also, most tellingly, there was a tiny gleam of triumph.

I knew all before he had opened his mouth.

'Eddy doesn't live here any more, Margot,' he said. His glance flicked away over his burly shoulder to a shadowy form I could just make out in her own dressing gown, standing at the foot of the stairs. 'He moved out.'

I resisted the temptation to follow his eyes with

every nerve, every muscle, every twitching impulse in my being. In my belly, something was squirming, with a terrible kicking energy, like a wounded animal.

'Oh,' I said. I hadn't the faintest idea what to do or say next, and Evan seemed to understand, waiting patiently for me to find my way. Within, I could see the shadowy figure move restlessly. She wanted me to bugger off, I'm sure. She's trashed my marriage and now has buyer's remorse, and my presence is damaging her rapprochement with her old favourite.

'When did he move out?'

'I don't know,' Evan looked over his shoulder, and she murmured something in the semi-darkness of her curtained hall. Her voice was husky, almost hoarse. Did Eddy find it part of her charm? 'Last week sometime,' he supplied.

Last week. He was at my house, unannounced, on Friday. Definitely Friday, for it was the day I'd come back late from the police station, the day I'd received the first letter from Bethan Avery. Dressed in his best. Come to talk about the settlement, tried to get me into bed and I'd blown him out. Why had I blown him out? I had often in my lonely hours wished him back again. Or thought I had.

Because I must have sensed something about him, I realized. Known that he wanted something.

'Do you know where he's gone?' I asked.

Evan shook his head.

He couldn't go back to the flat – he'd rented it out for less than its worth to some other chancer from Sensitall Labs, the extra-academic start-up business they were all involved in. Ah yes, of course, work was going to be very awkward for them all now, and as I seem to remember from Eddy's departmental gossip, Ara has a longstanding reputation for elegant ruthlessness. I scrubbed at the back of my head with one hand while I thought.

I'm not proud of what happened next.

I distinctly heard that husky voice murmur that it was very early and Eddy wasn't here, so could I please leave and let them get on with their day?

I glanced up, sharply, at the shadowy figure, caught the flash of the whites of her eyes.

'Don't you dare even speak to me, you filthy fucking bitch.'

Everybody froze. It would have been comical, but I was now some other Margot, and I think if Evan hadn't been standing in the way, I would have launched at her and ripped her eyes from her face with my nails. The lines that define the normal and forbidden are tissue-paper thin, after all. She has torn through my life, casting out all of the contents, all of the work, all of the memories, like rubbish spilled out of the bin during a high gale, and now she has grown bored of it and wants me to leave.

Evan moved, and with a jolt I realized I had actually taken a step forward.

'I think you need to go,' he said. That trace of sympathy had vanished now, his jaw set.

I didn't miss it, treating him to a contemptuous raise of my eyebrows. 'Well, good luck with all *this*.'

He set like concrete.

'Bloody mental,' hissed Ara from the shadows.

'I can see what he meant now.'

It was a cheap shot and aimed wide. I daresay Eddy said a lot of things about me to engage her sympathy. I wondered if he'd told her we didn't sleep together any more? Part of me now really wanted to ask her. Isn't that what married men always say?

I blew them a kiss as the door slammed shut, abandoning me in her fussy garden, which someone else was clearly paid to look after.

But by the time I got back to the car, my triumph was looking exactly like the sordid, mortifying encounter I'd promised myself from the very beginning that I would move heaven and earth to avoid. God, what did I say to her? Why was I like that? What did I hope to achieve? And anyway, selfish and heartless as she was, Arabella had never stood up in the pergola in an overpriced country hotel in a rented morning suit and promised to love me all the days of my life. I could call her all the names I wanted, but it changed nothing. Ultimately, this was Eddy's fault. He was the traitor.

I curled up in the front seat of the Audi and wept, not with grief, but in a kind of bitter, gnashing rage and embarrassment. At first, when Eddy left, when I wept at all, it was mostly through shock, as though I was in some liminal state that it would be easy to reverse, a bizarre mistake. He was going to come home, obviously. This was something we were going to work out.

I applied the scrunched-up napkins stuffed into the driver's door to my face, happy I had not made myself up that day. I needed to get to school, but I just wanted to howl and howl.

65

So this was love, apparently.

I would be better off teaching the kids about this, rather than *To Kill a Mockingbird*. It would be of much more use to them in the future.

The night before I was due to meet Martin Forrester, as I lay wide awake in bed, it struck me that I should cancel my appointment with him. Why did I want to talk to anyone about this? Why couldn't I just post him the letters? In the cold hours before dawn it seemed an increasingly gloomy, ghoulish errand to run, and I did not want to talk about Bethan Avery's suffering face to face with anyone.

Why did he want to meet me? How had he known about the school?

The prospect of engaging any further with this filled me with increasing unease. I should forget about Bethan Avery and make an attempt to save my marriage, to move past my humiliation and anger, to try to see things from Eddy's point of view. The alarm clock by my head said it was three in the morning.

Where was Eddy now?

Where was Bethan Avery now?

Was I a victim of a hoax in a way that its perpetrator never dreamed of?

One picture of her stood out in my mind. It was in Moore's book and it was the very first one. She is in it, sitting on a white pony at the seaside. Her grandmother, Peggy, is holding the reins, looking up at her, grinning with pride. She was a big, jovial-looking woman with stained teeth. Bethan glanced askance at the camera, smiling shyly, her head turned away a little. Her eyes are huge and very dark, and her long locks hang over her small face. Her hands are knitted tightly into the horse's mane. Perhaps she was scared of falling off.

But she wasn't the most interesting thing in the photo. Peggy was. The unfeigned expression on her face lit the picture with joy.

And I, who can be eaten up with jealousy, could search out this picture again and again and look at it – and at her – I who can't stand an even vaguely sentimental film, can take in all this, this feast of love, again and again.

Perhaps it's because I know it will all end so badly for this lost girl. That's rather in my character, I'm afraid to say. But maybe not this time.

Maybe ... she wouldn't be a girl any more, but she might be alive. That dark orphan, that dreamchild, that lost Persephone, might call to me across the decades yet, to be a mother to her, to be a mother to my own selfish self. And that's why I had to see it through.

I lay there a couple of hours longer, turning it all over in my mind. When the alarm clock flicked to five I rose silently and dressed for a run. Sleep was impossible, so I might as well seize this quiet, cold, magic hour.

I let myself out into the dark morning and allowed the breeze and the birdsong to blow away my doubts as I pounded down the drowsy roads. I was on a quest to save my cold and troubled soul, and tossing and turning through the dark night, I had realized how important it was that I succeed.

6

'You must be Margot.' He got to his feet, extended his hand. 'How d'you do?'

I had cycled into work today, as the weather had held its bright, sharp sunshine. I feel a constant nagging guilt that I don't do this more often, a sort of moral toothache. It would be good for the environment. It would be good for me. Cambridge, everybody will tell you, has cycling built into its very DNA.

I cycled everywhere once – when I was a student here, naturally, as even those who could afford them were forbidden cars in college, and then for years afterwards I would keep cars I only ever drove when shopping for groceries or when the weather rendered the bicycle too purgatorial to consider.

Then I married Eddy, who is much more a Porsche than a Raleigh man, and increasingly I found myself following suit as we dropped one another off and picked one another up – which was fine, as we were car-pooling, which made us less obviously ecological terrorists, but then before long I was driving in expecting to pick Eddy up, either from the Metallurgical Sciences department in West Cambridge or the Sensitall Labs out in the Science Park, and he was cancelling on me, leaving me to go home alone as he 'worked through the night'.

Worked through the night, indeed. I crushed down the fiery little prickle of anger and pain this consideration gave me. I am moving past this. Watch me move.

That morning, after my sleepless night, I had decided that, all things considered, it was time for me to get back on my bike, as they say – to resume my old life, my old habits, to close the yawning space that was Eddy's absence. It would be good for discipline.

Though it did mean that when I appeared in the Copper Kettle after my brisk journey from St Hilda's, I was windblown, shiny with sweat and sporting a bright red flush.

I recognized Martin Forrester immediately – he had obtained a table near the window for us, and he was gazing through it, seemingly oblivious to me, lost in contemplation of the delicate stone arches of Kings College until he caught sight of me self-consciously hitching my bike up to the rack outside. He offered me a wave and made a gesture both welcoming and beckoning, though he didn't smile.

I felt as though I was being summoned to see a tutor.

I came inside, wending my way past the busy tables full of gossiping students and laughing tourists, feeling nervous and flustered. He rose to meet me and offered me a firm, warm hand. His fastidious academic dress from the image on my computer had been replaced with a slightly stubbly chin, a pair of distressed skinny jeans and a neat dark blue shirt that skimmed over surprisingly defined musculature.

69

And yet, despite this casual attire, there was something harder-edged about him in person, something a little dangerous. His most striking feature, one that didn't appear in the photo, was his unsettling jade green stare, hooded under a strong forehead with thick black brows.

He waited for me to settle opposite him, summoning a waitress with a friendly nod that she quickly returned – I had the feeling they knew him in here.

'You recognized me,' I said, trying to hide the fact that this had unnerved me.

'There's a picture of you on your school website.' He shrugged, but those intense eyes didn't leave me, and there was something deeply calculating in them. 'Digital spying. It's the new black. Ops, that is.'

He smiled for the first time.

Of course – he'd looked me up, I told myself, and tried to relax. It's what professional people do. The fact that there's a picture of me on the school website isn't the same as him standing next to me while I called Arabella Morino a bitch on her doorstep.

Nevertheless, paranoia lingered over me, making it hard to return his frank gaze. I shrugged myself out of my grey coat, trying to avoid it.

The waitress, a little blonde whip-thin girl with black eyeliner and a Turkish accent, came over to take our orders. I chose a pot of tea, and while he discussed coffee with her, I took the opportunity to slyly study him out of the corner of my eye. He was taller and more rough-hewn than I'd expected. He wore a gold TAG Heuer watch that

70

looked oddly ostentatious on his darkly haired wrist, as though he'd stolen it. I found myself unexpectedly and inappropriately interested in it. Someone had bought him that – it was not the kind of watch you buy for yourself. I scanned his broad hands, their backs lightly covered with hair, for a wedding ring, and came up blank.

How intriguing.

I bit my lip, refocused. I was here on a mission. Not to be sidetracked.

'Did you come from nearby?' I asked, as the girl withdrew and I pushed my coat over the back of my chair. The atmosphere in the cafe was warm and close, the ambient chatter and clash of crockery almost but not quite loud enough to require me to raise my voice. It was an excellent choice of venue, I realized – we were unlikely to be overheard.

His reply was a crisp nod. 'Very near. I'm at Corpus.' He gestured down the street towards Corpus Christi, a pretty little college I had been inside a couple of times with an old boyfriend. 'I'm in college on a Monday. I run a postgrad seminar in the afternoon.'

'And where are you the rest of the time?'

'At the Institute, near the Law Faculty on Sidgwick Avenue.' He shrugged. 'Unless I'm travelling, of course. I do that a lot.'

I couldn't place his accent – it was professional and precise, but with a broad Northern burr beneath it. Geordie? Yorkshire? No, Lancashire. North Manchester or Bolton, if I was any judge.

'I know Sidgwick Avenue well,' I said. 'I did Classics.'

71

He grinned suddenly, and his teeth were white, sharp. With that and his piercing eyes and hirsute hands I suddenly realized what he put me in mind of – a kind of civilized werewolf. 'Ah! I pass that faculty every day,' he said. 'I often wonder what folk get up to in there.'

I laughed, clutching my handbag and the precious letters contained therein on my lap. 'Other than secret rituals and delirious bacchanals? Nothing much.'

'You disappoint me.' He raised an eyebrow at me. 'But why Classics?'

I shrugged, surprised at the question. I hadn't anticipated that I would be talking about myself so much with a handsome man, and my blush burned deeper, spreading down my throat in a wave, making my ears tingle. Damn, damn and double damn. He can *see* you, you know. 'It spoke to me the most. And I was lucky – I had a very good private teacher before I came up.'

'A private teacher? Your parents must have been keen.'

I shook my head. 'No, it wasn't like that. I was looked after by nuns. But one of them was very learned, and she gave me a head start. I took my A levels at night school.'

Our drinks arrived, and there was a flurry of business involving spoons, sugar and milk, with the waitress making two trips to our table. We sat in patient silence, under a kind of unspoken agreement not to say anything about the letters until she was gone.

'So,' he began directly, the minute we were relatively alone (on the table behind him, an older

72

woman in a green duffle coat attacked a slice of cheesecake with a fork, a copy of Camus' *L'Etranger* in her free hand, and across the aisle three medical students from St Catherine's, a girl and two boys, were chattering excitedly about a party they'd been to at Peterhouse the evening before, passing a mobile phone between them, each new picture making them burst into increasing laughter). 'I wanted to meet you in person and explain exactly why I'm ... why we are interested in your letters from Bethan Avery.'

'I was wondering about that.'

'Justly so.' He raised the coffee to his lips and drank deeply, like a man who was in a constant hurry. 'And I know you have limited time, so I'll be brief.'

I sipped my tea, waiting.

'As you've probably guessed, what we do at MHAT – the Multi-Disciplinary Historical Analysis Team – is historical analysis of crime data.' He replaced his mug of coffee on the table, gesturing with his broad hands for emphasis. 'We have a statistician, three criminologists, two psychologists, lawyers, police and social services liaisons ... the idea is that we pool our expertise and come up with something that is greater than the sum of our parts.'

'Hence multi-disciplinary.'

'Exactly so.' He nodded. 'Most of the analysis we do in our day jobs deals with general trends, rather than specific cases. It's used to inform police investigative procedure, and every so often public policy. It's big brushstrokes stuff, as a rule: poverty is an indicator in drug-related crime, or opportunistic robbery drops when you install street lighting.' Again, the grin. 'Common sense, if you like, only they have to pay us to look into it, since common sense – as I'm sure you're aware – frequently turns out to be complete bollocks.'

I stifled a little laugh. 'Indeed.'

'So we do the work, write a report, send it off, and governments and others use the report to justify spending money.' He shrugged. 'Or not spending money, as is more often the case.'

I waited, perplexed. 'I still don't...'

He cocked his head at me with taciturn sympathy, as though he understood my bemusement.

'It's like this. That's what we normally do. But we don't always work on big projects. Sometimes we'll do a little project – for instance, what happens to a sample of secondary school-age girls known to social services in the East Anglia area between 2001 and 2007 – it's literally a little project for a local care trust we hand off to a PhD student to work up for us – and then our student comes back with something interesting. For instance, she finds out a few of these girls have been misplaced over the years.' He leaned back into his seat and his eyes flicked out towards the street again. 'Misplaced in similar ways.'

Suddenly I thought I was beginning to get it.

'You discovered a pattern.'

He gave the tiniest acknowledging nod. 'Well, my student discovered an anomaly, in the first instance, so credit to her. The team worked up the pattern.'

I pondered this. '2001, you say? But Bethan went missing in 1998...'

'Yes, that's right. Bethan Avery was not the girl we first became curious about.'

'I don't–'

'Do you follow the news, Margot?'

I shrugged, a little apologetically. 'Not as much as I should, I daresay.'

'I daresay not.'

Something in his tone made me go still.

'What? What is it?'

'Believe it or not, you are not the first person to bring up the subject of Bethan Avery recently.'

'I don't understand.'

'Well, here's the thing. Nobody ever found who killed her. They found bloodstained clothes, but no body. There was an enormous manhunt and nothing ever turned up.' He leaned forward. 'But now this other girl has gone missing...'

'You're talking about Katie Browne,' I breathed, realization dawning.

'So you knew Katie?'

'She was a student at my school.' A beat, then I corrected myself. 'Is, I hope.'

'Most people think she just ran away,' he said. 'Problem child, and...'

'I know.'

'But not you,' he said, as though appraising me. 'Why is that?'

I felt there was something I wanted to say, but then I had the peculiar realization that I didn't quite know what it was yet. There was something about Katie, something about the way she had disappeared, but...

'You think it's the same man.' I thought hard. 'That's what this is about. But there's nearly twenty years between them.'

He winced a little. 'We identified some similarities. And let's just say, we know a lot more about this type of criminal than we did then. Once is never enough.'

'But if it is the same man,' I said urgently, 'it would make more sense that Bethan is writing now. She must know that someone else has been kidnapped, perhaps to replace her. She...'

'Then why doesn't she say that in the letters?' he asked. 'If it is her at all?'

'I don't know, yet, but...'

'You need to realize that we have a different sense of scale here, Margot. You think this might be the second time this has happened.' He motioned at the waitress as she passed. 'But there is a growing body of opinion that this has happened at least six times since 1998.'

'What?' I could feel the blood draining from my face.

'At least six. That we know of.'

'What do you mean?' I blinked. 'And who is *we?*'

'We...' he said, casting a sideways glance at the woman reading Camus, who, though her eyes were still fixed on her open book, was clearly no longer reading. 'You know what? Maybe we'd be better drinking up here and heading back to my office. Somewhere more private.'

7

Corpus Christi is literally a two-minute walk from the Copper Kettle. It's a tiny but ancient college, its inner jewel-green sward of lawn penned in on all sides by a beautiful sandstone quadrangle that does what it can to keep the town out on the busiest tourist route in Cambridge. To pass through its gate is to go from King's Parade with its fudge shops and whirring cameras and brash young men cheerfully touting for business for punt tours and to enter into a semi-monastic hush that has hung over that space for the best part of a thousand years.

Except when the balls are on or the bar is open, of course. I have very happy memories of Corpus, if rather mixed memories of Hans, the Classics postgrad I was dating at the time and who finished with me on Christmas Eve and then wanted to get back together on New Year's Day. I suspect there was another woman involved in that case, too, but I never got to the bottom of it, preferring instead to not return his phone calls or emails.

Christmas Eve, I ask you.

In any case, it wasn't Hans on my mind as I drifted along after Martin Forrester into the college, too deeply shocked to think straight.

The porters nodded polite greetings as he led me through the gate, and then across New Court and up the wooden staircase to his office, the steps creaking beneath our feet. The staircase itself was chill, the air still. From far away I could hear voices in the court below making arrangements to meet in Hall for lunch.

As we crested the final flight, with its quartet of doors, the names of the dons inhabiting them painted neatly on the walls next to them, I saw that there was a pair of chairs on the landing and that one of them was occupied by a lanky, dark, curly-headed youth I recognized.

'Daniel!' I burst out, pleased and surprised.

'Miss Bellamy!' He stood up, grinning though nervous, and we went through that strange moment when one of your old pupils realizes they are now expected to greet you as an adult. I decided to make it easier for him, and swooped in to shake his hand, but instead I found myself, with surprise bordering on almost-alarm, clasped in a hug.

It was proving to be a very strange day.

'It's awesome to see you!' he said. 'What are you doing here?'

'I...' I stammered for a moment, lost for an easy way to explain my errand, and touched by his enthusiasm. 'I'm taking some advice for a column I write.'

'Wicked,' he replied affably. With a start I realized I hadn't seen him since he'd left St Hilda's three years ago and that he was now at least five inches taller than me.

'Enjoying uni?' I asked.

His gaze slipped uneasily from mine to Martin Forrester's.

'Yes,' said Forrester drily. He did not smile. 'Mr

Collier is enjoying uni enormously, possibly a little too much. Are you here about your missing essay on penal theory, by any chance?'

Daniel blushed. 'I just need another day; it will be in your inbox first thing tomorrow – I swear, Martin. I won't let you down again.'

Forrester frowned at him, his sharp dark brows contorting, his face like granite, and for a second I was worried for Daniel. 'All right. Count yourself lucky I have more interesting visitors today. That essay needs to be in my inbox when I switch on my computer tomorrow or I won't read it. Now bugger off.'

'Thanks, Martin, you're a star. Bye for now, Miss Bellamy!' He bounded off down the stairs with a wave.

I smiled after him, bemused but pleased, while Martin Forrester unlocked his office door. When I turned back to him, he was observing me with a hidden, calculating expression.

'Is something the matter?'

'*Miss Bellamy*,' he said. You didn't correct that boy.'

I felt a hot blush stealing into my cheeks and up my throat. 'Ah. *Ah*. No, I didn't. Possibly because I'm expecting to be Miss Bellamy again before too long.'

It was suddenly his turn to look embarrassed and flush redly. 'I see. Of course. Sorry.' He pushed the door open, and something on the other side seemed to be offering resistance of sorts. 'Come in.'

His office was light and airy after the darkness of the staircase, his window overlooking the roofs and gables of Old School Lane. Crows occasionally fluttered up out of the trees, like raised dust devils. The room itself smelled of furniture polish and leather. The resistance to opening the door had been provided by a huge tower of tottering books, piled on the floor against an overflowing bookcase that had no further room for them. Most of them looked brand new, as though they had never been opened, and many of them sported the legend 'Ed. by Martin Forrester'. As I settled into the chair he offered me, I saw that they were all on roughly the same subject: *Serial Sexual Abuse in Care; New Perspectives on Caring for the Disadvantaged Youth; Raised by Wolves – the State as Fosterer*. On the walls were posters for conferences, a couple of blown-up photocopies of *XKCD* cartoons, and a big print of the Horsehead Nebula. Postcards from all over the world peppered a noticeboard next to the tall, groaningly full bookcase.

I saw no photographs of women or children on his desk, then told myself off for looking for them. Bad, nosy girl.

He settled into the chair opposite me and sighed. 'Any tea? Coffee?'

I shook my head. 'No thank you.' I let my handbag, with the letters inside, rest on the red rug beneath me. 'So, what's the next move? I give you the letters, I guess.'

'Yes. The guy we're planning on showing the letters to is called Mo Khan,' he said. 'He's based in London. He's agreed to see the letters tomorrow at ten.'

I nodded.

'You have the letters with you, right?' asked Forrester.

'Oh yes,' I said.

I reached into my bag and handed the buff-coloured envelope containing Bethan's letters over to him. He opened it and gently shook them out. I noticed he was careful not to touch them. In the muted sunlight slanting into his office they looked creased and pathetic.

'Interesting,' he remarked, more to himself than anybody else, and peered down at them, almost close enough to smell them. 'Very interesting.' Then he said, 'These weren't written in any cellar. These were written and posted recently.'

'Yes. It's very strange. It's well over fifteen years later, why the present tense? She'd be in her thirties by now.'

'Well, that presupposes she wrote them. I have to tell you, Mrs ... Miss Bellamy.'

'You know what? Call me Margot. Titles are a moral minefield right now.'

'Margot,' he said, raising an eyebrow, and there was a glitter of something beneath it that took me aback for a second, raised butterflies in my stomach. 'Call me Martin. I suppose what I'm saying is that there are many more reasons to assume it's the work of our killer rather than any of the victims.' His lips twisted into something rueful, something compassionate. 'I think you need to brace yourself for that possibility.'

I didn't reply. The thought was repugnant – but I saw his point.

He perused the letters for a few moments longer and scratched his stubbled chin with a thoughtful

81

unselfconsciousness. 'Still, all of these new details... Hmm. I suppose it would be pointless to ask if you had any idea who'd written them?'

'I've no idea,' I said, shaking my head. 'Absolutely none.'

'There is something you could do for us on that front, actually,' said Martin, as though deep in thought.

'Which is?'

'I imagine,' he said, 'based on your column, that you have relationships with mental health professionals who provide you with feedback and advice.'

'I do,' I said warily.

'You could take a copy of the letter around the local psychiatric hospitals. See if any of the staff know anything about it.'

I rubbed my tired eyes, careful not to smudge my mascara. 'I suppose it's worth a go,' I said, 'but I don't know how successful that'll be. There is such a thing in the world as medical confidentiality.'

'Hmm,' said Martin, absorbing this, his piercing gaze falling upon me once more.

'Though,' I said, thinking, 'what I could do, now you mention it, and probably should have done already, is go back through the files I keep of all the letters I get on the column, and see if the handwriting in any of them resembles these. I think that'll be a dead end, too, but it would be stupid not to try. I mean, I think we can assume she's a local woman, if it is a woman. The *Examiner* isn't exactly the most obvious place to send a letter like this – if it has a circulation of more than twenty thousand I'd be amazed,' I said.

'Yes,' murmured Martin. He seemed lost in thought, looking at the letters again. 'I wonder what Mo will say,' he muttered. 'Lovely forgeries...'

'Are you so sure they're forgeries?' I asked, then instantly regretted it. Of course they were probably forgeries. I was letting my imagination run away with me for the thousandth time – the notion of the captured girl, now a woman, trapped and trying to write her way out of her fate possessed me, made my heart thud dangerously in dread.

But now I'd asked the question, I had no real desire to retract it.

He raised a heavy eyebrow in surprise. 'Well, I suppose I can understand that you want to believe...'

I cut him short. 'I understood that the assumption of death was never much more than that. An assumption.'

I think I was giving him a fairly wild stare at this point.

'Yeah, it's an assumption.' He waved a hand in dismissal. 'And it's true that there's a lot we can't assume – because we simply don't know what happened to her. But the overwhelming preponderance of evidence suggests that she was held against her will somewhere, probably by whoever murdered Peggy, and that she received a serious injury, possibly while trying to escape. It all suggests that whoever attacked her finished the job and buried her somewhere. And then moved on to the next girl.'

'But you can't be absolutely sure,' I said. 'What

if she is still being held somewhere? We know she was injured, agreed, but what if she was recaptured... What if whoever it was treated her for her wounds? There are tons of cases where kidnapped women and girls have been held for decades, in some instances. Maybe that's what's happening here...'

'Then how is she sending these letters? Is her kidnapper providing her with stamps? And here's the big question – why doesn't she just write to the police? Mrs Lew– Margot, listen to me. I don't know if these letters are forged or not, or whether Bethan Avery is alive or dead. That's why we're showing them to Mo. These letters interest me because they're strange and very similar to Bethan's journals, and I've never seen or heard of anything like them before. If this is a scam, it's a very elaborate one.' He held out his hands in appeal, inviting me to see reason. 'But it doesn't prove she's alive. Far from it. So far, it only proves that someone wants us to think she is.'

I sighed.

'Or rather, for *you* to think she is.' I was pinned down again by that green stare. 'These letters could have been sent to any paper, local or national, and got a response. And yet somehow they've ended up with you.'

I thought about this for a long moment and shrugged. 'I have absolutely no idea why.'

He leaned back in his chair, then let out a sigh, lightly misted with compassion and barely hidden exasperation.

'You know' – his gaze rolled up to the plain plaster ceiling – 'it would be fun to imagine that this girl had somehow managed to survive for seventeen years. It's not that I'm...' he was choosing his words carefully, '*immune* to the imaginative appeal the idea has,' he said. 'But until someone can prove it...' He shrugged.

I sighed. 'Of course you're right.'

He regarded me with a thin sliver of suspicion for a long moment, as though he was trying to work out whether I was humouring him.

Suddenly he was on his feet. 'Come on, you'll be late. I'll walk you out.'

We strolled back across the courtyard, which was starting to fill up as students and staff wheeled back into college for lunch.

'Margot, I wouldn't build too much upon these letters. Even if we do find out they're real, what good does it do us if this woman won't tell us what she calls herself now? Or where she lives?'

I felt a pain in my chest, and realized it was my heart beating against my ribs. Martin was talking to me as though I were an overexcited child. He sounded momentarily like one of the counsellors at the clinic. I shuddered. Maybe life really is as simple as the people at the clinic suggest. I always have trouble believing it. I expect that's because I know it's not true.

'Perhaps she doesn't know where she lives, if she's being held captive in this place. She doesn't know she's been forgotten. I'm sorry,' I said as we reached the heavy darkness of the gatehouse. 'But somehow I believe in the letters.' I gave a tiny, apologetic twitch. 'I just do.'

We faced each other. The cool air blew between

us and I could feel myself anchored to the ground by the stony weight of my conviction. 'This woman, Bethan Avery, could still be alive. I'm not even saying she's being held prisoner. She believes she is, though. She's still the girl kidnapped twenty years ago. She wants to be set free.'

Martin rubbed his chin once more, seemed about to speak, then fell silent, with a sharp shake of his head, a policy decision in action. 'I'll take the letters to Mo tomorrow. There's no point discussing anything until then.'

We had reached the gate, and with an old-world courtesy he reached out and shook my hand. Again that warm, firm grip, surprisingly gentle from such a burly man.

'It was genuinely lovely to meet you, Margot. And I'll let you know the minute we hear anything,' he said. 'In the meantime, if there are any more letters, don't hesitate to call.'

'I will.'

He turned away, but before he could leave...

'Martin, wait.'

He paused mid-step, regarding me.

'You said that there was something else interesting about the letters. In your first email. I meant to ask you what it was.'

His face set a little, smoothed into something almost defensive.

'The handwriting...?' he mused out loud, and for the first time I had the sense that he was not being wholly honest – that he knew exactly what I meant.

'No, you said something else. That there were "other reasons" the letters were of interest.'

He froze, and then, as though considering, glanced quickly over both shoulders, then moved to rejoin me at the gate.

He bent low, next to my ear, and there was a strange, ambiguous moment during which I wasn't sure if he meant to kiss me or not. I was about to draw away when he whispered, 'The second letter mentioned soundproofing.'

'What?'

'Soundproofing,' he repeated. 'They found fragments of insulation material on Bethan's nightdress, they think it was used for sound-proofing.' He stepped back, with a little shrug. 'It was never made public.' He beetled his brows at me. 'So please keep that to yourself.'

It was over and I was back on King's Parade, in the mob of tourists, hurrying academics and office and shop workers in search of some lunch. I wandered, in a kind of weird, anxious dream, back towards the Copper Kettle and my bicycle. A big tour group was coming towards me and I stepped out of their way. As my groping hand reached out to steady myself it touched glass, and I became aware of a loud ticking, sinister and yet familiar.

I was in front of the Corpus Clock. I glanced at it, caught. Behind the glass a huge rippling gold disk, backlit in bluish-pink, the edges ratcheted with teeth, moved in fits and starts. Above it was a large gleaming metal locust – the Chromo-phage, the time-eater – who rode the teeth as they moved beneath its chrome body, each one issuing a harsh metallic click.

I have stood here for up to a quarter of an hour at a time before now, entranced by its slightly irregular, sinister movement, which is only absolutely accurate every five minutes. On one of our first dates, Eddy taught me to read the markings on the gold-plated disk to translate the hour. I sighed and glanced down at the inscription in stone below it: '*Mundus transit et concupiscentia eius.*'

'"The world passeth away, and the lust thereof"' I murmured.

I considered Martin Forrester, his piercing eyes, his thick dark hair, before firmly shaking my head and trying to dismiss him from my thoughts.

I had to go.

Work passed in a dream, and then there was the Classics Club after school – we were doing the third of our Conversational Ancient Greek nights this year, which is normally hugely amusing, but somehow I felt a little distant, a little lost, and had to work hard to hide this from the kids. We were doing an improvisation with Demeter asking in various shops and public amenities whether anyone had seen her lost daughter Persephone – the goddess of the fields looks for her daughter, the goddess of spring growth, who has been abducted by Hades, Lord of the Dead and the Underworld.

It was the sort of thing the children found funny and as a consequence their language skills raced ahead – in their version, Persephone has lied to her mother about where she's gone and is instead hiding with her unsuitable boyfriend underground – but tonight everything about it, especially the ribald undercurrent, grated upon my nerves.

It was late when I got back home, and there

were no further letters from Eddy's lawyers. The bedroom was slightly chilly, and I hurried into the bathroom, anxious to huddle myself into my bed as soon as possible. I pulled the cord dangling from the bathroom ceiling, and the light came on with a hum and a click.

My face was thrown back at me from the fluorescently lit mirror. I looked dreadful. A light sheen of sweat covered all the visible surfaces of my skin. My nervous lines had returned – they never really go away – but right then they were pronounced. When they get worse, the muscles they bind start to jump. Then they are twitching cords running from my cheeks to my chin, framing my nose with its rumpled bent bridge, making me look like a gargoyle or a damned soul.

I washed my face carefully, and then fumbled through my bag, finding the right bottle of pills. I was tired, so it took a few minutes. 'ZORICLOR-ONE – TAKE AS DIRECTED', and then my name. I unscrewed the lid and shook one into my damp palm. It was snow white against my pink skin.

I raised it to my mouth. The woman in the mirror mimicked my actions, my greedy haste. I suddenly stopped and so did she. What the hell was I taking it for? I looked terrible but I felt ... I felt fine. I could take my quiet heart and clear mind to bed to a just sleep, as deep and refreshing as a baby's. I couldn't remember feeling so good for a very long time.

The harried, nervous woman in the mirror raised a sardonic eyebrow at me, wondering what I would do next. She glanced down at the pill she held in her palm. Then she carefully tipped it back into the bottle, screwed the top back on and yanked decisively at the cord hanging from the ceiling, dismissing me with darkness.

I left the bathroom and stumbled through the gloom to my bed, barking my shin against the bedside table in the process.

But I slept like a baby.

8

Luisa Martinez's Facebook feed

Luisa Martinez: *Crying all morning – really missing my bae Katie now whose been missing for nearly 5 weeks! I hope the angels in heaven are watching over you, my beautiful bae and wherever you are hope you're OK.*

Charlotte Finley: *Sorry to hear you're upset, I keep crying too! Hopefully there will be news soon. :(*

Amber McGowan: *You're such a spaz Lu you hardly knew her and anyway everyone knows she's obvs gone off with her gyppo boyfriend. You're so thirsty for attention and its pathetic.*

Sorcha Malone: *Katie finished with Nathan before she went missing and he's still around. Check yourself Amber cos her Mum can see this page.*

Amber McGowan: *It's not me upsetting Katie's mum but Katie the selfish bitch, and IDK what you're so righteous about Sorcha cos you never liked her anyway.*

Sorcha Malone: *You lying cow! I NEVER said that! And Luisa is allowed to like her and miss her if she wants. What's it to you anyway? Stop being such a bitch for once in your life.*

Luisa Martinez: *I can't beleive how horrible your being to me. I was just being worried about my bae! I have been crying for weeks!!!*

Sorcha Malone: *Stop it Luisa you're just embarrassing yourself. Amber is right you hardly knew her tbf.*

Amber McGowan: *It's always about YOU isn't it La-La Lulu, and you can stop being 2-faced Sorcha. We all know Katie Browne's probably gone off to have an abortion or because that stepdad of hers has buried her under the patio, or whatever these social housing types do LOL!*

Brian Morris: *is that what they teach you to be like at that posh school you stuckup little madam how dare you talk like that about our katie where my wife can see it you heartless little sod!!! see you in school amber mcgowan i have took a pic of this scren bfore you dletee it and that posh school is goin to be hearing all abot you!!!!!!!*

And Brian, being as good as his virtual word, had

91

done precisely that, and so here we all were.

'My account was hacked,' Amber said, tossing her blonde head, though the two burning patches of red on her cheeks betrayed her as a liar.

Ben, our headmaster, had Luisa Martinez's Facebook page open on the laptop on his desk. Though he's quite content to bully Lily, Estella and me in meetings, the girls at the school, particularly the pretty ones, tend to reduce him to pusillanimous mumbling.

Today he had a problem, however. Brian, Katie's stepfather, had been in the office for over an hour, and Estella, who taught in the class below, had been hard pressed to stop her students from muttering and giggling at the low boom and roar of Mr Morris's voice as he, in the parlance of the day, 'Tore Ben a new one'.

Accordingly, Ben solved this problem by calling me in. I must have appeared a suitable enforcer to him.

'Clearly that's you,' I said coldly to Amber. I haven't taught for years without picking up a few social media tricks. 'I can tell it's you. Once you've finished libelling Katie and her stepfather, you then go on to "like" Tabitha's party photos and post the stats for your latest game of Bejewelled.' That rage, that Stygian rage that bubbled up from within me on Arabella's doorstep, was roaring at the gates of my ears. That man. That poor man, having to read that about Katie. And her mother. The thought of it smote me.

It was all I could do to stay calm. 'It was absolutely you.'

Something of all this must have shown in my

face, as within moments Amber paled and her defiant jaw unclenched.

She took a step backwards.

'ISN'T IT?'

Ben stirred, as though I was frightening him too.

But she nodded, once, and her eyes flicked to the ground.

'I just...' She swallowed and blinked her eyes hard, trying to conjure tears. 'I was just so angry at Luisa, because ... because Luisa didn't know Katie at all and yet there she was, trying to get attention, trying to get everyone to feel sorry for her, and I just had a go and then Sorcha, who is supposed to be my friend, was pulling me up in front of this idiot, trying to make me look bad, and I just ... I don't know, I just wanted to show them both up.' She blushed hotly. 'I mean, I'm not stupid. I know it looks bad.'

'Her father could read that.' I folded my arms. 'Did you not even consider that?'

'Her stepfather...'

'Her father to all intents and purposes. Don't try to excuse your behaviour on those grounds.'

She glanced up, her eyes red but dry, despite her best attempts, and I have to confess I did, in a warped way, understand her, even if it was an unforgivable way to behave. In the same way that Luisa was a slave to attention, Amber was a slave to her status. Sorcha had challenged her while she'd been in the process of putting Luisa down, and Amber had had to prove that she feared nothing and no one and could not be ruled by mere beta females, which meant not appearing to care what she said.

Neither she nor Luisa cared about Katie. Katie was a cypher, an alibi, something they could hang their interpersonal politics upon.

The girl herself remained missing, a footnote in their lives, just as she would become a footnote in a dreadful book like *Snatched in Plain Sight*.

Like Bethan Avery had.

I felt very tired suddenly.

'We'll need to discuss what we're going to do with you, Miss McGowan.' Ben stood up. 'And contact your parents.'

For the first time Amber's eyes grew round, and then pooled with genuine tears.

'No! You can't tell my parents ... you don't understand. They're very ... stressed right now...'

A flicker of sympathy shot through me. Amber got all of this from somewhere, after all.

'Come on, you,' I said, guiding her towards the door. 'It's no good crying now. What do we tell you in pastoral care? About the Internet?'

She screwed her lips tightly together. 'Don't post anything anywhere that you wouldn't be happy to repeat on television.'

'Hmm. So you do listen to me sometimes.'

After school that day I decided to follow Martin's advice. I took the second letter with me, and half an hour later I was parked outside Narrow-bourne Hospital.

The hospital made me cringe like no other place could. I had spent two weeks in an institution like this during my breakdown after university. I could still remember what it felt like to

94

be totally dehumanized – mashed down to my lowest common denominator – with very little effort. I could taste the never-ending rising panic of those wretched days on the tip of my tongue.

Maybe, if someone here recognized the letters, something good might come out of it, and with this in mind I climbed out of the car.

I had come to this particular hospital again as an out-patient three years ago, after a series of mis-understandings that would have been comedic in other circumstances. I accidentally overdosed on my medication – it's one thing to take too much aspirin, quite another to take too much Zori-clorone. No one at the school ever found out about that – about me being a Narrowbourne patient, that is.

'Hello,' I said. 'Is Staff Nurse Marriott on duty?'

The receptionist looked up. I remembered her. 'What's it in connection with?'

I pulled out the ID card Iain had provided me with shortly after I started work at the *Examiner*. 'I just need to ask her advice on something for the paper.'

'Do you know which ward she works on, love?'

'Chamberlain,' I said, and waited as she dialled through. I was wasting my time and I knew it. There was no way Lisa would instantly recognize the writer of these letters, even if it was one of her patients. But what else was there? Even if the letters were genuine, finding Bethan was going to be a huge, huge task. And, anyway, I had to be able to tell Martin that I had completed this errand.

For some reason his good opinion mattered.

I was trying to think of a fresh approach to the

95

problem when Lisa appeared.

'Margot, how are you? I haven't seen you for ages! How're you keeping?'

'I'm fine,' I replied, truthfully. I'd never felt better. 'I'm actually here on business. You knew I did some work for the local paper, didn't you?'

Lisa nodded. 'I gathered there was some reason for all those secretive phone calls requesting leaflets and so on. What were you up to?'

I laughed. 'I must have surprised you a few times – sterilization one week, alcoholism another.'

'The one that got me was Sickle Cell Anaemia,' remarked Lisa drily.

I smiled. 'The thing is, I was wondering whether you knew if someone in here had written this,' I said, producing a photocopy of the first letter. 'We've been getting a few of these at the paper.'

She scanned it, tiny lines crinkling the corners of her eyes. 'I've not the faintest,' she said after a long moment. 'Spooky, isn't it?'

I took the letter back.

'You could ask around,' she suggested. 'If these things are a real nuisance. But I don't think it's from here, to be honest.'

'I thought as much,' I said.

'I'm on my break now,' she said. 'Coming for a cup of tea?'

The place made my skin crawl and even Lisa's pleasant face brought back unpleasant memories.

'I'd love a cup of tea,' I said, smiling right through the heart of my fear.

Perversely enough, I went to the *Examiner* before I went home. I turned my office key in the lock

96

and was surprised to find Wendy there, even though it was Tuesday and seven o'clock at that. She was bent over a piece of paper.

'God, Margot, you're efficient. This has been every day this week.'

'I was passing,' I said with a shrug. 'Thought I'd call by for my post.'

She eyed me curiously. She reached behind her into the cubbyhole. It occurred to me that she never let me check the cubbyhole myself if she was in the office. 'Here you go.'

I glanced through the letters. I was wasting my time, I told myself. Then the familiar shaky, childish handwriting leapt out at me.

I was on the brink of asking Wendy when it had arrived and only just stopped myself. I shoved the bundle of letters into my bag. I could feel her staring at my back. I daresay she thought me very strange. But then, what the hell was she doing here?

As I straightened she looked away.

'Working overtime?' I asked, hefting my bag over my shoulder.

She nodded ruefully.

'Well, I'll probably see you tomorrow, then.'

'Bye.'

Her eyes bored into me through the office window as I walked down the steps of the building. Perhaps she'd realized that something interesting was happening in my correspondence.

Dear Amy,

I hope you're getting these letters. I can't let myself

think about what it would be like if you weren't. I think I would just lay down and die.

There isn't much time left. I'm sure he's going to kill me soon. He gets angrier and angrier all the time.

I realized that I've never described him – well, not what he looks like. He has blond hair and blue eyes. I don't know his age, but he might be something old, like over thirty.

He told my nanna and me when he came to visit us that his name was Alex Penycote and he was my social worker, but I think he was lying. He says he is part of a gang. I've never seen anybody else but I believe him, because he knows things about me, and about my mum and my nanna. When I was at the hospital visiting my nanna after her accident, he said I had to come with him. Now he says that he is very rich and powerful and anywhere I go in the world he will be able to find me, because he can pay people to kill me and they will.

Yesterday I tried to run away again. I got as far as the steps but he caught me. I was sure he would kill me, he just kept kicking me and kicking me and now I can barely move for the pain.

He keeps saying that I must be grateful for all he does for me, but I will only be grateful to see him burning in Hell.

Please look harder. It's not that I'm not thankful for all you do but I have to be rescued soon.

Love,
Bethan Avery

P. S. Be careful because he's very sly and I don't think he'd have a problem hurting people other than me. Don't let anyone in your house you don't know.

P. S. again – I'm being very serious.

The next day, my enquiries were getting me frankly nowhere. I'd gone through my back files and, as expected, there'd been no other letters comparable to Bethan's. The other psychiatric units in the district were no more help than Narrowbourne.

In the days that followed, there had been no more letters.

Perhaps there'd be nothing else now... Maybe we'd had our lot.

I was thinking about this possibility, funnily enough, when the doorbell rang.

I was cutting up vegetables for a wickedly spiced peanut stir fry, and musing to myself that even the deepest emotional wounds can have an upside – Eddy had never been able to stand the stuff.

'Hello, Mrs Lewis?'

Two people were on my doorstep, a man and a woman, lit only by the lamp on my hall porch, so it took a second or so to make them out. The man wore a casual suit and raincoat and was youngish, with thick, gelled hair and a petulant, rosebud mouth; the woman had on a dark dress and dogtooth jacket. Her hair was short and white-blonde, to set off her aggressive permatan, and she had soft cheeks and large grey eyes.

I had a sudden flashback to the scrawled post-script on Bethan's letter – 'Don't let anyone in your house you don't know.'

'We're so sorry to bother you – I'm Detective Inspector Hayers and this is Detective Constable

Watson. Would it be possible to have a word?'

'I...' I was stymied by the warrant card he held up before my face.

He'd glanced down at the knife in my hand, and my own gaze followed his.

'We can see that you're in the middle of making your tea, and I promise it won't take long.'

The knife. In my distracted state, I'd carried it to the door. I blushed hotly. 'Oh, God, sorry! Yes, I was cooking. Come in.'

I hurried into the living room as they followed me, remembering to put the knife down on the kitchen counter. I turned the fire under the pan down. ('Something smells nice,' said the woman. She had a broad Essex accent. 'I love a bit of Thai myself.')

They took a seat on the squashy leather sofa while I perched on the edge of the armchair, and tried not to look a) guilty or b) nervous, my default settings when confronted by the police.

'It's nothing to worry about,' said the man, whose name I had already forgotten, it being lost in the alarming prefix of his job title. 'But we understand that you've received some letters that have since been entered as evidence in a crime.'

I blinked. Had they? 'I spoke to a man, an academic, who took them away to be analysed...'

'Yes, Dr Forrester, we know,' he said, and smiled, a brisk professional expression, designed solely to reassure the fretful. 'We don't want to alarm you, but this is now quite a serious matter. We know there's a limit to how much you can help us and that you've already spoken to our colleagues at the station a couple of times now, but we just need to get a statement from you about these letters.'

The woman nodded, watching me, 'And there are things we'd like you to do if you receive any more of them.'

'What? Oh, yes, of course, whatever you need. What do you want to know?'

The man, the detective inspector, did the talking, asking me once again to tell the story of how I'd received the letters, what my job at the paper was, who I had spoken to about them, whether I had any idea where they had come from or why they were addressed to me. As he'd predicted, it was all material I'd covered before, but I didn't have the same undivided attention focused on me then as I seemed to merit now. The man's pen scratched quickly over the pad, while both of them kept nodding encouragement at me.

'So,' I said, once they seemed to finally be satisfied. 'I suppose the letters must have turned out to be real?'

They exchanged swift looks. 'I'm afraid I really can't tell you anything about that, Mrs Lewis,' he said.

'Are they going to reopen the cold case on Bethan Avery?'

'I'm sorry...' he said. 'I just can't...' He paused, as though reconsidering. 'The investigation you're referring to was never closed, because of the serious nature of the crime.'

I frowned. 'But if Bethan Avery is alive, how is it...'

'But Peggy Avery isn't,' interjected the woman gently. 'And we suspect this crime might be linked to others.'

The man nodded, as though in agreement.

Of course. Of course. There were other girls.

Possibly even Katie Browne. Katie who had been missing for nearly five weeks now.

'Mrs Lewis, are you all right? You look a little pale,' asked the man. 'Can I get you a glass of water?'

The woman was peering at me with concern, as though I might faint.

'Me? No, no, I'm fine. I'm just – I'm just a little shocked at how everything has accelerated.' I was shaking, I realized. 'So what do I do if I receive any more of them?'

The man put his pen back in his jacket, secreted the notebook into his coat. 'If you get another letter like this, we'd like you to let us know and we'll come down to get it. Even if you're not sure, but think it might be from the same person, still tell us. We'd rather a wasted trip than see evidence be impaired. If you see one in your post, try not to touch it, and just let us know.'

I nodded. 'Yes, of course.'

Wendy will be beside herself with all of this drama, I thought. I'll never live it down.

'Thanks for your time,' he said, rising.

'Enjoy your dinner,' added the woman with a quick grin. 'God, the smell alone is making me starving.'

I closed the door after them and returned to the kitchen.

I considered switching the heat back on under the pan for a long minute, the knife clutched in my hand once more. Instead, I picked up the phone.

'Hello,' I said.

'Hullo, Margot,' Martin Forrester sounded a little breathless, as though he'd just come in. 'I was about to call you.'

'The police were here.'

'Were they now? Who came?'

'Oh, I can't remember their names, I was stunned that they showed up at all. I wasn't expecting that.'

'Well, this is a bit of an emergency,' said Forrester. He sounded brusque, distracted, as though he were talking to me but paying attention to something else. 'Are you free this weekend?'

I blinked. For a ridiculous moment I thought he was trying to proposition me. I pulled up one of the pine chairs and lowered myself into it.

'What?'

'Listen to this, it's what Mo Khan sent back: "It is my opinion that Bethan Avery's journals and the letters submitted to me by Margot Lewis were written by one and the same person."'

'One and the same? Are you sure? There's no mistake?'

'Oh, there might be a mistake ... at the end of the day it's just his opinion. None of this stuff is cut and dried. But it's an opinion that carries more weight than mine does.'

'Jesus,' I said. I was lighter than air. 'Where are we going?'

'If you can get away there's a DS who worked on the Avery case when it happened. He lives in London. He was running the review of the cold case.'

'The what?'

'The cold case – well, not so cold any more – I told you this. He can tell you about the other girls. He might be able to offer us some help in tracking down our mystery correspondent.'

At these words a cold thrill shot through me, numbing my hand as it curled loosely around the telephone receiver.

'Can you make it this weekend?' he repeated.

'I ... I don't know. I think so. I'm involved in rehearsals for a school play but I'm pretty sure I can wrangle something.' I trapped the phone under my chin. 'Listen. I'm thinking of putting an appeal to whoever is writing the letters in the *Examiner* tomorrow.'

'An appeal? What sort of an appeal?' he asked sharply. I could almost see his dark brows drawing together.

'Nothing very exciting. Just a line inviting Bethan to get in touch.'

'A line?' he asked. 'Just that?'

'Yeah, along the bottom of the column. In caps, usually. I do it when I think someone is in danger – the last time, someone wrote to me in the midst of planning their suicide and we got him to speak to the Samaritans. Runaways get in touch sometimes, wanting to pass on messages to their family...' I tailed off, uneasy with this line of questioning. 'When we can't contact someone directly we use it. We never get specific about their issues, though, to preserve their confidentiality. Nine times out of ten, the reaction of the people around them to their problem is ten times more worrying to them than the problem itself.'

'You couldn't make this appeal bigger?'

'What do you mean?' I asked, puzzled. 'Bigger how?'

'I ... look, I think this is a great idea, but I need to check in with a few people. Let me call you back.'

'OK, take care.'

'I will. You too.' He hung up.

The next day at school, when I came out into the corridor, buried beneath a massive stack of grammar textbooks I was trying to hold steady with my chin, someone was waiting for me.

Sorcha Malone was standing in the corridor, her freckled face pale and her wiry red hair twisted up untidily at the back. Her nails were in her mouth, her white teeth worrying at their tips. Nail polish is forbidden at St Hilda's but the girls get around this by having meticulously buffed and shaped nails.

If Sorcha was chewing hers there must have been a serious problem.

She straightened up quickly when she saw me and dropped her hand, as though she'd read my thoughts.

'Sorcha – what can I do for you?' I peered at her around my bulky burden.

She darted a quick glance at me, before turning her face to the floor. 'Can I talk to you, Miss?'

'Yeah, sure, of course.' I had a sinking feeling. This must be about her own role in the debacle with Amber and her Facebook meltdown. To be truthful, I had been expecting Sorcha to turn up at some point. 'Let's go to my office. Take some of these.'

I handed her half of my enormous pile of books, in case any of her friends, or others, should see her. This way she would appear to have been drafted in to help me, rather than seeking my advice. She received them gratefully. Appearances are of vital importance when you're that age – my personal conviction is that this is something we are all supposed to grow out of, and yet so few of us do.

We joined the general melee in the corridor, all in genial chaos now that it was lunchtime. I led, aware of her shuffling behind me, taking her up the stairs and towards the Classics office, a tiny room little better than a converted broom cupboard, with a single small circular window, like a porthole. The office makes me claustrophobic so I try to spend as little time as possible here, but it's the one place I can be guaranteed a degree of privacy when I chat to the students.

'Just set them here on the desk,' I said, and her pile of books joined my own. Silently, I closed the door behind her.

Sorcha actually has an assigned pastoral care teacher, but for some reason they all come to me. I'd love to tell you that there is some deep-seated reason for this, that it's to do with the fact that I am so cool and approachable and down with the kids and all, but to be honest, while I have no idea why it is, I am pretty sure it is none of the above.

'Sit,' I said.

She did so, almost hesitantly. She was in two minds about being here, I could tell.

'Is this about Amber and the others?'

She nodded. 'Yeah.'

I waited, letting her collect her thoughts.

'I'm not speaking to Amber right now,' she said.

106

'I see.'

'You knew?'

'Well,' I said, shrugging – Amber's carpeting in Ben's office was not really any of Sorcha's business – 'it was pretty obvious that there was trouble in paradise in my English lesson last week.'

Her face was heating up, becoming redder, and she wiped at her wet pink eyes with her sleeve. I offered her a tissue from the box I keep on the desk for this purpose.

'We fell out over Katie Browne,' she said, and as she said it, she let out a little sob.

'Yes. Amber got into a little trouble over that,' I concede.

'I mean, she's really nice sometimes – I mean Amber – and to be honest, I didn't have that much to do with Katie, she was kind of on her own a lot, you know? I mean, other than the swimming, she didn't really hang out with the rest of us.'

'Yeah, I know.'

'But me and Amber,' she said, and her loneliness was so poignant I wanted to hug her, 'we ... we're best friends, and we have a great laugh, and everything would be fine if it weren't for Laura egging her on all the time.'

I sighed and crossed my legs. Laura had not been in evidence during Amber's Facebook fiasco – she'd managed that all on her own. Girls like Amber play the Lauras and Sorchas of this world off against each other, to bring out their worst selves.

What I really wanted to say was this: 'Sorcha, you may not believe this now, but as much as Amber feels like your best friend and you can't imagine life without her, I promise you faithfully that the minute you leave for university you will not exchange more than a hundred words with her for the rest of your life. And what's more, this will be a source of enormous relief to you.'

But of course I can't say that. One of the more glorious aspects of the column is that I can be a little more forthright.

'I know Amber said those terrible things,' said Sorcha, her hair twisting in her hand, 'but she didn't mean them.'

'Why would she say them, then?' I asked.

Sorcha twitched out a little distressed shrug. 'It's just showing off that she's not scared – but it *is* scary, you know?'

Her gaze sought my own.

'Yes. It's scary.'

'I mean, everyone's been saying Katie ran away, but what if ... what if she didn't? What if something has happened to her and nobody is looking for her?'

'Who told you no one's looking for her?' I asked, trying to sound calm, but my spine chilled with a frisson of alarm. Only Ben and I had been in the office when the policeman had arrived to say that they were investigating the possibility that Katie had left willingly due to trouble at home and that we could scale down the security measures the governors had put into place.

Sorcha shrugged. 'Isn't it obvious? They stopped coming around asking questions. She's not in the news any more.' She swiped at her face. 'It just ... terrifies me that she could be out there and nobody is looking for her.' She glanced up at me, her eyes filled with the heart-breaking seriousness that only children can possess.

'Yes,' I said, and with real feeling. 'It terrifies me, too.'

I was writing a reply to an email from a girl who was convinced she was pregnant as a consequence of wearing her boyfriend's underwear. It was quite amazing, the number of letters I received in this vein. It's like the Internet never happened, though it may be that my correspondents are clever enough in their own way: Internet searches can be traced. Can I get pregnant from a toilet seat, a dirty towel, if I don't have an orgasm, if it's my first time? Am I safe if I drink a bottle of gin and sit in a scalding hot bath afterwards? If I take a contraceptive pill beforehand?

Am I safe?

These letters depress me immeasurably for all the obvious reasons.

All of these prepubescents and their endless terror of pregnancy. But I suppose I can see it. Social stigma, tearful parents, fleeing boyfriends, finally being shunted into a council rat trap with a screaming incomprehensible little monster, their frustration aggravated as opposed to palliated by the odd benefit payment.

Maybe if we all, men too, looked after everyone's kids then I wouldn't feel like I do, and they wouldn't feel like they do – an idealistic thought, I acknowledge, but it keeps recurring.

'The whole reason you want kids,' I said out loud to myself, in the mistaken belief that this will make me take what I am saying more seriously, 'is so you can make it up to yourself for having such a lousy childhood. And that's selfish.' Maybe so. Maybe. Well, no maybe about it, really. It's not some deep-seated instinct. Just a psychological gratification, sharpened by the fact that I can't have children.

I looked at the clock. It was already 3 a.m. I hit *Send* on the email, CCing in my private work account. Then I encrypted the work file, turned the light off and headed upstairs to bed.

I fell asleep straight away.

I dreamed of Bethan Avery.

In my dream I was lost in a maze, a dread-haunted Demeter searching for her Persephone.

There were corridors everywhere – a hospital that looked exactly like Addenbrooke's – vast, sprawling, a lino-floored labyrinth. There is a monster in the centre, I understand in my own dream logic, a minotaur that is always searching for me.

The place was full of bustling faceless figures. None of them seemed to pay me the slightest attention as I drifted along, my quest offering no real impetus, instead just a woolly sense of foreboding. If I glanced from side to side I could see strange things through the windows to the wards – doctors and nurses slithered in and out of their uniforms as though shedding skins, and open doors breathed, slow and deep, as if nameless things slept behind them.

'I don't know where we are,' I told a young woman who confronted me in the corridor, arms folded.

'I know.'

'I'm looking for Bethan Avery.'

She glared back at me, dark eyes bright in their surrounding thicket of clumpy mascara, her peroxide blonde hair a messy halo around her head, and for a nightmare instant I thought she would hiss at me like a serpent.

'The world passeth away and the lust thereof,' she answered. And then she let out a single mirthless bark of a laugh, and there was something familiar about it.

There was something familiar about *her*.

'Please,' I said.

She frowned. 'I don't know where she is,' she said, tapping her sharp teeth with her pen. I thought this terribly unhygienic, even by dream standards, but held my peace, tantalized by the possibility of a forthcoming clue. 'Why are you asking *me* about Bethan Avery anyway?' she snapped, her mood changing, brittle with malice, with fear. 'Who are you?'

And though I had been offered no violence, when I awoke I was shaking, like a leaf in a storm.

I lay there on my back in my lonely bed for a long time, meaninglessly following the twitching shadows of the tree branches that the streetlights cast on to my ceiling.

Now I was awake I understood that I had indeed known that girl, but had not thought of her for years and years.

Angelique.

After that, sleep was a lost cause.

9

Katie thinks that somewhere in the house above she can hear the doorbell ring. It's a deep sonorous chiming, and it plays in several rooms at once, through some kind of intercom system. She presses her throbbing, bruised ear against the drainage pipe, where it stands proud from the cool stone, and listens. Her walls are lined with decaying soundproofing material, but the exposed pipes carry vibrations and voices down to her, here in her prison.

As she recognizes the doorbell, tinny and faint, for what it is, alarm, confusion and a dart of incredulous hope pass through her, each in quick succession.

In all the time she has been here, she has never heard anybody come to the door before.

She listens intently. He must answer it, surely; she knows he is up there, as she heard him walking over the trapdoor just a few minutes earlier, his heavy tread smothered by the covering rug.

Within her breast she feels a tightening dread, a profound nausea. She faces a choice, one with possibly terrible consequences. She has to take a risk. Who knows if she'll live long enough for another such opportunity?

The chimes sound out again, and the cold rusty metal scratches at her sore ear.

But there is only a perfect silence in reply, like

a held breath.

Perhaps about sixty seconds later, the phone rings. It's the house phone, as it is louder than any mobile would be and, like the doorbell, it carries through several rooms and down the pipes, down to her – it's the ghost of a phone call.

She has only ever seen a couple of rooms in the house other than the big living room, and those in snatches, when she was first brought here, kicking and biting against her gag, her leggings soaked where she had wet herself in terror, the hood over her head having fallen askew. He had stunk of stale cooking and sweat, the house of mould and dust. The rooms were big, wood-panelled, with gigantic stone fireplaces and antique ornaments. This and the intercom make her think that it's a big house, the sort of place that should have servants, but for all of his talk of gangs, she has only ever seen him here.

The phone rings and rings, and then stops. Then it rings again.

Katie has been trying, not very successfully, to manage her hope. You need hope to survive – she knows this, instinctively, but she also knows that to allow yourself hope is to invite her twin, despair. For instance, she could believe, if she let herself, that this determined assault by the outside world on the house after so many weeks of silence was a sign that they had tracked her down, thought to look for her here. Police and scientists and clever, driven detectives in long coats had been pounding beats, questioning suspects and viewing CCTV until they found something that had led them to the door of this house.

Her freedom could be minutes away.

Or maybe it is nothing and she is going no-where. It is unbearable to contemplate.

The phone ceases, leaving a ringing stillness in its wake.

There is nothing more, but she cannot bear to stop listening.

But now it's the doorbell again, and because she is tuned in, focused, it seems much louder than earlier. And someone is banging on the door at the same time, with their fist. They must have been calling on a mobile, from outside.

They *really* want to get in.

After an age, while the world and Katie hold their breath, she hears his clumpy tread, the creak of heavy wood opening, murmured voices. She can't hear words, not at first, but after a few moments of pressing her ears against the pipes, she realizes that whoever they are, they are coming inside, into the living room with its blue rug and square stone fireplace.

'Yes,' says the stranger's voice. 'You've been quite difficult to get hold of.' The newcomer is male, and his accent has a cross, posh edge. Not a local.

'If you had made an appointment–'

'I don't have to make appointments to see you.' The newcomer sounds annoyed. 'You report to me now, as I explained. I told you I was coming up from London today. As a courtesy you were offered the chance to set a date and time at your convenience, and you've done nothing but put me off.'

Katie holds her breath. Is this another member of the gang he keeps talking about?

114

'I've been busy here,' snaps back her kidnapper.

'I'm sure you have,' says the newcomer, and she senses a mixture of impatience and pity in his tone. The floor creaks beneath his feet. 'But I'm afraid that now Mr Broeder has died there will have to be changes. The family feel that his assets aren't being managed as proactively as they would like. As their management company, we agree with them. It's absurd that this huge house should sit empty in the current financial climate, as I'm sure you realize.'

'I don't–'

'The surveyors are coming a week on Friday, sometime in the morning. If you could be on hand to let them in, please.'

'But I have work to do on the garden...'

'I wouldn't worry about it, Mr Meeks. We expect the structural work to start very soon.' There is a closing briskness in his tone. 'In terms of your role, of course, there should be news later this week. Now, would you mind showing me round?'

With a little blast of shock, Katie realizes that whoever this person is, they are not part of what has happened to her.

Before the decision is consciously made, the handcuff tightens around her right wrist and she bangs it against the pipe, again and again, helplessly, and though she is gagged she screams anyway, through the wet sweaty barrier of the duct tape. She doesn't stop; she doesn't dare stop and listen to see if it's having any effect, or think what will become of her if this attempt fails. She bangs on the pipes until her bruised wrist is cut and bleeding against the ring of steel, but it becomes apparent that nobody is coming, and when she finally lets her head rest against the pipes again, she hears the muffled sound of the giant front door closing.

Her exhaustion and despair are almost instantly replaced by freezing terror. What if Chris ('Mr Meeks') had heard her making this noise? His rage was terrible to contemplate.

She waits, in the darkness, but he does not come. She crushes down her disappointment and fear and allows herself to relax a little and think on what she has learned. Surveyors a week on Friday, whenever that was. She cannot tell the days apart, except that there is one day a week when the house is awash with classical music, and he sometimes lets her out, into the room above. She thinks this might be a Sunday. A day like that happened... Oh God, she can't remember. It wasn't yesterday, or the day before...

He seems to take a long time to turn up with her daily offering of food. Tonight it is soup, tomato, and microwaved to a blistering, volcanic heat.

He comes down the steps, carrying the bowl carefully in his hands, and her mouth waters at the smell despite herself. He switches the light on, and she blinks helplessly under the glare of the single light bulb swinging from the ceiling.

'Hungry, are we?'

She nods.

He smiles, and then, just as carefully as he carried it down, pours the soup into the drain near the door, it leaving a sad little plume of steam as it vanishes.

116

'Do you think I didn't hear that racket you made earlier?' Within moments her hair is gathered into his fist, yanking her forward, and the first blow lands.

10

I picked nervously at the lapels of the olive green suit I'd bought the night before from a tiny but very expensive boutique on Rose Crescent. My eyes had watered as I'd handed over my card – with Eddy gone, such purchases were on an emergency-only basis from now on.

And yet there was a tiny part of me that was almost, I don't know, relieved. I would be my own mistress again. I would see a way through to becoming Margot once more, Margot before she was abandoned, before she was humiliated. Margot might not have the money for many suits, but what she did have was at least all hers.

I'd dressed for this meeting, and Martin gave me a sideways glance and raised eyebrow as he jumped down from his brown Range Rover and opened the door for me. A hank of his long dark hair had fallen out of the band at the back, brushing his face, and I wondered for a long moment what it would feel like to reach out and tuck it back behind his ear.

'You look well, Margot,' he said, and treated me to a vast, wolfish grin while I climbed up into the leather seat. I felt a variety of competing and comingling emotions – nervousness, pleasure and, in the midst of these, a vague, hot little flicker of desire, out of place and inappropriate but not unwelcome. Martin himself wore a Ted Baker T-shirt and jeans, and I could surreptitiously admire his fine, well-muscled arms while he drove off.

'Is the suit too much?' I asked, with a stab of self-consciousness. Easy on the eye or no, his casual wear alarmed me.

'No, not at all.' He glanced into the rear-view mirror. 'You look … it's very nice.'

'I felt I'd better make an effort to look respectable.'

He shook his head, pulling away down Huntingdon Road, carefully avoiding the wobbling arcs of cyclists. 'There's nothing to worry about. But I need to warn you, there's a change of plan. It'll be the psychologist, Greta, and O'Neill might join us later. Greta is going to give you some copy for your column, and you just need to get the paper to publish it under your name.'

Something about his speech felt a little stilted, as if there were something he wasn't telling me.

'Sounds like a plan,' I said, settling into the seat.

He turned down Storey's Way, and we drove in silence past the newer colleges – Fitzwilliam, Murray Edwards (it was New Hall in my day) and Churchill, with their Sixties architecture and modern sculptures.

'So Bethan Avery is writing the letters,' I said after a few moments.

There was a pause. 'Yes,' he said eventually. 'She is.'

'What does it mean?' I asked.

118

His intense green gaze flicked away from me, out of the window, through the trees shielding the lane to the Astronomy Institute. 'I don't know.'

Silence fell between us again.

'Gerry seemed a little freaked out,' I ventured after a while. Gerry was the *Examiner's* managing editor, a very grand title indeed considering only ten people worked there, including me. He had regarded me with polite amazement and just a hint of reproach as I explained what had been going on, as though I had been engaged in some unsavoury activity behind his back.

Martin shook his head again. 'Nope, all squared with O'Neill. Remember, if something comes of this, there will be an opportunity to sell on the exclusive. This could be a big deal for him.'

My lips thinned. 'Charming.'

If he heard my own air of reproach, he shrugged it off. 'If we find Bethan and can get her to help with the search for Katie, it's going to be a win-win for everybody, including her.'

I sighed, only slightly mollified. I don't know why I was surprised, or even disappointed. Of course there were engines of self-interest and opportunism at work here. That's just the way the world is. But it was a consideration that made Cambridge a little greyer, a little flatter. 'I suppose.'

He raised an eyebrow at me, but didn't reply.

Around us London honked and hissed and hammered. It had begun to rain – a faint sodden drizzle, and smart umbrellas were beginning to snap open on the pavements, hoods were drawn

119

up, heels struck a little faster as they passed by. After the long drive, suddenly a wealth of secret energy seemed to surround me and buoy me up. There is something about London that always makes me feel more sharply alive. Every time I come here, I wonder why I don't live here any more.

And then, just as suddenly, I remember why not, and a little puff of coldness blows across my heart.

We pulled into the underground car park beneath a squat grey block of offices, after a sceptical guard opened the barrier to let Martin drive through. Then there was a steel-grey staircase, then a steel-grey lift, and finally a steel-grey reception area with two bored middle-aged women in police uniforms. Their eyes flicked up and down Martin, and then up and down me.

'I'll tell her you're here,' said one; a lifetime of heavy smoking growled deep within her voice, like a lifting portcullis.

We were left to mill in the lobby together.

After what seemed like an age but was probably merely two minutes, while I fiddled with my bag and Martin stood, muscular arms crossed, a side door opened and a tiny woman with a tightly styled short red bob emerged, her heels making sharp little taps as she crossed the marble. She was dressed in a cool blue dress and pink cardigan, her identity pass dangling from a lanyard around her neck. Her face was smooth and youthful, her eyes hazel and twinkly behind ironically chunky horn-rimmed glasses.

'Martin!' she said, as though his presence was a

delightful surprise, despite the fact that she must have been expecting us.

'Greta,' he said, leaning in to kiss her cheek decorously. 'Good to see you.'

'And you,' she said. 'Who's this?' she asked, turning to me.

I don't know why, but there was something disingenuous about both the question and the lilt in her voice as she asked it, and it rattled me. Of course she must have known who I was, and this was merely a simple way to guide Martin into introducing us. Even though I was little more than a messenger, I felt the subject of intense but cloaked interest, and I didn't like it.

'Margot,' I said briskly, shaking the proffered hand. 'Margot Lewis.'

'Margot,' she said, as though sounding my name out for falsehoods. 'Of course. Follow me.'

We were led up a dingy stairwell and through a series of corridors lined with offices, glass windows offering views inside them. Within the offices, towering piles of manila files balanced everywhere on desks and filing cabinets, and every so often I caught a glimpse of something intriguing – a map covered in pins, or an anatomically correct cloth doll.

'Just in here,' said Greta, pushing an already open door wider and letting us into a fusty-smelling room. Her office (it must be hers as there was a photo on the desk of her younger self with two small girls) was a little larger than the others I'd seen, and much tidier – though she still had to clear a chair free of books before Martin could sit in it. She wheeled her own chair out from behind the dark obstacle of her desk to face us, and I recognized a practical strategy meant to put me at my ease.

Unaccountably, it seemed to have the opposite effect. I have had many dealings with people who work in mental health, and I'd wager I can recognize all of their strategies, at a pinch.

'So,' she said, and she had the bright chirruping accent of someone from the Home Counties, who had doubtless played a sport like lacrosse at some discreetly expensive private school. 'I understand you've been receiving some distressing letters, Margot.' She laced her plump little hands on her lap, and I realized that the thing I'd been dreading was this – that I was once more going to be given the third degree.

I nodded.

'How upsetting for you.'

'It was a shock initially, but it doesn't upset me,' I answered, quickly and possibly somewhat impatiently. 'Or at least it doesn't upset me as much as it appears to upset the person sending them.'

She peered at me, as though I had just said something very interesting. 'I see.'

The silence gathered, and I fought the urge to babble out something to fill it. Next to me, Martin shifted a little uncomfortably in his seat.

'I suppose I'm wondering,' she said, after a minute or so, 'why you're the one receiving these letters.'

I shrugged. 'I'm sorry, I've no idea.' I gestured over at Martin. 'I've gone over my notes from the *Examiner*–'

'The *Examiner?*' she asked sharply.

'Yes,' I said, aware that she must already know this, but deciding to make it easy on myself by volunteering everything up front. I explained about receiving the first letter, the steps I'd already taken to find the author, while Martin sat with his arms crossed, refusing to meet anybody's gaze. Something was bothering him.

As for Greta, she leaned forward, regarding me with bright, brittle attention as I finished. She wore a slight smile, as though she was waiting for me to inadvertently blurt out that I was the one holding Bethan Avery captive.

'You checked in with the local psychiatric units, then?' she asked. 'Do you have contacts there?'

I eyed her. 'Yes, I do. They've been very forth-coming with advice and materials for the column.'

'And how did you meet them?'

I paused at this, a thin squirmy stirring moving across the tiny hairs at the back of my neck. Martin was frowning at Greta, deep lines framing the corner of his mouth. 'I think most of the staff would help someone out with information on request,' I say carefully, evading her more obvious question. 'Educating people about mental health issues is part of what they do there.'

'But do you know them socially?'

'No, not socially,' I said, keen to get this show on the road and myself out of this dingy office and away from her scrutiny. 'Anyway, my under-standing of the plan is that I am to publish some-thing in my section of the paper that might make this woman reveal more about herself, or possibly come forward. I think the officer in charge of the case spoke to my boss at the paper about this yesterday and squared everything away with him.' I crossed my legs, which felt chilled in the unfamiliar short skirt. 'So I suppose all that remains to do is find out what I put in the paper and how you want me to handle any response.'

She watched me for another uncomfortable ten seconds and finally let out a little sigh. 'Yes, I suppose so.' She opened a drawer, getting out a pen and paper. I was annoyed to see that the paper was blank. Martin had seemed very sure that the appeal I was to publish had already been written. I also realized that I had been expecting the supervising officer in charge of the case – O'Neill – to be here as well.

Beside me, Martin's brow furrowed more deeply but he said nothing.

As for myself, I began to get a sinking feeling.

'I just wanted, before we do this,' said Greta, 'to ask a few questions. We don't want this to appear at all staged, and it would be far more convincing if we composed it together.' She smiled again, as if sensing that I was becoming more and more uncomfortable with her.

'By all means.'

'So you live in Cambridge?'

'Yes.' I tugged down the hem of my skirt. 'Well, Girton really. It's a village just outside the centre.'

'Are you local to Cambridge?'

'After a fashion,' I said. 'Once I left the university I got work in London and then came back to live in the town itself. I went into teaching.'

'Oh,' she said. 'A teaching job in Cambridge? You were very lucky.'

I had achieved a double first in Classics from

Cambridge University, and I am fluent in Latin and most flavours of Ancient Greek. Recalling the fraught hours of revision, the late-night reading and stammering my way through my *viva voce*, I was tempted to remark that there was a little more than luck or even talent involved. It had all been bloody hard work.

For God's sake, Margot, calm down. She's just being polite.

'Which of the colleges were you at?' she asked now.

'St Margaret's.'

A sharp little light came on in her eyes, as though she'd caught me in a lie. 'Isn't St Margaret's a graduate college?'

'Graduates and mature undergraduates. I was twenty-two when I came up. I studied my A levels at night school.'

One of her dark red eyebrows lifted. 'And from there to Oxbridge.' She let out a little laugh. 'Such an achievement! Though I imagine you felt a little out of place with the usual hothouse flowers at Cambridge. It must have been very alienating at times.'

'I did all right,' I said, trying to keep my voice even. 'I got by.'

I was treated to another maddening pause while she considered this, as though I had blurted out something incriminating. But this was all a Rubicon I needed to cross, so instead of giving my impatience its head, I did a little trick I'd been taught by Mother Cecilia years ago in another life, whenever things weren't going my way: I concentrated on my breathing, letting it silently slow down, pausing just before the inhale. I should not always be the Fury.

It would have done me good to have remembered it when talking to that trollop Ara, but hey-ho.

'So you would have been in Cambridge, what, from around 2007?'

'Yes.'

'And in all that time you've had no contact with anyone from the case? Anyone at all?'

'Not to my knowledge.'

She offered me a prim little smile. 'And have you been contacted by missing persons before?'

I blinked. 'I'm sorry, I don't understand.'

'Through your work on the paper?'

I thought about this. 'Well, yes. Sometimes I get letters from people who have run away from home. Certainly never from a potential kidnapping victim before.'

'I did wonder,' she said, clasping her little hands in front of her, 'why you got into that line of work on the paper. Do you feel you empathize with people with problems?'

I frowned at her. 'Yes. Don't most people?'

'And you like to help them out? This satisfies you?'

My frown deepened. 'Is there any reason it shouldn't?'

Again that tiny smile.

Oh, fuck this. Seriously, my inner Fury whispers to me. Take the fight to her.

'Is this about the addiction? Or my breakdown?' I asked, just a touch more loudly than I'd been speaking up until this point.

'I...' She was startled and glanced at Martin, tried to resume the smile, resume control of events.

'Because it really, *really*, feels like it is,' I continued. 'And that's fine, you know. I'm happy to tell you about it...'

'I didn't mean to imply–'

'So basically I started a brand-new job writing copy at some wretched PR start-up in London where I was working up to eighteen hours a day, and before long I became a lot less fun to be around,' I said, as though her answer had been, Please do. 'Anyway, the business went under after the director decamped to the Caribbean owing me two months' salary and bonuses, which I'd already spent. None of this was particularly good news, but it was all doable, or so I thought, until in the middle of it all Mother Cecilia, who got me off drugs when I was a teenager and was, to all intents and purposes, my only family, was stabbed to death three days before Christmas in the women's refuge she managed.'

'Margot, I–'

'That effectively did for me for a little while, and I went to bed and didn't get up, and then continued not to get up until someone broke in to find out what had happened to me and I attacked them.' I inspected my dark red painted nails for an instant, then leaned back in the chair, meeting her gaze head on. 'And so I found myself in the uncomfortable position of being sectioned under the Mental Health Act.'

Greta had stopped smiling now, so that was a plus. I didn't dare look at Martin.

'I muddled along for a little while with drugs and therapy and it became clear that celebrities and copywriting and the bright lights weren't for me. I wanted to be a teacher and work in Classics, like Mother Cecilia, because she was always a real person.' I crossed my legs again. 'She didn't need a *reason* to help people. She just did it.'

'Now, Margot–' she began a little nervously.

'The rest you know, as you have access to my social services files and have clearly not stinted from using it. The short answer to your original question, and the only relevant one, is no, I have no idea who is sending me the letters.'

I shrugged into the resulting ringing silence.

After all that, the rest was an anti-climax. Greta produced two lines of distant appeal – 'Dear Bethan, please get in touch. I can't help without more info' – and it occurred to me, in a snarl of anger, that I had been summoned all the way down to London for this.

I changed it to 'Bethan A – don't be afraid – to help I need to know more about you' and there was some pointless toing and froing ('Are you suggesting that she should be afraid?' I snapped at Greta after she had resisted this minor point for a good ten minutes) but in the end the resulting text was something we could both live with.

They also wanted to publish my picture, and as Greta talked, I realized that this was the one good idea that she was likely to have. A picture would give Bethan someone she could connect with. They suggested using the one from the school website, which cast my rather bent nose into unattractive relief, but I had a better idea – Lily dabbled in amateur photography, and could take a black and white one especially for this purpose. I have always found my school photo a little corpse-like, and the death's head grin I wore wasn't likely to encourage confidence.

'There's nothing wrong with that photo,' observed Martin, with a gallantry that verged on the confrontational. 'I like it.'

My heart lifted its head fractionally from where it lay in the basement of my ribcage.

But by the end of the interview, after my initial lively annoyance, I had sunk into a kind of low funk, and I wanted out; away from her, away from him. How foolish of me to think that I would ever escape the low looming shadow of my past, that in any case where it mattered I would ever be taken seriously. And yet, while I sulked as Greta fired off the email with the approved text and Martin stirred to stand up out of his cheap office chair, I could not repent embarking on this journey. Wherever Bethan Avery was, her own misery was greater than mine.

After Greta's fulsome and false goodbyes, I trudged after Martin back past the twin gorgons at the reception desk and into the lift to the car park. He was silent and thoughtful, and I could feel the mortified blush rising in my cheeks.

You would think I was past shame by now, but you would be wrong.

As I slid into the passenger seat beside him, I could bear it no longer. I turned to him and opened my mouth to speak.

'Margot, I'm so, so sorry about that,' he said,

his arms crossed on the top of the steering wheel, his forehead resting against them. 'I thought she might poke around you a little, but to be honest, I wasn't expecting anything like ... well, what we got.'

I stared at him. 'You *knew?* You knew about me?'

He nodded wearily, not looking at me. 'Yeah. I mean, I did tell you I'd checked you out before I met you...'

'You said you'd looked at the *school website.*'

His mouth thinned. 'Yeah. I may have done a little more.' His fingers danced a nervous tattoo on the steering wheel. 'Personally, I don't see the big deal myself. You're someone who went through a tough time and bounced back. I'm not sure it justifies all of this drama but, you know, Robert and Greta are coppers, and they think like coppers...' He shrugged again, and his hands fell to his thighs with a soft slap. 'They're just being cautious.'

I looked away. 'You know, Martin ... there are things they don't know about me at my work. About the...'

'Suicide attempts?'

'There was no suicide attempt,' I said quickly, suddenly very alarmed. 'The Narrowbourne thing was an accidental overdose of my anxiety medication. All they know at work is the one, isolated breakdown that happened years ago when I graduated and was living in London.'

They can't actually fire you for having a history of mental illness – it counts as illegal discrimination under law. Thus, it doesn't appear in your DBS check, which is what they call the old Criminal Records Bureau or CRB check that all

130

teachers have to pass before they are allowed access to children or vulnerable adults.

He raised an eyebrow. 'I thought you were hospitalized twice ... once in London and once here, in Narrowbourne hospital.'

'The second time was hardly anything,' I said, and I could feel my cheeks heating up again. 'They were over-cautious. I was actually fine. Not that it even matters, because if they find out about the second forced admittance at Narrowbourne, I'm done at that school.'

'But it would be discrimination if they fired you.'

I shook my head, annoyed at his denseness. 'You don't understand. The first one was years ago, in the distant past, but the second was relatively recent, while I was working at the school, in fact. They never found out the full extent of it.

'They couldn't fire me. But if they found out about it, they could make my life very awkward until I quit.'

'Would they?' he asked.

I paused, thinking about Ben. 'I don't know.'

'Are you sure that's all?'

'What do you mean?'

He rubbed his face. 'I get the impression there's more. You can't seriously think they would fire you just for the things you describe.'

I raised my hands to my temples. I was trembling.

'Margot?'

I put my hands in my lap, faced him. I had no choice.

I had to trust him.

'I... Martin, before the nuns took me in, I'd run

away from home. I did a lot of things. I got hooked on heroin – I was injecting it by the end. The nuns got me off it, but I've still got an affray arrest from when I was a minor.' I ran my hands through my hair, frantic. 'The school can't find out about that.'

The arrest had resulted in a caution because I'd been under seventeen at the time, and it had never turned up in a background check. I understand they've relaxed the rules since and my caution is less likely to turn up than ever before – but again, if the board of governors found out about my scandalous past, it wouldn't matter. They couldn't fire me, but I would be well on my way to some sort of constructive dismissal. After all, we couldn't have all the little darlings at school exposed to my depraved and debauching influence. And just because they couldn't boot me out directly didn't mean they couldn't make my life a misery until I left.

No, no, no. This can't happen.

When I took my hands away from my eyes Martin was looking at me.

'I don't know what you're panicking about, Margot,' he said. 'Who's going to tell your employers about this? You haven't done anything wrong. You passed the background check, so it's not like you'll fail it now.'

I took a deep breath. I wanted to shake him.

'I'm panicking because information always wants to escape.' I sighed. 'That's the way of the world. My past, Bethan Avery's fate – it all wants to escape. That's why this is happening, after all.'

His reply was a sympathetic half-smile. He knew it was true.

'I just ... if that cow ... sorry,' I say, stopping myself. 'I realize she's a friend of yours.'

'She is a friend of mine,' he said mildly. 'But you're right, she was a bit of a cow today.'

'If she or anyone else starts poking around in my life asking questions...' I closed my eyes, let my head sink back. 'I just need to publish this damned appeal, and Bethan Avery will either come forward or we'll never hear from her again. Right?'

'Right.' He sat back in the driver's seat, regarding me. 'Unless you don't want to do this any more.'

'What do you mean? You think that I should just drop it?'

'You've done your best, I'm not sure anyone would blame you.'

'No.' I took a deep breath, steadied myself. 'I would blame me.' I met his gaze. 'Katie's still missing, isn't she? *I* would blame me.'

He didn't reply for a long moment.

'Come on,' he said, turning the key in the engine. 'You look like a woman that could use a drink.'

11

I cannot remember how I came across the nuns. I only know that I fell into their eccentric orbit, somehow. They used to send a plain-clothes nun or one of the lay volunteers to hand out cards at coach stations, in an attempt to rescue the young flotsam and jetsam of the provinces as they washed up in London, and I must have taken one.

But I remember my little bunk in the upper dorm of St Felicity's, with its thin but rigorously boiled sheets, and the wailing sirens and roars of night buses that came in through the sliver of open window.

St Felicity's, or Flicks as it was more commonly known, was run by the Sisters of St Mary of Good Counsel. In those days they wore habits – pale grey knee-length dresses, with short white wimples and veils, ugly taupe stockings (I asked about this and was told black was considered too racy) and sturdy brown shoes. They smelled of clean sweat and plain soap. Even after years of living with them, they never lost that aura of consecrated otherness, which I could admire but never had any desire to emulate.

They were managed by a woman called Mother Cecilia, who was from a little town in Fife called Lochgelly, and spoke with a soft accent. She seemed ancient to me, and was grey and ivory and paper-thin, and rustled wherever she walked – she made me think of spun lace, or fabric so worn that the sun shone through it. That said, it would be wrong to imply that she was in any way infirm or weak; she ruled St Felicity's, and the nuns, with a kind of strident ferocity and energy, like a female Gandalf.

There were two parts to St Felicity's – one was a pair of large, rambling Victorian semis that had been knocked through and into which homeless women were buzzed via the triple-locked door on the left side of the building. The front door on the

134

other side, peeling and weather-stained, was never used and the bolt had rusted shut. ('That's the Golden Gate, child,' Mother Cecilia replied one day to my puzzled question. 'Like the one in Jerusalem. It won't open until the Messiah knocks.')

The second part of their portfolio was a modern low-rise with six flats in Surrey Quays, the address of which was kept secret. When I was with the nuns for a while, I saw more of it. A high wall surrounded it, pierced by a single electronic gate, the top of which was fleeced with barbed wire, like a command post in a hidden war. It was a refuge for victims of domestic violence, particularly women with children, and nuns with business there changed into street clothes before setting off, lest their distinctive habits lead danger to the door. The world is a perilous place for women – that is the other thing the nuns taught me.

I remember going there on an errand with Mother Cecilia once, who appeared like a stranger to me in a serge skirt and lumpen black jacket, her short grey hair covered by a rose-printed scarf, as though keeping her head uncovered, even for a short time, might fry her delicate hothouse brain.

And it was a delicate hothouse brain. She had, at some point in her life, been extensively educated, and knew Greek, Latin and French.

To me, then, her powers over history and language seemed nothing less than alchemical wizardry, the sort of thing that centuries ago would have seen her burned. She would read things aloud in Latin and Greek, if asked, and I would listen, amazed, soaking in its magic, the music of the names of lost heroes and villains and aeons,

135

buried under tide and dust.

I don't remember how I stumbled on this hidden facet to her in the midst of a loud, busy, chaotic homeless shelter. I just know that I did, and somehow, for some reason, she took me under her wing. It turns out it's true, you never forget a good teacher. I devoured the books she lent me – simple elementary grammars and course books designed for children at first, before moving on to others, many of them surprising possessions for a nun – the poetry of Catullus, for example.

She's the reason I became a teacher myself. If I could pass on her gift to me to just one person, I would consider my life's debts paid.

And I believe I have run up enormous debts in my time.

'The secret key to the history of the world,' she said, 'is to know its mother tongue. That way, my dear, you'll always get to the living heart of a thing – the voices out of the past will speak directly to your soul. Your life and thoughts should never require a translator.'

I thought about this all the way home as Martin drove.

And the more I thought about those lost years, and the people I met in the warren of that shelter, and in the fortified flats of Surrey Quays – those places where the world's female driftwood washed up – the more I wondered whether I had, perhaps, met Bethan Avery before.

'Who can tell me who Nemesis is?'

I was back in my Classics class on Monday morning – this was the Year Tens who were study-

136

ing, for their sins, the Oresteian trilogy by Aeschylus. I was priming them, ahead of time, with a little ancient Greek cosmology before they started reading. I'd already done a whistle-stop tour of the Olympian gods, and was about to start on the more exotic parts of the pantheon.

I really liked my Year Ten class, who by a happy accident were sprinkled with cheerful, interested kids and the occasional genuine wit.

I liked them more than usual this morning, because Saturday's adventures in London had demonstrated that I was nearer than usual to losing them. I hadn't slept a wink all weekend.

Hands went up.

'Nemesis is your worst enemy, Miss,' supplied Oliver Monto, a tall youth with a massive dark afro, once I nodded at him. 'The thing that gets you, like, because of your own flaws.'

I nodded and then shrugged. 'Yes and no.' I tried not to think about how apposite this summary was to my own situation. 'I mean, you're right, but that's only what "having a nemesis" has come to mean nowadays. But it wasn't always that way. The word itself comes from ancient Greece, and is the name of a goddess. Does anyone know what she was the goddess of?'

There was a pause. 'Revenge?' someone ventured at the back, not wishing to put their hand up and commit.

'Yep, vengeance. But a particular type of vengeance.' I wandered over and drew a large cross on the board. In the upper left-hand corner I wrote Nemesis. 'The Greeks imagined two major categories of crime that needed punishment,' I said,

137

counting them off on my fingers while the class watched. 'There are the crimes mortals commit against the gods – crimes such as hubris, or personal arrogance in the face of divine will,' I tapped on Nemesis's name, 'and there are the crimes that are committed by mortals against one another despite the gods' injunction.'

I tapped on the right-hand upper quadrant of the cross. 'So, who do you think punishes mortals for the crimes they commit against each other?'

The room was silent while everyone frowned. Outside, a lorry honked angrily on Trumpington Road.

'All right,' I said. 'The goddesses that punish mortals are called the Erinyes, or you might have heard them called their other name – the Furies. Erinyes literally means "the Angry Ones", though they are sometimes called "the Kindly Ones" out of respect for their powers.'

There was an approving gasp somewhere, as if something had made sense.

'The Furies are ancient goddesses of the under-world – older than the Olympian gods – and it is their job to punish sins. Traditionally, there are three of them and they are named. First is Alecto,' I said, writing her name in the lower right-hand quadrant of the diagram. 'And her name means "unceasing anger". Next is Megaera, and her name means "the grudging one" or "the jealous one". And finally,' I said, still writing, 'There is Tisiphone. And Tisiphone's name means "implacable revenge". Together they punish the most serious crimes, such as murder or rape, particularly when those crimes involve family members.

'So,' I said, putting the chalk down. 'How do you think the Furies punish criminals?'

'They chase after them and rip them apart,' said Charlotte, a tiny blonde wisp of a girl.

'Sort of, though it's a little crueller than that. Aeschylus tells us they locate their prey by smelling upon them the blood of those they've harmed...'

'Eww,' someone said at the front.

'They then pursue their quarry day and night with shrieks and curses, wielding iron whips...'

'They nag you to death!' chipped in Malek Singh from the back of the class, making scattered laughter ripple across the room.

'You may find it funny,' I said, though I was smiling when the chuckles settled down. 'But when you think about it, what the ancient Greeks are describing here is the psychological effect of a guilty conscience, and the terror of exposure–'

With a sudden crash the bell rang and I had lost them.

'All right,' I bellowed over the clatter of books and shifting chairs. 'I want you to be up to speed on your Olympian gods and chthonic goddesses for next week! Which means I want you to know what "chthonic" means!'

12

They had placed the line at the very bottom of my column, which I was now reading over in the staff room. My picture seemed huge, irrelevant and a little saccharine. I wondered if I might have scared Bethan off.

You're being ridiculous, I told myself, which is something you are very good at. The thing only went in the paper on Saturday night. Give it a chance.

Through the staff room windows I could hear the distant yells and shouts of the children, and a quick breeze was swiping yellow-gold chestnut leaves off the trees, and they fluttered down in whirling drifts onto the lawn outside. I looked down at the message I'd put in the paper. I was trying, desperately, to keep a hold on my world – my job, my vanished husband and my column – but I was disconnecting. The ties to my ordinary life were loosening, snapping, and the dark world of Bethan Avery was becoming more real than my own. After all, what were my petty griefs against the irresistible pull of her stricken letters?

I dreamed of her regularly. Sometimes I saw her, but more often than not she was a presence, a person I knew was in the room but who was never quite in focus, shadowy and plaintive and wisp thin; a cloud, a vapour.

A ghost.

Once again, I reminded myself not to chew my nails.

I wasn't well and I felt fine. I breathed easily but far too quickly, my eyes were bright – too bright; I'd dispensed with the pills that slowed down my thoughts, but now they raced away out of control.

I was living in strange days.

All I ever knew about drugs I learned from Angelique.

I met her while I was in St Felicity's. She was in the bunk above me in the dorm – a slight teenage girl who dyed her dark hair white-blonde, and who was roughly the same age and height as me. Her skin was pale and spotty, her lips dry, and she perpetually dabbed at them with a tube of cherry Chapstik. She did not really sleep the first night she arrived, instead tossing and turning endlessly above me, making the old planks creak. I did not really sleep either, as a rule, so it didn't trouble me, but I wondered at her pathological restlessness.

At eight the next morning in the shelter cafeteria, I was eating my frugal breakfast of roll, jam and butter. I was surprised this morning to find my upper neighbour had brought her tray over and was settling in next to me, straddling the bench and arranging her long, pathetically skinny legs under the trestle table. With her big eyes and narrow body she resembled a distressed gazelle, and her clothes were hanging off her.

I regarded her suspiciously.

'Morning,' I said.

She did not reply, but nodded, not meeting my

gaze. We ate in silence, and after she had picked at her roll, tearing tiny holes out of it, like a bird might, and licked the jam out of the little packet and drained her tea, she got up and left without a word.

'O'Neill wants to do a reconstruction,' said Martin.

We were back on King's Parade, only this time we had graduated from coffee to lunch in the Cambridge Chop House, somewhere I'd passed dozens of times but never eaten in. I wore a dark green jersey top and rust-coloured skirt and boots, all the while persuading myself that I had not dressed with any extra care for this meeting. My make-up was also an afterthought, I had explained to myself, while I carefully slicked my lips a muted dark pink.

I paused, my fork suspended over my cod and cheddar fishcakes. 'What sort of reconstruction?'

'A crime reconstruction,' Martin replied, slicing into his calves' liver with gusto. 'Filmed, and broadcast on television.'

'For Bethan?' I asked in surprise.

'Yep.'

'After so long? I thought I read that there had been one already, in the nineties, why don't they show that one again?'

He was chewing now, so shook his head silently. 'No. They want a new one,' he answered after a few seconds. 'They want to include some details from the letters. Alex Penycote and his description, for one.'

I didn't know what I felt about this. On the one

hand, good, but on the other hand, Katie had been missing for nearly six weeks, during which time nobody had been looking for her, and now ... this – this sudden escalation in the hunt for what could be the wrong girl.

Suddenly, I wasn't so hungry.

'Are you all right?'

I shrugged, helplessly.

He seemed to understand. 'Remember, Margot, we still have absolutely no evidence that Katie was abducted by the same man.'

I clucked my tongue sadly. 'Same location. Same type of girl. Same social background. And now Bethan Avery is writing letters.'

'All circumstantial.'

I knew this. I tried not to sigh.

Then, surprisingly, his hand was over mine, and he gave it a light squeeze.

'Margot.' His green gaze was hard to meet, but I made myself do it. 'You've already made a huge difference. You've provided new evidence for the historical case, and this has lit a fire of new evidence under the investigation into Katie. Everything that's happening is happening because of you.'

I stared down at his hand, charmed by it.

He let mine go quickly, as though he had surprised himself in some guilty act.

There was a moment of silence. Then he picked up his glass of red, setting his shoulders, clearly determined to bluster his way through this odd, intimate transgression. 'We will find her, you know.'

I smiled wryly at him. 'Which one?'

143

'One, either, both,' he said. He cocked his head at me. 'Can you meet me Saturday morning, probably obscenely early?'

'Why?'

'That's when they're filming.' He grinned. 'I thought you might like to see it.'

I shrugged, as though it meant nothing to me. 'Yeah.'

For a long moment, I considered mentioning what had occurred to me on the drive home from London in his car – that maybe, in that lost, hidden past of mine, I had crossed paths with Bethan Avery.

But I didn't, and the moment passed.

'So, what happens in one of these things?' I asked, rubbing my hands together in their mittens. Our breath steamed in the cold, still air.

We stood outside Addenbrooke's Hospital, surrounded on all sides by enormous buildings, a brisk modern city within a city, inhabited mostly by people in pale uniforms – though not many at this time of the morning, a little after seven. Dawn had only just departed. Thin, tremulous sunshine trickled down into the narrow lanes and pathways between the towering medical skyscrapers, far too weak to provide any warmth. I craned upwards, peering into the lemon sky, tracking the flight of faraway birds. Nearby, trendily dressed young people were carrying bulky black and chrome equipment into lifts, muttering amongst themselves about proper brass monkeys weather, this is too fucking early, careful – careful with that!

'Have you seen the previous reconstruction?

144

The one from 1998?' asked Martin, seemingly untroubled by the weather and looking snug in a dark grey fleece and jeans.

I nodded, my chin lost in my chunky knitted scarf. 'Yeah. It was on YouTube.' I did not add how disturbing I found this. Who went about loading old footage of obscure child abduction reconstructions on to the Internet?

On the other hand, it had been there for me to watch, so I suppose I should be grateful. Bethan's fate had not been wholly forgotten it seemed.

'This will be a little more in-depth. We're going to try to widen the search to include this Alex Penycote character.' Martin steered me towards the lifts. 'Come on.'

We followed a worried middle-aged woman and her husband, who appeared to be nothing to do with the reconstruction, and three burly young men carrying cabling and cameras, into a large steel lift, and then followed them all out again a few seconds later on to a long, chilly skywalk.

'They're going to film in four locations – Peggy's ward, the adjoining corridors where Bethan was last seen, the lobby where the tea and coffee used to be served, and just outside the grounds.' Martin took my arm, noticed my shaking. 'Margot, are you all right?'

'I'm fine,' I said. 'It's just a bit cold.'

He contorted his brows, an unspoken question.

'I'm not a big fan of hospitals, generally, if you're after full disclosure.'

'Who is?' he replied. 'But seriously, are you all right?'

'I'm fine,' I said. I smiled at him. 'I'm actually

sort of excited. The smell of the greasepaint and all that. I have no idea how these things are done.'

He smiled back, but there was something else in it, something speculative.

'Good,' he replied. 'Come on, it'll be warmer once we're in the building proper. I'll introduce you to the production team.'

We passed through a warren of corridors, descending stairs into a lower, older level of the hospital, where the modern skywalks and steel gave way to more Victorian brick. The intense rasp of disinfectant and the bland wafts of institution cooking followed us throughout, the clatter of heels and squeaking of trolleys trailing us like curious ghosts.

When we reached a crossroads, stairwells and wards spiralling off on either side, Martin came to a stop.

'They're too rammed for space, yeah?' a brightly dressed girl with a long golden-brown ponytail was telling a small crowd gathered around her. 'They won't close off the corridor for us. So we can film, but we can't show anybody's faces. Anyone wants to come through here, we need to stop filming, yeah?'

There was a collective groan. 'Does that include nurses or patients or both?' asked an older man, stood at the back, pushing a big light on a tripod.

'We need to be out of here in an hour,' she continued, as though she hadn't heard this, 'so jump to it.' She tossed her long ponytail. 'Where have Thea and Roddy got to? Are they ready? Ah, Dr Forrester, hiya! And you must be Margot, yeah?'

She dropped the clipboard and came forward,

shaking our hands with a brisk dispatch completely at odds with her querulous turn of speech, as though we were soldiers in the field come to report further intelligence to their commanding officer.

'Hello Tara,' said Martin. 'Nice to meet you in the flesh at last.'

'Yeah, yeah, you too.' She smiled and turned to me. 'Now, Margot, you don't mind doing an interview with us, do you?'

'What?' I asked, astonished, not quite sure I had heard right. 'What could I know?'

She shook her hands at me, as though to bat away the depths of my misunderstanding. 'No, no, you're not an expert or a witness, yeah? We'll just ask you about the letters, and you can answer a couple of questions about how the person who wrote them isn't in any trouble, yeah? You just need to talk, and then re-state the appeal from your column in the same words – Pete or Dr Forrester can brief you if you've forgotten them. We might not use the footage, depending on time, but since you're here, it would be a shame to pass up the opportunity, yeah?'

'Absolutely, if you think it will help,' I said, though in truth I was more staggered than anything. I hadn't harboured any ambitions to appear on television before now.

'Great. I'll get Sophie to you with a waiver to sign. Got to get back to it – need to find my director. Laters.'

I nodded towards the blonde girl's departing back. 'Is she a policewoman?' I asked, possibly with a touch of scepticism.

Martin shook his head. 'No. She's the producer.' He gestured to one of the group; a short, stocky young man with dark hair in a buzz cut and black eyes and a pale mouth, rubbing his small chin and gazing at an iPad. Next to him, a tall bearded man with tousled hair was pointing and poking at the screen. 'The little guy is Pete Wilkins. He's the police liaison; he's here to oversee everything. He won't get involved unless things go really wrong. The full brief is written up beforehand and given to the production company – what shots are re-quired, where they should be – it's story-boarded in an office long before anyone arrives here.'

I considered this while the lighting men started to set up, pushing us gently but firmly out of the way as the brightness of the floodlights filled the gloomy space, giving it the aura of a studio, or perhaps an operating room. We moved back, by common consent, to rest against the cream-painted wall, which was a cold, unyielding presence against my shoulder blades.

'I suppose it makes sense,' I offered. 'All that forward planning. Something like this needs to resemble reality, if it's to work at all.'

'Yes and no.'

'What does that mean?'

He gestured towards the bright space in front of us. 'There are multiple reasons to film a reconstruction.'

I waited for him to elaborate on this.

'Jogging memories is only part of the plan,' he said. 'After all this time, it's unlikely anyone remembers anything new.'

'Then why do it?' I frowned, trying to understand. The crowd buzzed around me, busy as bees with their bulky, shiny equipment. 'It looks expensive.'

'Because there's always the hope that someone who does know what happened – either the abductor themselves, or someone else who perhaps suspected them or even shielded them – will have their conscience pricked and come forward.'

I thought about this for a second or two. 'Could someone like that have a conscience?'

'Probably not. But it's worth a go. These things–' he gestured towards the set, taking in the working men barking monosyllabic commands to one another, the lights, 'these kinds of crimes – they invite you to be part of the story. Someone who is already part of the story might be tempted to get swept further into it.' He nodded towards the police liaison, Pete. 'This is why they do them. A re-enactment is very psychologically powerful – it puts incredible pressure on people who have information, and it motivates others to interrogate their own experiences.'

I nodded, as though I understood.

At the far end of the corridor, near the lintels of a set of fire doors, a nurse accompanied a very sallow, very drained man curled into a small ball in a wheelchair. His hair was a smoke of thin grey, curled up in disordered shapes; from the neck down he was covered by a bright orange blanket. He was being pushed by an orderly, who was chatting to the nurse who giggled back, both appearing to be utterly unconscious of all the unusual activity around them, yet both betrayed themselves as utterly captivated by it. I heard the whispered words, 'It's a *Crimewatch* thing, for some old missing persons case,' from the nurse.

Martin was on to something, I realized.

The crew stepped out of the way with bad grace as the small group approached, and as he passed me, on his way into the ward on the left, I heard the old man whisper in a small, mucus-cracked voice, 'I'm ready for my close-up,' and then, with a swift, surprising vitality, he offered me a bawdy wink and smile.

I smiled back, amused and charmed.

'Look at you. Already flirting,' said Martin. There was warmth in his voice. 'There's someone I want you to meet.'

He led me gingerly past the men setting up equipment to one of the stairwells, where one of the most beautiful girls I have ever seen was deep in conversation with a blond man. The girl had long dark hair and an exquisitely fine complexion, which, now that I looked, I realized was the result of several layers of expertly applied make-up. She wore a school shirt and skirt, purple V-necked pullover with a grey stripe trim, black tights and ugly shoes. Her plain brown mascara had been lightly oiled, as though to suggest tears.

'This is Thea, who's playing Bethan,' Martin said as we drew near. 'And this gentleman is Roddy, who's going to be Alex.'

Roddy was in nondescript jeans and jacket. I realized that in her letters Bethan had never offered much information on how he dressed.

The pair acknowledged us with distant little smiles, but did not pause in their urgent conversation, which appeared to be about regional accents.

'So, Ian says go neutral,' said Thea, in an achingly upper-middle-class actressy voice, 'but I'm thinking that since her family was a bit *Jeremy Kyle Show* I should do something more Normal for Norfolk,' then the pair of them burst into tinkling, affected laughter.

A sharp little stab of dislike shot through me.

Martin squeezed my shoulder. 'Drama students, eh?' he whispered to me. 'Shall we find a seat and wait for the show?'

The morning passed in a kind of constantly interrupted tedium, as nothing much happened, but it kept having to be halted while staff and patients moved through the corridor on their business. Again and again, the scene reset as extras dressed as nurses, doctors and visitors ambled up and down the corridor, while Thea and Roddy marched towards us, a rolling camera preceding them, Roddy walking swiftly about ten feet behind Thea, while she stumbled and wiped at her face in distress.

Then there were a few takes of them talking while people passed them by. In a few they argued; in a few he appealed to her, one hand curled around her arm possessively; in one he grabbed her, holding her close, the implication clearly being that he had a weapon tucked against her belly or back and was frog-marching her discreetly out of the building.

'I need to go to the loo,' I murmured to Martin. 'Be right back.'

It took me about five minutes to find the ladies', and I felt chilled, queasy that someone could just grab a girl like that. It could happen to anyone.

151

Alone in the toilets, I fell prey to a slippery spurt of paranoia, and quickly splashed my face with cold water, keen to return to the safety of the herd. My heart pounded beneath my jacket.

When I threw open the doors, Martin was waiting for me.

I nearly jumped out of my skin.

'Are you all right? You looked pale.'

'I'm fine,' I said. 'It was just a little upsetting to watch. It felt so...'

'Visceral,' he supplied. 'When you see it like that, it becomes so much less abstract. You see how it works. What happens to people.'

I gazed back up at him. He was standing very close.

'Yes. Exactly. Visceral.'

For a moment I thought he was going to put his arms around me. I wanted him to, in the worst way – I wanted to be enfolded by him, to rest my head against that muscular chest, to set this burden down. I could feel myself starting to grow flexible, limp, waiting for his touch...

But it didn't come. I stole a quick glance at him, at the peculiar way he had frozen, as though stopping himself.

We both cast our eyes down, pretending that each had not seen the other's reaction, though my flush must have been apparent, as was his.

Of course he shouldn't be hugging me, or encouraging me, I reminded myself stiffly. He knew things about me. I was not a suitable girl.

'Come on,' he said, with a warm, only slightly stilted, tug of my arm. 'It's time for your close-up, Mrs Lewis.'

13

Today must be Sunday, because Katie has been allowed out of the cellar room and up into the lounge for the evening, with its patterned blue rug covering the wooden floor, and the old-fashioned fireside chairs, built of black studded wood on a monumental scale, and the low couch with its deep cushions. The news is on, and an earnest man in a suit is on television talking about some company that has either lost millions of pounds or lied about having it in the first place. Her hands are clasped around a chipped mug of thin hot chocolate. She's enjoying its heat far more than its taste.

She's sitting next to him on the couch, and the sense of stuffing and cushions is strange after days of incarceration. The patterned silk is slippery against the backs of her legs.

Outside brisk autumnal winds thump against the windows, making low moans as they rattle through the rotting frames, the draft raising the light hairs on her arms into goose pimples, stirring the brown leaves on the trees shading the house into a crackly susurrus.

He is watching the television but she can sense his boredom, and his hand reaches out and casually begins to stroke the back of her neck. She stiffens, as she always does.

'Is something wrong?'

'No,' she says, biting the end of the syllable off. Her bare thighs are still dappled with the bruises he gave her the day before yesterday, when the man had called by and she had tried to alert him – huge blossoms of brown and green and violet-blue.

'You know, this is supposed to be a treat,' he says, his tone clipped and offended. 'If you'd rather go back downstairs...'

'Sorry,' she says quickly. As the word slips out, she realizes that she isn't and that, more importantly, she doesn't sound it. What's more, she needs to do something about it: it's tiny incidents like these that set off the runaway train of his rage. What starts with hurt looks, curt speech, agonizing stretched silences and a purply-pale colour marbling his cheeks, has ended before now in him grabbing her hair and smashing her head into solid objects while he shrieks like a crazy person, white spittle gathering at the sides of his mouth.

Now is the time to say No, I'm really sorry, and perhaps lean into his hated touch, and even elaborate on how grateful she is that he has saved her from the others. Then his hand will return to the back of her neck before moving down her spine or on to her lap, and dreadful though the sequel will be, it is better than when he is violent. Everything leads to the same outcome anyway. There is nothing she can do to avoid it. She tries and tries, but every response just serves his ends.

Today, however, the honeyed words will not come. They stick in her throat, in the place just under the collarbone.

His attention has turned back to the television,

154

which is now showing the weather – bright but getting colder, with snow expected before too long – and she can sense his growing displeasure. She drinks the cheap chocolate quickly, as who knows when it will be taken away from her. The mug is patterned with Wedgwood-blue flowers, and chimes faintly when her ragged fingernails strike against it. It's a twin of the one she smashed over his head.

On the stone mantelpiece, two silver candle-sticks glint back at her. When she's in this room, she thinks about those candlesticks and what she could do with them to a person whose back was turned. She thinks about that a lot.

Now it's the regional news. As a rule, she is for-bidden to watch or read the news unless expressly invited to, usually as he shows her the paper and its lack of any mention of her as evidence that his 'associates' have hushed up her disappearance.

But she realizes that she has caught him at a crossroads – he can't decide whether he wants to get angry and fight with her – if you can call it a fight since he always wins – or whether he wants to give her a little longer to submit and play along, and while he thinks it over the local news keeps going, and something extraordinary happens.

'Yesterday filming completed on a reconstruc-tion of a decades-old mystery, the disappearance of fourteen-year-old Cambridge schoolgirl Bethan Avery, who vanished without trace in 1998. Colette Samson gives us this report.'

'Thanks Tim, and here at Addenbrooke's, early on Saturday morning, the hospital is replaying one of the darker scenes of its recent history.'

There is a long shot of a dark girl in an old-fashioned school uniform walking along a hospital corridor, a man shadowing her, his face vague, his hair blond.

Next to Katie, her captor has gone very still.

There is a cloying hit of stunned panic and swarming hope in Katie, and she moves her eyes away to the rug, wondering for a single mad instant whether she has let her face or body betray any of this.

Bethan Avery. That's the name scratched on the cellar stones beneath their feet.

She waits, for one beat, two, for the blow, or for hard fingers pinching into the hollows of her shoulder; for him to become aware that she is watching this, too, and that he absolutely should not be allowing that to happen, but there is nothing.

There continues to be nothing.

'On January fifth, 1998 the town was turned upside down by a terrible, seemingly motiveless assault on sixty-one-year-old Peggy Avery and the unexplained disappearance of Bethan Avery, her young granddaughter, who, it is believed, was lured away from her grandmother's bedside and abducted, then presumed murdered when bloodied clothing was found on the Fens near her home.

'However, Cambridgeshire Constabulary have confirmed they are reopening the case in light of new evidence, and are commissioning a brand-new reconstruction of the tragic events of early January 1998.'

It's a film of the same girl from the hospital, only

this time she and another girl are walking along a street of new, cheap houses, talking and laughing. They are replaced suddenly by a picture of a policeman in uniform, wearing a peaked cap that betrays him as quite high-ranking.

'We have never given up hope of finding out what happened to Bethan, and of finding and prosecuting Peggy Avery's murderer,' he says. He has rheumy pale eyes and reddish skin, as though he's been outdoors in the cold for a while. 'And we now believe that someone out there has evidence that can help us.'

'Is it true that there is potentially new information on this case?'

The policeman nods vigorously. 'Yes indeed. We have been given the name Alex Penycote in connection with Bethan's disappearance, in relation to a blond-haired, blue-eyed man. We suspect it might be an alias, but we'd be extremely interested in hearing from anyone who has met this person, or heard this name in any context, possibly from somebody representing themselves as working in health or social services. And of course, if you *are* Alex Penycote, we'd be delighted if you could get in touch with us so we can eliminate you from the inquiry as soon as possible.' Katie steals a sideways glance at him through her lank, overhanging hair.

He has gone ghostly white. She does not think he is even breathing.

Now on TV it's Mrs Lewis, who teaches English, and Classics to the posh kids who sign up for it; the one who's got the agony column in the local paper.

What's *she* doing on TV?

157

Katie is familiar with the column. Last year one of her exes, Joshua Barrett, and his best mate had tried writing their own stupid fake problems to the email address in the paper, but Miss had never published any of them. It was like she knew.

'Yes, my name is Margot Lewis and I edit the advice column for the *Cambridge Examiner*. I'm just here to say to anyone out there watching who may know something about what happened to Bethan – you don't have to be afraid.'

Katie thinks that if anyone looks afraid it's Mrs Lewis – her hair is slightly skew-whiff and her eyes are huge.

'I'm waiting to hear from you again. You can come forward and you will be protected from whoever it is you think is looking for you. If you don't want to talk to the police, then you don't have to, there's a victim support number you can call, which is going out with this report, or, if you prefer, you can use the anonymous Crime-stoppers number. Even though it was such a long time ago, we all desperately need to hear from you again, before anyone else gets hurt.'

'Thanks, Margot, and that number is at the bottom of the screen. Back to you, Tim, in the studio...'

Katie has forgotten to breathe, forgotten all caution, and the next thing she knows his hands are around her throat and he's shaking her like a rag doll as she yelps in terror.

'Is this you? Did you talk to someone? Did you? *Did you?*'

His eyes are tiny blue marbles of madness. His face seems to be all yellowing gritted teeth. Her hands flutter like birds, trying helplessly to push him away, push him off as she gasps for air, as everything goes grey. It's like someone is turning the sound down and it hurts, *it hurts,* then finally he releases her and she falls backwards on to the couch, and they're both wheezing with effort into the silence.

She flinches again as he reaches down and pats her arm.

'Sorry,' he gasps, but it is with the same distracted air as her own reply earlier. He is not thinking about her at all. 'Sorry.'

Katie does not dare move.

He has switched off the television with the remote and is staring ahead of himself, his bottom lip moving, trembling a little. She has no idea what it means, except that...

'12/1/1998 BETHAN AVERY'

Jesus, she realizes, they think Bethan Avery is *alive.* She must have written to Mrs Lewis's column, that's why she was on TV.

But what did that mean for Katie?

'Sorry,' he mumbles again.

He is on his feet and hauling her up, barely look-ing at her, and though faint and fighting still to fill her lungs, she gets up quickly, keen not to provoke him. He is pushing back the rug with his foot, lifting up one corner, and the trapdoor is there.

There is a second, perhaps two, as he bends down to lift it up by its heavy ring and swing it open, during which the candlestick on the right edge of the mantelpiece seems almost to wink at her over his bowed, balding head. She is perhaps ten feet from it. She could never reach it in time, particularly while he has hold of her arm.

You couldn't reach it this time, you mean.

Then the moment is past and she is being pushed ahead of him down the narrow steps that yawn before her and thrust through the open doorway of her cell. The stone is cold beneath her feet, the darkness absolute as the door shuts behind her, and yet she cannot be sorry.

He did not touch her – and he does not. It is the first time since her arrival that he has left her alone, and something within her tentatively resets, is allowed to breathe, to think, to cautiously inhabit her own skin.

Once again, she wrestles with the dangerous illusions of hope, while she lies wrapped in her blanket in the dark. Above she can hear his footfalls moving relentlessly up and down the ceiling. He is pacing, and it goes on for a long time.

He feeds her late, much later than usual, providing her with her usual Sunday 'treat' of a microwaved ready meal – some kind of meat and rice; it's impossible in the dark to judge what it's supposed to be – a can of fizzy drink and a small sweet pastry, but he does not speak to her.

When she falls asleep at last, her head buried against her arm, she is sure she can hear something from the rooms above that may be the wind, or may be him – a kind of low but rising howl, such as might come from a dangerous wounded animal.

14

'Ah, Margot.'

The deputy head, Jane, had bustled up to me and was giving me a strange look, as though she had caught me napping. 'Are you all right?'

I smiled, a little confused. 'Yes, I'm fine. Just distracted. Is something wrong?'

'There's been a call for you,' she said. 'Someone for a Margot Lewis.'

I offered her an apologetic look. I was buried in calls, mostly going to the *Cambridge Examiner*. There had been a constant stream of them, true, though nothing promising by way of leads, Martin had told me.

That said, it was still very early days, and the reconstruction hadn't yet been broadcast.

'I'm sorry, Jane.'

She let out a half-sympathetic, half-annoyed sigh. 'Well, he didn't mention Bethan Avery. He said he had something of yours that you'd lost.'

I frowned. 'I don't think I've lost anything. My mind, maybe. Did he leave a number?'

She shook her tight curls. 'No. He said he'd just call back. He wanted your home phone number but I wouldn't give it him. I told him to talk to you.'

Curiouser and curiouser.

'Did he say when he'd call back?'

She shrugged expressively. 'No idea. Told him

161

not to bother in class time.'

'I see. Thanks, Jane.'

'Probably a reporter,' she said. 'Trying to find out what this "new evidence" is.' She threw me a speculative look.

I sighed. 'Well, he's on a hiding to nothing. Even if I knew what it was, the police say I'm not to talk to people about the letters.'

It was a delicate hint, but she took it regardless.

'By the way, Margot, can you do Biology with Year Ten in the lab? Rob is going home at two; he's got a hospital appointment.'

I nodded. I didn't have a choice.

'Good,' she said. 'See you later.'

'Bye,' I said, lost in thought. Whoever this mystery caller was, it wasn't Martin. He had my home phone number already. Could it have been Mo Khan, or the police? Surely they'd contact Martin before me.

Something I'd lost? Like what?

I searched through my bag – my wallet, my keys, my phone, all present and correct. Whoever it was had known I was a schoolteacher, but not where I lived.

Not where I lived *yet*, I thought with a sick little start. And he'd been after my phone number.

I'd been very naïve, I realized. I had been worried that this business might follow me to the school. I hadn't suspected that it might also follow me home.

Whoever they were, they still hadn't phoned back when I left for the *Examiner* offices. I was back in the car again, idling my engine at the painted, wrought-iron gates of the school, as I had a supermarket run to do – I loathe supermarkets, so plan each trip as comprehensively and rarely as possible, as though they were expeditions to the summit of Everest. Lily is constantly telling me to have my shopping delivered, but something about this seems, I don't know, decadent.

I was waiting for a cream-coloured station wagon to get out of my way so I could pull out. Also idling at the kerb was a scruffy dark Megane with a single man at the wheel. He was casually dressed, but something about his demeanour seemed to suggest that he would be more at home in a uniform. His back was straight, his shoulders squared, and he stared at nothing so intently that he distracted me. When I looked back at the road the station wagon was gone and had been replaced by another car. I thumped the wheel in annoyance.

Gaggles of children swarmed out of the gates, making it even more difficult to drive out of the school. I scratched my scalp, leaning on the wheel, as someone pulled up right in front of me, boxing me in, and swung wide their car door, inches away from my front bumper. Bloody madmen – their children had to run into the middle of the road in order to get in. One, Alice Wright, turned to wave at me. I smiled in a strained fashion.

As the idiot took off I pulled out right after him, managing to cut up the guy in the Megane, who pulled away from the kerb at the same moment I did. I waited for the expected honk of rage on his horn, but it never came. I glanced in my rear-view mirror, and saw him, his face im-

163

placably calm, hidden behind large sunglasses and a baseball cap, his thick knotty arms crossed on the wheel.

I supposed I had wished the traffic upon myself. Usually I wait around at school, marking a few essays, until it thins out. But I very badly wanted to go home after shopping. I was tired, nervous, and I wanted a long bath, and then afterwards to sit in my bathrobe, drinking tea and watching *Sherlock*. The gridlock improved after the bridge, as the road forked. My temples were sore and I rubbed them. I must have been frowning again without noticing it.

It wasn't until I'd actually got to the *Examiner*, or it might have been a little before, that it occurred to me that there was something strange about the man in the Megane. He'd parked at the gate, running his motor, for all the world just another dad come to collect his children from school, but when he'd pulled out after me there'd been nobody in the car with him.

There were no letters from Bethan, though there were a dozen messages from helpful folk who had watched the news segment, and while having no inside knowledge they definitely had opinions, which they were keen to share. Some claimed Bethan had murdered Peggy for an inheritance. Or that Bethan had had a boyfriend who murdered Peggy. Or that she had been mixed up with Satanists.

Wendy looked at me very strangely indeed.

Once I got home, and the shopping was unloaded and stowed away, I made myself a thrown together salad of halloumi and spinach and ate it at the counter in the kitchen, washing it down with a glass of Merlot. In the maroon depths of the wine I could see my own loneliness reflected back at me. It was the sort of thing that Eddy and I had always drunk together.

It was eight o'clock by now and it was dark outside. On the table were a pile of marked essays – I'd worked steadily to catch up on them – so all that was left were the letters for my column; the non-Bethan letters. I was looking forward to them. I could lose myself in them; pretend to an objectivity that I could never seem to apply to myself.

First, however, I'd have to go to the corner shop. I had bought pallet loads of supplies but forgot milk. I finished the salad and grabbed my coat, which I'd left carelessly lying on the back of one of the chairs. I took a tenner out of my purse and pocketed my keys.

It was freezing outside. I thrust my hands deep into my pockets and set off at a fast clip up the street. I could see the lights on in Marek's shop, a friendly glow in the cold black night.

'Hello,' he said, as I entered the shop. A buzzer grizzled briefly, then silenced as the door shut behind me. Marek was seated at the counter – a large, roughly triangular-shaped mound of heavy-jowled middle-aged man with a perpetually mournful downturned mouth and thin, flat hair. With a little frisson of alarm I saw that the *Examiner* was open before him, with the feature they'd run on the filming of the reconstruction. A picture of me, looking wild-eyed and waylaid in the middle of my interview, was under his right hand.

'Hello there,' I nodded in response, and quickly picked up a plastic jug of milk from the shelf. 'It's bloody cold outside,' I observed while he carefully poked the amount into his ancient till.

'Hah. This is not cold,' he said, frowning at the keys. 'I have seen what real cold is like.'

Behind him, his teenaged son, who was stacking cigarettes along the back of the counter, rolled his eyes at his father's back and offered me a grin.

'Are you still off the fags?' asked Marek.

'Yep.'

He let out a tiny disappointed sigh.

'I gave up three years ago, Marek. I think it's going to be a permanent arrangement.'

Again he sighed. 'People worry too much about being healthy,' he said with disapproval. 'You should enjoy life more. Buy more cigarettes.'

He held out his hand for my tenner, which I surrendered.

'I see your picture was in the paper,' he said, while he very carefully counted out my change. 'You look good.'

'Why thanks, Marek.'

'Is that husband still gone?'

I felt the blush rise to my cheeks. 'Um, yes.'

'Not coming back?' asked Marek, checking my change again, while his son looked pained and shrugged at me.

'No,' I said, and felt the truth of the words. 'I think that's going to be a permanent arrangement too.'

Marek rumbled out a long hmmmm that could have meant approval or disapproval. 'A good-looking woman like you will not be single for long.'

'I'm in no rush,' I said, sparing him a smile, the jug of milk dangling from one hand. 'Good night.'

'Good night,' he said, following me to the door to lock it for the night.

As the light went out behind me, the street seemed a more threatening place. The night was still freezing, at least to me. Whoever was it, I thought, that invented orange street lighting? It makes everyone look evil and the sky goes a horrid, lurid violet. It's unnatural.

I was musing on this, and other, less weighty matters as I walked home along my street when I realized, with a shock, that someone was sitting in their darkened car, right next to me, as I passed it. I'd assumed that I was totally alone, and now there was a person, not three feet away, separated from me only by a car door. The engine was off, the headlamps were dark, but there was a man in there, in complete darkness, doing nothing, merely staring straight ahead, as though waiting for something. I stole a surreptitious glimpse of him as I passed by.

He turned away as soon as he saw me looking, but it was the man who'd waited outside the school, the man I'd cut up in the car. I knew him by his squared shoulders, his unmoving form. The baseball cap was still on his head. At first I'd thought he belonged in a uniform – my quick glance saw an almost military precision in his bearing, although his features were hidden in the darkness.

I walked on, not varying my pace, and not looking back, trying to give no sign that I perceived that anything unusual was happening.

I checked out the houses as I went, calculating which door to bang on if this strange man should get out of his car and come after me. I listened for his engine to rev up, or his door to open. I heard nothing, the nothing you hear when you are convinced someone is watching your back.

I'd reached my own house. My keys were already balled in my fist, sticking out from between my fingers, more vicious than knuckledusters when used correctly. I preferred not to speculate as to whether this creature knew I was in the house alone. I jammed the front door key into the lock, twisting it so hard that for a horrid moment I thought it would snap. Then the door opened, letting me into light and relative safety. As I turned to shut it behind me, I risked a look up the street. He was still there, unmoving; simply waiting.

I don't think he realized that I'd recognized him, or even noticed him. I put the milk down near the kettle and tried to sort myself out. I was breathing hard, and my heart beat a skipping tattoo beneath my jacket. I felt light and panicky.

I ran upstairs to our, or rather my, bedroom, which overlooks the street. I didn't turn the switch, but instead crept forward to the window. Fractionally, I pushed aside a tiny fold in the curtain and peeped out.

I could just about see him, at the very edge of the perspective the window gave me. He was still in the dark Megane, though it looked brown in the sodium light. Other parked cars near him hid his registration plate from me. He was still waiting.

I don't know how long I watched him watching my house, as my breath condensed slightly on the cold glass and my legs started to cramp. Then, with appalling suddenness, the engine started with a faint roar and the headlights came on, dazzling me.

I held my breath.

He shot away from the kerb with a growl, and headed off, at speed, past my house and off to the main road. He was gone.

I breathed again. The street was blameless and empty once more. I waited and waited, but he did not return. Eventually, I got up and went downstairs to make a cup of tea and phone Lily.

'Following you, you say,' said Lily, leaning back on her shabby couch, pausing to yank a small green stuffed dinosaur out from behind her back before settling in. There were tired lines around her eyes, and I realized guiltily that it was late, and she had a sick toddler to look after and school in the morning. 'Are you sure?'

Lily has three small children that she has pretty much raised alone, with occasional input from her harried, perpetually gloomy mother. She specializes in short, passionate, fraught relationships with desperately unsuitable men. The last one was a married master at one of the colleges who was on the brink of resigning over her, and the one before that had to leave the country after he was caught trying to sell cocaine to the bevy of privately educated female under-grads he was coaching in tae kwon do. Perhaps, all things considered, there's a good reason that Lily's mother looks old before her time. If the single life is an urban jungle, Lily hacks through it with a giant machete, and engages romantically only with hungry jaguars and cannibal tribesmen.

I moved my hands through my hair and sighed. 'It was the same guy that was at the school today. I'm positive. And I think he was probably the same guy who phoned the school looking for me, but I'm not sure about that.'

'Whoever phoned probably had nothing to do with it,' she replied with a flick of her ochre-painted nails. 'Did this guy in the car follow you all the way home from school?'

'I didn't go straight home. I went up to the paper first. Then Waitrose.' I was exhausted.

'But did he follow you there?'

'I don't know!' I burst out in frustration. 'I don't keep a constant lookout for sinister types spying on me!'

Lily frowned at me.

'I'm so sorry, Lils,' I said, mortified. 'I'm bang out of line, I know. I'm very tired and maybe I'm imagining the whole thing.'

She rubbed her chin thoughtfully. 'Maybe. But you know, perhaps you want to be careful. People see you on TV, and...'

'How do you mean?'

She opened her mouth, as though about to say something, then shut it again. 'Did you see his face?' she asked.

'I did the first time. It was too dark the second. But it was definitely him.' I shrugged helplessly. 'And there's something else.'

'What?'

'I'm not sure,' I said, 'but I'm starting to wonder whether I've met Bethan Avery before.'

She did not reply, merely stared at me.

I found this unaccountably difficult to discuss. I do not enjoy talking about my past, even to Lily, who doesn't know the full extent of it.

'It's just ... I met, well, I met a lot of very, very damaged people in those years with the nuns,' I say. 'And now I'm starting to wonder whether she was one of them.'

'Have you told this to the police? Or that friend of yours, the criminologist?'

I shook my head. 'Not yet. I mean, I *can't...* What would I say? I have no memory of ever meeting her.'

Lily frowned, her jaw jutting slightly. 'It doesn't change the fact that this is a man following you, not a woman. You know, I think,' said Lily, about to pronounce her final word on the subject, 'that you should phone the police if you see this creep again. Get them to come over and ask him what the hell he thinks he's doing.'

The drive home passed in a strange kind of dream. I reflected not on the man, but instead on the hostel and the girls I had met there, trying to recall any nugget of information that would help.

But mostly I thought about Angelique, the Queen of the Night.

I was sitting in a church the second time I met her.

I had wandered into the church after being shooed away from a library, and then the blissfully warm lobby of a department store. I was huddled in a pew at the back, contemplating the stained-glass window behind the altar.

I still had four hours to kill.

St Felicity's had strict requirements for those receiving its largesse. First and foremost, if you weren't back by nine at night, you lost your bed. No ifs or buts.

Furthermore, no single women were allowed to stay in the hostel between eight in the morning and six at night, while the nuns and volunteers scrubbed the cheap linoleum in the rooms and boiled the sheets in their constant and bitterly fought rearguard action against lice and bedbugs.

As a consequence all I remember of that first week, before the nuns took me in semi-permanently, was a cold, dreary nomadism where I shifted from place to place, looking to wear out the hours until I could return – eat, wash, go to bed, get up, eat, leave, and do it all over again.

Now I was in one of those tiny dark churches London is littered with – medieval boltholes over-shadowed on all sides by high industrial buildings. This one was dedicated to St Eugenia who, from what I could see, had been some sort of martyr, and perhaps cross-dresser, who had disguised herself as a man if I understood the mosaics correctly.

I've never been a particularly religious person, though I have my beliefs. But I was drawn to the church's shelter and peace, harbouring me against the bitter wind outside. Above my head, someone was practising on the wheezy old organ – some elaborate classical piece – and a trailing fugue of falling notes came from above.

I was thinking about nothing, my habit during such hours, when I was startled by somebody throwing themselves into the pew next to me

172

with such force that the wood creaked and I nearly leapt straight up in the air.

It was my neighbour from the upper bunk, grinning at me, her dark eyes gleaming in the dusty candlelit space. One of the teeth next to her right canine was missing, a spot of blackness in her face.

'Well, hello there!' she said, her voice and laughter shattering the calm, clearly very amused by my shock and surprise.

'Are you mental?' I snarled, still light-headed and shaking. 'You nearly gave me a heart attack!'

'Sorry. Sorry. But it *was* funny. You should have seen your face.' She offered me a pleased smile, as though contemplating a job well done. She had a strangely refined accent, at complete odds with her appearance. I wondered if it was real, or if she was making fun of me.

I crossed my arms over my chest again. 'What are you doing in here?'

'Avoiding people.' She gave me a cool look. 'Like you, probably. Are you going to steal that?'

'What? What are you on about?'

She nodded over to a battered collection box, attached to the centre of a wrought-iron stand containing rows of shelves filled with sand and tea lights.

'Am I *what?*' I asked in horror. 'God no. I was just looking at the stained glass...'

'Yeah, yeah, I'm sure you were.' She got up, those long legs unwinding endlessly as she did so, and strolled over to the candles. She did not even look round to see if the coast was clear. She tugged at the battered iron corner of the box, which rattled but didn't move. 'Bugger.'

'Stop that!' I hissed at her, appalled, but also secretly thrilled at her heretical daring. 'There's somebody up there!'

'Who's that, *God?*'

'No, whoever's playing the organ, you muppet!'

'That's a tape recording...' She flapped a dismissive hand at me, inspecting the fixture holding the box.

'It bloody isn't! They've stopped in the middle and restarted at least two times.'

She shrugged and retreated back to the pew after a few seconds. 'It's bolted on anyway,' she said, as though to make it absolutely clear that she had not desisted because I had commanded her to, and that she feared neither God nor the organist.

She was silent for a few seconds, giving me the opportunity to study her out of the corner of my eye while the music continued above.

In profile she had fine features, big black eyes, a petite nose dusted with freckles, and plump, sensuous lips. She could have been beautiful, in fact, but the most obvious thing about her was her state of deep disrepair. Her peroxide-blonde hair was dyed to the point of colourlessness. Angry red spots dotted her brow and cold sores bracketed her mouth. Her lips were slightly feathery with peeling skin, and she was pale, too pale, almost a sallow green.

Her arms, bare from the elbows, were dusted with little blue fingertip bruises, and in the crook of the right nestled an ugly mass of red and purple, pocked with little black marks.

'If you're cold you should go to the Southbank Centre,' she said suddenly.

174

I threw her a surprised glance.

'They keep it heated all day. And they can't throw you out unless they catch you up to no good, like begging.' She gestured expansively, not looking at me, as though demonstrating that it cost her absolutely nothing to tell me this. 'It's, like, one of those public space things.'

I considered this for a long moment. 'Thanks,' I said.

She was still looking away, but she nodded, once.

'What happened to your face?' she asked.

I froze.

I was aware of the effect I had on people at present, and suspected it was why I had been moved on from the library and the department store. My face, and the reason I was homeless, had a very close correlation.

'I tripped,' I replied stonily.

She glanced back at me then, no doubt taking in my two black eyes and swollen, broken nose.

'Yeah. You "tripped".' She snickered. 'Of course you did.'

'It's true.'

She seemed to be thinking, her finger now at the corner of her mouth as she worried at the nail and its cracked casing of peach-coloured varnish.

Or perhaps, looking back on it, she was merely nervous.

'Do you want to come to a party?'

'A party? What, *now?*'

'Well it will have to be now because we have to be back at Flicks for nine or we'll lose our beds.' She didn't wait for my answer, rolling once more to her feet, her sleeve falling to hide her wounded arm. Her back was straight, tense, and I realized that despite her affected accent, dramatic mannerisms and recklessness, that this was because she feared my refusal, my rejection. 'Come on, if you're coming.'

I couldn't tell you how my relationship with her developed, how I got her name out of her, even whether we were friends or merely acquaintances forming our own pack for survival. I knew her name at this point – Angelique, which she pronounced carefully, lingering over each syllable as though it were music, which made me think it was not her real name at all – and before long we were staying out later and later each night before returning to the hostel. She was universally admired and introduced me to her friends – a grimy circle of skinny people I did not particularly like and who didn't like me, though that might have been to do with the taciturn way I refused to answer any of their questions. They offered me draws on spliffs while Angelique vanished into the back rooms of their filthy squats with them before returning, her eyes dull, her limbs languorous. Before long she stopped hiding what she was doing and started shooting up in front of me.

I can't remember when I started to join her in this. I just know that I did.

15

It was Tuesday night, and the reconstruction – ten minutes' worth of vague acting and the appeal from me – had aired. I could barely watch it, caught between the twin poles of dread and exposure. Lily had wanted me to come round, for us to watch it with her mother; I had gently declined.

There had been no further communications from Bethan Avery in the meantime. Or Messrs Calwhit, Blank, Mettle. Or Eddy. Or Martin.

This last, funnily enough, seemed to rankle most of all. I fought the absurd feeling that I was being discarded for being insufficiently attractive to traumatized kidnap victims.

Yeah, that's right, Margot – its all about you, I thought ruefully. Pull yourself together. It's only been a day or two.

I sat down on the couch, in front of the grey and silent television, and looked at the clock on the cable box. It was six, and it was dark outside, dark early today in these days of early darkness, because of the fog. I don't like fog. Apart from being inconvenient and dangerous, I dislike it on principle. Walking through it, there is the sensation of veils lifting and falling behind you, white gauzy veils, but there is no final one that is lifted, leaving what you are really looking for completely exposed.

Perhaps this is why I objected to the fog more today than I would on other days.

I stared at the blank television and kidded myself that I was thinking.

I kicked my shoes off and pulled my legs up under me on the sofa. I had a bag full of essays and a couple of letters for the column to answer, so I thought about them for a few minutes, without getting up. I couldn't just sit here and helplessly watch the work pile up.

After all, I'm not helpless.

'I'm not helpless,' I said aloud.

The silence in the house mocked me.

I had never felt so worthless.

I had received a commission, an imperative, a cry for help ... and I'd got nowhere. I'd learned that the plea was genuine, shortly before it had been smothered by my own bull-headed carelessness, insensitivity and stupidity. I hadn't found out anything at all about where Bethan was now, or come any closer to learning about her state of mind. The void that Bethan had vanished into was still a void, issuing nothing but a trio of backward-looking letters. I could not shake the feeling that I'd failed somehow – the sensation one must have when one runs to a panicked shout heard in a wilderness, only to find a bloody garment nosed by wild animals, or a piece of rope hanging over the edge of a precipice, the frayed end wafting in a mountain breeze.

I tried to tell myself that the reconstruction had literally only just aired, but my spirits would not lift.

She was still with me; she was almost tangible. But I knew, in my heart of hearts, she would offer no more material help. The distance between her-

178

self and me bristled with tension, and her badly contained panic as she waited for her rescue; waited for the eyes hunting through the darkness to light on her, for the first and last time.

I walked into the kitchen, and switched on the light. The kettle rested on the counter, empty, and I picked it up, pulling out the plug. I took it over to the sink, placing the red and chrome spout under the tap. Before me was the kitchen window, looking into my back garden. I peered through it, swiping at the condensation on the cold glass.

There was nothing out of the ordinary, just the night and the fog.

What had I expected?

Disquieted, I turned off the tap.

The house phone rang – a sudden shrill squawk of electronic noise. Shocked, I dropped the kettle, which crashed into the stainless steel sink, water gushing everywhere. I swore and lifted it out, sure it had scratched the metal. Wiping my wet hands on my trousers, I hurried out to answer the phone.

I moved into the dark hall and swiped up the handset.

'Hello?'

There was no reply, just a dense electronic silence.

'Hello, can I help you?'

Nothing. But not quite nothing – there was breathing; not heavy, but light, silent, controlled. Expectant.

'Who is this?' I asked, though I knew by then they would not reply.

The click and purr of the receiver being replaced was my only answer. When I hit 1471 on the keypad, I was told that the caller had with-held their number.

The next morning, I was walking through St Andrews churchyard after my run, on my cooldown, and the bells were ringing. Today I felt a fierce, sharp optimism.

Watery daylight touched the shrivelled grass, the sky was pearly grey and thick as cream. Nearby, an old couple, smothered and muffled in heavy winter clothes, negotiated the broken and buried graves. The woman held a stiff brush of sturdy flowers, a no-nonsense winter bouquet. They were making their way to the newer part of the graveyard.

A pair of magpies fluttered down from the church tower, to strut and bob over the bodies of the ancient dead. I smiled at them, and they ignored me with cavalier indifference.

I paused by the old church door, and sat down on the step, delaying the start of my morning, with its fuss and bustle, just wanting to breathe in the peace and space. The bells chimed happily into the white sky. The magpies paused, too, as though listening. Then they hopped up into the cold air and in a few quick flaps were gone.

I had to go too.

I should have been terrified, or at least nervous. But I can honestly say that I wasn't. These swinging fits of despair and hope seemed normal to me. I suppose Eddy would say that I wasn't in my right mind. Maybe I wasn't; maybe I was in some other mind – a mind that was more my own than any other. I think I was excited, more than anything, terribly excited. Perhaps I was terrified, but I enjoyed the terror. Is that strange? I was menaced, but for once it wasn't the ghosts of my own mind that haunted me so tirelessly, so inconclusively, but something active, something evil, something cruel and decadent, something I could hate with a will.

I was sitting on the church steps, and instead of being in a frenzy of fear, I felt tensely calm and utterly vindicated. Let them do their worst. I was hunting for lost things, and if I could find Bethan then I would prove to my doubting and querulous heart that nothing was lost for ever. That peace and contentment and innocence and justice were not lost for ever. That *I* was not lost for ever.

I stood up, dusted my hands on my sweatpants, and went home to get changed and get into work.

When I got back to the house, Eddy was there.

I had a little warning beforehand, but not much – I had been strolling along our road in the morning sunshine, enjoying the cool breeze against my hot, sweaty skin, and the birds as they flitted through the tree branches while I wound the cord of my headphones around my iPhone.

I was wondering if there was any way to go in and check Dear Amy's post without having to run into Wendy, who, since my first television appearance, had raised her game in terms of passive-aggressive digs. I had been led to understand in no uncertain terms that all of this extra work and fuss I had put the staff through was extremely inconvenient.

And yet, when I came into the *Examiner's* office

181

last night after school, looking for any more letters, she had practically run from the other side of the office, shooing away the intern standing directly in front of the cubbyholes and reaching to fetch my post, in order to hand the bundle to me herself with the maximum possible bad grace.

In short, I was deeply preoccupied that morning, so I didn't spot Eddy's smoke-grey Porsche Carrera parked up on my right until I was nearly on top of it – I could have reached out and touched the bonnet. The driver's seat was empty.

I felt a little giddy, a little sick. What now?

I shoved my phone into the pocket at the back of my running leggings and pulled out my house keys while considering my strategy.

The truth was, I didn't have one. I simply didn't want to fight with Eddy at the moment. I had things to do, things to think about. The idea of it exhausted me and left the fragile accord I'd come to with myself on the church steps in shreds.

Why couldn't he just sign the arbitration? If he signed the arbitration, we could talk about the rest. I didn't want anything unfair. Why was he behaving this way?

I was going to have this conversation with him now, and ask him. Like a grown-up. There would be no repeat of the scenes at Ara's house the other day. I forbade it.

I turned on to my path, past the high hedges of unruly leylandii, and sure enough he was waiting on the step.

'You're still running?' he asked. The sun gleamed in his golden hair. 'I keep telling you it's terrible for your joints.'

His voice was faintly hoarse.

Straightaway I could see that something had changed, and not for the good. When he had appeared here last time he had been impeccably turned out, as was his habit when going to or from work.

This new Eddy looked as though he'd been out all night. His shirt was crumpled and limp, his coat thrown over it, the jacket missing, the tie just a little off-centre, his shoes dull with a slight patina of dust. I daresay anyone else would have found him respectable enough – he'd shaved and his hair was neat – but I'd had four years of getting to know all of Eddy's idiosyncracies. Something was wrong.

'And yet I still persist in it,' I said, coming to a stop before him. 'Like you. Why are you here?'

'What, we can't talk any more? Do I have to book an appointment with you now you're a TV celebrity?'

'I thought we were doing this through your lawyers.'

'We could still discuss it like reasonable people.'

I folded my arms. I was shaking a little, and it wasn't just because I was cooling down.

'We could indeed,' I said, 'but I'm left wondering why you'd buy a dog and bark yourself. What are you up to?'

He offered me his tight, crooked smile.

'You're being very paranoid, Margot.'

'Not paranoid. *Direct*. It's completely different.' I cocked my head at him. 'Did you call me last night?'

'What?'

'Call me,' I supplied again. 'Last night.'

'No,' he said, but there was a rising note in his voice, and I wasn't sure he was telling the truth. 'Are you going to invite me in?'

I considered him for a long minute. 'This isn't a good time. I need to get to work in an hour and a half.'

'It won't take long.' His hands fell into his coat pockets. 'And it's urgent, Margot.'

I raised my eyebrow at him, but I was already applying my key to the lock. 'Really?'

'Yes,' he said, with a little shrug. 'I need your help.'

So once again he was in my kitchen, and I was making him coffee. He took a seat at the pine table, and as I stole surreptitious glances at him in the reflection of the kitchen window, I could see he looked older, tired, and there were dark pouches under his eyes when his face tilted forwards.

Despite myself, something within me clenched in pity. I wanted to go over, put my hands on the tense muscles of his shoulders, knead the knots out of his hard flesh, feel the warmth beneath my palms; in short, to get on with pretending that none of this had happened.

It was impossible, but I wanted it anyway.

'You said it was urgent,' but there was a soft note in my voice.

'Yes. I need some money,' he said.

This was so frank it took me a second or two to parse it. I put the kettle down.

'You want *me* to lend *you* money?'

He shook his head. 'Yes. No. In a way.' He

184

sighed, leaned back in the chair, and there was no disguising his tiredness any more as he rubbed his eyes. 'Ara and Gareth are trying to force me out at Sensitall.'

I blinked at him. This was very bad news for Eddy. Everybody knew the company was going to do very well indeed in due course, but for now, things were still building. If he was forced out, a great deal of his work would have been for nothing.

'Gareth has issued me with a parting offer that's worth about...' he paused, as though catching himself before saying too much, and there was a flash of banked cunning in his expression that hardened something in my heart, '...about a third of my real share.'

Gareth was the other partner in their start-up business, who contributed capital and had got them the lease for the offices. My mind ticked and whirred – of course, he'd been an 'old friend' of Ara's, and she'd brought him in.

I'd met him a couple of times at dinner parties and company social events at expensive restaurants and hotels – a squat, short man with thinning ginger hair and a pronounced underbite beneath his moustache. He'd always been extremely charming and gallant with me, exercising a flirtatious banter that seemed to maximize my personal vanity without ever crossing over into insolence.

That said, charming or not, he was Ara's man at the end of the day. She had called and now he was answering.

'Tell them you won't take it,' I said. On the face

185

of it, it seemed a simple enough riddle to solve, if you weren't too greedy about it. 'If they want rid of you that badly they'll raise their offer or liquidate the company under you. Get them to up your share offer, so you'll see a profit when the business does.' I shrugged at him. 'In any event, I don't see what this has to do with me any more.'

I put the kettle back on the stand, snapped it on.

'Margot, you don't get it,' he said, with a deathly earnestness. 'If I can get the retainer together, there's a solicitor in London who thinks she can get my offer doubled...'

'Then complete the arbitration I sent you and mortgage that flat of yours,' I said as the kettle switched off, gouting steam into the air.

He raised his chin, his eyes meeting mine, and a hateful light burned within them.

He had become someone I didn't recognize.

'I didn't work and sweat like a fucking bastard for two years just so that pair of twats can kick me to the kerb now.'

His voice was low, harsh and very cold. I found myself a little afraid of him.

'That's great,' I said, moving to fill the mugs with boiling water, so I didn't have to look at him any more. 'But, like I said, it's nothing to do with me.'

'If we hold off on the divorce we could get a loan out on this house,' he said.

'Hold off?'

'I mean, forget about the divorce.'

I had been about to pour water into the waiting mugs.

'What do you mean, forget about the divorce?' I asked carefully, my back still to him.

'You know what I mean,' he said. 'Stop pretending you don't.'

I wanted to be reasonable. I had promised myself that I would be reasonable, and calm. And to be honest, there was something in me that had wanted him to show up here again, for us to talk.

It was tough doing this alone, this life, to sit in here in the dark at night, to be haunted by thoughts of shadowy stalkers and lost girls and silent phone calls.

If this had panned out some other way, I would probably have taken him back, I realized.

I turned to face him.

'I don't want to forget about the divorce, Eddy.' I crossed my arms.

'Margot, I know I–'

'I don't want to be married to you because I don't think you love me.'

And as I said it, trembling as I was, I realized that it was completely true.

'In fact, if we're doing full disclosure, I'm not sure you ever loved me, but be that as it may, I'm really quite positive you don't love me now.'

'Oh come on,' he said, and he was clearly angry, his chair squeaking as he drew back, 'I made a mistake, I admit it! I know I was a bastard, and you're still furious about Ara, but–'

'No,' I said, and felt the truth of it. 'I'm not furious about Arabella, not any more. You didn't love her either.' I pulled the band out of my sweaty hair, to let the cool air nearer my burning brain. 'You're a liar – it's the company you really want.'

'What?'

My promised calm was fraying and snapping

187

like a weak tent in a strong wind. 'You went after that woman for her money and now you're bricking it because she was more than a match for you. And there is no way in hell I'm going to risk my house because your sexual takeover of the company went tits up.'

He looked stunned, as though I had slapped him.

'Everyone makes mistakes, Margot. You should know that better than anyone. And you might want to think about that before you decide to get all self-righteous. What if they found out about your old mistakes at that school of yours?'

I gripped the kitchen counter behind me, numb with horror. 'Was that supposed to be a threat?'

'Oh for God's sake, I was just pointing out a fact.' He had gone an angry scarlet. 'What's the matter with you? You're twitching all over the place. Are you off your meds again?'

I flinched inwardly. I had forgotten that he knew me just as well as I knew him.

He pointed his finger hard at me, with something like triumph. 'I *knew* it! I knew it when I saw you on TV!'

'I think you should leave.'

'Margot, you don't realize this, but you need me—'

'Get out. Get out *now*.'

He looked about to say more, but instead merely held up his hands and shrugged. 'Suit yourself.' He got to his feet, snatched up his coat and offered me a bitter smile. 'But if you need someone to ring next time you're thrown in the loony bin, you might want to remember this conversation.'

I kept utterly still until I heard the door slam after him. I didn't start crying until I was quite sure he was gone.

16

Wednesday night is late-night shopping in Cambridge, and I'd been elected by a jury of my peers at school to buy Rosa Vidowski her leaving present. This meant I was back in the car today, as I don't like cycling late at night, and I'd parked under the Grand Arcade.

I'd no idea why I had been chosen to do this rather than anyone else. I would have made an excuse, but they caught me on the hop. So, after my obligatory and pointless visit to the *Examiner* offices, with its sudden thickets of letters from people who weren't Bethan Avery but had something to say on the subject, I found myself aimlessly roaming around the china and fancy goods department of a large department store.

I listlessly sized up saccharine china figurines of beautiful women dancing, flirting, reading and fanning themselves, bedecked in the ribbons and stays of dead ages, the store lights making their glazings gleam. Apparently this was the sort of thing Rosa liked. I could not, for the life of me, imagine why. The glass cabinet that held them slowly revolved, showing them all up to their best ceramic advantage.

I glanced away at a table nearby, where several

larger objects in china and metal were displayed. Quite a few of these were representations of women, awful art deco women, nude or almost nude, or wearing carved drapes under which their nipples stood out stiffly, and which were slit open to reveal long bronze or pewter legs. Soft porn in a perfectly respectable department store: some of them were even bent over, or exaggeratedly arched, to hold stupid trivial things in their long thin badly carved arms, objects like ashtrays or sockets for light bulbs.

I was growing angry; a hard, cold anger. I thought of Linda Moore's book, describing Bethan's 'porcelain good looks', and I looked back at the clay dolls going slowly around in their glass cabinets. They were connected, these china virgins and pewter whores, I knew it instinctively. They were opposite sides of the same coin; they defined women in lies and half-truths; they were Everywoman and consequently No Woman.

Maybe I read too much into things. Eddy always says I do. But how could I misread something so obvious, so tangible? I hefted my bag and walked off, leaving them all in their foolish poses.

I ended up purchasing a pair of fancy glass candlesticks, shot with blue and pink. Well, I liked them, so Rosa better had, too.

I paid for the candlesticks and joined the desultory queue on the escalator down, packing them into my big floppy black bag. I was heading for the doors when the perfume counters caught my eye. I was running out of my regular perfume and fancied a change. Since Eddy wasn't going to be buying me the usual bottle of Coco for Christmas this year, maybe it was time to update my scent along with my last name.

These thoughts all made something hitch painfully under my ribs.

You could have him back, you know. If you called him, he'd come.

He would.

But would you have him, under such terms?

Perhaps it's not how you think. Perhaps he's lying on someone's sofa right now, mourning your loss, his own foolishness. Perhaps he is missing you. If you don't yield a little, check in with him, how would you ever know?

Lying on someone's sofa? In their bed more like. You never did trust him. And with good reason, in the end.

I sighed so wearily that the woman on the escalator ahead of me turned to stare at me as I blinked back tears.

Shopping for things like make-up and perfume has always been tough going for me. I can't stand a hard sell. So I had to drift lightly between counters, just taking a little squirt out of the tester bottles, then moving off quickly before I got hammered with a strident, 'Can I help you?' from one of the breezy girls behind the counters. Obviously they can't help me. If I'd made my mind up, I wouldn't have to test their wares, would I?

I was just sniffing something in an outrageously elaborate glass bottle when a man caught my eye. An anomalous enough creature to see in a perfume department, but I'd noticed him because he'd been looking at me keenly when I'd glanced up, then immediately looked away.

191

Hmm. So much for the art of flirting, I thought, rounding the counter and heading off for the next one, where I tested something that smelled like cat's urine and violets. Urgh. Definitely not for me.

Or, more embarrassingly, perhaps he'd seen me on the television and wanted to strike up a conversation about it. I was constantly being asked about this 'new evidence' that had turned up in the column, and sometimes no amount of declaring that the police had sworn me to secrecy was enough to deter people.

I backtracked as I saw the girl behind the counter put down something in preparation for pouncing on me. I stepped backward and turned, and I saw that the man who'd been staring at me before hesitated, not knowing which way I was going.

He was dressed in a suit and long coat, and he had dark hair and a smooth face. He was following me.

I was breathless, lightheaded with fear, and I paused near the counter, clutching the edge, perversely wishing the girl serving would engage with me now so I could whisper to her to call the police.

I stole a glance at him in one of the multitudinous mirrored surfaces on the counter.

It's not the same man.

I couldn't tell you exactly how I realized this, but I did. The shape of his face, his build, the way he held himself – it wasn't the man who'd parked outside my house. I would have sworn on my life.

I started to breathe again.

It struck me then that he didn't want to approach me, just to follow me. He must have been a store detective, who thought I was a shoplifter. I wanted to laugh suddenly with embarrassment and relief. On the other hand I felt strangely guilty – I don't know why. I suspect there is a secret shoplifter in me who reacts the same way when confronted by authority. I pulled my bag up on my shoulder as the colour rose in my cheeks.

The cool night air was soft after the air conditioned heat of the shop. I paused outside the door, at something of a loss.

I hadn't had a very good week so far, and this evening was proving no exception.

I would treat myself, I thought, heading off down Market Street. I would go into Heffers and buy myself a new novel. I would choose one packed with incident, erudition and sex, in a shiny dust jacket. It would be pleasantly heavy in my bag as I walked back to my car, and when I got home I would cuddle up on the sofa with it, with a packet of biscuits and a bottle of wine, and read it right through. It would be a sensual pleasure. The anticipation of it was already erasing my embarrassment.

I walked on past the brightly lit shop fronts, the coyly illuminated pubs and cafes, the stony grandeur of the colleges – Emmanuel, Pembroke, Peterhouse, St Catherine's, Corpus, King's, with gargoyles growling at me from their cornices, each splendidly overdressed in fluted railings and manicured lawns. I love this place – opulent, medieval and alien as it is, it nevertheless stretches out its arms and includes me. It was here that I first learned to breathe freely, to express my thoughts with confidence. Cambridge is my *alma mater* in truth, and I do tend to cling to her skirts, despite Eddy's disgust. 'It's just a bloody school,' he would say, as gown-clad academics hurried off to some Formal Hall at Christ's and confused foreign students practically cycled under his front wheels on Downing Street and King's Parade, only their lack of speed saving them. 'A school with pretensions.'

'Yes and no. It's a world within the world.'

He would merely sigh impatiently. 'You should try working in it. Your romantic memories of it would last two minutes.'

I didn't reply. Mother Cecilia had been so happy when I'd told her I'd got in. The memory still made me smile.

It's ironic that Eddy should be so cynical, as he is the one that never left. He is still a senior member of his college and we would turn up for Formal Halls together in their vast vaulted dining hall about three times a year. He was desperately angling to be elected a Fellow, though the disaster with Ara wasn't likely to help his chances.

I spent an hour browsing through the bookshop, poring over covers full of blurb, hearing the books creak as I opened them, smelling fresh ink and cut paper. I forgot about my embarrassment with the store detective. It had been something and nothing, one of the momentary weirdnesses that life is full of.

When the staff at Heffers eventually threw me out at closing time, I had a bulky novel nestled in my bag and a small smile on my face. On the other side of the tiny cobbled street was Trinity College, dark but for the homely glow of the entrance. Porters moved within, sporting their trademark bowler hats, nodding acknowledgement at a lone student hurrying through the gateway into the inner quad. I looked up into the night sky. A few stars poked spikily out of the clear, sharp air. What a bizarre night. I felt disorientated, but it was not unpleasant. In fact, I actually felt carefree … as though a great weight had lifted from my shoulders. When I got back to the underground car park beneath the Grand Arcade I practically bounded down the steps.

My car was on the second sub level of the multi-storeyed edifice, and as I approached it I became dishearteningly aware that it had been a stupid place to park. The light was dim, the place was utterly deserted – the other shoppers had all gone home – and I was a long way from help or hope of it.

I gripped my car keys firmly and marched up to the Audi, attempting to look less intimidated than I felt. What a stupid, stupid, prizewinningly stupid place to park...

Then I was angry. Why couldn't I park where I liked? I'd paid, hadn't I? Was I expected to be under some kind of curfew after dusk, just because I was female?

I was at the car, and quickly opened it, after having a peep into the back seat. There was no one lurking in there. Once in the car, with the reassuring smell of upholstery and air freshener, I felt secure. I'd just have to remember to be more careful next time. I gunned the engine, its roaring alarmingly loud in the echoing concrete surroundings. Time to go home.

I glanced in the rear-view mirror.

195

The man from the department store was crossing the deserted concrete towards me. I craned around to stare at him.

He saw me looking and smiled at me, a big toothy grin, then waved a friendly hand, as though asking me to wait. His other hand was in his pocket, and his shadow, grotesquely elongated, was approaching the back of my car.

He wanted to tell me something.

I knew, with utter, iron certainty that I was in deadly danger.

I let out the handbrake and raked the gears into reverse. The tiny reflection of the man in my rearview mirror started to run towards me, the smile dropping a few degrees. I squealed into reverse and he stepped back, mouthing something I didn't hear but presumed was an obscenity.

Then I revved forward, shooting towards the exit ramp. In my mirror, I could see the man scurrying away, becoming smaller and smaller before vanishing down a stairwell, his coat trailing after him.

The whole incident had lasted perhaps three seconds.

I drew up to the road, my fingers trembling around the wheel. I checked my mirror again. The mirror reflected the car park, empty and harshly lit, framed in concrete. He was gone.

I swerved violently into the road and drove to the police station.

'So what did they say?' asked Lily.

The kids were in bed, and her mournful mother had retired upstairs with a low-voiced goodnight.

My hands shook around the mug of tea she'd

made me.

'They just asked me if I knew either of these men. I said no, and they said that unless they'd actually spoken to me, that was it. They said he sounded like a mugger.'

'So it was definitely two different guys?'

'Yep. I'd swear to it. This one was ... more personable, if that makes any sense in the context of a weirdo that follows you into an underground car park. And I ... I wouldn't swear to it, but I think he was younger, too.'

Lily folded her arms and sighed furiously, making the little tendril of hair hanging down from the crown of her head blow upwards. I smiled weakly at her from the sofa and shrugged.

'So you have to be raped or murdered before they can shift themselves to do anything?'

'That's it,' I said, 'in a nutshell.' I leaned back into the soft cushions and closed my eyes.

She drummed her fingers on the armrest, regarding me thoughtfully, and as she did the rapid little tattoo she was beating out slowed, moved into something more speculative. 'Fancy something stronger than tea?'

'I've brought the car with me,' I muttered dolefully.

'That's what taxis are for,' she said, getting to her feet. 'Red or white?'

She moved off into her kitchen and I rubbed my face with my hand. It was still trembling.

'But here's the thing, Margot,' she called back from the kitchen. 'Why would anyone follow you?'

I started, a little surprised. She knew all about the business with Bethan Avery, of course. 'It must be something to do with the letters,' I said. 'I can't imagine why else I'd be so interesting.'

'And you told the police this?'

'Well, yes.'

She reappeared at the kitchen door with a bottle of Sauvignon Blanc, which she was uncorking while she talked.

'Margot, can I ask a question? Without you getting mad?'

Half of her mouth was screwed up in a tight little grimace.

I shrugged, or I might have shivered. 'Sure.'

'When was the last time you went to the doctor's?'

I blinked. 'About a fortnight ago. I don't know. What's that got to do with anything?' But I saw, with horrible sureness, what she was getting at.

'Don't you think you should make another appointment?'

I licked my lips. No, I thought, I don't.

'I don't see how it's relevant,' I said, trying to sound calm, measured and reasonable.

She nodded, as though a personal theory of hers was being proved.

'Look,' I said, 'it's not just me. There's all sorts of ... take Martin Forrester for instance, he doesn't–'

'I'm not being funny, Margot – really I'm not. It's just that sometimes...' She sighed, as though considering an unpleasant task. 'Something can feel very right when you're in it, and then...' she trailed off, as though searching, 'But it can turn out that the things driving your interest are not what you thought they were.'

'I don't understand,' I said, a little coldly, even

though I think I did. 'There are other people who...' I was about to add, 'believe me', but hearing the pining, apologetic slant in the words, I stopped myself.

She sighed.

'But this Martin Forrester doesn't know all about you, does he?'

You bitch, I thought, with something like wonder. This, I had not foreseen.

'He doesn't have to know about me,' I said angrily. 'This isn't about *me*.'

'I don't know if you realize you're doing it,' said Lily, raising a silencing hand, 'but the fact is that you keep doing the same thing. You start feeling better, feel better enough to stop the pills, and then once you do, things start to fall apart for you.'

'They're only sleeping pills...'

'They're not only sleeping pills. They're antidepressants. You were given them to help you sleep, true, and they're a lower dose, but you've talked yourself into believing that they're simply sleeping pills.' She bit her lip. 'You do this a lot, Margot. You *minimize*. You ignore the obvious and hope that sending your problems to Coventry will somehow make them evaporate.'

'Maybe my problems would evaporate,' I said with chilly preciseness, 'if people would stop reminding me of them whenever I feel I am starting to outgrow them.'

'That's not fair.' She was making an effort to keep her voice even, but the high spots of colour were starting to bloom in her cheeks, and her eyes were narrowing. The wine bottle had stilled in her hands. 'I am merely suggesting that you have been off your pills for three weeks, and now you are being written letters by dead girls and followed by masked gunmen. You write for an advice column, for fuck's sake – of course you're going to get crank letters. It doesn't mean you have to make it all about you.'

I was speechless, though my mouth opened, moving helplessly.

'You think I'm making this up?'

Her lips thinned, and inside her head I could see that determination warred with diplomacy.

'Margot, I'm not saying you are imagining these things, or at least imagining all of them. I am just asking you to consider the possibility that you being off your meds and these things suddenly happening to you might, conceivably, have a correlation.' She held out her palms, as if to demonstrate she had no more concealed weapons. 'That's all.'

But she didn't need any more concealed weapons. She'd already stuck me, hard enough for blood. I was recoiling, and all I could think was, I need to get out of this house right now.

'Margot, no, don't, don't leave like this–'

I'd already snatched up my bag and pushed past her, through the door and back out into the night; with its freight of sinister and perhaps delusionary predators, its memories and its acid cold.

17

I drove home. My phone rang. I switched it off. I remember almost nothing about the journey – the next thing I recall is being sat at my own kitchen table, with the desk lamp on, wiping the tracks of tears from my face with a furious energy that burned the skin beneath my fingers.

I'm a crazy person.

And so we're back here again.

I don't know who I am. I've never known, it seems, but the world is full of opinions on the subject. I had a breakdown. Well, one and a half, if we're heading towards full disclosure. A few people know about it, because it is good to have friends, good to confide, is it not?

But telling people things about yourself is always, always a mistake – like a drug, in a way – the euphoria of communication and trust is always followed up by the regret of paranoia and suspicion. You describe yourself shrieking and being dragged backwards into rooms with gurneys and hypodermic needles – horrible, horrible needles – and there is a part of the other person that will always see you that way.

Things, once known, can never be unknown.

No matter how hard you try, I add to myself, perhaps nonsensically.

I considered the possibility of opening a bottle of wine, but dismissed it.

I leaned back in the chair, stretching out my shoulders. I was shaking with shock, and for a long moment I actually considered going out and buying a pack of cigarettes, before recalling, We had this discussion, Margot, remember? You quit. A big part of being a non-smoker is not smoking.

Yeah, I told myself, I remember. I don't smoke.

I tried to calm down and think about Lily, painful as it was, and then I realized that while her words smarted and burned me, I wasn't actually angry with her. Not angry like I had been at that, yes, let's say it again Margot, bitch Arabella.

I may not have liked what Lily had to say, but she wasn't trying to hurt me. Which only made it worse, in a way.

I didn't know what to do. I would apologize to her in the morning, I decided, but before that, I would briefly entertain the notion that there might be something in what she said.

I thought about the letters. I thought about Martin Forrester and that ghastly police psychologist. The letters are real, I told myself. Other people think the letters are real. You are not imagining the letters.

But was I imagining my pursuit?

I made myself think back, to the man in the dark Megane, and the man in the car park who I'd encountered that night, and I had a clean sharp memory, of Mr Megane pulling away from the kerb the instant I did, even though he hadn't answered a phone, or collected anybody, and once again its strangeness was compelling – his upright posture, his cap and dark glasses.

No, I did not imagine that. I did not imagine

Mr Car Park either, but now that I am sat here in my own house, I realize that the man in the car park was a different type of threat. He wasn't wearing an obvious disguise.

That does not, however, mean he wasn't following me.

Oh no, there was something here, all right.

I didn't want wine any more, and certainly not cigarettes. I wanted good black coffee, and lots of it. I stood up, filled the kettle, and the rushing tap was shockingly loud in my silent kitchen. My brain was whirring. I was being shown something, something important, and Lily and my self-doubt were suddenly beside the point.

Bethan Avery was out there, and she was as real as her letters. This, being true, meant something else. It meant that whoever had seized Bethan was somebody who could exact nearly twenty years of silence from a fourteen-year-old girl, a silence so absolute and heavy that it was sacred even now.

The pale net curtain stirred over the kitchen window, motivated by some draught in the house. I frowned. There should be no windows open in here. I peered into the garden. Absolute darkness. It did not mean the garden was empty.

As I did so, I suddenly understood what was happening.

We had broadcast an appeal to Bethan Avery, Martin Forrester and I, but she was not the only person that had seen it. Whoever had taken Bethan had seen it, too.

She had warned me, after all, in her letters that there was a gang. That this might happen.

Bethan's kidnapper thought I knew Bethan.

And not through anything as impersonal as letters, but that I knew her now, that I'd spoken to her, that I knew where she might be...

That was what this shadowy following wanted – the man parked outside the school who'd followed me home, the smiling man in the concrete car park – they wanted me to lead them to Bethan.

The woman herself had eluded them, but it would be easy enough to trace me from my column in the *Examiner*. All that remained was for them to find Bethan through me and renew her twenty-year silence...

And perhaps they could find Bethan through me.

My growing suspicions refused to be silenced, crowding into my thoughts, driving all else out, till it seemed there was nothing left but a kind of screaming behind my skull.

You could have met Bethan Avery in that hostel years ago. You could. And she's reached out to you now.

Because she knows you.

I covered my mouth with my hands in a sudden thrill of dread.

I had to tell someone! I had to tell them every-thing, all about Angelique, the hostel, the drugs, that old life I had tried to bury and forget for ever. Furthermore, I had to make them believe me while I did it. This was fast becoming a matter of life or death.

Martin Forrester.

I realized that I wanted to talk to Martin For-rester right now more than anyone else in the world.

I glanced at the kitchen clock. Would he mind me phoning this late? I doubted it, not with what I had to tell him. I could ask him whether we should go to the police. I could talk to another human soul about this, and hear him speak back to me.

I stood up. My shoulders ached and my back was stiff. I must have been sat there for hours.

I walked over to the phone, and picked it up.

Something was wrong. It took me a second or so to realize what it was, as I hunted for the Post-It note containing Martin's number. The phone was utterly silent – there was no dialling tone. It was dead.

I followed the cord to see if it was plugged in – maybe I'd pulled the plastic out of its socket – but it was connected, all right. I wiggled the plug in the socket, to see if this made any difference. Still nothing. I replaced the handset, then went into the hall to try the phone there. It, too, was dead. I suppose I'd known all along that it would be.

I stood in the darkened hall, trying to shake off my sick, frightened feeling. The mobile. Where the hell was my mobile? Oh yes, I remembered now. I had switched it off and thrown it contemptuously on to the back seat of the car when Lily had tried to call me on the drive home. Not that my mobile would do me much good here – there was hardly any signal out at this end of the village.

I listened intently, but there was nothing but the faint creak of the house settling about me, the tiniest rustle of dead leaves in the cold still autumn outside. Perhaps the phone was nothing, some glitch with the cable company – or perhaps, whoever they were, they were waiting for me outside, waiting for me to realize the line was dead, and to panic and run out into their grasp.

Why on Earth had I come back to the house?

You know, maybe Lily has a point. Maybe I am insane.

I lifted the phone again, but it was still dead.

That draught, that draught in the kitchen when I'd filled the kettle – where had that been coming from?

'What now?' I whispered.

I had to get out of here. I had to get my mobile.

I retreated back into the kitchen, the dizzying vertigo of unreality making me feel as light as air, horribly conscious of how the window framed me by the lamplight, displaying me to anyone who might be watching from the night-shrouded garden. There was a steak knife lying in the sink, slightly greasy from the cooking I'd been doing yesterday. My knuckles whitened around the black plastic grip.

'Calm down,' I whispered to myself, but the knife shook anyway.

Now I was back in the kitchen the idea of leaving it appalled me. The rest of the house was silent and unlit – the only sound was the hum of the refrigerator, constantly startling me.

I moved to switch the kitchen fluorescents on, to chase the darkness infesting the house back outdoors and into the night, but found I didn't dare. My hand covered the switch. It was sweating on to the cold white plastic, leaving salty smears.

There was a sudden sound, a momentarily unidentifiable change. I leapt away from the wall

206

and raised the knife – I didn't think about it, some part of my reptile brain must have done it for me – then realized it was only the fridge motor winding down.

I remembered to breathe again. It was like the first breath I ever took; air flooded my parched lungs. I sighed in relative relief.

Then the table lamp flickered uncertainly.

Surely the bulb couldn't be going now. Not now, for God's sake... Gripping the knife, I resolved to hit the switch for the fluorescents. I would not be left in total darkness. I would *not*...

The table lamp winked out, and the room vanished.

I think I screamed, if you could call it that. It was a dry, choking noise, a high-pitched cawing, like a crow's. I'd thrown myself back against the kitchen wall, and now the chilly plaster ground against my shoulders.

My hand snaked out frantically for the light switch, but it had disappeared in the darkness. My fingers slid over the paint, making whispering noises as they brushed against it. Then one finger caught on the tip of the fixture. I jabbed hard at the flat switch, which clicked several times, uselessly.

I slid down the wall a few inches, sagging with terror and despair.

I don't like the dark at the best of times. A little of the streetlight and the vicarious lights of other houses, shuttered in warmth and safety, lightly limned the larger objects in the kitchen, or it may have been my eyes adjusting to the dark.

You must get out of here. Get out. Get out...

The front door was nearer to me than the back. Besides, my car was out front, with my discarded phone lying in it. I would be safe in my car. Or I could go to a neighbour's house. The nearest was over the garden wall, but the wall was too high to climb in a hurry and the odds were good that if I screamed, no one would hear me.

I would go out the front way.

I tried to stand up properly, but this was impossible. My body absolutely refused – it was as though I'd been nailed to the wall. The same instinct that had had me jump and brandish the knife before now welded me still, locking my joints.

The wall behind me shook, or it might have been me, desperately wanting to move and not daring to. My ears sensitized to the silence to the point where I could hear the tiny, minuscule tick of the kitchen clock and the roar of the occasional traffic on the main road, several streets away. My shoulders were cold and damp, and cramped sporadically.

I tried to swallow, but my throat was simply too dry.

They had cut the phone and the electricity prior to coming into the house to get me. It was obvious, apparent, so why couldn't I move?

I held the steak knife before me with crabbed white hands.

There was a sound; my head whipped round in its direction. It was coming from the back of the house – someone was trying the handle of the back door.

This broke the spell. I stood up, the now

violently juddering knife held ahead of me, and sidled towards the hall doorway, glancing each way. A faint glow suffused the frosted glass of the front door, enough to silhouette my jackets and coats, hung neatly on their pegs, the spaces where Eddy's would have been louder than bombs right now. My work jacket, containing my car keys, was in the middle of them, and my hand drifted soundlessly into the pockets, searching for them. Behind me, the living-room door was a rectangle of opaque blackness, and through it came the creak of a window being tried – wood squealing against wood – carrying towards me through the blackness clearly and precisely, like notes of music.

My hand closed over the keys.

The sound of the window being raised stopped abruptly, only to be followed by deceitful silence.

I blinked at my front door. One hand let go of the knife to unfasten the latch.

A shadow might have flickered over the front of the door.

I wanted to weep. I was trapped.

What do they want? I screamed at myself, in the roaring quiet.

Suddenly I made my mind up. To linger in the house was impossible. I must brave the door, shadow or no. If I was quick enough, I might surprise him – he would not be able to see me from outside, through the frosted glass.

I gripped my knife and my courage, and wrenched it open.

There was nothing out there but my lawn and my fence, and my red Audi parked on my street-lit driveway.

I practically fell through the door, jerking it back behind me. The glass shattered as the door was flung against the inner wall, swinging wide. Instantly I knew I was not alone. Something cut down through the air, a line of cold fire, down my shoulder, over my collarbone, heading for my heart, my pounding heart ... it was a knife, glittering in the icy air, wielded by a man who had appeared from nowhere, a man who must have been waiting for me, a short stocky man with a black coat and furious eyes staring out of a woollen balaclava.

I thrust my own knife forward into his unprotected middle, shrieking as his flesh resisted for a second, rubbery and tough as the steak I usually used the knife upon. I jerked back in horror.

The air left him in a low animal grunt. He doubled over, his weapon clattering uselessly away. I kicked at him, feeling hot liquid running down my breast.

'Help!' I screamed, but it was such a thin, strangled, pathetic noise that no one could have heard it. My vocal chords were knotted with fear. The blood on the knife I held was black and gleamed sickly in the orange light.

'You fucking bitch...'

It was the man from the school gates, Mr Megane – or at least I thought so; he was wearing the same leather jacket. He seemed about to rush me when he noticed what I was holding.

'Stay there,' I croaked, backing away from him towards the haven of my car.

He eyed me speculatively from my own doorstep, doubtless calculating the best way to disarm me.

Blood sopped heavily into my shirt, from my cut shoulder.

'Just stay away.'

Holding the knife at arm's length, my right hand dipped into my pocket, alighting on a crumpled piece of paper and a sea of keys. I would have to take my eyes off the man in order to find the right one for the car. I very badly didn't want to do that.

The man on my doorstep took a hesitant step towards me. His posture was a study in objective cunning, his exposed lips curling as he concentrated – I might have been a wild animal he was hunting.

'You've cut me, you fucking bitch,' he said. He had a broad accent that sounded oddly familiar, though I couldn't place it. I expect I had other things on my mind.

'Get away from me!'

He took another step closer, as though testing my resolve.

'Get away!' I howled, and then the fat black plastic surface of my car key was in my hand. I squeezed it hard, and my car barked out a little beep and flashed its lights as it unlocked.

He chose this moment to rush me.

Had I tried to retreat, undoubtedly he would have over-powered me. But I couldn't. The car was behind me. So I lunged at him with the knife, as he came forward. A flash of terror distorted his visible features and he stopped in his tracks, sizing me up again.

I jammed a hand into the door handle and

wrenched the car open.

'There's no need to get so het up,' said the man.

'Get away from me. *Right now.*'

'We can discuss this like calm, reasonable people.'

The voice. There was something familiar about his voice.

'Get the fuck away from me,' I breathed. 'I'll *kill* you.'

And it seemed he believed me. He backed off a pace, his eyes swivelling towards the left, betraying his intention to circle around the car, to the other side, the minute I got in. I could see him minutely, in my perfect state of panic, despite the darkness. His lips gleamed lightly with saliva, which he licked over them with his pale tongue.

I ducked into the car, slamming the door shut and the lock down just in time. My shoulder was still hot but my breast was cold, chilled with some cooling liquid, as I revved up the car. The man had vanished.

I stared around wildly, but he had gone. I had no time to worry about it. I had to get out of here. The car squealed backwards, and I caught one last fleeting glimpse of my redundant front door, swaying restlessly back and forth over the entrance to my dark and empty house, and then roared forward into the night.

My hands were nerveless jelly around the wheel, and the bloodied knife lay next to me on the passenger seat. It was not dripping in gore, just lightly laced with it, blood beading minutely on the stainless steel. Blood...

My shirtfront was a huge crimson stain, gently

spreading. I had to go to a hospital. But I was so tired ... so very tired and faint. Not frightened at all now, just tired. The hot liquid was gelid now, settling on my skin.

The bleeding was stopping. I was too exhausted to be relieved.

The uneven road shook me slightly ... I was so tired. I couldn't go on. I would faint over the wheel ... a horn blared at me out of nowhere, and suddenly a man in another car was making an obscene gesture and screaming at me. I had to get off the road. My eyes kept rolling shut. At least the bleeding was stopping. Stopping ... I had to stop. The engine thrummed gently in my ears, like a lullaby, and the road rocked me like a baby. I had to stop...

When I woke up, I was in pitch blackness and absolute silence.

18

Katie wakes in darkness, as always, but there is a strange burr in her sleep-dazed brain that tells her she is not normally awake at this time.

Something is different, but she doesn't know what it is. It is cold, true, but no colder than usual, and in any case, now the nights are drawing in, her captor has recently upgraded her thin blanket with the addition of a musty-smelling candlewick bedspread.

She sits up, stretching her wasted limbs, and

suddenly realizes what it is.

The house is in utter silence.

She cranes her face upwards, towards where the ceiling is, forcing herself to become perfectly still as she concentrates.

Normally, at any time of night or day, Chris is in evidence through his media spoor. Rubbish TV plays loudly round the clock – talk shows all day, old movies all night, and she suspects that he sleeps in front of it. Certainly all of the bedrooms he occasionally takes her into have the perfect, sterile look of a show house or museum. Even when he works in the gardens, facile talk radio carries through the air, its lively mutters audible even down here through the medium of the pipes.

Sometimes she can hear him swearing explosively at these electronic voices, and at one point he threw something hard and the television went silent, which produced even more angry outbursts until the problem was corrected.

The music he sometimes plays on Sunday is his only concession to peace – but even then, it is not listened to, it is merely noise, an aspirational ambience.

Katie thinks of something Brian always says – wise men speak when they have something to say; fools speak because they have to say something. Chris cannot bear his own company, and since she cannot bear his company either, this makes perfect sense to her. This cocoon of empty, oblivious one-way chatter and white noise exists around him so that he is never alone with himself, and yet never in danger of being confronted by anyone else.

She wonders, darkly, if she is also a part of this strategy.

The silence now, however, is absolute.

Wrapping the candlewick bedspread around herself, she shuffles over to the door and, as carefully as she can, conscious that this might be a trap of some sort, she tries the lock. It is as thoroughly bolted as ever.

The thought comes to her, in a blinding instant of panic, that perhaps he has abandoned her. The message to Bethan Avery has sent him running, and he is never coming back.

She is to starve to death in this cellar.

No. No. She refuses to believe this. She is going to get through this. She has given up too much, lived through too much, for any other outcome, and besides, she is going to see her mum and Brian again. Her mum and Brian, who must be going frantic, who maybe even believe those stupid lies spread about Katie running away.

When she thinks about how she spoke to Brian the last time she saw him, before she charged out of the house on that fatal night, a hot runnel of shame flows down from her head to her gut, burning everything in its path.

Brian, not her dad, was the one that had always been there for her.

She has to get out of here. She has to make it up to him, and to her poor mum.

Katie crushes down these thoughts as they are too painful – she can barely manage her own horror and dread; contemplating her mother's is more than she can bear. She raises her chin in the darkness and grits her teeth. She is going to get out of here. She is going to make it up to them both.

As though she has conjured him, she hears his feet on the stairs – not his usual heavy tread, but something quicker, more irregular, and when he throws up the trapdoor she can hear his ragged breathing from where she sits, and the click of the switch in the passage. She remembers to scrabble back to her bed and lie down just as the cellar door swings wide and blinding light floods in.

She blinks, slowly, deliberately, as though he has just woken her. She is amazed to find, considering her fears of being entombed alive a few minutes ago, that she is pleased to see him.

The feeling lasts roughly ten seconds, ending as he stands over her, pulling off the candlewick bedspread with greedy haste. His face is in shadow, the light behind him, but the lit planes of his cheek and neck are shiny with sweat and, she thinks with a little burst of horror, she can smell blood.

'It's all right, sweetheart, it's all right.' His hands are freezing. 'I'm going to fix this. Don't worry. Now, come here.'

19

My first thought was that I was dead.

I was curled into a foetal ball on the driver's seat of my car, and I was shivering violently with cold – I'd shivered myself awake, in fact.

I put my hands out to lift myself up and felt the hard matte plastic of the steering wheel. It was

216

smeared thinly with something viscous and sticky that had a familiar smell. As I raised my arms even this slight distance, the pain wound about me like a serpent. My left shoulder was jelly, exquisitely painful jelly. It could take no weight at all, not even the weight of my arm. I touched it lightly with my other hand and it was boiling hot.

I wanted to cry. I couldn't get up. I couldn't move. I had no idea where I was, and it was dark – the hateful darkness was following me. The last thing I remembered was trying to drive to the hospital and then realizing, with the giddy objectivity of a dream, that I would never make it that far, and I would need to call them on the mobile to come and get me. That's the last thing I remembered thinking; that I'd never make it. The last thing I remembered *feeling* was hunted – even as I'd left the man on my front lawn, I'd had the mounting paranoia that he was right behind me.

Had he caught me?

Was that why I was here? And where was here?

After a minute or two feeling completely helpless I decided I had best try to do something.

With my good hand I made a few vague weak passes at the car door handle beside me, without much success. Just as I was about to give up for a brief rest my fingers recalled the movement to open the door and it swung wide with an echoing creak.

I rested for a moment in the faintest moonlight. The car was pulled up beside a big building, a warehouse, and there were some gigantic trucks parked nearby, blocky and silent. Their wheels were as high as my chest, or they would have been had I been able to stand up straight. There were a couple of thin windows in the very high walls of the building, and that was all I could see in the miserly amount of moonlight. I was parked before a huge roller shutter bay door, now closed and padlocked for the night.

Laboriously I turned myself around on the driver's seat, until my legs rested gently on the ground outside the car. My keys swayed slightly as they dangled from the ignition.

I turned them experimentally – I wanted to switch the headlights on. Nothing happened except for a pathetic coughing noise – the battery was dead. I had left the lights on while I was out cold. I swore gently under my breath, trying again, and then again.

I was wasting my time.

My mobile lay in the passenger footwell, and I let out a little gasp of happiness. I reached down to pick it up and hit the Wake button. Nothing happened. The battery was dead.

I turned it over in my hand, trying to think despite my muzzy head. It had been charged this morning. I must have been talking to someone to wear out the battery like that, though there was no way, at the moment, to find out who.

Damn it.

Shooting pains went up through my legs as I climbed out of the car, until finally I was upright.

I was suddenly dizzy. I grabbed at the car for support and pushed my hair out of my face. My forehead felt on fire.

I looked around. I tried to understand where I was. Next to the building was a dirty yard full of disused machinery, which stopped abruptly at a hedge. After the hedge there was nothing but gently rolling silver streaked fields.

I needed help. And to call for help, I needed to be able to tell them where I was.

Walking was just as harrowing as standing up, maybe a shade worse. I was breathing too quickly.

I glanced back at my little car, huddled close to the iron shutters. I looked out over the fields, and examined the back of a huge noticeboard, erected next to a gap in the hedge that issued out into a small lane.

I had never seen this place before in my life.

I plodded up to the board, my breath curling foggily before my face. As I suspected, I was in the yard of some kind of plant or industrial site. The board said that the place was called Farrell's Distribution Ltd. I blinked at it, uncomprehendingly.

According to the board, Farrell's Distribution Ltd was located in Rainham, Essex. I didn't recognize the telephone code.

There were no houses nearby, just the warehouse, the yard and then fields. If I could make the car start, there would probably be a farm eventually, or a village. As it was, I was stranded.

How had I got here?

Well, I said to myself, I must have driven here in the car. But why here? The last thing I remembered was wanting to drive to a hospital... I touched the noticeboard tentatively, to make sure it was real. The wood was freezing beneath the tips of my numb and bloodless fingers.

The moon was round and fat, bloated with white light, as it sailed amongst the needlepoints of stars.

I had the feeling I was falling, even though I was standing upright. The winter air coldly searched my wound, knifing into its unhealthy, unhealing heat.

As I returned to the yard, I noticed that the trucks were gently rusting, their body parts removed by long-gone scavengers – I had driven into a graveyard of sorts. Perhaps this was a scrapyard. I couldn't imagine what Farrell's Distribution distributed, and I didn't much care right then. My shoulder was pure agony, and my vision was blurring and warping.

I picked up my dead mobile and sighed. I could have charged it from the car, except, of course, the car wouldn't start.

I drifted painfully off to circumnavigate the place, hoping to discover something useful, and almost immediately I was rewarded. Next to the big shutters, hidden by a corner of the warehouse, was a little brick extension, and a window with a Venetian blind pulled shut – it must be the office.

I would try its door and see if there was a telephone. I wouldn't be able to walk far in my current condition.

And, I thought with a sudden flicker of cunning, if I broke in, I would be able to trigger the alarm. I could see it, a tiny blue firefly of light flickering in the eaves of the flat steel roof. The security company would come, or even better the police, and however awkward the conversation would be initially, it was better than bleeding to death or dying of exposure amongst the rusting hulks in the fields.

Breaking the glass with a piece of broken steel

produced no sound other than the terrifyingly loud crash of the thick pane. Perhaps it was a silent alarm.

I cleared the sill and awkwardly straddled it, climbing into the dark space. There was a chair and a light switch. I clicked it. There was a tinkling hum and then the strip light came on. I sighed in relief.

I put my hand up to cover my eyes from the intrusive, shocking glare. I sat down in the chair, thick with black dust that had been deeply ingrained by a succession of overall-clad bottoms. An ancient desktop computer, its casing yellowed and smudged, faced me. The office was still used for something, but I couldn't think what. There was a pale Bakelite telephone on the desk, covered with black smudges. I picked it up and, amazingly, a clear, loud purring issued from it.

There was a dirty pad of paper, of a light green colour with the letter heading 'Farrell's Distribution Ltd' on it, with the address and phone number of the place. It was sticking out from beneath a pile of well-thumbed soft-core magazines for men. Semi-naked women smiled at me in encouragement. I pulled the pad out and studied the address.

My fingers negotiated the stiff and heavy keypad of the telephone with difficulty. I tried Eddy's work, even though I knew it was shut. The phone rang. And rang. I listened dully to it. After several minutes, it became slowly apparent that I was wasting my time. When nobody answered, as I'd known they wouldn't, I still managed to be disappointed. I tried to remember Lily's number, but couldn't. Or didn't want to.

I had the absurd fear that I'd died, and that this was my Hell – to spend forever in a juggernauts' graveyard, phoning people who never answered, under the unforgiving glare of a fluorescent strip light that made my puffy white hands and arms look like marbled meat. I shook my head, but only succeeded in making my shoulder twang painfully.

I leaned my throbbing head on the back of my hand. I should call the police. I should pick up the phone and dial 999 and tell some stolid citizen in a dark blue uniform exactly what had happened to me. But in my weak and fevered condition the prospect horrified me. I felt the same way about the hospital. The thought of strange hands touching me, and unknown faces leaning over me, questioning me, challenging me, a myriad of voices buzzing in my ears like a nest of wasps... The idea repulsed me.

Of course, this was stupid. My home had been ransacked, I had been attacked and nearly killed. I lifted the receiver again.

I replaced it. I did not want to entrust myself to the police. It had never worked before. I remembered Lily saying, 'But he doesn't know all about you, does he?' in that horrid, insinuating tone, during our argument, that smug tone that undermined my reality regardless of the facts. The police would do the same...

Well, I thought, some kind of resolve thickening around my dreamy head, they can *try*. My house has been broken into and I'm injured, I'm cut, and it's swollen and hot in my shoulder and it's making me giddy and I've got to call somebody.

222

But in a minute.

I rested, to muster my courage and word my explanations, which was proving difficult. My head swam deliriously, and just then, one last sharp idea shot through it, like a little silver fish through a thick sea.

'What city?' said the bored voice of the operator.

My mouth, when I opened it, was as dry as dust. 'Cambridge.'

'What's the name?' Her voice was flat and contemptuous. She thought I was drunk, most likely.

'Martin Forrester,' I said, then tacking on needlessly. 'It might be Dr Forrester.'

'I see,' she said. That in all of my terrors, borne of fatigue, pain and loneliness, the only human company that I could lay claim to was a woman who despised me sight unseen made me want to weep.

I think, as I phased in and out of consciousness at this point, that I must actually have cried, because I remember that her voice became somewhat softer as she gave me the number. I wrote it down on the pad with a well-chewed pencil. My hand was feather light.

He was in.

My head felt on fire, the four walls seemed to buckle around me. The tape on my bandages cut into me like a vice, the thin shirt I wore seemed like a tent designed purely to keep heat all over me. Heat, heat, too much of it altogether and it was everywhere. The sheet was soaked. I looked at the floor, with its unfamiliar carpet. The floor would be cooler. I tried to get out of the bed but it was just too much work. Gravity itself had changed, and a pillow weighed a ton, a sheet a thousand tons, a blanket a million tons. My shoulder throbbed ceaselessly. I wanted to cut it off and be rid of it, for good.

I closed my eyes, and when I opened them Bethan Avery was there, which seemed perfectly natural. She was dressed in a little hooded Parka and a short tartan skirt over black cotton tights. She obviously wanted to continue the conversation we'd been having while I'd been waiting for Martin to pick me up.

'When will you see me?' she asked with exasperation. I thought she was being a bit preemptory, since she was already here.

'Oh, soon, soon.' Speech was an effort. The ghastly heat had filled my mouth and dried it all up. 'Soon, darling.'

'Margot, you can't lie about in bed all the time.'

'I know, I know...'

'He'll come to get me soon. We have to do something or I'll die, Margot, we–'

'I know!' I shouted.

Her face softened. I wanted to cradle her in my arms, her bottom lip seemed so tender, her eyes so large and dark. But I couldn't raise my arms just then so she remained remote and hazy.

I thought she was about to leave. I couldn't have borne the heat and timelessness alone so I reached out a supplicating hand, which rose for a moment and then fell weakly to the bed.

'I'll get you, Bethan. I promise. I'll take you home.'

'Home,' she said, considering the word.

'It'll all be all right.'

'It'll never be all right.' She rubbed the side of her face thoughtfully. 'I can never go home. But I know what I want. I want a future. Bring me a future. Do that and I'll let you go.'

'What kind of future?' I asked dreamily, not really following her.

'Any future will do.'

I sighed and shut my eyes, and Martin was there, with a couple of pills and a glass of water. He looked exhausted, and there were tiny tight lines around his eyes.

'Where is she?' I asked, pushing at his hand, which was gently offering the pills. 'Where did she go?'

'There's no one here, Margot. Open wide and stop scaring me.'

'No, no,' I said, still weakly resisting his warm arm. 'Didn't you hear us?'

'I didn't hear anything,' he said. 'Take these. You'll feel better.'

'I don't like pills.'

'They're only painkillers.'

'They keep telling me to take pills. Everything will be fine if I take the pills. Well I prefer things not to be fine. I prefer them to be real. I won't take any fucking pills.'

'You took them before. And see, you're better already. You know who I am, that's a start. Just take them. They're nothing sinister.'

I wavered. 'All right.'

I opened my mouth and he poked them in. They stuck to my dry tongue. He held the glass gently up to my lips and I took a few weak sips of water.

He tried to take the glass away but the water turned to nectar in my mouth. He patiently held it still while I drained it very slowly.

'Want some more?'

I nodded. My head felt heavy on my neck.

He left me and I could hear a tap being turned. He came back with a full glass. I drank greedily.

'D'you know where you are?' he asked eventually.

'No. But I think this must be your house, so we're in Cambridge, right?'

'You are a lot better. Do you remember getting here?'

I sighed, suddenly exhausted again. 'No. Wait. *Yes.* There was a hospital, and a doctor who said he was from Tobago. And policemen came.'

'Quite right,' he said. He took the glass away. 'No more for a few minutes. No need to overdo it.'

I thought for a moment. The mist seemed to be clearing. God, thought a nonsensical part of my head, that stuff's hot shit.

'So, how did I get here?'

'The police picked you up from the warehouse, remember?' He looked very kind in the dim light, his long hair loose around his face. 'They took you to the hospital in London.'

'No, I don't remember that part.' At least, I didn't remember anything that I hadn't just imagined. 'What was I saying to you?'

'Nothing that made much sense. I thought you were dying. I was trying to get you to phone the police and you were getting hysterical.' He shrugged. 'So I ratted you out to the ambulance service. Sorry. Then I thought, she sounds ter-

226

rified, I'd better go up there and see her.'

I frowned. 'You drove all the way to London?'

'No, not London. Essex. Well, what else was I supposed to do? Just hang up on you? I thought you were going to die on me just when our acquaintance was becoming interesting...' He pondered the empty glass in his hand. 'Fortunately, it's not that bad ... your shoulder, that is. It's just a cut, not too deep. It needed a few stitches.' That intense green gaze turned on me. 'They say that the reason you, um, are feeling a little strange right now is that you've discontinued your medication.'

I lay back and sighed. 'I know.' To be honest, I'd suspected a chemical cause to my swinging bolts between optimism and despair in the days following the broadcast. I just hadn't wanted to own up to it.

Though now, here in this quiet house with this man, the prospect of admitting it did not appal or terrify me as much as it had.

'It'll wear off, they say.'

I nodded.

'You didn't want to go back home or contact your husband, and I couldn't really blame you under the circumstances, so I brought you back here.'

'Oh,' I said. 'You shouldn't have.'

He set the glass on the floor and smiled. 'That's not what you were saying before.'

I grinned sleepily to myself, and licked my lips. 'Sorry. How do you feel about being alone in a room with a dangerous lunatic?'

'Pretty relaxed.' He pulled the sheet I'd kicked off back over my legs. 'Rest.'

I shut my eyes. 'OK. And Martin?'

'Yes?'

'Thanks,' I said. 'Thanks for coming for me.'

He smiled and opened his mouth, as though about to add something, but instead he simply shook his head. 'Good night, Margot.'

I was terribly tired and hot, but I was still curious. I kicked the sheet off when I saw he was gone, and lay back, thinking furiously. But all my thoughts were muddled and strange with pain-killers, and after a few minutes I was asleep.

I was following Bethan Avery through the corridor in Addenbrooke's, and on all sides the film crew were packing away their equipment, chatting to one another. Martin was deep in conversation with Thea, the actress who had played Bethan, and she was flirting back at him, with her tinkly little laugh.

Bethan walked quickly, stumbling a little, look-ing neither right nor left, the hood on her parka drawn up to cover her dark hair.

I wanted to shout out to someone: 'Stop her, stop her, that's her!' but my mouth was sealed and I could make no sound at all. I could only run after her, unable to call her name.

And though she was only walking while I was running, I couldn't catch up with her, no matter how hard I tried to make up the distance, my feet heavy and slow over the hospital's tiled floor. She remained just thirty feet ahead, as though she was a bright mirage in the desert of my subconscious.

I was aware of the walls of Addenbrooke's grow-ing darker and more narrow, the light increasingly dim and orange, and there was the smell of incense, disinfectant and cigarette ends, switching in and out. Voices came from ahead, from the unknowable distance in front of Bethan, a sort of loud chaotic hubbub echoing against the red bricks, and the gold and scarlet murals painted on the ceiling showed a female saint in a man's toga.

I emerged into a richly decorated space filled with dark wooden pews, and the stained-glass window with its image of St Eugenia, the woman in disguise, let variegated light fall on to all present.

I lingered at the back, unsure of how to proceed. Someone in priest's vestments was at the altar, but I didn't want to look up, to meet their gaze. I understood that it was vitally important that he didn't see me.

The candles flickered all around and the organ began to play as I stared about myself, utterly lost. Bethan appeared to have vanished. The congregation all seemed a little familiar, and I felt that something was insisting that I look at them, notice them too, but then I saw the back of Bethan's hood, from where she slouched in the front pew, her legs crossed lazily before her and poking sideways into the aisle, her toes in their black Mary Janes flexed skywards.

I hurried up the aisle to the nave, my chin pressed to my chest, careful not to look up and attract the notice of whatever creature was officiating. I pushed myself in almost roughly next to Bethan, determined to get her to come with me away from all of this danger, or at the very least to adopt a more respectful posture in church.

I seized her elbow, and she turned to meet my gaze almost lazily, her hood falling back to reveal her peroxide white hair.

'Heya, Amy,' she said, and her eyes were glazed and dead. 'Want to come to a party?'

I found my voice and I screamed, screamed so loudly that the congregation grew still and everything was silent, except for the ringing, deliberate footfalls of someone stepping down from the altar and slowly coming for us both.

20

I was woken by church bells and the raucous cries of crows.

My shoulder hurt less, but my limbs were just as heavy. It was very restful, actually, to just lie there and be unable to do anything.

Then I remembered.

'Martin,' I shouted, or attempted to. My voice was tremulous and insubstantial.

My car was still in the juggernauts' graveyard. I had to get it back. I had to get to the police and describe my attacker. I had to get Wendy to forward my mail somewhere safe. I had to ... tell Martin that I knew who Bethan Avery was.

I couldn't see my mobile phone.

I touched my shoulder. It was still a little hot and tender, but the bandages felt far less tight. This gave me so much confidence that I got out of bed and stood up in one motion. I was in the process of taking my first step when the dizziness hit me and I collapsed to the floor. For a moment I couldn't move at all.

I was so frustrated and angry that I wept hard but silently into the coarse carpet for a few seconds.

Now, now, Margot, you were just a touch too hasty, that's all. If you stand up slowly then you'll be all right.

I sat up, slowly. Even this made me feel vague and numb. How the hell could I accomplish anything in this condition? If that thug burst in here right now I would be utterly helpless. This sobering notion gave me renewed strength. Sitting around and crying about it was quite simply not a luxury I could afford.

I tugged down the shoulder of my shirt to examine my injuries with my own eyes. I gently pulled off a little of the tape and lifted the bandage. Even this hurt, the cooler air stinging it. It was a knife cut, a long furrow beginning at the top of my shoulder, and coming down over my chest until it was level with my armpit. It was a perfectly straight line, about a quarter of an inch deep at its widest, with slightly raised edges that were white against the angry red skin surrounding it. Within the lacing of the stitches, the blood within had congealed to a dark ruby red. I peered at it. It looked ugly, but was hardly the death-dealing injury I had mistaken it for. I replaced the bandage carefully, the tape refusing to stick properly again. Sod it.

I stood up, slowly. Far better. I still felt weak and dizzy, but it would pass. I tried to smooth down my tangled, sweaty hair.

The room, now that I saw it in daylight, was small but pretty, with pale blue curtains and a sanded grey wood dresser. This supported a warped antique mirror that threw my reflection back at me at a slightly queer, fun-house angle. A conch shell rested before it.

Nudging aside the curtains, a tiny but beautifully maintained scrap of garden lay below me, edged in dark green hedging. Blue tits and chaffinches were darting in and out of a bird feeder. Beyond the garden were fields, their stubble ploughed under, bounded by a thin ribbon of trees. The landscape was flat, the sky wide – this was the Fens, I understood immediately – but where in the Fens?

It was a beautifully cold, sunny day on the very lip of autumn, before it turns to winter. With my good arm I opened the window. There was a squeal, then the fresh tang of a cold breeze ruffled against my face.

Where was I?

I made it, one foot at a time, to the top of the stairs. On the landing, a trio of plastic crates full of papers, folders and other bric-a-brac stood one atop the other, the debris of a house move, if I was any judge. Getting down the stairs was the worst thing and took the longest time.

Eventually I found myself in a small living room, low ceilinged and crammed with bookshelves. Books burst untidily out of these, stacked up in rows two deep in places, every available nook and cranny full of them – non-fiction, literary novels, a smattering of crime and thrillers with their titles in large block capitals. There was lots of twentieth-century literary biography – De Beauvoir, Sartre, Miller, Hemingway – clearly Martin had a thing for Left Bank writers.

There was also a record collection comprised of real records near the wide-screen television – vinyl, stacked in their own cabinet and with the names on the spines. As I hobbled nearer I could make out the Sex Pistols, the Stranglers and the Clash, which made me smile. So Martin spent his leisure hours mourning the fact he was too young for the punk rock revolution, did he? How adorable.

Stop that, Margot, I told myself sternly.

Everything looked slightly amazed, a little jumbled, as though this was the condensation of the contents of a much larger home.

I had never heard Martin talk of a Mrs Forrester, but to me this looked like the pad of a divorcee rather than a bachelor, with its sense of belongings decanted into a smaller space than they were used to.

A pair of glass doors led to the little garden, and in the middle of the room stood a low coffee table surrounded by a sofa and chairs. A remote for the expensive stereo and a glass bowl full of coins and keys lay on top of it, but despite the genial messiness, there was no sign of any dust – I suspected he got someone in to clean as he didn't strike me as a neat freak.

There was also no sign of my phone, though.

I sighed.

'What are you doing downstairs?' Martin asked suddenly from behind me.

I started, shocked. He had emerged from the

hallway, and behind him I could see a door standing open, displaying a vast, very expensive iMac, and an ergonomic desk chair with a mesh back. It must be his office.

I blushed hotly, aware of myself as nosy and furtive.

'Um, where am I?'

He furrowed his brows, as though in disbelief. 'You ... well, this is my house. In Little Wilbraham. Why aren't you in bed?'

'Oh.' I bit my lip. 'I have to make a phone call,' I mumbled, feeling very vulnerable standing there, sticky and dishevelled and sheet white.

He raised a finger, as though I had a point, and vanished back into his office before reappearing a second later with my iPhone, fully charged. 'Here you go.'

I accepted it without looking at him. I was embarrassed, very embarrassed, for a variety of reasons. The circumstances of my presence here created a peculiar kind of intimacy with him, one I hadn't thought I wanted but did not resent.

'Martin,' I began awkwardly.

'Yeah?'

'Um ... thanks, you know. For everything. I'm sorry about...' I twitched my shoulders vaguely and the hurt one twanged. 'Well, you know...'

'You thanked me already.' He put his hands on his hips and looked down at the floor. 'So don't worry about it.' His head snapped up suddenly, as though he'd had a burst of inspiration. 'Are you hungry yet?'

Before I tackled Martin about what I had realized

in my dream, I wanted to talk to Lily, to whom I owed an apology. I might have been right about the fact that strange men were after me, but I had still behaved disgracefully, and unlike Ara, I thought with a little stab of shame, Lily did not deserve to be spoken to in that way.

She didn't answer – and when I thought about it, I realized she might be in class. In fact, I ought to be in class, I remembered with a gut-lurching spasm of guilt.

'What?' asked Martin. He had stopped by my shoulder while I sat on the sofa, in order to put a fresh cup of hot coffee in front of me. Bless him, he'd remembered I take it black. The smell of it immediately made everything seem fractionally more manageable.

'I need to call work. What time is it?'

'Don't worry about that. The police took care of it.' He flicked a tea towel back over his shoulder and vanished into the kitchen. 'Toast? It's all I've got, I'm afraid.'

I paused, frowning at the coffee, then at the door he had gone through.

'The police called my work?' I could hear the suspicious note in my voice. 'Very obliging of them.'

'I told them you weren't in a fit state to bother yourself.' I could hear bread being sliced in the next room. I was starving, I realized. 'You weren't, at the time.'

'I'm surprised they let me leave with you.'

He chuckled drily, then stopped dead.

'What?' I asked, craning my head round towards the kitchen.

Silence.

I stood up, hobbled towards the open door to be met by him.

'What?' I repeated. 'What's so funny?'

He glanced down, embarrassed again. 'I was the only person you *would* leave with. You wouldn't give them the names of anyone to call.'

I met his eyes as they came up. They were very green. 'Tell me.'

He licked his lips. 'You were on their system, and since you were obviously distressed they wanted to send you to Narrowbourne, and then I said, you know, you could stay with me in Little Wilbraham overnight, and you liked that plan, and after some very fast talking, and getting O'Neill out of bed and running it past him, they reluctantly agreed. So, here you are.'

'I don't understand. Why would they send me back to Narrowbourne?' A cold dread and fury was starting to hammer against my breastbone. 'Good God, I was the one that lunatic attacked, why would–'

'No,' he said. 'It's not like that.'

'I mean he broke into my home and tried to kill me,' I continued, feeling the ignition turn in the engines of my rage. 'I didn't imagine that, did I? Or did I?'

'Margot, stop. Stop–'

'I mean, maybe I did, maybe this is–'

He raised a quelling hand. *'Stop!'*

I paused, waiting, as my chest rose and fell.

'It's exactly what you think it is,' he eyed me keenly. 'Whoever kidnapped Bethan Avery saw your picture in the paper, or you on TV, found

236

out where you worked, followed you home and attacked you there.'

My mouth snapped shut. I was so unused to people agreeing with me lately that I think I was astounded.

He offered a little bounce of a shrug. 'That's exactly how it went down. And it's something that should have been anticipated, given everything we know.'

I considered this and sighed. My anger was draining away. 'Well...' I took a deep breath, tried to force some calm back into my lungs. 'Why should it have been anticipated? Why should these people come after me? If I knew where Bethan Avery was, we wouldn't need to pay drama students and film crews and get underfoot at hospitals making movies about her, would we?'

Something queer came into his expression then, something both sympathetic and yet speculative.

And increasingly, nothing about this whole incident and its fallout made any sense. If, as I had suspected before the attack, I was being hunted because Bethan's kidnapper thought I knew where she was, why had he not tried to question me about her whereabouts? And what about the other man, the one from the car park? Was there really a gang after all? And why had the police wanted to send me to Narrowbourne? I couldn't go home, obviously. I probably had come over as a little hysterical (and who could blame me) but why not keep me in hospital overnight? I mean, I know the NHS is under pressure, but still...

I felt sick. I couldn't remember much at all about the previous night. The hospital had been a blur. When I don't remember things, it's never a good sign. I don't remember drinking, so there wasn't even that for an excuse.

Oh Jesus, maybe I am really crazy.

'These men...' I began.

A faintly embarrassed look stole over his face. 'Well, man.'

'There were two...'

'No. The other fellow who followed you to the car park was, um, an undercover police officer.'

'What?' I asked, stunned.

He shrugged, his mouth twisting ruefully. 'Yeah. The police have had you under surveillance for a couple of weeks now.'

'They ... *surveillance?*'

'Yes.' He was rubbing at the back of his neck with his hand.

'I don't ... they think I knew who was writing the letters, don't they?' I drew a sharp intake of breath. 'Martin, I think they're right. Listen, I've been thinking about my time with the nuns, and there was a girl there who could have been Bethan Avery. Someone I knew at the hostel. Her name was—'

'Margot, I don't think it was anyone you knew at the hostel. We found Bethan Avery. Last night.'

I couldn't reply. I was absolutely amazed.

'You have? I don't understand... Martin, tell me. Honestly. What's going on? Who is it?'

He looked at me then for a long silent moment, before he threw down the tea towel. 'Come with me.'

I pulled my arm around myself and shivered,

despite the cheery warmth of the house.

'Take a seat,' said Martin, bending down to clear papers off the mesh-backed office chair.

I couldn't, not straight away. I was transfixed.

On the wall opposite, a map had been put up – a gigantic view of East Anglia, scattered with pins. Over the top of this was a collage of sorts – a diagram of missing girls. They smiled out with guarded shyness from school portraits, they glowered from mug shots, they lay curled and sunken on steel gurneys or wrapped in rotting blankets.

I blinked, overwhelmed, horrified. Then I began to distinguish what I was looking at out of this carnage. There were six major hubs of photographs, connected by arrows. Some of these pointed at the girls, some at random locations, and all were dotted with notes – Cambridge Methodist Youth Club, St Hilda's Academy – with an icy shock I recognized Katie Browne in her St Hilda's uniform.

In the upper left corner was Bethan Avery, and I was struck suddenly by how similar the two girls were, with their dark hair and suspicious, keen dark eyes.

'What is this?'

Martin came to stand at my shoulder. His heat was palpable, even through my shivering cold.

'The other victims,' he said, almost gently. 'I mentioned them before, remember?'

'The ones you think he killed?'

'The ones we're now sure he killed.' He placed a hand on my good shoulder. 'Or at least the ones we know about.'

I tried to parse this. 'There's ... good God...'

'Six, yes. Six we know about. Two more that we suspect.'

I was shaking. 'But...' I pushed my hair out of my face. 'They're all so *young*.'

'Let me talk you through it,' he said, releasing my shoulder. His tone was still gentle, but there was something glittering underneath, some hard edge of determination. 'It works like this. In 1998, he kidnaps Bethan Avery while she is visiting her grandmother in hospital. He keeps her for no more than two months, but she escapes.'

I nodded.

'There's no evidence,' he continues, 'and the case dries up. No body, though everyone assumes she must be dead because of the blood loss on the nightdress they found.'

'Yes, I know,' I said, trying to rein in my impatience.

'Fine, so we'll come back to Bethan. Because I think that's what's happening in this case. We're coming back to Bethan. The next one that we know about is Jennifer. And there's a long gap – about three and a half years – which makes a few of us very nervous, as someone like this, well, three and a half years is a long time when you're that driven.' He scratched his stubbled chin thoughtfully. 'I think that when we catch him we'll find there was another victim during that period–'

'Or that Bethan's escape frightened him off for a while.'

Martin let out a short *hmm*. 'Possibly. But yes, sorry, Jennifer Walker.' His finger nearly fell on the face of a heartbreakingly young girl in a pink

240

sundress, seemed to reconsider and then touched the photo margin below instead. 'She was only twelve. Like all of them, she was known to social services, in this case in Norwich. The social services thing is going to be a theme, I warn you. She was put into residential care for six weeks when her mother refused to leave her father after his conviction for breaking her jaw. He got out of prison, moved back in, and Jenny was moved out in very short order.

'So, Jenny is bullied in care and wants to run away. Tries a couple of times, is brought back. She's a sensitive sort, finds it very hard. This is also going to be a recurring theme, incidentally. She's last seen in a McDonald's with a strange man before vanishing. It hits the media. Search parties, press conferences, the works... Sorry, are you cold?'

'I ... a little.' My teeth were beginning to chatter.

'Try this.' He put a heavy Barbour jacket over my shoulders, and leaned over and switched on a mobile heater by the window. 'It won't take long to warm up.'

'Thank you.'

'So,' he continued, 'after ten days a family out camping find her buried in a shallow grave near a picnic ground in Thetford Forest. She'd been strangled, and buried in a white nightdress that wasn't hers. Again, there were no hair or fibres really, as she'd been washed post-mortem – but not well enough to take out all the DNA, so we do have a profile on him if he's ever caught. The nightdress is still creased from the packet it came out of. Everyone thinks of Bethan Avery, and there's talk about a serial killer, but even though Jennifer and Bethan have their own *Crimewatch* special and there are a billion people and their dogs phoning in with leads, nothing comes of it.

'So a couple more years go by, and then in 2003, the summertime again, Lauren Jacks goes missing. Lauren is from Newmarket, about fifteen miles up the road, and she's another girl that appears to have absconded from care. Her body isn't found, and it's not clear whether she just ran away.

'Then two years after that, something changes. Sarah Holroyd, who's twenty-one and three months pregnant, is found dumped by the side of the A11, near Mildenhall.'

He stabbed the point on the map with his finger, but I didn't see it. I was staring at a photograph near the pin, and couldn't actually breathe or speak.

'No attempt to bury her – she was nude. She'd been beaten to death. But her body was suggestive – she'd definitely been kept alive somewhere in poor conditions for a significant period in the run-up to the murder, and more than that – she looks, physically, like the others. Well, she doesn't there, obviously, poor girl … sorry, are you all right?'

'I … I could do with sitting down.' I thought I was going to faint. I've never fainted before.

He was so obviously mortified, I pitied him. 'I'm *so* sorry, Margot, I'm used to looking at these kinds of pictures, I forget that other people...'

'No, it's fine.' I swallowed, let the mesh chair take my weight. I deliberately turned my eyes away from the gruesome photo of the dead girl,

242

with her misshapen jaw and open, staring, blood-shot eye. 'I'm fine.'

He peered at me, and there was concern, but also something else – that speculative tilt to his head, as though I was being tested for something. 'If you're sure.'

'Yes. Go on.'

'Well, Greta, who you met in London recently...'

I suspect my face spoke volumes.

'Well, she thinks Sarah and then Becky, the next victim, made him angry somehow, so their remains are treated far less respectfully – they're literally dumped at the side of the road near rubbish bins – and they die more violently. Sarah was pregnant when she was abducted – we think, perhaps, that this would have made him feel she was promiscuous and unworthy, and Becky, from all accounts, was a notorious firebrand. She would have fought him all the way down.' He twitched his head sideways. 'You may not have had much time for her, and with good reason, but Greta worked up a profile on our man and it's very convincing if you are an aficionado of those sorts of things.'

'Since I'm not, I'll take your word for it.' Believe it or not, I didn't say this to be snippy. I don't even like watching this sort of thing on the TV. I find it too disquieting.

He acknowledged this with a tiny nod and a twist of his mouth. 'Regardless, Greta suspects he is someone that would appear very affectionate to his victims initially. He would believe he's in a romantic relationship with them.'

I treated him to an incredulous raise of my eye-

243

brow. 'So he seduces them into coming with him?'

'No, absolutely not. Or, rather, not ultimately. What happens, we think, is that he befriends these girls somehow, or passes himself off as something he is not, and through doing that he is able to get them to accompany him somewhere he can abduct them. Of the girls that are found, every single one of them has injuries that are consistent with some kind of forcible imprisonment, forcible assault – broken nails, restraint marks on the wrists and ankles, malnutrition. However crazy he is, he must know that all things considered, they don't want to be with him. And the injuries we find are always as old as the girl's disappearance – the incarceration happens straight away. Greta thinks the incarceration is the whole point. It's all about control. He gets to have a person in his power that he can dominate totally, someone who is not in a position to reject or abandon him.'

I let out a disgusted sigh.

'I know,' he answered. 'He'd also, however, have very poor anger management and next to no ability to brook any kind of defiance or resistance from them. There's a reason he chooses girls so young.'

'Heaven forefend,' I said, in bitter irony, 'my rape victim dared to be cheeky with me.'

'He's a psychopath, Margot. He's incapable of seeing any point of view but his own. He thinks this is a romance, and so it is, to him. But the worst part is that the violence escalates every time he imprisons a girl, and with each girl it takes less time for him to become disillusioned with them.' He sighed. 'That's bad news for Katie: she'll be coming to her cut-off point.'

I couldn't think of a single thing to say to this. My heart hammered against my ribs.

And beneath it all, my fury coiled and rustled, like a fanged serpent. How dare you, whoever you are. How dare you.

'I won't labour this; though there have been no more bodies, we think there were two others between Becky and Katie – Hannah Murphy went missing after a youth club disco in 2011, and Chloe Firth in 2013. No evidence, but they haven't been heard from since and they fit the victim profile – dark-haired white girls, both from East Anglia.' He shrugged. 'And then, Katie Browne. Katie from Cambridge, where it all started.' He rubbed his chin, regarded the girls on the board. 'Started with Bethan Avery.'

'Who is writing letters now,' I said. I felt exhausted. The heating was now far too high. I let his coat drop off my shoulders and on to the chair back.

'Yes.' He came and sat down opposite me, on an old trunk pushed up against his office window. Next to us, his wall and its web of misery sprawled away on either side. 'Bethan Avery, who is writing letters now. But why now, after all these years?'

I felt very sad all of a sudden. 'You think that she's an accomplice, don't you? That's what this all must mean.' I let my gaze stray up the morass of photographs, the notes, the maps. I was close to tears; it was as though Bethan had betrayed me. 'She's been helping him in some ghastly way, and twenty years in she's had an attack of conscience. She writes as a child to garner sympathy, perhaps, but can't commit to finally giving him up.'

Because really, it was the only thing that made sense. I just hadn't wanted to admit it. There was no way, in the situation that she described herself being trapped in, she could post letters to a newspaper. This could only mean one of two things. Either her captor was in on it, or she was lying about the situation.

'No,' said Martin briskly. His gaze was very direct, unnervingly so. 'Nobody thinks she's an accomplice.'

'Then what?' I growled wearily, rubbing my temples. One of my migraines was lurking around the back of my head, considering whether to strike or not.

'Greta and I think,' and he seemed to choose his words very carefully, 'that in a very fundamental sense, she is exactly who she says she is. She is a frightened girl who lived through a terrible ordeal and has never recovered.'

'Fine,' I snarled. 'But why can't she just say what happened to her so we can catch the bastard?'

'Whoa, calm down,' said Martin, putting a hand on my trembling arm.

'I'm sorry.' I bit my lip. 'But it's such a fucking huge ... *mess*, Martin. I didn't think helping this girl out would have such a massive effect on my life. I thought I'd tell the police about the letter and someone would sort it out, and now everything I have is in jeopardy, it's all in free-fall. My house is in pieces – my house, which I love – I was nearly killed, and my employer's going to find out about my past – Jesus, if they haven't already.'

'No, not at all,' he said, then winced. 'Well, *maybe.*'

I threw myself back in the chair with a horrified sigh, and covered my eyes with my hands.

'I'm sorry,' I said. I seemed to be saying it a lot lately. 'I must sound like a perfectly selfish creature to you.'

'No,' he said, 'you really don't. I don't think for a moment that when this started you imagined the consequences would escalate as quickly as they have.'

I uncovered my eyes and let my head flop back against the chair. 'I just can't see my way through to the end, now, not at all. It's a labyrinth.'

'Well, yes,' he said. 'But the thing about labyrinths is that you're always at your most lost just before you get to the centre.'

In the quiet, I could hear a clock ticking, gently, somewhere in the house, and as always there was the background whisper of the wind; and the fine, lost strands of the croaking crows.

'What do you mean?' I asked. His gaze was not on me any more, it was on the map on the wall. He had a calculating squint.

'One thing hasn't changed,' he said, as though I had not spoken. 'He's keeping them all in the same place, wherever that is.'

'But where would that be?'

'Well, Bethan Avery was the first – it will be near her. It's a cellar or basement, certainly the walls are stone and there are particular kinds of mould found on the girls' bodies that only exist in cold, humid conditions. They've nearly all got some kind of lung infection in autopsy, depending on how long they've been down there. O'Neill thinks that after the initial abduction in winter the killer switched to summer for that very reason.'

'But Katie went missing in October.'

'Yes. And Katie wasn't known to social services either, which makes her a little different. Something has changed. Maybe his supply dried up somehow. Or he had a brush with the law, or a conviction of some sort recently, which means he doesn't have the same access to girls. Cambridgeshire Constabulary and MHAT have been running a mile a minute to analyse all the data we've got. There are a few good leads in there, too. And believe it or not, the reconstruction did turn up some interesting nuggets from the general public via the hotline number – the one they're most excited about is an Irish hitchhiker.'

'What?'

'Yeah. She says she encountered someone very like our man outside a service station on the A12 near Ipswich in 2006. He offered her a lift.'

I stared at him. As far as I'd known, the reconstruction had been a bust.

'A hitchhiker?'

Martin nodded. 'Yes. She accepted, but as he opened the car door, there was something about him she didn't like, so at the last minute she declined his kind assistance and he went for her, tried to drag her into his car. She saw the reconstruction in Belfast, of all places, and gave the hotline a call.' Martin rubbed his head. 'She describes him as very friendly at first, as he talked her out of the service station and over to his car door, but then he changed to "absolutely raging

248

crazy angry" once he realized she was going back into the service station and he was going to lose her. She'd never seen anyone react like that before, and out of nowhere, from the second she turned him down. It fits our profile of him – he'll be able to hold it together to deceive someone for a short while, but no longer than that.'

'This girl didn't go to the police?'

He shrugged. 'She meant to report it, but never got around to it. She was nervous talking about it on the telephone ten years after it happened, according to O'Neill. She was only fifteen at the time.'

'He wouldn't need special access of the kind you're talking about if he's grabbing hitchhikers,' I mused.

'No, but we think he just liked the look of Miss Belfast, so acted on impulse. From what we can tell about her, she would have been exactly his type.'

I spared a glance at the wall. 'So, clearly, the rest of the time, he's choosing them somehow. They're mainly vulnerable girls in the social services system, and they share a certain physical type. Somehow he has access to a pool of these kinds of girls…'

'Absolutely.'

'So, a social worker perhaps, or a policeman.'

'No. The police looked into this, but there is nobody that had official contact with all the girls during the time period. It's far more likely he's an ancillary worker who moves around and works on short contracts, possibly a driver, because the girls are in different council catchment areas. He

249

almost certainly has more than one identity.'

'It doesn't necessarily follow that he's a driver,' I said. 'He could be a locum of some sort.'

'He could, but probably isn't,' replied Martin, with the sure conviction of someone who has had this conversation before. 'Greta and I think he's bright but not educated past secondary school. He'll be fundamentally incapable of taking any kind of orders, or tolerating criticism, so he probably works alone and for himself, possibly as a taxi or bus driver, or in catering, or as a janitor. Or maybe he just volunteers for a charity. Any of those could expose him to these girls.'

I shivered, imagining it. You never know who is in the background, watching you as you go through your daily life. 'Surely people are vetted if they're going to be working with vulnerable children?'

'They are now, yes – this is a post-Soham world – but they weren't always.' He let his head rest forward. 'And remember, vetting only works if you've been caught before, or your offences are still on file.'

I managed a weak chuckle. 'That I can vouch for.'

We exchanged wan smiles.

'So you've found Bethan Avery?' I asked.

'Oh yes,' he said, and he didn't look away. 'I think so, most definitely. Margot, I've got something to tell you. It may bother you.'

I shivered in expectant silence. Then I said, 'Go on.'

21

This was impossible.

This was madness, true madness, something my adolescent peccadilloes merely hinted at. I sat very still in his ergonomic office chair while Martin Forrester attempted to reason with me.

'Margot, don't you see? It explains everything.'

He might have been speaking in a foreign language. He was telling me that once I understood it all, I would feel better than I'd ever felt. It explained all the things that had ever troubled me.

'You're mad,' I said. I could think of nothing else to say. I was stuck out here in the middle of nowhere with a crazy person.

He explained it again, while I sat there, incapable of speech or movement, as though I was made wholly of wood. The sensation of being a spring wound down had never been stronger, and I was going to explode.

'All right,' said Martin. 'It does sound mad. But that doesn't mean it's not true.' He handed me the piece of paper, the piece of paper with 'Farrell's Distribution' on the letterhead.

I took the paper and read it again.

Then I read it once more, observing every character, every loop, every nuance.

'Margot,' said Martin, 'speak to me.'

He suddenly appeared genuinely frightened for me. I suspected that for some reason I struck that indefinable chord in him. I don't know why. We never know why.

All I knew was that after thirty-five years of being alive, thirty-five years of a varied and, I now realized, extensive existence, I had known him for two weeks and he was all I had in the whole wide world.

But that wasn't any help now.

'So,' I said to him, 'when did you work all this out?' I must have sounded cold and unfriendly. That's how I felt.

He sighed, then gave me a long look. 'I suspected it from the first moment I Googled your picture on the school website.' His head turned back towards the wall, with its freight of woe. 'I wasn't lying when I said I live with these pictures all day. Your nose was badly broken at some point and healed without being reset, and it changed your appearance, but the rest...' He gave me a little smile, and a shrug. 'I wasn't that surprised when the analysis on the handwriting came back.'

I examined the piece of paper again without speaking.

'When did I write this?' I asked, not looking up from it.

'You were writing it when they came to pick you up at that place, that warehouse,' he said softly. 'You were delirious ... you don't remember. I found it in your jacket pocket when I put you to bed...' He tailed off.

I stared at the cold sunshine beyond the window. It was hard to see. My eyes were blurred. I managed a vague, cynical smile at Martin. Something was ticking urgently and precisely in my head, like a bomb. I handed him back the piece of paper, so I didn't have to see the horror of it again.

The horror. I could not even deny it.

I shut my eyes.

It wasn't Martin that was crazy, it was me. It's always been me.

The paper was in front of me again behind my closed lids, the one I'd written on in my fevered delirium, while my shoulder ached and the world warped and I waited for rescue, but I'd forgotten that. I'd forgotten Margot, I was writing the fourth letter to Dear Amy, in the childish, fussy script I knew so very well.

The words stood out like knives.

Dear Amy,

I am so frightened now, so very frightened and so sick, and I know he means to kill me very soon and there is nothing I can do. I know that no one knows where I am and that no one will rescue me, and I am so scared and I don't know what to do. Please help me,

Love,
Bethan Avery

Then the ticking in my head stopped, and the bomb went off.

'Fine,' I snapped, leaping to my feet, my hands balling into fists. I no longer felt the pain in my shoulder. 'Fine. I'm a head case. I've wasted everybody's time pretending to be Bethan Avery.' I could hardly breathe with terror, with shame, and also with pure rage – the rage of Furies, the rage I can never quite let go of. 'Was it really necessary to bring me all this way? To humiliate me like this? I had no idea I was writing these things, that I was this ... this *disturbed*. This wasn't just some shitty little plot for attention, you know. I genuinely thought...'

'But you're not pretending to be Bethan Avery.' He was unmoved by my anger, his hands resting on his knees as he stared up at me. 'That's the whole point. You *are* Bethan Avery.' His mouth twisted into a half smile, but his eyes were sympathetic. 'That's who you've always been. And your suicide attempts and your breakdowns and your pills are all down to one thing: you are pretending to be Margot Lewis.'

My mouth worked, soundlessly.

'Stop this,' I said, and the mortified tears sprung, unheeded, and gushed down my face, as if they were something utterly separate from me, entirely outside of my control. 'I'm sorry. I'm sorry I led you on like this. But there's no way in the world that I'm her. That's just insanity.'

He stared at me for a long moment.

'All right,' he said briskly. 'Come with me.'

He was standing now, and steering me towards the door. 'Do you have everything in your bag?'

'Um, yes, yes I do...'

I was being led out of the house, through the door, into the bright, brittle sunshine. His Range Rover was parked outside, a thin film of fallen leaves lying over the bonnet and roof. 'Get in the car.'

'What?'

'Fine, you're not Bethan Avery. Get in the car.'

254

'But...'

'I have something to show you.'

'What do you mean?' I was growing alarmed by him, by the steely change in his attitude.

'You may not be doing this deliberately,' he said, 'but that doesn't change the fact that there are consequences to your actions. Get in the car. *Now.*'

I don't know why I did it, but I did. Perhaps it was due to the complete collapse of any and all moral authority I might have pretended to, but I let him push and prod me into his chocolate-brown Range Rover and sat meekly while he drove away from his house down the winding country road through the village, heading south.

I was absolutely poleaxed.

I had written letters pretending to be Bethan Avery, a likely long-dead murder victim. It was morally repugnant and very likely illegal. Most horrifyingly, now that I had been confronted with this, I could guess for you exactly when I had written them. The last had been in the warehouse, in Farrell's Distribution. I didn't even have drink to blame. The second had been after Eddy's visit, when he'd tried and failed to seduce me. And the first...

The first had been after the police had visited the school for the final time. Katie Browne had been missing for nearly a month. They'd told the headmaster that they could find no evidence that she'd been kidnapped – she'd packed a bag and taken some personal effects and money – so they were scaling back the search. She was sixteen, after all. I had been in on the meeting, and listened with increasing ire. So what if she was sixteen? So what if she had problems? If she'd been lured away from her house and had concealed why, not even leaving a note, then clearly something wasn't right.

'If she's just absconded with some boyfriend,' I said, aware that my cheeks were red, and I was shaking slightly, and that I was scaring the others more than a little, 'then why wouldn't she just say?'

The policeman, transparently alarmed at my apparent lack of self-control, had coughed and harrumphed and shrugged and said that ultimately it wasn't illegal to leave your home when you were of legal age.

'But it is illegal to bail out of school,' I said. 'And it is very suspicious and out of character that this girl would behave that way. She was very committed to her swimming, for example.'

More mumbling and blushes. I suspect, looking back, that the young officer hadn't agreed with me about this. There was more information that had come up, which he couldn't disclose, family troubles, etc., that led them to believe she'd left voluntarily. Other forces had been notified, and they just wanted to let us know, thanks very much for the tea, get in touch if you hear anything else.

So much for the search for Katie Browne.

Martin drove in silence and, having nothing to say in the face of my epic humiliation, I did nothing to break it.

We barrelled down the M11 for an hour, passing the turn-off to Stansted, before rolling off the motorway and taking a series of increasingly narrow country lanes.

'Where are we going?' I asked eventually. When he'd told me to get in the car, I'd thought we were only going down the road. My shoulder had started to hurt again, cold sweat trickling into the wound through my compromised bandage.

'Wastenley,' he said. His voice was neutral, and it was impossible to tell what he was thinking. 'We're nearly there.'

The name sounded familiar, as if I should know it, but in my confused, lost state I couldn't conjure its context. 'And where is Wastenley?'

He turned to me and narrowed his eyes, as if I had failed a test.

'You'll see.'

Wastenley was an expertly trimmed and planted Essex village – there was a sign on the road into it announcing it was a 1989, 1993, 1997 and 2012 winner of Britain in Bloom. I could feel my heart sink. I have never felt comfortable in these kinds of places – places where everyone knows one another, where people have deep roots and where everyone is expected to contribute and, in this instance, compete.

The village gardening committee was run like the Kremlin during the Cold War.

Who had said that? It sounded so familiar somehow.

Martin drove past picture-perfect thatched cottages with exquisitely tidy gardens, past a manicured village green only just beginning to go patchy with encroaching winter, and a twee little post office with a Victorian pillar box outside. A sign taped to the noticeboard advertised a Gilbert

257

and Sullivan revival from the Wastenley Amateur Dramatic and Operatic Society in the Meadhall.

Martin was looking for something, and every so often I would catch him glancing at me.

It was another test, of course. This place must have something to do with Bethan Avery (I couldn't think why, as its pristine and affluent order would have seemed a million miles away from Bethan's situation, raised on the edge of town with her impoverished grandmother). Martin, with this insistence that I was Bethan (an inexplicable madness – the handwriting expert was, quite simply, wrong) was expecting me to recognize something about it.

Well, I could happily swear to never having seen any of it in my life before. I had no idea why I had agreed to come, and I grew more and more morose, considering the scale of this monumental disaster. The list of things I needed to do to fix my life had started to grow exponentially. I needed to head off the police before they talked to the school about me – to throw myself on their mercy. I wondered if wasting police time came with a prison sentence. On the other hand, other than the incident with Greta, which I now viewed with a new, horrible sense of shame – she'd seen through me, of course – I wasn't sure how much time I'd wasted. Mo Khan had analysed the letters, but he clearly hadn't done much of a job of it, and so here we were.

The letters had caused all of this, and I had written them; there was no escaping from any of that.

Unless Martin had written them, and planted the final one on me.

Or laid hands on them after someone else had written them.

The thought flashed coldly through my brain.

I'd seen the stacked books in his office – the vulnerabilities of young girls in care. If anyone knew how to work the system, to get access to these girls, it would be *him*.

My heart thudded in horror.

Why did I agree to get in a car with him?

We rolled slowly to a stop in a tiny close of three cottages. On the left was a white plaster and timber confection, built, I would guess, some time in the eighteenth century, and lovingly updated and restored. I got out into the cold wind, and it ruffled my hair as I followed Martin through the squeaky timber gate and along the garden path to the front door.

He gave this door a single, authoritative knock.

I stood back, increasingly alarmed and uncomfortable, and waited. The smell of burning bracken was in the air. What would Martin want out of me to keep silent about all of this? I was at his mercy too.

I was in real trouble.

After a minute or so, just as the silence between us grew unbearable, someone approached slowly through the diamond-shaped spyglass set in the door, moving with the tell-tale carefulness of old age.

Martin raised an eyebrow at me, just before the door opened, revealing a tiny old woman with a perfectly white bun of hair balanced on top of her head. She was gently fat and a pair of cat's eye glasses perched above her forehead, as if just pushed back rather than removed before she returned to whatever task had been absorbing her. Her hands were white with flour and she was rubbing at them with a tea towel.

'Hello?' she asked.

Martin's expression had changed almost magically into that of polite puzzlement and just a hint of embarrassment, but I saw too that it wasn't real – as though he were an actor, waiting until now to play his part.

'I am so sorry to bother you. My wife and I are looking for Kettle Lane, and we've been driving around forever. She suggested I stop someone and ask, and frankly the village is deserted...'

Strangers at the door would trouble many old people, but not this spry little bird with her blue apron and flour-dusted fingers. Her bright eyes alighted on us both, examining us with fearless curiosity. 'Oh, that's fine, most people get lost. You need to go back out, and straight ahead until you come to the main road, past the Green, keeping it on your right, and then turn left down a very narrow little road – it looks like a private drive, but that's Kettle Lane. You'll know you're there when you see the graveyard just before it.'

Her accent was as beautifully polished and precise as cut glass.

'Thanks so much,' said Martin.

'My pleasure,' she said, with a grin full of even but yellowing teeth. 'If you run into trouble, just ask in the post office. They're practically next door. They'll point you straight.'

They exchanged polite goodbyes and the door

closed, leaving me absolutely bewildered but relieved. I don't know what I had been expecting.

'So,' said Martin, guiding me back to the Range Rover. 'Remember anything?'

'No, of course not. I've never seen this place before. Who was that?'

His eyes narrowed, and a faintly cruel smile played around his face, though whatever the joke was, he didn't seem to find it that funny.

'Well,' he said, 'if you're really Margot Lewis, then this is your childhood home.' He spared a glance over his shoulder at the cottage. 'And that was your mother.'

I don't really remember what happened next. I felt faint, and suddenly Martin caught me under my arm and helped me back into the Range Rover, his face stricken with concern.

'I'm sorry,' he said roughly as he closed my side of the car. I could tell I was alarming him, that he felt he'd overreached himself.

He climbed in next to me, and the door thumped shut on us both, sealing us into the silent cell of the interior.

I wanted to say something, but couldn't. To deny it all. To ask where the hell we were, what all of this was about. My mouth felt loose, my skin numb.

He sat next to me, his fingers tapping the steering wheel.

'I...' I swallowed. All the saliva had dried up in my mouth. 'Who is she?'

'She's Flora Bellamy.' He did not turn to me, instead glancing back towards the house. Behind one of the leaded windows, a curtain twitched.

261

'Her daughter, Margot Bellamy, left home in 1997, when she was sixteen. Took up with an older boy who got her into some unpleasant scenes. Got into some unsavoury scrapes with the law. Turned up high as a kite for Christmas dinner that year and was told by her angry father never to return.'

I breathed in, breathed out.

'She never did. Police showed up a few times, looking for bail, statements, asking questions. Then nothing. Nothing that lasted for years. The father, Bob, was ex-army and something of a martinet by all accounts; he never forgave her...'

'He ran the village gardening committee,' I said softly, this nugget reappearing to me like a flickering spark falling through darkness – but where from? I know this because I know it, surely, however much I've tried to block it out.

'Did he?'

'Yes,' I say with certainty. 'Because it was good for discipline. It was all *good for discipline*...' I trailed off.

Why was that all I could remember? I couldn't even see his face. I couldn't see hers – the woman in the cottage. She had been an utter stranger to me.

Martin waited in silence.

'Anyway, the daughter's name wasn't even to be uttered out loud in the house,' he continued, 'but after he died ten years ago Flora contacted the Salvation Army looking for Margot. She was their only child.'

A kind of burning shame was falling over me, like a veil of fire.

'And the Sally Army found her. Living in London. Didn't take long. Didn't do any good. Margot refused contact and refused to say why.'

A silence fell again. I realized, in my shocked condition, that this statement was actually a question, and an answer was expected.

You know, he made me get up at six every morning of my life. He stood there and watched me wash and brush my teeth until I was fourteen. To make sure I did it properly, he said. Stood and stared, with his arms crossed. What father does that?

And then laughter, a peal of bitter laughter, and that too had a jangling note within it, like cut glass.

'What do we do with women that let their children be abused?' I asked. 'Women who live in fear, who daren't rock the boat? Should we forgive them? Should we, shall we say, cut them a little slack? Blame their parlous mental state? Pardon all in the great wailing cry, "But I love him ..."' I looked out of the window and shook my head. 'If you can't be strong for your children – if you can't get it together for your children – then what purpose do you serve? Why are you even alive at all? What possible comfort could you be to them?'

I said this last dully, staring out of the window, and out of the corner of my perception he shifted uncomfortably.

'That's very harsh.'

'It's a viewpoint refined by experience.'

He tapped the steering wheel gently for a moment, as though considering this.

'So,' he asked quietly, 'whose experience? Is this Margot or Bethan that's talking now?'

What an excellent question, but I could barely compass what it meant, never mind answer it. I

263

am not Margot Bellamy. I am not Margot.

Dear God, if I'm not her, then who the hell am I? What's going on? How is any of this even possible?

I shut my eyes. They're wet. Something was coming. A sea change. I felt it in my quaking heart, my sinking stomach.

Perhaps I don't know who I am, but there is somebody, somebody I remember.

I could see her in my mind's eye, cigarette in hand, tracing airy figures in smoke as she talked and gestured, as though she was summoning the spirits of the demi-monde. Her short, peroxide hair stuck up in spiky angles, and that scent of hairspray went everywhere with her, like a following ghost.

And that sharp, cut-glass accent – soaked in indifference and noblesse oblige, as though she was a grand duchess in exile. Everyone we met in those squats and communal hostel rooms remarked upon it. As I had come to know her better, I had dismissed it as an obvious affectation, like her alias.

'Angelique,' I whispered.

'What?'

'I don't know if this is my house.' I wiped at my eyes impatiently with the back of my hand. 'I think it might be Angelique's.'

22

'Hello, my darling. Did you sleep well?'

Katie blinks awake in the sudden daylight flooding down the steps, which she can see is low-angled, cool, tinted a faint pale yellow. It must still be dawn. He has opened the door and is carrying something carefully in both hands.

'Yes,' she says, filled with terror, wondering what this could all mean.

Then she smells what he is carrying on the tray. It is *breakfast*.

There is sausage and beans and toast and a fried egg, burned lacy around the edges. This all sits next to a mug of hot, sweet tea. Her mouth fills with saliva, almost gushes with it.

'Tuck in,' he says, giving her head an indulgent pat.

She does. She tears into the meat first with ravenous desire – she has been starving for meat, has dreamed of meat. Chewing it hurts her sore gums, burns her mouth going down, but she doesn't care.

'Greedy girl,' chuckles her captor, as she scoops up the microwaved beans with the thin white toast. 'You keep this up, you'll get fat.'

Katie, too busy devouring the feast before it can be seized from her, does not reply.

'Ah,' he sighs after a while, 'what am I going to do with you?' He squeezes her arm affectionately.

His hands are clean, but his sleeves and trouser legs are covered in damp mud.

He sees her looking. 'Yes, just doing a bit of digging in the garden while you slept, you lazy little loafer.'

She manages a wan smile.

'You know, when we move away from here, you'll need nicer table manners than this if we ever eat out.'

This gets her attention, though it doesn't stop her from folding the fried egg in half and popping it in her mouth, letting the warm yolk melt on her tongue as she swallows it. 'What ... moving?'

'Yes, yes, I'm afraid so,' though he won't meet her gaze. 'They're turning this place into some kind of hotel or convention centre or some such thing. The surveyor's coming tomorrow, they say. And anyway, I'm getting bored of working here. Done it for too long. It was all right once I left the army, but you can get tired of a place.'

Katie's head is ticking and whirring.

'Bored of working here'... 'All right once I left the army.'

He has never once volunteered a single detail about himself or his past life that has sounded authentic before today. He has tripped up, forgotten his own lies – or perhaps merely abandoned them – as liars are wont to do. Previously, he has only ever admitted to owning this house, being its master, being part of a sordid cabal of high-powered kidnappers.

Something has changed in him. Or more properly, something has happened; she understands, young as she is, that Chris does not change

266

or evolve the way a normal person might.

He is reacting now to some outside stimulus of which she knows nothing.

Whether this is good or bad news for Katie remains to be seen.

'Maybe we can go abroad, like to Spain. Or maybe even further, Thailand or somewhere like that. Would you like that?' he asks her, smiling.

'When?' she asks, and as she says it she realizes that she's been too quick, looked too interested. His eyes narrow at her. 'I mean,' she adds, as though merely making small talk, 'will it be before Christmas?' She forces herself to dredge up some facsimile of girlish enthusiasm, and butter her voice with it. 'I hear that Thailand is one of those countries where Christmas comes in the middle of summer. They do barbecues on the beach. That sounds so mad. I've always wanted to see that.'

He chuckles again, strokes her dirty hair and then rubs his thumb along her cheek while she lifts the tea and drinks deeply. 'I'll see what I can do. But we'll be leaving very soon. Now, would you like a bath?'

She nods yes, injecting her voice with all the enthusiasm she can muster for the idea. Katie would love a bath; give the world for a proper bath, though a part of her suspects that even should she scrub herself raw between now and the end of the world, she will never, ever feel clean again.

However, she does not love the baths Chris gives her, which he calls his 'favourite time with his favourite girl'. The thought appals her.

She sets the mug down – not on the tray, next to herself – but he quickly scoops it up to join the paper plate. Bugger. He never forgets the mug, the only potentially sharp object she is ever entrusted with.

She wonders whether any of the others before her hung on to their mug. Like Bethan Avery. She wonders whether other girls were given knives, forks, plates, bowls and glasses, small freedoms, and each and every one has been used in an attempted escape and taken away from her successor, and then after that her successor, so that now Katie eats with her hands from paper plates.

When was Bethan here? 1998? An unimaginable aeon to Katie, who had not yet been born then. How many girls have been in this cellar between Bethan and Katie, in all of those long years? Girls who tried to escape; girls who were cunning and bold in the face of evil; girls who dissembled, who fought; girls who had plans?

What became of them all?

Katie is starting to guess.

She tries to control her trembling as he takes the tray with its paper plate, and wipes at her fingers with the wet napkins he has brought down.

'Now the shops are open, I'm going to nip out and get you some clothes for the journey,' he says. 'Something pretty to wear. And when I get back I'll run our bath.' He stands up, the tray in hand. 'So sit tight.'

The door closes behind him, and after the rattle of the keys in the locks, he is gone.

Katie cannot account for it, but she is rigid with terror.

She tries to talk herself into calm. Yes, it was strange he brought breakfast. Yes, it is not her

268

usual bath day. Yes, his disappearance last night was odd, his reappearance stranger.

It's no use. Her mind ticks inexorably onwards, to realization. Nothing about his words this morning have made any sense. There is no way he can get her as far as Dover without being caught, never mind Thailand. He's not maintaining his cover as the house's owner because there is no longer any point.

The important things she must take away – the indisputable truths – are that tomorrow, Friday, surveyors are coming to the Grove and she cannot be found here. That Mrs Lewis has been on TV looking for Bethan Avery, whom people believe is alive, and if Bethan is alive, then she will lead the world right to Chris, and right to this very cellar.

And Chris has been digging in the garden.

She puts her hands to her face, barely able to breathe, as she realizes that what she has so quickly devoured, what he so carefully cooked for her, was her last meal before her execution.

23

'Who's Angelique?'

I didn't answer him straight away. Part of it is that I didn't want to answer, but the other part is that I was not entirely sure what the right answer was.

'Margot, who's Angelique?'

'I don't...' I trailed off. It was gone.

There was a long pause, while he sighed and I stared out of the car window. The sky was a cold, deep blue.

'Margot, do you know anything about psychology?'

'I've read plenty of pop quizzes in *Marie-Claire*.' I folded my arms, trying for defiant, but instead feeling weary, beaten, hunted and utterly bewildered. 'I'm an agony aunt. And I've been sectioned as a danger to myself and others before today. That might be relevant.'

'Do you know anything about PTSD?'

I frowned at him and swiped at my drying tears. 'A little.'

'The interesting thing about post traumatic stress disorder,' he continued, glancing sideways, towards the house – the curtain had twitched again – 'is that it's a form of extreme anxiety. Soldiers in the field get it. Victims of terrorist attacks.' He paused, 'Ra–... Assault victims.'

'Thanks, yes, I get the general idea,' I snapped. 'It's the one where you relive the event over and over.' I flounced back in the seat, not interested in helping him out. Not interested in having this conversation. Why were we talking about this?

Inside me, a reasonable, rational voice was pointing out that we were having this conversation because *I* have done something bad, not him.

He thinks he is trying to help you, Margot.

I did not want to be helped. I did not want to be helped in the worst way.

'Well, yes. And no. Most people relive the events. But sometimes, according to our good friend Greta, when someone is in an unbearably trau-

270

matic situation, especially a young person, and there is absolutely no escape for them, they stay sane by cutting their ties to what's happening to them; they cease to engage with reality and devise a new reality of their own. The mind can only stand so much bad news.'

'So then what happens?'

He thought for a moment. 'It depends. Sometimes they simply choose to forget who they are and what happened to them. It's called dissociative amnesia.'

'You can do that?'

'Yes, you can do that. But there's always a price. You'll always be fractured, a thing in pieces, with no continuum. You'll never be whole.'

'Perhaps wholeness is overrated. We are all different people at different times, a variety of competing ego states,' I replied. 'The Greek philosophers were right. No one's ever really themselves – they are a reflection of their Platonic ideal.'

'I am not interested in discussing Greek philosophers with you, Margot,' he said sternly. 'They are beside the point.'

I sighed. 'So, what else happens apart from amnesia?'

'Fugues,' he said. 'There can be fugue states. When you wake up somewhere and hours, days, weeks have passed and you can't account for where you've been or what you've done.'

I did not reply. I was more troubled than I had ever been.

'They happen, apparently, in response to triggers.'

'Triggers.'

'Yes, triggers. Things that make you remember the original trauma. Which, in your case, is very interesting. Because Bethan is writing letters now, which she did not do before, or at least if she has, you have never contacted anyone about it as far as we know. And Bethan appears out of your fugue states. Somehow, something has triggered her. Deep inside you, in the Bethan Avery part, you know much more about what's happened to Katie Browne than you realize with your conscious mind.'

I still did not reply.

'And,' he said, turning to me, now actively trying to catch my gaze, 'this girl's life may depend on this knowledge, so I need you to try and work with us on this.'

I let him catch my gaze.

'What's this *us?*' I said, with conscious cruelty. 'You want me to work on this because you'll get a fucking paper out of it and pay the mortgage, Martin. That's what you want. That's why you've been so much in evidence.'

There was a long second of molten silence between us.

His face was white, set. I had cut him, it seemed.

'Margot, listen to me. I understand that you do not want to have this conversation. I understand that you're running, and that you've been running all of your adult life, and that you believe, in your heart of hearts, that if you ever stop, you'll die.'

'I...'

'You have made escaping what happened to you, consigning it to oblivion, your life's great

272

work. You have laboured and slaved to do it. You have made tremendous sacrifices in every aspect of your relationships so that you never have to be Bethan Avery again. And you have so very nearly succeeded.' His hand nearest me moved, and then stilled, and I realized that he wanted to reach out, to touch me.

I glared at the offending limb.

'But the goal is impossible, Margot. You can't escape who you really are...'

Panic engulfed me. He understood nothing.

I had no idea who I really was, if I was not Margot.

Then hard on the heels of panic: fury.

I threw open the Range Rover door, hard enough to feel the joints creak. He was calling after me, 'Margot, Margot,' as I stormed towards the door of the cottage.

There was movement through the net curtain, as I banged on the door knocker sharply and stood back.

It did not take nearly so long for her to reach the door this time. Her fearlessness had gone, and her face through the crack was pale, the tiny creases of age in her lips compressed together, rumpling her skin.

'Do you know me?' I demanded.

No reply. I realized that she must have heard Martin calling my name, and that that name has unlocked something inside her, something feral and desperate that I would never have anticipated when I first met her.

'I am asking you if you know me!' I shouted at her, tears springing up within me. 'Am I your daughter? Am I? AM I?'

Her eyes widened, her mouth compressed even further, but left a glint of yellow teeth – a snarl of fear, or perhaps agony. She was a perfect picture of pain.

'How dare you! Get off my property this instant, before I call the police, do you hear me? How dare you!'

Then Martin was there, and he had hold of me, trying to pull me backwards while I fought and shrieked in his arms.

'Am I your daughter? *Am I your daughter?*'

'NO!' she shouted, as though this single word contained all of her being. The door swung wide and I thought that she was going to launch herself at me in the perfection of her rage. 'I don't know who you are! And if I ever see you again, I'll kill you!' The white bun had fallen loose, the strands framing her furious face.

It was as if she had struck the blow already. I felt suddenly empty, slack, drained of blood.

'I am so, so sorry,' said Martin to her, dragging me back as I became limp in his arms. 'Terribly sorry.'

I had ceased resisting him, and let him lead me back to the car and strap me in. There was only white noise in my head. Her resounding 'NO!' – her rejection – had blown all other sounds away.

She did not leave her door until we pulled away and she finally slammed it shut.

'We need to get out of here before the police come. It'll complicate things,' he said, driving as quickly as he dared out of the drive. In the house opposite the cottage, a younger woman ran out

274

on to her step, no doubt drawn by the shouting. With a slicing hand and a command she ushered back a small cloud of children who wanted to follow her, and in the rear-view mirror she hurried across the road, heading for Flora Bellamy's house (Flora who is Margot's mother, but not my mother), her face full of obvious concern. Halfway across she stopped, watching us go for an instant, before carrying on to Flora's door.

My shame and horror were absolute.

As was my utter bewilderment.

'This is impossible,' I said earnestly. 'Martin, this is a mistake.'

'Oh, it was that all right,' he replied. His eyes flicked up to the rear-view mirror and away again.

'This ... this can't be happening. It can't be *real*. Look, I have no memory of that woman. You've got the wrong...'

'The Margot Bellamy that lived there had your National Insurance number, date of birth, your schools...' He sighed, as though considering, and then seemed to calm down. 'It's Margot's house. But you're *not* Margot. That's why you don't remember Flora.'

He pulled over, outside the post office, and I was trembling now.

'Listen–' he said.

'No, you listen. Do you seriously believe that for one moment, for one solitary second, that I would keep up some kind of fraud, keep up this pretence, if I thought Katie Browne's life depended on it?'

'I didn't–'

'Do you think I'm so selfish a monster that I would let a girl be raped and tortured and mur-

275

dered just so I could keep my fucking shit job? Is that what you think is going on here? Is that what I *look* like to you?'

'No, I don't think that, but–'

'I have no idea what you're talking about, Martin! None! When you say Bethan Avery to me, nothing comes back! Nothing! You sound like a crazy person! I swear to God, I have no memory of–'

'I know,' he said with sudden urgency, and he reached out and grabbed me hard by the wrists. 'Listen. I know you think you don't remember anything. You've spent years excising her and you've become very good at it. That's not what I'm asking.'

I could only stare at him, dumbfounded, his hands warm on my skin.

'I am asking you to take a leap of faith. To be open to the possibility that Bethan Avery may be in there, locked out of your conscious mind, and that everything that's happened to you so far is because she is banging on the windows and desperately trying to tell you something. Something important.'

I took in a deep breath.

'A leap of faith?'

'That's it. That's all I want from you.'

I couldn't speak, not straightaway. And when I did, my voice was tiny, like something I was hearing from the other side of some enormous distance.

'All right.' I licked my lips. 'I have my doubts. But if you think it helps, I'll try.'

He released me then, slowly.

'All right,' he said.

We paused then, our conflict exhausted.

'So,' I said. 'How do we do this?'

'I don't know.' He opened the door and pulled out his phone. 'Wait here. I need to call Greta.'

He was on the phone for nearly fifteen minutes, during which time I watched him pacing urgently in front of the post office, listening far more than he was talking. Every so often our eyes met through the windshield and he offered me a wan smile.

While this happened, two thoughts circled one another relentlessly in my mind, like dogs chasing one another's tails.

Firstly, this was all utterly impossible and insane. I cannot be Bethan Avery. Yet it had been proved impossible for me to be Margot.

Who am I? Who am I?

And alongside this, even if it wasn't impossible or insane that I was Bethan Avery, or even if it was impossible and insane, but was still, nevertheless, true, then how were we going to find Katie Browne?

I felt sick, nauseous with anxiety, and just when I thought I could bear it no more, and was about to leap out of the car and grab him, he was suddenly jumping back into the driver's seat, slamming the door after him.

'Well?' I asked.

'It's difficult. There are three ways to treat you. There's psychotherapy, which takes months. There's hypnosis...'

I widened my eyes. Of course.

'But with such an entrenched trauma, it's more

277

likely to produce false memories than real ones.'

'I don't understand...'

'The past is a country you really, really don't want to visit, Margot.' He turned to me. 'Events have proved this. Greta thinks you'd need hypnotherapy under a chemical trance. It's all very specialized, and very high risk.'

I shrugged. 'If it helps, I don't care. I'll do it.'

'It's not that simple,' he said, starting the car. 'They need to find someone with the expertise to perform the procedure, and then convince them that the result will be worth the potential risk to you.'

'Risk to me?'

He nodded, not looking at me, pulling out into the road. 'Yes.'

'What kind of risk? I mean, comparatively speaking, how bad can it be considering what we're up against?'

He shook his head. 'I didn't get into it. It's pointless until she finds someone prepared to help us. She's got a few names in mind, and a couple of them are in Cambridge, so with any luck we'll hear back from her soon.'

'What do we do until then?'

He had turned out of the village and was heading north fast. For my own part I was glad to see the back of Wastenley.

The pause was so long that for a moment I thought he'd forgotten my question, until he said, 'We could do things while we're waiting. We might find something useful there.'

'Like what?'

'We could look for triggers.' That bright green

278

gaze was on me again. 'It can't hurt.'

I nodded, as if I understood.

'And where do we start?'

He turned back to the road, and his smile was small but genuine, spiked with camaraderie, and perhaps something else.

'The best place. We start at the beginning.'

The clear blue sky clouded over as we headed back to Cambridge, but it had become a little warmer.

'Snow,' I told Martin as he punched through the digital buttons, trying to get a radio station that played actual music.

'You think?' he glanced upwards, peering at the clouds.

'A fiver says it snows tonight.'

'You're on.'

With a burst of noise, my mobile leapt into life. A picture of Lily in Halloween costume – a vivid blue-green mermaid with shells in her hair – was glowing on the screen.

I swallowed hard and swiped to accept the call. 'Hello there. I'm surprised you're still speaking to me.'

'Margot! I just got your message, are you all right?'

Well, no, I wasn't all right, but it was too much to get into over the phone. 'I'm fine. I'm with Martin. We're heading back to Cambridge.'

'The police have been here. They're asking about Katie Browne again...'

'I know.'

This stymied her. How could I possibly know?

'They think it's...'

But Martin was gesturing, drawing a finger across his throat. I understood immediately. Lily would share this all over the staff room, who would share it all over Cambridge. It might do no harm, but better safe than sorry.

'Sorry, Lils, I meant I knew the police had called. I didn't know there were new leads on poor Katie. Look, the battery on my phone's dying so I'll call you when I get back, all right?'

There was a pause. She could tell I was lying about the phone, I was sure, and she was hurt. Perhaps she thought we were still fighting.

'And,' I sighed, trying to put it into words, 'I just wanted to say that I was sorry about last night.'

She didn't reply for a minute. 'But you were right,' she said. 'You were attacked ... the police said...'

'I know, I know – what I mean is, I'm sorry I stormed out like that. We're good friends and we should have been able to talk about it, and if I had, well, maybe last night wouldn't have happened.' I rubbed my eye. 'You know, you've been a good mate, and before ... well, before things kick off properly, I just wanted you to know that.'

'Margot, what are you talking about?' Her voice was still, quiet. I had alarmed her.

'I can't say now. When I get back I'll tell you everything.'

'Are you in some kind of trouble?'

'Yeah, maybe. But not as much trouble as some. I've got to go, Lils. Bye.'

I hit the button to end the call.

'Recognize this?'

'No.'

'You mean you would drive miles and go to London and undertake all of this trouble and danger, but you were never tempted to visit the neighbourhood where it happened, even though it was only ten minutes away in the car?'

'Apparently not,' I said coldly.

He opened his mouth, about to take me to task, then stopped, his jaw clicking shut. There was something in him then, a glint of pity.

'What?' I asked.

'I'm sorry, Margot. I keep forgetting. Of course you wouldn't come here. You're always running away from all this. You're the Red Queen from "Through the Looking Glass". You have to run with all your might, just to stand still.'

I didn't know how to reply to this, so I said nothing.

We were west of Cambridge, further west than the sumptuous gardens and greens of Barton, with its multi million-pound houses. This was a poor, lonely little pocket of council housing, forested in regular rows of planted trees, a desert island before the Fens begin again, spreading flat and green-grey as an ocean under a massive gunmetal sky, which was ramping up its threat of unseasonal snow.

Beneath these clouds the village itself huddled unprepossessingly, as though cold in a cheap coat too thin for the weather. There was a drab single-storey prefab community centre, a GP's office, a late-night Co-Op whose outer bin was filled with empty bottles and crisp packets. The streets and drives wound in around themselves in mathe-matically correct curves, giving the impression the place had grown organically rather than been dreamed up whole by a council architect.

Greta had not called back yet.

The buildings themselves were mostly maison-ettes – flats pretending to be houses, stacked in long terraces and made of pale brick and brown painted timber. Brass numbers adorned some of the glass doors, but many had been replaced, or fallen off, leaving just the shadow numerals behind.

'So, this is her street, is it?'

I was starting to get angry again. After my failure to recognize Flora Bellamy, I was now about to fail to recognize yet another putative childhood home. This was happening because this was *not* my child-hood home. This Bethan Avery stuff was madness. Yes, writing the letters was clearly wrong, and likely to ruin me, even though I had no idea I was doing it. And Martin was no doubt on to some-thing when he identified my personal blindness as being borne of a personal darkness. But this was just wasting time. More to the point, it was humiliating me.

I bit my lip.

I had promised him a leap of faith.

'Yes,' he said, determined to remain blithe and neutral. He pointed to a house on the corner, with a scrawny garden. 'You lived there.'

'Did I now?'

'Yes,' he said, unmoved by my obvious, restless anger. 'You did.'

I had promised.

'Do you want to get nearer?' he asked.

'No.'

'Margot...'

'Fine, let's do it.' I stalked off towards the house, with the rolling, determined gait of someone about to put a Molotov cocktail through the bay window at the front. What the hell was the matter with me? I'd agreed to this. I...

'I'm not trying to be a bitch, you know,' I told him.

'I know.'

'I'm ... I'm frightened.'

'I know.'

'I mean, if it's true, it turns out that everything I have told people about myself, everything I have told myself about myself, is a lie.' I thought about this for a moment longer. 'In fact, even if it isn't true, it's all lies anyway, isn't it?'

He didn't reply, but waited for me to speak as we mounted the pavement and paused before the shrivelled lawn.

'I have no idea who I am any more.'

'I know.'

'It's not a state of mind that encourages relaxed positivity.'

'I can see how that would be.'

We stood there, side-by-side, like patient ghosts. There was no movement from within the house.

'Do you want to try and get in?' I asked.

'What?' He looked shocked.

'I don't mean break in. I meant knock, ask to look around. Perhaps it will help. If we're going to do this...'

'They won't let us. When I started researching

283

the case I called by and was given my marching orders. I think the same people live there.'

I frowned. 'What people?'

'The Gallaghers, they were called. They thought I was a ghoul. Fat angry man, skinny angry wife, three angry kids – mind you, the kids are probably old enough now for their own houses. They got this place after Peggy, Bethan's grandmother, was killed here – well, attacked here. She died in hospital. Can't blame the new family really. They had all sorts calling on them in the early days. Everyone wants to see the murder house.'

'Peggy,' I said, as though trying out the name. Nothing answers me from within.

'Come on,' he said. 'Let's walk to the top of the road and back. At least we'll get a chance to stretch our legs.'

I nodded. In silence we ambled up the winding street to the nearby sounds of traffic.

'Are you cold?' he asked me.

I shook my head.

'You're shivering.'

He was right, I was. 'It won't kill me.'

We reached the junction, and the pair of us gazed disconsolately around ourselves. I was tired, so I perched my bottom on the low road sign and crossed my legs.

When I glanced up, Martin had an odd expression on his face.

'What?' I asked.

'Do you often do that?'

'Do what?'

'Sit on a sign like that.'

I opened my mouth, closed it. Because I didn't.

It's something kids do when they hang around after school.

'When was the last time you did that?' he asked me.

I didn't know. And now I was self-conscious, confused. I could trust none of my feelings or memories.

But I had promised him a leap of faith.

I tried to recall when I had done this in the past and realized that I couldn't. In fact, I now felt faintly ridiculous. At my age, it's the sort of thing you would do if you were walking home drunk and needed a little rest.

Indeed, as I sat there, I could see a balding man in a dark blue car on the main road slowing down to stare at me. I glared back in challenge and he instantly sped off.

The edge of the sign was damp and probably crawling with mites, the old wood behind the plastic facing decaying and likely to leave dark stains on my trousers. If one of the kids from school were to see me, I would be an object of derision.

And yet...

And yet...

It felt *right*.

'What are you thinking?'

I was thinking that the ancient Greeks believed madness was sent to a person by the gods. Madness leads to prophecy. To be sane is merely human, says Plato in his 'Phaedrus', but to be mad is to be touched by the divine.

Martin had been wrong. He *should* be interested in Greek philosophers.

I will stop second-guessing myself. I will let my madness lead me.

'I've been here before,' I said.

'You're sure?'

I nodded, rose to my feet. 'Yes. Very.'

Martin's phone rang suddenly.

24

Chris can't breathe.

He can't breathe and he can't think, and as he tears along the little country lane to the Grove he nearly hits an oncoming van, whose young driver honks furiously at him, his tattooed neck leaning out of the window to scream at him. The accompanying words, however, are ripped away by the wind.

On any other day, Chris would have turned around, followed him, bellowed his own insults, tailgated him – nobody treats me that way, no fucker! – but right now it's like something that happened to somebody else, in a foreign country.

And besides, the wench is dead.

Where had he heard that before?

Well, it didn't matter where he had heard it before, because the wench was not dead, despite his best efforts last night. She was still very much alive, thanks very fucking much, and walking around – those vast dark eyes; that abundant hair he'd seized in his fist so many times, now cut short around her shoulders; that full, cheeky fucking mouth.

Just sat there like the little girl she'd been, talking to some twat in a leather jacket. As if she knew he'd be passing. As if she *knew*...

Now calm down, Chris my old mate. If she is here to get you, then the place would be swarming with coppers by now, wouldn't it? She'd have straight up handed them the cellar years ago, and Katie, and you'd be in the cells waiting to go to prison for practically fucking forever. She could have sent them round this morning.

But none of that's happened.

She was supposed to have died. I thought she had died. Oh god, why isn't she dead.

No. Stop panicking.

He massages his face with his shaking hand. Next to him, on the front seat, is the bag with Katie's new nightgown in it. Poor Katie. She's been such a good girl. Better than that insolent whore Bethan fucking Avery ever was.

And yet, there was always something about Bethan. Bee. The first one.

She's come back.

His head rolls back hard against the driver's seat.

'What the fuck does she want?!' he bellows at the roof of the car.

Chris never forgot the first day he met Bethan.

He hadn't been living at the house then – nobody lived there – it was kept pristine waiting for whenever some scion of the owner's family wanted to visit. There was a woman from Cherry Hinton that came in with her daughter to clean

287

once a week, and they would chatter to each other in some alienating, nonsensical Eastern European language. Sometimes, in their sly glances and incomprehensible tittering, he caught the signage of their contempt.

He lived in the village full-time then, a mere half hour's walk from the house. And walk he did, rain or shine, through the narrow streets and drowsy houses with their smattering of trees, until he reached the gravelled track to the Grove. The trees stopped there, and he joined the Fens – flat, bleak, washed with rain. In ditches on either side of the raised drive secret weeds grew, and overhead every so often flew fat black crows, or the large, streamlined shapes of swans. The wind howled here, knowing no impediment, all the way in from the North Sea. Its icy ruffling felt like a kiss against his face.

The house belonged to the Fen. Years ago the family that owned the Grove had farmed these lands, but no more. Now their patrimony was the house and the walled garden and the keeper's cottage in amongst the outbuildings. What would have been an undulating landscape of walks was now under the industrial plough. The house was empty most of the time, an afterthought in the life of the family. It existed liminally, the vanishing relic of a lost way of life.

Chris could sympathize. He was also part of a lost world, where men like him had no place.

In his dusty backpack he carried his usual lunch – a cheddar cheese sandwich on thin sliced white bread, a Penguin bar and a bag of prawn cocktail crisps. It was what he had eaten for lunch every day, more or less, for the last fifteen years.

The backpack also contained two unopened letters, thrust into its bottom, to be read later. One was a thin envelope from the Avon and Bristol Police Force, and its smallness and slightness already told him to expect bad news. Another rejection.

The other was A4-sized, made of stout brown paper, and about a quarter of an inch thick. His hands had shaken slightly as he'd packed it. It was risky to take it out of the house, even though the odds were good that he wouldn't see another soul today. That envelope could get him into a lot of trouble, should it fall into the wrong hands.

Its weight against his back made him sigh. It might not be strictly proper, but a man needed his pleasures. Chris did not have access to this new thing, the Internet, and what he heard of it did not fill him with confidence, but the magazines and newsletters of his earlier years were getting harder and harder to get hold of, and consequently the risk involved in getting them was growing. More and more of them were shutting down production, or featuring muck-brown foreign girls instead of the decent English ones he liked, or using older tarts to play young girls. None of it would do. English roses, that was what he wanted, barely more than budding. A man couldn't help what he liked, after all.

'Come on, Bee, we've got to get to school. We can look for it later.'

'I know, I know, just give us a sec.'

He had been so lost in his reveries, thinking about what might be in that brown envelope, waiting for him, that he had utterly missed the real thing.

Two girls stood in the ditch on the side of the road; they'd been hidden from him by a bend in the track. One was short and plump and mousy blonde, though the way her school skirt skimmed over her generous bum was not without interest as she bent to inspect something in the thin ditch water. Had she been alone, he might have approached her, engaged her in conversation, manoeuvred himself into accidentally-on-purpose touching her through the taut grey serge, letting his fingers flicker over her. That was the trick, leaving them so they weren't sure if it had been an accident or not.

And out here, on her own, what could she have done about it? Or said about it afterwards, to others?

Had she not been so near to the village, depending on her reaction, he might have ventured more.

But she was not alone. The other girl stood, her arms folded disconsolately around herself, her face hidden by her overhanging dark hair. She was tall, but not too tall, and slender, but not too slender, and her stooped posture and neglected unhappiness, something he'd taught himself to recognize, shone out like a dark sun.

He could feel something within him start to pulse, urgently, and when she raised her face and he saw her sad dark eyes, her full mouth, he could hardly breathe.

'Can I help you?' he asked suddenly, treating them to his most disarming grin, the one he practised in his mirror at home for exactly this kind of occasion.

The dark girl, Bee, shrugged silently, but the little blonde one offered him a sunny smile, full of repulsive pert confidence. He immediately realized that touching her would have been a bad idea, and swallowed down a little spurt of dislike.

'It's all right. Bee's lost a necklace. A little silver cross. We was walking back this way last night and it must have broke.'

'It was my mum's,' said the dark girl, this Bee. Her voice was low and sweet, and full of unspoken appeal. Those heavy brown eyes were upon him. 'I don't suppose you've seen it, Mister?'

'No, no,' he rapped out quickly, trying to control his hammering heart, his shortening breath. Her lips were a perfect deep rose. 'But why do you think it's in this ditch? Surely you'd be better looking on the road.'

'We thought we saw a kingfisher down here,' said the blonde girl. 'But it weren't.'

He didn't even look at her.

'Yeah,' said Bee. 'I wanted to show Nat. She's never seen one.'

'And it was definitely around here, then?'

They nodded, though the dark girl did so a little hesitantly, as though not sure. The corners of her eyes were crinkled a little, the whites red with distress. How old was she? Fourteen, fifteen? He longed to slide his arms around her, to comfort her, to pull her close. He drank in the sight of her, trying to think of something to say, something that might detain her.

'A little silver cross, you say?'

'C'mon Bee,' said the blonde girl quickly, her

voice strained, flat, oddly neutral. 'We'll be late for school. We can come back later.'

He glanced at her, impatiently, and realized his error – her suspicion was writ large on her face, before being quickly hidden. She didn't know what she suspected yet – she was a little too young – but she had picked up on his eagerness, his interest in her friend, and realized it was not quite … normal.

He cursed himself for a fool.

'Yeah, yeah,' said Bee, reluctant to leave and seemingly oblivious to her friend's alarm. 'We should go.'

It would be a mistake to try and keep them now; it would only compound his bungling.

'Very true,' he said, affecting the tones of a concerned adult, the-fun-and-games-are-over-now type. 'You can't be late for school, girls. But what should I do if I see your necklace?'

He grinned at the object of his desire, waiting for the gift of her address, her phone number.

The blonde girl's gaze narrowed at him.

'You could leave it at our school, St John's. It's only in the village.' She took the dark girl's arm, pulling her after her, towards the lane, leaving him behind in the ditch.

'Leave it for Bethan Avery.' She tugged. 'C'mon, Bee. We're late.'

As they moved off, he had heard them murmuring, their voices carried further than they would have expected by the still flat air of the Fens.

'Sorry about your cross. But what a creep.'

'Aw, come on, Nat. He was only being friendly.'

He searched for hours before he found the necklace, glinting at the side of the lane. He had been about to give up. It was a sign, he realized, turning the fragile links over in his hands, running his finger down the cheap thin silver cross. It was a sign that fortune was finally answering his prayers. He squeezed the broken link in the chain closed with ease. The thing was probably worth a tenner, if that. Its value was clearly sentimental.

He didn't reach the house until nearly eleven. The gardener, Malcolm, was already packing tools away and treated him to a curious wave.

Chris returned it, with a brusque good morning, but didn't stop for conversation. He could barely breathe, the little silver necklace tucked into his fist. He retreated up into one of the first-floor bedrooms, and when he was sure Malcolm was gone, he thrust his hand into his unzipped jeans and worked himself frantically. Twice in the ditches by the lane had failed to slake his burning desire, had only increased it. He heard her voice again – 'I don't suppose you've seen it, Mister?' – that gentle entreaty, the way that Mister turned to Master in his memory, and it was over in seconds.

Later he turned the pages of his magazine, sprawled on the carpet, and the girls in the black and white photographs all had her face. He hung the necklace over the bedpost, so he could look at it and keep his hands free. The afternoon's setting sun lit it into a little silver blaze, a star shining against the antique Jacobean wood.

Bethan Avery. Even her name was like music.

After all of these lonely years, these furtive gropings, there would be love at last. He could be anything she wanted. She was too young to know what she wanted, anyway, so he would be able to teach her, to mould her into whatever he desired. He imagined returning the necklace to her at some point during their special intimate times together, fastening it around her naked neck while she lifted her abundant dark hair up, and her pleased, grateful smile glowed more brightly than the silver.

He did not go to the school. That would have been madness. Instead he waited, hiding in plain sight, on pub benches and at bus stops, slowly piecing together her route home, his face hidden in newspapers as Bethan and her friend, who he took to calling The Gnat, sauntered by, too caught up in their girlish gossip even to notice him.

The Gnat left her on the corner of Church Road, and sometimes if their conversation had not quite finished, they could loaf there for hours, through the growing snow and rain, half-sat, half-leaning on the street sign, laughing at nothing, their hoods up over their heads. This both pleased and infuriated him – though it meant he spent more time with her, it also meant that some other man might see her there, as she twirled in her little grey school skirt, black cotton tights and cheap nylon coat, showing some dance move to The Gnat. Some spotty rival might appear and steal her away. When she was his girl, there would be no more exhibiting herself on street corners, that was for sure.

He didn't have a car then – he'd been taught to drive in the Army, before he'd jumped/been pushed, though he'd never needed one – but he saw now that the time had come to get one, as surveillance was becoming impossible without it. There was nowhere to sit and wait on the rest of her route home without curtains twitching. All of this would be much easier with a car, especially now the bad weather had arrived, and sitting outdoors in it only attracted attention. Time to dip into his hoarded savings. He bought a neat but old Ford Fiesta from a taciturn man in a baseball cap on Milton Road, sold with the implicit understanding that it was going to fail its next MOT. Chris thought its sassy red colour might please her – and in any case, it suited his cover.

A plan had begun to form in his mind.

Snow fell and the freezing winds turned to ice. The Indian summer of a mere three weeks ago, when he'd first met Bethan, was little more than a memory. His hunger for her grew dangerously, explosively. He drove out to Ipswich, to Newmarket, to Norwich, picking up small, malnourished prostitutes he could pretend were her, thinking that soon, soon, he would have the real thing in his arms.

The rest of the time he spent working on the old priest-hole below the main sitting room. It was filthy and full of layers of dead cobwebs – not suitable for a young girl – but he swept the flags, took measurements for a bed, a toilet, some soundproofing material. While he was sure that Bethan would come round, there was probably going to be a little girlish reluctance at first, until she understood the full force of the love and desire she had raised in him. And once she knew, how could she fail to return it? This was just a temporary measure, to stop her from running off home in a strop, he told himself. Once he was sure of her, he could move her into one of the main bedrooms. Or perhaps, considering her age and how near they were to her home, they could flee together, to the continent. Live together on the Costa del Sol, run a bar maybe. They'd serve runaway gangsters on the lam from England, who'd be unlikely to dob them in.

He lay in bed imagining scenarios where he mixed freely with these violent, dangerous men in their silk shirts and golden sovereign rings – besting them at poker, hiding their contraband from the corrupt Spanish police chief, defeating them in gun battles and being acclaimed their leader – and then returning to his adoring Bethan as she lay in bed, weeping at the thought of him almost being killed; vulnerable, tender, and entirely and utterly *his*.

Surely such love was worth risking everything for.

25

Chris waited, watching the police station in an agony of suspense. Bethan and her man had suddenly gathered themselves together and headed off in a hurry back to their car – a big Range Rover, a car for people with big heads, in his opinion – and he had followed them here at a discreet distance, which had been difficult considering how hot on the pedal the other man had been.

They'd parked round the back of the cop shop, then walked in through the front door.

Finally, Chris had pulled up in the car park opposite the police station – he didn't know what they did in the offices the car park belonged to, it looked like law. In amongst the gleaming Beemers and Mercs his dusty blue Megane stood out, and he attracted jaundiced looks from the suits that walked past him. Parking in Cambridge was always hotly contested.

Well, let them try and contest it with him now. He had an illegally imported canister of Mace in the dashboard, which he kept in case any of the girls had ever required a little extra encouragement to get in the car for the first time, and he was in just the right mood to use it. After all, you couldn't build proper relationships with all of your sweethearts at first – the world was full of nosy beggars and troublemakers, endlessly wanting to see ID or get you to sign in or run fucking criminal background checks. That was the latest thing – this is what you got for volunteering to help underprivileged kids in today's society; no wonder the country was going to the fucking dogs – sometimes you had to admire your girl from afar before you were ready to let her into your life. Sometimes that was safest – for both of you.

On the other side of the street, people streamed in and out of the police station and students cycled by, but Bethan and that fellow she was with didn't come out again.

Oh, Bethan. What am I going to do with you?

Well, if she was dobbing him in he was safer here than at the house, he supposed. It was hardly worth rushing back to his little Katie if they were heading that way anyway. He'd already withdrawn what was left of his savings while he was out buying Katie's nightdress, and it was wadded in his jacket pocket. There wasn't much money left after all these years – these girls, they bled a man dry.

On the other hand, it would do nobody any good if they got talking to Katie. He should end it decently with her. If he left now for the Grove and got it finished with, he could be on his way to the coast, or the wilds of Scotland, with Katie tidied away and nobody any the wiser.

And now this one, his first love, who'd broken his heart. What did she think she was playing at? He'd watched the house CCTV, no one had come while he was out last night; there'd been no one while he was digging the new patch by the rhododendrons to put poor Katie in. Katie loved rhododendrons – well, he was sure she would, if he asked her. No sign of the police. No sign of anyone.

What was Bethan playing at?

He let his forehead fall on the steering wheel, ignoring the besuited tart that scowled at him through the car window.

Was she torturing him? Did she know he was following her, and she'd come here to bait him? Inside, she was probably describing a lost cat or stolen bicycle, aware of him out here, sweating, watching her.

Oh, you wicked minx.

He'd been so wrong about her. He'd had clues,

298

early on, that there would be trouble in paradise, during Phase One. But did he listen? Did he pay attention? Did he buggery.

Phase One, as he called it in the little black notebook he kept with his stash of magazines, began on 15 December 1997. He had arrived at this date after considering various practical factors. It would be nice to have everything cleared away and spend Christmas with Bethan, after all, and see the New Year in with her.

A new start for a new year.

The Fates had smiled on the venture early – his phone call to the UK Border Agency had quickly seen the Eastern European cleaning duo removed from their weekly slot. Old Mr Broeder had charged him through the agent, Mr Merrills, with finding replacements, but it was easy enough, with Christmas coming up, to fob him off. Everyone knew Old Mr Broeder, in his Knightsbridge lair, had no interest in anything but his club and his antique collecting, and Young Mr Broeder, his grand-nephew and the ersatz heir, who was allegedly a student, had no interest in anything that wasn't turbocharged or in skirts.

At the Grove, Chris was effectively the Master.

And there was no reason to tell Bethan any different once he got her here.

He'd bought a new outfit that made him feel awkward and clownish – baggy jeans, a hoodie, a stupidly expensive pair of what his mother would have called tennis shoes. It was what trendy liberal do-gooders wore, apparently. He had his shaggy blond hair cut into the longish style that was popular for men, just like that one out of Oasis, the group with the two Manc brothers that swore all the time. They were inexplicably popular with Bethan and The Gnat, though The Gnat had loudly declared to Bethan that she preferred Blur, who were just more of the same as far as Chris could make out. He had to remember to forgive Bethan for her immature tastes and poorly chosen friends – she was only young, and had no father figure in her life to correct and guide her ... at least not yet.

He parked up the street from the dumpy little brick maisonette she lived in, trying to control his pounding heart, his mouth dry as he walked out of the car and towards her door.

It was all about confidence. Fair heart never won fair lady, and all that. Christ, years ago, before his mother's latest boyfriend, Derek, had made him join the Army (it had been that or dobbing him in to the coppers), he had been a past master at chatting up old people on the doorstep and getting inside their houses. If Derek the Dick hadn't started noticing the money and stuff coming through the flat, he'd have got clean away.

The flags leading to the door were cracked and uneven but weeded, and there was a bright little planter by the front, though the flowers in it were gone, of course, their dead remains already in compost. Peggy was particular about the garden, it seemed, if not about herself.

He knew there was no mother, hence Bethan's distress at the loss of the necklace. He had braced himself for the presence of a father, though hopefully one that would be in full-time work.

But his surveillance had proved that there was only a grotesquely fat old woman, clad day-in and day-out in the same leggings and one of three baggy tunic-like shirts. These all bore the names of holiday destinations she could never possibly have visited in big letters, as though by force of will she could persuade herself this was Barbados or Fiji or San Diego.

Most days she didn't leave the house, but every so often his binoculars had caught her hobbling her doughy self out with her cane to the post office to collect her pension, or to the shops for cigarettes if Bethan wasn't around to run these errands for her.

The doorbell produced no response, as his nervousness grew. Finally, he knocked loudly, twice.

'Give us a minute!' came back the cracked, hoarse reply, and through the dappled glass he could see Peggy coming towards him, her gait halting. He could hear her breathing even through the door. The disgusting fat pig...

The door opened, showing a sliver of the woman's face.

'Hello ... Peggy, isn't it?'

'Yes.' In their folds of flesh her eyes were deep-set, bright and suspicious. 'Can I help you?'

'I'm Alex Penycote. From South Cambridgeshire Social Services.'

'Yes?'

'This is just an informal visit. Can I come in?'

'Of course, yes, yes.' She shuffled backwards. Her accent was different, something Northern, possibly Geordie. 'Sorry I was a bit abrupt. Thought you were here to sell me something. Or convert me. Come in.'

And just like that, he was inside the sanctum, being led through the tiny, neat house with its smell of boiling potatoes and roasting beef pie. She hadn't even asked him for ID.

His heart soared.

'Is this about Melissa?' Her voice was rasping and the breathing harsh. It was not just exertion – something was wrong with her.

'Sorry?' he asked.

She turned, her knuckles whitening on the cane's head, and the suspicion was back. She knocked on the wall, just under a hanging photograph of an exquisite brunette with a wavy perm and Bethan's fathomless black eyes – a photo that had clearly been taken by a professional. 'Bee's mother. My daughter. Melissa. Have you found her?'

'Oh, sorry, no. This is just a follow-up visit to check that everything's OK with Bethan.'

'What d'you mean, checking on Bethan?' she asked, her voice rising. 'Nobody's come for years. We're fine here. Just the pair of us wondering where her bloody mother is, that's all.' She breathed in hard, her eyes narrowing. 'Did some interfering bugger call you lot up?'

'What? No, no, nothing like that. It's purely routine. It's just that since she'll be leaving school in a year or so, and our care, we just want to manage her transition...'

'She's not leaving school.' Peggy had dropped her anger as quickly as she had picked it up, and was once again moving into the kitchen. 'She's staying on. She's bright. Aren't you, pet?'

302

'What's that, Nanna?'

The kitchen was as small and pokey as the rest of the house, but bright and clean. A pot bubbled merrily on the stove, and the oven made a gentle humming. At the Formica table in the middle of the room sat Bethan, surrounded by books.

He could hardly breathe at the sight of her, her dark hair drawn up in a ponytail, the top button of her school blouse unfastened, the tie discarded, showing the white flash of her neck. And those dark, bottomless eyes...

'Hello, Bethan,' he said. His throat was dry. Smile at her. Do the smile.

'Hello,' she answered politely but distantly, her eyes moving over him once, and then back to her books.

'Pet, why don't you take your homework upstairs so...' she gestured impatiently at him. 'Sorry, forgotten your name.'

'Alex. Alex Penycote.' He hitched the smile at Bethan a little higher, aware that it was desperate, almost a rictus.

'...So Alex and I can talk.'

'About me.' She fixed Peggy with a look. There was something Chris didn't like in that look – cynical, knowing, older than her years. But it was also affectionate, full of shared understanding. A strong bond, in other words. Together they would have borne the burden of the missing Melissa over long years.

Bethan had no business having strong bonds she would only have to learn to break. This was a complication.

'Aye, we'll talk about you,' went on Peggy with

a hacking laugh. 'But if your ears start to burn then shout down.'

Bethan shrugged and swept to her feet. 'It was nice to meet you,' she said to Chris, with the same throwaway civility she'd greeted him with.

And then she was gone, books in hand, her light footfall tripping up the stairs.

'Always in such a bloody hurry, aren't they? Cup of tea?' It was as though a bomb was going off between his ears, a ringing silence of shock and humiliation.

She hadn't recognized him.

He'd prepared a story to explain their meeting, was braced for her opening burst of surprise, her follow-up questions about the necklace – but nothing. Bethan had looked straight through him. As though he was some sort of stranger.

'I said, a cup of tea?' reiterated Peggy, her brows coming down. The glint of suspicion returning.

'Oh yes, milk and three sugars please,' he beamed up at her, through the gut punch feeling, his sick disappointment and his growing rage.

Peggy rambled on, as she shuffled slowly around the kitchen, turning off the potatoes and the oven, boiling the kettle, carefully placing the cup before him with a shaky hand. Telling him about Melissa, who'd run away to London to be a model and had come home with more than she'd bargained for; dumping the daughter on Granny and heading off for Amsterdam and another vague modelling contract – in Chris's opinion Melissa sounded like the sort of self-absorbed wastrel better off un-found – and how tough it had been taking on Bethan at her time of life. But she was no trouble, not really, a very good girl. Chris nodded along and smiled and let her talk and tried to calm the storm of misery at work in his heart.

She had obsessed him, taken possession of him body and soul, to the point where she was his first thought in the morning and his last one at night, and for her part she did not even recognize him.

He was nothing to her.

Well, all that would change.

He let Peggy talk – the point of the exercise was to establish Peggy's trust in him, after all, and not Bethan's – but it was very hard to pay her any kind of attention, and he had to work to stay civil and focused as she slurped her tea and breathed in her laboured, noisy way, whinging on about the failure to track down Melissa, as though this was Chris's fault somehow. He had no sympathy. If Peggy hadn't wanted a runaway child-abandoner for a daughter she ought to have raised her better.

For his part, he rifled through the forms he'd taken from the post office and put in the folder under his arm, tutting that he'd forgotten the right one, careful to make sure that Peggy only saw the official printing in the briefest of snatches. Of course Peggy didn't look, not really. That was the wonderful thing about the power of authority.

He was terribly sorry, he explained. He needed to complete the right form. He would have to come back and talk to both of them some other time, and with Bethan alone at some point, and in any case, he could see that he was interrupting their dinner. Could he have their phone number? He wrote it down in his folder as she read it out, trying to control his triumphant tremor.

305

And then, because he couldn't bear to leave without seeing Bethan again, even though she had so wholly disrespected him, he asked to use the toilet and was directed up the stairs.

The stairs creaked beneath him, the cheap carpet worn and frayed with countless steps. There were three doors at the top of the landing, as he'd been told – one lying open at the end, which was the bathroom, one on his right, door closed, with a little novelty sign saying, 'GONE CRAZY – BACK SOON!'

On his left, the door was open, and Bethan Avery lay upon her belly on her pink bed, while walls of posters of gleaming-toothed young men surrounded her on all sides, like an admiring audience.

The air left his body in a low whoosh.

She was poring over a textbook lying open before her, her legs raised up and crossed at the ankles, a pair of headphones against her ears, holding back the dark tide of her hair. She was oblivious to his presence, and he could hear some kind of distant tinny sound, obviously the music, being piped into her head while she chewed the end of a ragged pen.

And then, as though some sixth sense had prompted bet, she glanced up.

'Hi,' she said, though the word had more of the character of a question, and she did not smile.

'I was ... sorry, I was looking for the bathroom...'

'Oh,' she said. 'Straight ahead of you,' and pointed towards the end of the landing with the pen.

'Thanks.'

He was rewarded with an equally brisk smile that vanished as soon as her head dropped once more to her book. He had been dismissed.

He was trembling as he shut the thin door behind himself. He splashed his face with cold water and rubbed it dry on one of Peggy's foofy little pink guest towels.

Scraping his hands through the ridiculous haircut, he imagined going into her room, seizing her about her mouth, straddling her back, teaching her a good hard lesson while that fat sow waited downstairs, oblivious.

No, no. He was here on a mission. A time was coming when he would get to see all of Bethan whenever he wanted; it would be stupid to spoil everything now. He was the hunter, the stalker, the wily one. He passed by her door again, pleased that he managed not to steal another glance at her, aware only of Bethan as warm periphery, of the tiny beat coming out of her headphones. He managed a friendly but professional smile at Peggy, a few parting words, and then he was outside and letting himself back into his car. He was shaking, shaking with terror and desire and fury and elation at his success.

Fumbling to fit the keys in the ignition, teeth gritted, he replayed her again and again in his mind. He had been mistaken about her, he realized, and she was not the imploring waif he remembered shedding tears on the Fens. She was cheeky sometimes, and distant, and would be in need of some correction if she was to be his dream girl again.

Who did she think she was, treating him that way?

He sighed. It was hardly her fault, he supposed, considering how she'd been brought up by that pig in a dress, but it made a difference to how he would have to deal with her. He would have to put the fear of God into her. He would have to...

And it came to him, whole and of a piece. The Grove, the girl, and what he would tell her. As he played it in his mind, he could feel himself believing it.

He was a rich man, a powerful man, and he was in a club that exchanged young girls amongst themselves. He had kidnapped her and was supposed to pass her on, but he had fallen in love with her, and he was going to keep her.

But these others, oh, they were rich and powerful too. If one let the side down, they would all be in trouble, so they would do all they could to punish both her and him if they caught them. So she would not be able to leave him, he would tell her, because they would kill her loved ones – her granny, and that friend of hers, The Gnat.

They had done the same to Melissa, after all.

That was it. He would tell her that they had killed Melissa – beautiful Melissa, who had run off to London to be a model, then given birth to her and vanished, never to be seen again. After all, neither Bethan nor Peggy had any real idea of what had become of Melissa – only suspicions.

And this shadowy cabal; they'd ordered him – well, not ordered him, because he was rich and powerful, nobody ordered *him* around – but strongly suggested that they pick up her daughter too. And he couldn't say no, because they would ruin him, but now here she was and unless she helped him conceal her then...

His shame at his reception was going out, like a fast tide. That was it. That was the answer. And perhaps he would tell her the truth eventually, one day, when they were both far away and he was sure she knew who really held the whip hand over her.

When the car started, he felt much, much better. He was already glad – so very glad – that he had come. Everything was falling into place.

He didn't get Bethan for Christmas, or see in the New Year with her. He arrived at the Grove the next Friday afternoon, 19 December, and with a sinking heart recognized the glossy 4X4 in the drive, its front tyres crushing the lawn, and the cheerful bellow of Young Mr Broeder. Phase Two, it seemed, would have to wait.

Young Mr Broeder (or Caspar, as he insisted upon being called) would be staying for a long weekend, with two Hooray Henrys he rowed with and an icy posh self-assured blonde called Julietta who Chris detested on sight. He threw out their champagne and Cognac bottles and their empty trays of takeaway, listened to them yowl and chatter to one another in the house while he busied himself in the grounds, their ghetto blaster filling the cold winter air with meaningless pounding noise that they never seemed to tire of. Dubstep, they called it. Apparently Young Mr Broeder had composed it, out of a selection of dustbin lids banging together from the sounds of things. What the fuck did they teach them at university, anyway?

When Christmas Eve rolled around and they finally buggered off, it was too late to move to Phase Two. Christmas came and went, and then New Year, and he sulked at the inherent unfairness of his life. He knew social workers had this time off, so despite endless and furious thinking, he could come up with no reason to contact the Averys, and stalking Bethan was too dangerous.

It had been the longest he had gone without seeing her since that day he had first laid eyes on her, and the absence was killing him. First thing Monday morning, he was calling that number of Peggy's.

He had, when he started, no clear idea of what he intended, other than to get close to her and wait for an opportunity to suggest itself. He had half-formed the conviction that she should go willingly with him – which was not to say, fully informed, that would be a little too ambitious – but there could be no question of trying to force her into the car or using violence against her, at least anywhere where he might be seen. Some ruse would have to be devised.

But the cold lonely Christmas had hardened his dreams into plans, and the closer he came to realizing them, the more he had to bleakly consider the danger they put himself and Bethan in. Especially him. Unfair as it was, they wouldn't be sending her to prison.

On the other hand, nobody but Old Mr Broeder knew about the hidden cellar, and good luck if they wanted to get any sense out of him. When the hue and cry went out, as it almost certainly would, the police had to be in a position to search the house and find nothing.

If they even got this far. He had a plan for that too, now he thought about it.

He used up the soundproofing material he'd purchased, and bought more just in case, driving for miles so as not to arouse suspicion, being constantly jostled by a post-holiday crowd of shoppers. He queued patiently in Marks & Spencer in St Albans with his lacy bras and panties, his cotton nightdresses in the basket. He surveyed the other women in the queue around him – not one of them was a patch on his girl, he thought with quiet satisfaction. His glee seemed to fill him up, threaten to spill over. *His girl.*

He bought ready meals and cans of soup and individual pots of yogurts. He pondered whether to buy games, or books, or chocolates, before deciding that he would let her earn them first. The thought made him smile.

In the final load of soundproofing and rope he purchased from the building supplies store in Stevenage, he also threw a ball-peen hammer into the cart.

In the car, in the here and now, Chris tried to ease out his tensed, cramped shoulders, rolling them in their sockets, feeling his wiry muscles sing and stretch.

Nothing from the police station still.

All right. Ten more minutes.

If nothing happened and she didn't come out, he was heading back to the Grove.

To Katie.

311

26

I rested my weary chin on my hand.

Through the high barred windows the snow was falling, the first snow of winter, whirling past and down in huge, diaphanous pieces. It had been snowing for a while, doubtless the ground outside was now soft and white. I wouldn't have known, I'd been sat in a cheap plastic chair for the last two hours, being mercilessly grilled like some kind of criminal.

I suppose, technically, I was some kind of criminal.

Martin stood up and offered to get me a coffee, and I nodded assent. The policeman sat opposite us leered unpleasantly.

Also with us, finally, was the legendary Detective Superintendent O'Neill, who was running the investigation, though at the moment he was largely (very large – he must be at least 6 foot 5) silent, leaning against the desk, regarding me with a curiosity that was not quite hostile, not yet, but was far from friendly, the vast surface of his forehead wrinkling at me. The reflection of myself I saw in him merited no better response. What kind of selfish nutcase, who could be able to finger a rapist and murderer of young girls, uses pitiful ruses like letters and fugue states to call attention to herself first?

I shifted uncomfortably. I had no answer for

this. I had no answers at all, until somebody finally hit on the right question.

I had been astonished by the amount of personnel involved. Various people, most of whom were police officers, had come in at junctures throughout the day, wanting to speak to O'Neill about some aspect of the case, and drawing him outside the room for circumspect conversations. At one point the woman detective who had come to my house appeared. I had smiled at her. She did not smile back.

Greta was the one standing next to O'Neill now.

And as for Greta ... well, the less said the better.

'I am astonished at you, Martin. Abusing a vulnerable woman like this!'

Her complexion was marbled with red and white. She was really very, very angry.

'I'm not vulnerable.'

She threw me a look, and I met it with steel.

'I am not vulnerable. I don't know if any of this is true or not. I literally don't remember. But while my memory might not be up to much, there's nothing wrong with my intelligence. Or my will.'

'Margot.' She sighed before she could stop herself. 'Only last night you were raving...'

'Raving,' I repeated crisply. 'Thank you for that.'

She blushed, red winning over white, her mouth freezing into a tough little line. 'I only meant...'

'I know full well what you meant. What I'm telling you is that if this is real, we need to get to the bottom of it. If it's not real, well, that's a problem for a different day.' I held out my arms. 'So, if it was real, what would you suggest? Hypnosis?'

She paused, as though lost for words.

313

It was her first moment of silence since she'd arrived. I don't think she'd drawn breath before now, having hotfooted it from London by taxi and resenting the imposition every step of the way. Or resenting something. Her normally pristine little red bob looked vaguely disarrayed and her language so far, though couched in terms of Martin's irresponsibility, had come dangerously close to using some very interesting words to describe me – elusive, troubled, and I thought but couldn't prove that she had been within a hair's breadth of calling me 'manipulative' fifteen minutes ago, but pulled back just in time.

I was disappointed, as by then I was in the mood to have a proper stand-up row with her.

Insane as it sounds at such a moment, a quiet little corner of me suspected that the thing Greta so resented might be the attention Martin was paying to the crazed lunatic with the selective forgetfulness. As she pointed, shouted and slammed down her bag on the desk, I couldn't help feeling – from her cold glaring and the way she talked over my head, as though I were some kind of sentient vegetable – that I had achieved in a week or so what months of working lunches with Martin and jokey/borderline flirty email exchanges had not.

Furthermore, I could tell that Greta was the sort of person who considered herself relentlessly professional, because she lacked the insight to distinguish her own desires and prejudices from the diktat of authority.

As a consequence, her grudges carried to her the semi-divine fiat of law, and I had no doubt that she would go to extraordinary lengths to

314

ensure that they also carried its force.

This made her very, very dangerous, so I needed to watch my step.

I let my gaze rise to Martin's face as he placed the coffee before me – to his tired eyes, the little creases bracketing his mouth.

Oh, Martin. You need to watch your step, too.

'We need to start the DNA testing,' he said, and not for the first time.

The detective raised his head, as though a bell had rung. 'Test her against what?'

'The blood on the nightdress,' replied Martin. 'I know a sample was pulled off that years ago.'

'At the very least it wouldn't hurt,' I threw in, despite the fact that everybody was refusing to look at me. 'But I'm also betting that these things take a little while to be processed.'

O'Neill dismissed this as of no consequence. 'We'll do it. But if Martin's right, Katie Browne is in danger right *now*.' He uncrossed his arms, crossed them again. I was left with the impression of him as a huge, impenetrable fortress, and nothing useful would issue forth out of the gates until he was quite ready. 'I don't pretend to understand this whole dissociative amnesia thing. I always thought the trouble with bad memories is that you can't get rid of them, not that you could forget them all wholesale.'

I opened my mouth, to attempt to reply–

'You can't forget them wholesale,' snapped Martin, and there was a sharpness, a protectiveness in his voice and, wonder of wonders, I think it was meant for me. 'That's the point. You live in terror of remembering them. You have to work

315

and keep working so that they remain forgotten.'
He pointed at Greta. 'Am I right?'

'Martin, there are a lot of factors–'

'Perhaps there are,' he said, and now he was getting angry. 'And maybe none of this is anything to do with Margot. But as she keeps trying to tell you, that's a question for another day. What I want to know is, what are we going to do next?'

'What about hypnosis?' I said. 'We could do it now. You see it on the TV and in movies all the time...'

Greta exchanged a glance with O'Neill.

'What?' asked Martin.

'Several things,' said Greta. 'Firstly, the use of hypnosis in such cases is ... controversial. And possibly dangerous, in terms of Margot's therapy...'

'We're not doing it for my therapy,' I burst out. 'We're doing it to solve a crime and find a missing girl.'

'Secondly,' she continued, as though I hadn't spoken, 'you'd need a specialist – a psychiatrist, not a psychologist. There are medical implications.'

'Yes, Martin said as much. Handy that we're in Cambridge then,' I replied, 'as there's bound to be one knocking around.'

'And you'd be looking at using an injected opiate or barbiturate-induced semi-hypnotic state rather than a hypnotic trance.'

I went absolutely numb. 'Injected?'

'I don't understand,' said Martin.

Greta pushed a long strand of her bob behind her ear. 'The risk of false memory creation is too high with ordinary hypnosis. You'd require something like sodium pentothal or some kind of benzodiazepine, which doesn't eliminate the risk of false memory or confabulation, but makes it less likely. And I say again, though nobody wants to hear it, that there would be serious psychological risks for Margot in such a procedure. If Margot really is Bethan Avery, she will experience all the emotions that grew out of the original trauma all over again. And if she isn't ... all of that will be doubly true, as I have no doubt that *some* trauma is present – just not the one we need.'

'You'll have a go though anyway, won't you, Margot?' asked Martin.

I did not reply. I could not open my mouth.

'Margot?'

Martin's expression had changed. Something was wrong.

I was shaking. I was shaking so hard that the very floor was vibrating beneath my chair, and I was astonished that they could not feel it.

'I can't... I thought you meant pills.'

Greta glared at me, as though I were talking in some incomprehensible language. 'What possible difference does it make?' she snapped.

'I ... I can't have needles injected into me.' I felt frozen with horror. 'I hate needles. It's a gigantic problem at all the hospitals when they try to treat me. I just can't do it.'

Martin blinked at me. 'But that's... Margot, you told me that when you were on the streets you were an injecting heroin addict.'

I couldn't think of a single thing to reply. There was nothing inside me but a dumbstruck amazement, a confusion, but something ... something was becoming suddenly very clear.

'Except that ... that you *weren't*, were you?' he asked.

At that moment, I finally got it.

I had tried to comply, to take that leap of faith, but I had been resisting. I had not believed. Yes, my past was a muddy patchwork of experiences, frequently misremembered and often poorly understood, but still, you could say that about a lot of people's lives.

The woman in Wastenley this morning may or may not have been my mother, and after so long doing without her did it really matter? Did she disown me because she was angry with me, with my sudden appearance, the way I bellowed at her like a crazy person, yet another victim of that fathomless rage that keeps looming like a shark's fin out of the dark waters of my subconscious; an emotion I can neither enjoy nor control?

Or did she really just not know me?

I was quite sure I didn't know her. But that was not true. I remembered ... I remembered knowing *about* her. More to the point, I knew about her husband.

I remembered sitting on a street sign this morning, but does it follow that it was that particular one, on that particular street? Did I just want to make Martin happy, so my hungry, needy mind sought out this tiny detail – after all, I already knew that Bethan Avery had lived there – it would stand to reason that she would know this street corner.

But Martin didn't ask me to sit on the sign.

I had learned not to ask questions, to live in the

moment, and I'd been doing it all of my life.

I thought I did it rather well. I fooled everyone, but most especially, it turns out, I had fooled myself. My life wasn't a mosaic of dim memories, it had been invented out of whole cloth. It was all lies, lies which I cleaved to despite the fact that they hurt me, cost me my peace, could have cost me my job, could have cost me my life, if last night was anything to go by.

It was all just lies.

And the only thing to replace them with was unimaginable horror.

Before I knew what I was doing, I was plunging for the door.

Martin found me outside, standing on the steps under the awning, watching the snow fall. He didn't say anything, but came and stood next to me, watching the snow with me for a little while.

As far as I was capable of feeling anything, I felt grateful for this. I wanted him to put his arm around me, knew that he would not, because if it had been an unwelcome gesture it would have been an unconscionable thing to do to me at that particular moment.

Perhaps I needed to put my arm around him.

'Margot ... about...'

'I have an idea.'

He did not reply, waiting.

'I need some cigarettes,' I said.

'I didn't know you smoked.'

'I don't. Or rather, I don't any more. I gave up.'

Beside me, I could feel him wanting to object.

'Trust me,' I said. 'Trust me as I trusted you.

Come with me while I smoke a cigarette.'

We crossed the road to the little Co-Op opposite, and queued patiently at the counter while a man in front of us quibbled with the shop assistant over which scratch card he wanted.

Bloody hell, it was practically a tenner for a pack of twenty Silk Cut Blue nowadays. It only seemed like a couple of years since I gave up, and it was a fiver then. You could have knocked me over with a feather.

You could have knocked me over with a feather anyway.

I bought them and a pink plastic Bic lighter, which the boy behind the counter obligingly flicked into a flame a couple of times, just to check that it worked.

Martin observed all of this, and me, with an aura of bemused indulgence.

'What's this about?' he asked, as we emerged back on to Parker's Piece in the snow. It was growing, if not exactly dark, then dim.

I hadn't forgotten that we were on a clock. Far from it.

'It's about drugs. And memory,' I said. 'Sit on the bench with me.'

We settled on the bench opposite the fire station, with its new gleaming frontage. Behind the glass panels the engines were vast and quiescent.

I unwrapped the cellophane from the packet, willing myself to remember this action – I must have done this hundreds and hundreds of times over the course of my life.

'Am I interrupting something if I ask questions?'

'No,' I said. 'It won't make a difference. It's

beyond words.' I thumbed open the top of the box, regarded the tesseract of packed filters within for a long moment. At one point this sight filled me with equal parts desire, self-contempt, resignation – or even nothing at all, something I did without thinking.

'You're right,' I said. 'The minute you said it, I knew I could never have been a heroin addict. The thought of applying a needle to my own flesh makes my skin crawl. The thought of loss of control terrifies me. It had just never occurred to me before, because of course, I'd never had to think of it that way. I could remember how to do it, but I didn't long for it. It was just a fact, one I assumed was true.

'If I was truly addicted, I would have got past it. But no. There wasn't even the residue of desire. Now these,' I shook the box at him. 'Holding these, looking at these, smelling that herby scent, that ... that male scent – grassy, slightly bitter yet very rich – these hold the residue of desire for me.' I lifted them to my nose and inhaled.

He was silent, listening.

'Our minds are tricksy,' I said, gazing down at the box. 'But our senses ... our senses have memories, too, and they're harder to fool.' I pushed one of the cigarettes upwards, drew it out, put it between my lips. They pursed around it, adopting the correct shape, as if they'd been waiting to do this for years.

I was right, I knew it.

I lifted the lighter, ignited, inhaled.

It tasted horrible. But that was OK. I expected that. It tasted like a welcome from people that haven't recognized you yet, but will soon, and will be overjoyed when they do.

The smell of burning was like a little hearth, warming me. I blew out a puff of smoke into the cold air.

Martin's intense gaze followed it.

'I know everything there is to know about how to shoot up heroin,' I said. 'I know to crush the pills. How to cook the mixture, how to draw up the solution through cotton wool so the bits don't get sucked up into the needle. I know everything there is to know about it, because I watched Angelique do it.'

I inhaled again, the burning, sweet heat of it. It still tasted disgusting. But I had no desire to stop.

'Angelique's dad ... well, it wasn't sexual abuse, the way she told it, but there was a sexual component, or maybe that's not right.' I shook my hand, as though to conjure the right phrase, and it seemed to work: 'There was a *control* component. He made her get up at six every morning and inspected her. I mean, he watched her shower, and brush her teeth, and get dressed, until she was about fifteen years old. She kept a diary, which had to be submitted to him every week for his approval. She was allowed no friends that he didn't vet, and he didn't rubber-stamp any of them. They were all dirty, or sly, or ignorant, or rebellious. Basically, he had no chance of controlling them, so out they went.

'And Angelique went along with all of it, until she was fifteen. Then she met a boy on the way home from school, who offered her a lift in his car. By the end of the week, she'd run away with him. To London. Where I met her.' I let out a sad little laugh. 'Isn't that what everyone does, at least once in their lives? I did it, Bethan's mother – my mother – did it, and Angelique did it. She ran away to the big city.'

The glowing tip of the cigarette jutted out from between my ring and index finger on the right hand, as though it had never been away.

'I'd like to say she was happy ever after.' The smoke curled out of my mouth. 'But I'm quite sure that she wasn't.' I let my forehead sink down on to my hand. 'I know that she wasn't.'

He waited. The snow had stopped for a little while, but was now whirling downwards again.

I sighed.

'Somehow, I became Angelique,' I said. The words sat on the still air, in a little cloud of their own craziness. 'I can't tell which parts of me I've stolen from her, like the heroin, or which are really me, like the cigarettes.'

'It will be all right,' he said, putting a hand on my trembling arm.

I cast about me. The sun had set and the stream of passers-by was drying to a trickle. The street-lights had started to glimmer redundantly in the gloom.

I touched my hair and snow came away in my hands. I didn't feel cold though.

'You're right,' I said. 'It's about triggers. My mind doesn't remember, but my senses can feel the way, if I let them. I need to get up close and personal with more triggers. But first, we need to make that crew in there do that DNA. And the hypnosis. *Now.*'

'You're freezing,' he said after a minute. 'And

323

we do need to go back. We can't sit here all night.'

'Another minute,' I said.

'Let me get you your coat, then. It's only in the car.'

I nodded, these arrangements passing me by, like a dream.

I watched Martin walk up to the Land Rover, watched his feet plodding through the slush. He moved aside for a man passing along the inside of the pavement.

The cigarette had burned away practically to the filter. I dropped it, ground it into the snow.

Then something thudded into my head. I could feel my consciousness tremble and ripple, and Martin's receding back vanished into a mist of grey. I dropped like a stone through the ripples, into nothingness.

It didn't hurt at all.

27

There was something vibrating against my head.

My chin was settled into my chest, and my back ached, especially my neck. The vibration was quick and low, the throb of an engine. Through my half-closed eyes I could see the strands of my hair, falling against my face. My head was muzzy with pain, and each time the little muscles in my face moved it hurt.

I remembered that I was in danger.

I shut my eyes quickly.

I was lying in a moving car, jammed in the gap between the front seats and the back. My shoulders were against the door, my head sunk into my bosom. My hands were tied behind me, and full of furious pins and needles. The car's interior smelled musty, full of mould, and the seats were stained with it.

I started to wriggle my wrists carefully against my bonds, desperate not to signal that I was awake.

On my side was a wall of vinyl that was the driver's seat, or rather the back of it. Warm air blew at me from the gap beneath it. I saw all I could without moving my head, or any part of my body. My limbs lay loose, as carelessly as they had when I'd been thrown there, but they were full of secret tension, and I was in terror lest someone should accidentally kick or touch me, and it would be discovered.

There is a state of mind where one ceases to question the whys and wherefores of life, a state where all that can be done is to exist, from minute to minute, with only the physical world and the promptings of millennia-old instincts as guides. This was my state, in which one second followed another and preceded the next, and I thought of and saw nothing but the wall of black vinyl, hearing the growl of the engine and the roaring wind buffet the door.

I fought to lay still and relax, and picked at the tight little nylon knots in my bonds, as I was carried forth into the centre of the labyrinth for the final time.

My neck was aching. I could not take it much

325

longer, I would have to shift position. Whoever was driving would notice me, notice I was awake. As tortures go, it was an elegant device, scrupulously executed.

'Still fucking snowing,' said the driver. I froze, but there was something distracted but comfortable in his tone, as though he was someone that spoke to himself more often than others. He had a soft, low voice, which startled me. My hand might have twitched.

My cut shoulder itched abominably.

We were travelling at speed, and it was snowing. Dusk was settling, but there were no streetlights. I had to get out of the car. I had to escape. And when I thought of the word 'escape', a wild, fierce longing broke out in me; a bitter hurt. From prison to prison to prison, from cellar to refuge to office to hall of residence – from drugs to sex to marriage to work – an endless cycle of escapes, like a rat in a laboratory maze, or the flight of a magpie from grass to hedgerow to rusted railing.

A twenty-year fox hunt, pursued by hounds both real and imaginary.

Hounds...

...And the magpie.

It alighted in my head again. I could see it rise, its tail spined out against the English sky. Rain had been falling. It had hit my face in little splashes, cool and refreshing after ... after what? The rain. The rain had always been there.

My skin remembered the rain, even if I did not.

Back in the car I felt the driver shift against the cheap upholstery.

Like an answered prayer, the knot I was gingerly

picking at unravelled beneath the pincers of my nails. The twine slackened and fell off one wrist.

Long nails are always a good thing on a woman. Don't let anyone tell you different.

Now, I have choices.

I could try to overpower the driver, whoever he is (oh don't be stupid, you know who he is. He's Bethan's – your – abductor, the one who has Katie) or attract the attention of passers-by. But he's driving at speed and is likely armed, and the dim dusky sky I can see through the opposite passenger window whenever I dare to raise my eyes, which is just showing a few peeping stars, does not inspire confidence. I am not sure we have passed another car the whole time I have been awake.

The third choice is to flee, which presents its own problems.

There is only one way out of a car: through the door. I concentrated my already condensed attention on the hard thrumming I was leaning up against. I would have to open the door and jump. At this angle I would be 90 per cent sure of landing headfirst, then my body would somersault over it – my neck would almost certainly break, if the car was moving at any kind of speed.

This horrific option, however, was the only one I could think of.

My hands lay under me, and very, very slowly I started to move them apart, to my sides.

Through the door at my back I felt the intense chill of the wind, pregnant with snow and the slush driven up by the wheels. A strand of my own hair tickled my cheek, exquisitely.

There was the musical tick-tock of the indicators, and the car engine idled down a few octaves. He was going to turn. I might have tensed imperceptibly, as a voice spoke softly into my ear, It must be now.

Now it would be.

No jerky movements.

My right hand was retreating up the length of my body. The car was slowing, slowing to turn.

I had my instant – it was upon me. Act now or for ever hold your peace.

I threw myself over, belly down now, and seized the door handle. I had not even depressed it before there was a sudden panicked braking, a shout of, 'Oh no you fucking don't!'

His rage was paralysing, molten, and I was filled to the brim with a scrabbling animal terror, as though my senses remembered this too. Anything would be better than being in the car with him. Anything.

The handle clunked down, metal grinding against metal, and I pushed, though my instincts screamed against it.

I kicked wildly, my face full of the freezing wind gushing through the crack in the car door. The snow was deep and still flying away from me at a perilous speed, which was growing greater. The driver was speeding the car up.

I kicked free.

There was a long, flying moment, when everything was suspended, as though the turning world itself had hit some impossible impediment. There was neither sound nor sensation, just whiteness, and the flight of fate out of my hands.

Wheels rushed by, inches from my head. I

waited for death or mutilation, as I crunched back into time, cushioned and jarred by the thick snow.

But when I raised my bruised head, one side of my face stinging with the force of a hundred needles, the car was just a black blur, swinging round in the snow, sending a white wave over its bonnet, which thudded on to the metal like a tiny avalanche, glittering in the headlights.

I got up, staggering slightly. The car, some hundred yards down the road, was growing closer, nearer through the darkness and the veil of snow.

There were trees, iced in white, near the road. A tiny stand of woodland, an oasis of Fenland, stretching out under the sunless sky. I ran into them, as though pursued by wolves.

It had stopped snowing, but that was no help.

I had run and run for miles it seemed, through black trees sticking up like spikes through the white carpet, and then scrambled down into the narrow crack of one of the ditches lining a small lane, aware that on the flat Fens I would be visible for miles, even in the dark, and that the snow would hold on to my footprints. I was soaked to the bone, burning hot, scalding the snow into water that dripped over my skin and sifted through my clothing.

I paused. There was something like ground glass in my lungs, cutting me with each breath I took. The lane next to the ditch had come to a crossroads, both literal and otherwise.

Above me, the pitch-blackness was giving way to the inky points of stars. The muffled moonlight enjoyed a slightly freer reign. I listened intently, but there was nothing but the wind howling across the Fens.

Unless he'd had a flashlight, he must have lost me, I told myself.

I crouched ankle-deep in the thin ditch water, my feet numb. Another country road, lined with untidy hedges, stretched out from left to right, where it was joined by a footpath, which meandered into a diagonal bent from the fields at my left. A tiny wooden bridge with side slats crossed the water in front of me.

I recognized this bridge from somewhere – but where?

Just before the bridge was a pole, casting a sharp shadow now as the moon gathered its strength, with signs affixed to its top, and thrusting my hot hands into my wet pockets, where they ached with cold, I approached it.

The moonlight waned as I reached its base, but reappeared in a few seconds to tell me that Cambridge was four miles to the left, and Comberton two miles to the right. There was also a little sign, indicating that this was some kind of scenic walk.

Miles and miles of snow stretched away before me, meeting the stormy sky in a straight line – black meets white, with mathematical precision.

I stared up at the sign. Weren't suicides buried at crossroads? So the ghost couldn't find its way back home?

Each time the wind ruffled me it sent freezing gusts through my sodden clothes. I could hardly feel my feet any more, now that I'd stopped running. I glanced anxiously back but there was nothing there.

There was a house to my left, over the bridge, a big house, surrounded by walls. I blinked and held my breath. A single light was visible in one of the upstairs windows. It looked huge, rambling, with Jacobean chimney turrets standing stark against the moonlit sky, and big wrought-iron gates.

A house – oh thank God, thank God, some civilization at last! There was doubtless some well-heeled, slightly dotty family living inside, or at least some discreetly wealthy stockbroker or entrepreneur using it as his country retreat, or it might be another one of those language or residential schools that Cambridge is teeming with, full of harried supervisors and confused foreign teenagers with identical backpacks.

Someone who had a phone, at any rate. Though something about the place, with its Escher-esque eaves and iron gates, made me feel uneasy.

Or, as I observed tartly to myself, I could lie at the foot of the crossroads and freeze to death. Suicide or not, I think my ghost would find the way back home. She'd been very tenacious so far.

My teeth chattered. The house and I regarded each other. I don't know why, but the thought of going through those gates and approaching the faded white door on its porticoed plinth filled me with vague dread. Though perhaps it's not strange that I've been feeling somewhat paranoid lately.

The lane was thickly blanketed with snow. It would take me hours to get back to Cambridge, or even to reach Comberton in this condition, even if I didn't die of exposure first or my pursuer caught up with me.

And anything could happen to Katie in that

time, wherever she was.

I pressed my freezing hands into my armpits and shook my head, as if to clear it of irrational fear. The cold night air pinched my shoulder and my feet trod across the soft, deep snow to the closed iron gates.

At least I was out of the wind.

Walls of dark brick loomed up over my head. The yellow light coming out of the windows could not reconcile me to them. I scratched at my prickling scalp and my teeth chattered.

My shoes squeaked, leaving a watery trail of prints as I mounted the sandstone steps to the door.

There was a dusty bronze doorbell, the casing starting to crack with age. Now I was up close to the place, I understood what had made me think twice – there was an aura of shiftless neglect everywhere – from the weeds creeping through what had once been a careful, sweeping drive, to the cracked window casements and their crumbling putty, their distress plainly visible in the bright white motion sensor light that had come on the minute I opened the gates. A brand-new padlock with sharp steel edges on a shiny chain had swung from the gates themselves, unfastened, as though it had been opened in a hurry.

Comfort and aesthetics might have been neglected by the inhabitants, but there was an obviously new CCTV camera set up on a wall mount, pointed at the gates, and I could see its twin mounted on the side of the house adjoining the rambling brick wall surrounding the estate.

Red lights flashed on them in heartbeat time. Perhaps someone was watching me right now.

I pressed the bell.

A loud pure double chime rang out through the house beyond, electronically amplified in some way, as though the people who lived here were used to being too far away to hear an ordinary doorbell.

I strained to listen for signs of life, pressing my ear to the faded white surface of the door paint. My cheek stung against it – I had grazed it when I fell out of the car.

There was absolutely nothing.

Long moments went by.

I tried once more, pressing the button and letting the chimes ring out, again and again. This was an emergency after all. I didn't have to be intimidated by these people and their big house.

Then once more, I pressed my ear to the wood, trying not to weep.

This time, there was a noise.

I'm not sure I would have heard it in the usual run of things – if it had been daylight, and there had been rustling trees and birdsong, passing cars and aeroplanes. It was very tiny – an irregular *rat-tat-tat*, like someone tapping on something metal. The sound was buried deep within the house, more of a vibration than a noise.

Perhaps it was the pipes.

My ear still pressed to the door, I rang the bell again.

Again no ambient sounds, no sign of movement in the house, but that tiny rapping started again immediately, and its rhythm had an urgent, no, desperate, quickening – *RAT-TAT-TAT-TAT-TAT*...

A kind of horrible realization bloomed within me.

If I was right, there wasn't a moment to lose.

I circled what I could of the house, looking for an open window or unlocked door – faint hope, but better than nothing. Most of the windows were resolutely curtained, and under their sills were old rotting wires, the remains of an alarm system. The new alarm system was centred in a blinking red box at the back of the building, undoubtedly complete with sensors and linked to the cameras, to protect the house in its dotage.

I tried to come up with some sort of plan. My thoughts were slow and fuzzy. Perhaps the alarm system was switched off. Perhaps the red blinking box was all there was, a way to deter thieves. I was going to have to walk to Comberton on my numb feet.

But that was impossible. I had to get in there. *Now.*

I trudged from window to window, all resolutely veiled with damask or heavy cotton. The big ones at the front and sides were leaded in diamond patterns – I could never have broken in through them, so I circled round to the side, my feet crunching through virgin snow on the narrow path. Then there was a smaller window, and then another, but all had net or cheap polyester hanging over them, and I could see no lights in them. They looked like servants' quarters.

I stared up at the sheer brick walls. There were a few other windows above, on different floors, but they were also unlit and peculiarly forbidding. This part of the house outcropped a little from the rest, so it had presumably been an extension from its antiquated foundations. And there appeared to be no one in it.

At least not yet.

My fingers were curling up into two little blue crabs, and my neck and cut shoulder ached keenly with the cold. I needed to break the glass in one of the smaller windows at the back, but how...?

The padlock and chain, from the gates.

I was running to the gates when the security lights blazed awake with an audible click from somewhere up on the wall, bathing me in white light. Just a motion sensor, but I nearly screamed with terror. The chain and padlock threaded out through the bolt, their shiny steel newness at odds with the ancient, nicked wrought iron.

Beyond the gates, in the darkness, something moved.

I paused, illuminated, on the drive, blinded by the lights, trying to see any approaching cars. There was nothing. But that didn't mean there was nothing out there.

I ran back to the window and lashed out with the chain; the thin glass shattered into a thousand pieces with a musical tinkle, as though it had been waiting for this very opportunity.

In the back of my mind, I tensed for the shriek of the alarm. It didn't come – perhaps it was a silent alarm, or merely there for show.

Or it's been disabled in some way, I thought. Maybe whoever lives here can't risk strangers or the police turning up every time some kid tries to break in.

Which implies he probably has something on hand to take care of problems of that sort himself.

No time to worry about that now.

I gathered up the slack of my blue cardigan in my stiff fingers and pressed its sodden mass to the broken edges, snapping them off so I could crawl in. The pieces fell on to the floor of the room, with a glissando crash. It was all I could do not to cut myself in my terror.

There was a bed in the room, which was small and poky, and a chest of drawers with a cheap mirror mounted above them. A half-open suitcase lay on the bed, full of a mix of men's clothes, and a shoebox lay on top of them, the lid slightly open.

Inside were papers, a passport, two driving licenses, one for Tim Henry who lived in Barton and one for Christopher Meeks who lived in the village, and there was also an ID card for Chris Henry, a driver for North Cambridgeshire Social Services, which had expired eighteen months ago. All of these cards showed images of the same man, with sandy greying hair. Clothes lay everywhere, a flurry of packing halted and waiting to be resumed.

I sat down on the bed, burying my hands in the starchy coverlet. It was icy cold, but at least it was dry.

I smoothed the melted snow out of my hair. When I touched my cheek, my finger came away black with blood.

The mirror opposite showed a series of fine scratches across my face.

Looped across one corner of the mirror stand was a little tarnished silver cross on a thin chain.

For some reason, despite the danger, the need for haste, my eye was caught by this detail, and kept being drawn back to it, as though by some enchantment...

How had this man found me? Oh, I'd been so stupid. While I'd been arguing with the police over exposing Bethan Avery in the paper with the appeal, I had really been exposing myself.

None of it mattered, though. I needed to find the source of that tapping, to quieten that terrible suspicion in me. I needed to find a phone, and without a moment's delay.

Outside the door there was a smooth wooden corridor, with flat rugs laid on it, and at its end a big tiled and plastered space opened out. I waited for a few moments, merely breathing, listening – I guessed the corridor led into the kitchen. Perhaps there was a phone in there, and maybe some kind of weapon. I glided cautiously on to the rug, my feet making only the faintest of whispers against the coarse material.

I heard nothing, nothing except the sound of a big house from a bygone age, gloomy and neglected and falling into dust. The tapping had fallen silent.

Through the dusty, cavernous kitchen I moved, where the only thing that had the patina of use was a tiny ancient microwave, crusted with food stains, then through doors to a winding series of staircases with marble steps and steel banisters, the moon reaching down to me through a glass skylight. No sign of a phone still. I fought down my sense of panic.

The double doors ahead of me were shut, but I

337

knew I was heading to the front of the house, and to the room with the big leaded windows near the drive, where I had first heard the tapping.

This was where the light had come from that had drawn me from the path. It limned the shut doors in a thin line of gold.

I threw them open.

I don't know what did it to me where so many other things had failed, but the blue damask curtains, the black and white tiled floor with its thick, heavy blue rug, that velvet sofa – that fucking velvet sofa – filled me with a terror and rage so intense that I wanted to set light to it.

I knew, with the lightning ring of truth, that I had been very, very unhappy on that velvet sofa.

I remembered this room.

More to the point, I remembered what happened the last time I was in it.

28

It was early evening, and I was out of the cellar.

There had been, as there always has been, the cellar. I think even then I had become so damaged, so dissociated, as Martin might say, that I would have been hard-pressed to remember who I was; that I had once had a mother, Melissa; that my best friend was Natalie.

But some things I had not forgotten.

It was winter and I was always bitterly, bitterly cold, and I constantly thought I was going to die.

But I had not died. I had stayed alive because my nanna was terribly hurt and in hospital. I had to get back to her. She was in trouble; in danger.

I had not been allowed out for a long time, and I was so weak I could barely stand up. I was injured – something in my chest hurt and I think one of my ribs was broken. I'd done something to make him angry, but I cannot remember what it was.

In any case, I wasn't standing up. I was sitting, on that velvet couch.

He said his name was Alex, but I was sure this was a lie. He was skinny and middle-aged (or so I thought, though through the filter of my own experience I suspect he was no more than thirty-two or -three), had thin, sandy blond hair and didn't often wash. That fusty, sweaty-sour smell is clearer to me than his face. I cannot remember his face very well – I hated looking at him so rarely did, and I took the cues for my own survival from his voice. It was whispery; borderline obsequious, but could change in a heartbeat to a full-throated furious bellowing, usually accompanied by his heavy, driving fists.

He told me that he had rescued me from the men that killed my mother – they were looking for me, too, and for my nanna. He told me he was rich and powerful, and that this was his house. I didn't know whether I believed that, but I did believe that my nanna was in danger, and that somehow he knew what had happened to Melissa. I believed that he knew my teachers, and that some of them knew I was here, including Miss Costas. That he knew social services – how

else had he got my details? – that he knew policemen – that was why nobody ever looked for me.

He thought I should be grateful to him for saving me and my nanna, and that I should show it.

When he spoke to me it was as though he was
speaking to some other girl he'd mistaken me for,
some other girl called Bethan that he liked better,
which was bad news for her I guess. This other girl
was his girlfriend and she was in love with him;
they were very happy together, though it would be
difficult to tell this as she didn't often speak.

While they were together I simply went away,
deep into some corner of myself, and stood with
my back to them both.

The last time I was in this room he was being
very nice to me – uncharacteristically so. He was
sorry he'd lost his temper, even though I'd
schemed to escape behind his back, ungrateful
creature that I was, despite all he'd done for me; all
he continued to do to protect me. He was going to
make it up to me. He looked like he'd been crying
and his hands shook as they touched me on that
fucking velvet sofa. I didn't go away inside myself
that time. I stayed, because I realized that something had changed and that change was bad.

He'd bought me this white nightgown, made of
cheap slippery nylon lace, and he wanted me to
put it on. He watched while I tried to get it over
my head despite my cracked rib, as though I was
performing a private striptease for him. Then he
made me lie back on the sofa.

'That's it, my beautiful darling. Now shut your
eyes.'

I did, despite every instinct screaming at me to

340

leave them open. They stayed shut as he leaned in and kissed me, kissed my eyelids, and drew back.

There was a faint rustling from the bag the nightdress had come in.

I could not endure it, despite the risk of his rage. My eyes flew open.

He had a ball-peen hammer in both hands and was about to bring it down on my skull.

On the velvet sofa, something that had been lying coiled within me suddenly sprang into life, as though it had been there all along, despite the cold and this crazy man and the sense that I was fractured into a thousand broken pieces, none of which bore any correlation to one another any more.

The thing within me was much more awake than I. It knew not to waste precious energy on trying to defend myself against the falling hammer with my weak arms, or to try pleading for my life against his watery blue eyes, his trembling lip.

I knew I was in the last few seconds of my existence, so instead I lunged upwards, despite the sharp stabbing in my ribs, and jabbed my fingers into his eyes.

There was a shocked curse of pain and surprise, followed by another yell as he dropped the raised hammer and it crashed down on top of his head, the wicked claw tearing against his ear as it fell, leaving him momentarily stunned.

And that was how, suddenly, the hammer – smeared in old, dried bloodstains – was in my hands.

I smacked him with it on the side of his head, and he howled.

You might be wondering why I didn't go on and kill him with it, and I have to wonder that too. But I think I was wiser than I give myself credit for – he was merely dazed, and already grabbing for the hammer as I lay pinned beneath him, and once the element of surprise was exhausted there was no question of who would win a fight.

With all of my remaining strength, I twisted sideways beneath him, and as he tried to stop me hitting him again, he lost balance and fell off the sofa on to the heavy blue rug.

I leapt to my feet, my injuries forgotten, a creature of pure adrenaline, and made to sprint away.

He grabbed my ankle and yanked backwards. I was falling, and my face smacked down hard on to the black and white tiles where the carpet ended. Pain exploded across my nose, something crunching beneath the skin of my face between my eyes, and blood spattered outwards across the stone. The hammer flew out of my grip, skittered out of my hand over the flags, bouncing tinnily off a wall until it lay still.

With my uncaught foot, I kicked backwards, hard.

He yelled again and let go of my other foot. I scrabbled forward for the hammer, barely feeling the wetness of blood dripping down my nose, my mouth, out of my cut lip.

Get up, get up, get up!

It was back in my grasp. The swords of dead kings could not have had such a steely glitter to me. I gained my feet and snatched open the door to the hall.

He was after me in an instant.

I did not have time to try the front door, running instead for the back of the house, through the labyrinth of passages; the hall with the winding marble staircase, the corridor, the cavernous kitchen; while he, the monster at the centre, growling and bleeding and bellowing curses, came after, a mere second behind, so close I could feel his hot, fetid breath upon my neck, and when I did I whirled around with the hammer, screaming, and he would duck back, but only for an instant.

He's going to catch me. He's going to catch me and kill me.

I skidded into the kitchen, saw the knives.

No he isn't.

It was in my other hand just as his arms seized tight around my waist, and I was stabbing him in the hand, reaching back to stab him in the thigh, in the belly, anywhere I could reach despite the awkward angle, while he screamed obscenities and let me go.

I had dropped the hammer, keeping hold of the knife, and the kitchen door was in front of me, on a simple latch lock.

I flung it open and was through.

My bare feet touched wet grass, iced with early evening dew. The breeze I had wept for and dreamed of stroked my body, but I had no time nor thought to savour it.

I ran.

I ran as I'd never run in my life. The field seemed endless. No matter how my legs pumped down into the damp green, the trees remained elusive, receding from me as quickly as I approached them.

I ran in utter silence, my hard breathing and the susurrus of the grass my only company. There was a sharp howl, an almost inarticulate cry of baffled rage, rising to an insistent baying.

It was drawing closer.

I hadn't thought I could run any faster. I'd been wrong. I knew that if I looked back I would see him, tearing over the grass behind me, my death written on his face.

But I didn't look back. You should never look back.

Then the trees came to meet me. The muddy ground was strewn with treacherous roots, painfully jarring and tripping my feet. My fate was upon me. I looked up at the twining branches in desperation. The wind whipped cold droplets over me; it was raining.

Something started out of the brush. It contrasted sharply with the dusk, and the brown-grey bracken. It was black and white. It burst into the air, soundlessly. I saw with the perfect clarity of terror what it was. It was a magpie. A meaningless detail. A root tripped me up. I put my hands out to steady my fall, one still grasping the knife.

They met nothing.

The riverbank sloped away, hidden from all eyes by the trees and bracken surrounding the edge of the stream. I rolled down the bank, my fall half-broken by stray plants and long grass. Alex poised on the lip of the bank, shouting in fury, as I plunged, grabbing futilely for purchase on the river's banks, into the cold and swollen water.

And just like that I was out, as though I had been

344

bodily evicted from my own memory.

I was Margot again and I was standing on the blue rug, facing that fucking velvet sofa with its stained upholstery, its extra decades of desolation and dust.

Katie.

I knew where Katie Browne was.

The rug was heavy, terribly heavy, but I heaved a corner of it back.

Set into the stone tiles was a trap door; such as I had seen in innumerable plays and films. Its edges were lined in black metal bolted to a wooden frame. A thick black ring lay flat in a depression made to fit it.

I seized this, pulled, pulled again. At first I thought it was just heavy, until I saw the keyhole just under the ring – made to fit some big, antiquated barrel key.

I swore.

Nothing happened, except that from below, there was the *rat-tat-tat* again.

'Katie?' I shouted, dropping to my knees. 'Katie, is that you in there?'

There was silence. Then, very muffled but still audible, threaded with disbelief: 'Mrs Lewis?'

'Oh my God!' And weird and inappropriate as it sounds, I wanted to laugh with joy. 'Oh my God, you're alive! Katie, where does he keep the key?'

'The key?'

'The trapdoor is locked. Do you know where he keeps the key?' I shouted into the flush join between trapdoor and floor.

Her reply was inaudible.

'I can't hear you!'

'I don't know… I don't know!'

'Katie, look, listen, it doesn't matter. I'm going to call the police and they'll get you out, all right? I promise. Sit tight.'

'OK,' came the thin, muffled reply.

'Good girl.'

I stood up, rubbing at the back of my neck. The phone. Bloody hell, the phone would be in the hallway.

The hallway – where the hell was that? There was a door in the wall next to the velvet sofa, and I pushed it open. Bingo.

The handset was old and grubby, but it still let out a profound purring once I lifted the receiver to my ear.

I jabbed in 999, glancing towards the front door. It was open, just a crack.

My stomach hollowed out in dread. In all of the excitement, I had not heard anyone come in.

'Police, ambulance or fire brigade?' chirped the voice on the other end.

Something very cold pressed itself into the back of my neck. The receiver was being lifted out of my hands, and I let it go.

'Put your hands up,' he said.

I raised them, slowly. The wallpaper in the hall was dark pink, in a fleur-de-lys pattern, faintly stained.

'Turn around,' he said.

He still had that whispery voice.

I turned, hands raised, and there he was, in a dirty blue Parka, his blond hair now greying, shorn close, and missing up to the crown of his head.

His watery blue eyes met mine over the barrel

346

of the shotgun he was holding.

'Oh, Bethan,' he said, 'you've been such a bad, *bad* girl.'

29

'Move,' he said, motioning me back to the other room with the gun.

I was tempted, recklessly tempted, to tell him to go to hell, to shoot me where I stood, if that's what he was going to do, for I would do nothing to oblige him, contemptible bully that he was; not a single thing, not any more.

But there was more than myself to think about. Katie was in there.

I had to get Katie out somehow.

I let him walk me back, watched him unlock the trapdoor, the shotgun still trained on me.

I remembered something else – I never used to look at him; never used to dare, or desire to, but I looked at him now.

I gave him a long cold stare.

'Get in,' he said.

Hands raised, I preceded him down the stairs to the underworld, along the dusty corridor, to the door at the bottom. The black and white tiles were down here too, black and white like magpies, and flecked in places with tiny maroon spatters that I realized were old blood.

I wondered how much of it was mine.

My jaw tightened.

I was back in Martin's office, and his crowded wall of pictures and scraps of notes rose before me, like a rocky bluff before a rudderless ship.

All of those girls...

The barrel was a cold circle pressing against the back of my neck. He was handing me something. Down, past my elbow, I saw him holding out the key to the door.

He was breathing hard. On some level, he was enjoying himself.

'Hurry up. I haven't got all day.'

I bit my tongue and took the unpleasantly warm key from his sweaty hand. It turned smoothly in the lock.

'I don't understand it,' he said, and his voice was full of hidden rage and a whiny self-pity. 'Why did you come back here? Is it money? Is that what you're after?'

Within, Katie Browne pressed herself into the far corner in a filthy pink nightshirt, and her face was dirty and bruised. It was also horrified and hopeless.

I gave her a long cool look too. It's not over yet.

Her bruised bottom lip curled inwards.

'Don't you ignore me,' I could hear the approaching thunder of his rage in that voice – that childlike rage that could brook not an instant's frustration, not a particle of disapproval. 'Why are you back here?'

I turned to face him. 'You drove me here, you dumb bastard, when you dragged me into your car,' I said. 'You tell *me* why I'm here.'

He twitched, and his breathing was a little faster, and like lightning he slapped me across

348

the face, hard enough to make my ears ring.

But I was not afraid any more, because his rage was as nothing compared to my own. The memory of this underground room with its mouldy foam, the stench of terror, made my blood sing in my ears, my heart pound like a drum.

With this rage I would accomplish great and terrible things.

'Don't you dare get cheeky with me, you fucking whore!' he roared. His eyes were lamps lit with madness, and just for that second, he forgot himself, lowered the gun, just a fraction. 'We could have been a match made in heaven, but you ruined it!'

I let my tongue dab lightly at my lip, where he had cut me. I was rewarded with the taste of salt and iron; it was like a bit between my teeth.

I bit down hard.

'Oh, *you* are no match for *me*.'

There in the underworld, drawn by the scent of blood, I attacked.

The padlock and chain were out of my pocket in a flash, and I lashed out with it, hard, across his face; a metal scourge that tore into his flesh, his eyes. Blood squirted out, spattering me, and he let out a stunned yell, but I was possessed – I realized that all that really stops us from hurting one another is not strength of body but strength of will, and now every ounce of my strength was going into slashing him again and again with the chain, the sharp edges of the padlock cutting into him while he screamed and fought with the gun. It went off, but it was too close, firing wildly to the side. Its roiling blast was as vague and irrelevant as

349

distant thunder and all I could see was him, through a veil of fast-moving scarlet fragments.

How dare he touch me. How dare he touch those girls. I will kill him. I will *kill* him...

He was forcing me back, using the gun as a club, but he was blinded with his own blood and I cared nothing for my own safety. But still he was stronger, filled with a terrible stocky brute strength, like a bull, and he was bearing me backwards; he was going to push me over.

'Katie!' I screamed. 'Get out!'

There was silence behind me, but I did not turn to look at her. I saw only him; he filled my vision. He raised his hand quickly to swipe at his face, and his left eye was half-closed and torn, swollen; blood leaking out from behind the lid.

Suddenly the gun was dropped and both of his hands were around my neck; he was squeezing hard, so hard I could hear cartilage popping beneath his fingers.

I caught the gun and smashed the butt, full force, into his temple.

He let out a soft, sucking *ooph* sound and dropped slowly to his knees. Then, with a dumb animal groan, he toppled forward, his face striking the floor of the cellar with a sick wet smack.

I came back to myself then.

The gun was raised over his head, and I realized that I was moments away from dashing his brains out with it.

I paused, as though time was suspended, the very dust having ceased to drift in the light of that bulb. My discarded scourge lay at my feet, his strands of sandy hair matted with crimson gore.

I lowered the gun, and I was shaking now – shaking so hard that it seemed as though the very floor shook beneath me. My hands were smeared with scarlet.

'Oh,' I said out loud, though my crushed throat strangled the words. 'Oh.'

I have discovered what my enemy discovered all those years ago.

There is a killer inside me.

'Oh,' I said again, and raised my raddled hands to my mouth. They trembled against it. 'Oh.'

At my feet, he sighed out shallow, broken breaths.

Whatever force had risen up in me was now going – slinking away, its work done, back into the depths of my subconscious, leaving me there, utterly abandoned and alone.

Except I was not alone. Katie was with me.

Dear God, I must have scared her half to death.

We had to get out of there. I had to get to the phone. I had to tell people what had happened.

Oh, God, what on earth would I say?

'It's all right, Katie,' I rasped, not taking my eyes off the wounded man. I picked up the chain and began to wind it around his slack wrists as, half-dead or not, there was no way I was turning my back on him. 'It's over now. We're going home.'

From behind me, there was a soft choking sound.

'Katie?'

I turned.

Oh no. Oh no, no, no...

That single shot had found its target.

Katie was lying on her back, and her belly was a

gaping red hole, soaking through her thin cotton nightshirt. Her eyes were open, staring, and a little red rivulet was running out of the side of her mouth as she coughed again, then again, then was still.

30

After weeks of therapy, I think I remember the first part of the story.

I'm not being coy or peekabooish with you. I genuinely don't remember most of it, and the parts I do, well, they are strange and askew, like old photographs, badly stored. Some patches have faded into nothing. Some have curled and warped into weird shapes, as though exposed to open flame. In other places they are jewel-bright, vivid as the day they were taken, but without context, like single jigsaw pieces, unable to tell the story of the whole.

I am walking down a hospital corridor, looking for the toilets. I am very upset, very frightened. Someone I love is in trouble, and from glances, circumspect lowering of voices, ornate and contextually inappropriate kindnesses, I suspect that this person is about to die.

All they will tell me is that she's fallen. She slipped on the ice and hit her head.

But she looks terrible. Her head is a mass of bandages, her eyelids heavy and puffed over her eyes – and she lies in an attitude she does not even have in sleep, her lips pursed around a plastic tube that seems made of something more vital than she is right now. Not even her fraying mass of grey hair is visible. She is in some special unit, in her own room on the ward in a kind of glass box. Everything smells wrong; it's that hospital smell, and forever after that smell will make me batey and bitey, like a trapped, feral animal.

At her side, something on a trolley beeps in time with her heart. That and her slow, gasping breaths, her chest rising and falling, are the only signs that she is alive at all.

They've called me away from school. First day back at school, I'm sure it was, and the cheap uniform with its neat darning over the torn holes and hem feels strange on me, as though it must be worn in again. I think I had only been there an hour before the headmaster came to get me, before ... ah yes, I remember – before Miss Costas drove me here.

My heavy school shoes make a clumping sound against the linoleum. I am like a filled balloon, about to burst with dread.

'Ah, there you are!'

I look round, and about thirty feet behind me I can see that social worker, Alan or Alex or whatever his name is. He is doing his stupid smile at me, and waving, and speeding up along the corridor to meet me, practically running.

I, conversely, can feel myself still walking forwards, trying to pretend I didn't hear him though I obviously looked round, and I am aware that this is a shockingly rude way to treat an adult, particularly one who has power over me.

But I really don't want to talk to him, especially not right now. He gives me the creeps.

I don't have the courage to front it out, so I stop and wait for him to catch up with me. He's still doing the smile.

'There you are,' he says, coming to a halt in front of me, and his gaze flicks quickly up and down the corridor before resting on my face. 'They just rang me at the office. I've been looking all over for you.'

Since I have been where you'd expect to find me, I have nothing to reply to this. I let my glance fall downwards towards my ugly cheap shoes. I can feel his attention burning into the crown of my head.

'Such terrible news,' he says, rubbing his hands together. 'She was such a nice lady.'

I shoot him a look, before I can stop myself.

'*Is* a nice lady. So sorry. I meant, she was nice when I met her.'

I look away. My eyes are filling up again, too fast for me to control. His hand, when it lands on my shoulder, pats me awkwardly, heavily, while I dash furiously at my wet face, not wanting to break down in front of him.

He gives my shoulder a final squeeze.

'I hate to bring this up,' he says, lowering his voice, 'but we have to make arrangements for you while your grandmother isn't able to take care of you.'

'I'm staying here, with Nanna,' I say, blinking back my tears. 'I don't want to go anywhere else.'

'All right,' he says, after a couple of seconds. 'You can stay here. At least for tonight. Come on, now.'

He has hold of my arm, is guiding me forward.

I hesitate, digging my heels in, and I can sense the flicker of displeasure in him as I resist. 'Come where?'

The smile is back. 'You need to pack a bag to tide you over for your stay, and then we'll come right back here, I promise.'

I am suddenly aware of an overwhelming feeling of wrong – of fear – that bites hard enough for me to sense even through my misery. I do not want to go anywhere with him.

'But we have to tell Miss Costas first,' I say, my voice trembling. 'And the nurses.'

'June already knows,' he says, looking up and down the corridor again. 'It will only take a few minutes. You want to be back here when your nanna wakes up, don't you?'

I am imprisoned by doubt, by indecision. I do not want to go with him, but there is no way I can refuse that won't seem incredibly rude, that won't make me look like a crazy person. He hasn't done anything wrong, after all. And I remember what Nanna always says: 'Social services – never get on their bad side, pet. Watch what you say. They could have you off me in a heartbeat.'

For all his smiling, he looks to me like someone that would hold a grudge. He has the power to take me away from Nanna and put me in a Home. I do not want to antagonize him.

And after all, he knows Miss Costas is called June. They must have spoken. I'm just being stupid. I don't want to look stupid in front of Miss Costas, who is my favourite teacher.

I push down my misgivings – his constant

355

checking out of the corridor, the almost-caress at the end when he squeezed my shoulder, the way he stands too close – and nod.

'That's a good girl.'

In the front seat of his little red car, as we take the main road to the village, I reach into the pockets of my coat and suddenly realize that I have left my house keys in my school bag. My bag is lying under the chair next to Nanna's bed at Addenbrooke's.

'I've not got my keys,' I say. 'I left them at the hospital.'

He does not reply or look at me. I tell myself he must not have heard me, though I know in my heart he has.

In my heart, I already know everything.

I don't remember much more about the car journey.

Thankfully, I remember even less about what came after that.

31

My adventures with hospitals are not over. Perhaps they will never be over. Live in hope, says Martin, and I try to.

Once more I am walking down a long hospital corridor, and I am looking for somebody.

This time, though, I know exactly where I am going.

'Hey,' I say, knocking on the wooden door. 'Is now good?'

'Oh hi. Yeah sure. Come in.'

Katie Browne is lying on her hospital bed in a pale green nightshirt. She puts down the iPad she was holding. From the tinny sounds that issue from it, I guess that she's been watching *The Hunger Games* again.

Early on I lent her my iPad and told her to buy what books she wanted and rent movies on my account. Martin was sceptical, but so far she has always had to be pushed to spend any money on it.

It means, though, that I can see what she reads and watches – what she consumes – and what she consumes is fantasy Amazons, warrior-women skilled in sword and bow and laser pistol, protectors of the weak, champions of justice. Because I have access to the same books and movies on my phone, I've started to consume them too.

It's surprisingly therapeutic, and touching. Through her wounded, unspoken front I see into her dreamworld, and it fills me with hope for her recovery.

And, by extension, hope for my own.

Through her window I can look down on the swarming roads and towers of Addenbrooke's. She follows my gaze, smiles.

'Yeah. It is a cool view.'

I sit on the chair next to her bed. On the little bedside cabinet there is a riot of brightly coloured greetings cards.

'You know what I'm going to say, don't you?' I ask.

'Um, no.' Her smile falters and she turns away, as though shutters have come down across her soul. It has been nearly three months, but Katie is not yet ready to discuss the cellar, or what happened to her, to the frustration of her support team. I can hardly blame her, really.

But when she is ready, I'll be here.

'I was going to say happy birthday.'

'What? Oh, yeah!' Her relief is palpable. 'But you're a day late.'

'Yeah, I'm sorry. The meeting with the lawyers was yesterday.'

'You met the lawyers?' Her eyes widen. 'I thought...'

'No, not that meeting with my lawyers. I meant my divorce.'

Her dark eyes are wary. She does not know what to say about my divorce. Despite all she has been through, she is still essentially a child.

'It's OK,' I say. 'I'm over it.'

The meeting had taken place in London, which is where Stephen, my solicitor and newfound indispensable person, works from a smart office near Gray's Inn. It was already late afternoon by the time I arrived, my guts heaving, my stomach in my mouth, and I was conducted into the ultra-modern meeting room and shown into a high-backed chair.

Eddy was already there. His presence was a physical shock, and I felt myself grow numb and light-headed.

Stephen's assistant, Tanya, then moved to the sideboard. Behind her, London was visible in a

358

milky dusk, framed by floor to ceiling windows. St Paul's poked up tinily, like a novelty sugar bowl, and I almost wanted to lift up the lid and peek inside.

'Would anyone like tea? Coffee?' she asked in a small fluting voice, like a bird.

I shook my head. So did Eddy.

'Not for me,' he said.

Eddy looked the same, and yet also not – he was, as always, fastidiously neat, but his exquisitely cut white shirt and small lapelled black jacket made him seem like someone playing a part, perhaps that of a gangster or Bond villain, and his glittering cufflinks appeared vulgar, particularly in the context of our meeting and what it was about. It was as though he had lost the power to fill his own clothes. He was a generic version of himself, constructed of discount materials.

Or perhaps it was I that had changed, and I saw him with different eyes.

Who knows.

'Penelope, you've had a chance to discuss the agreement with your client?' asked Stephen.

Eddy's solicitor was a woman, an ash-blonde tigress with a steely gaze, clad in a titanium-grey dress-suit and terrifying black patent high heels. I guessed instantly that this was the person who had advised him to get back with me so he could mortgage my house and use the proceeds to fight for his share of Sensitall's innards.

This consideration really warmed me towards her, as you might imagine.

'I have,' she replied firmly.

'Any questions?'

'No, we're fine.' She glanced at Eddy, who was pretending to be engrossed in the highly polished table top.

Stephen flipped open a folder and took out copies of the documents.

'Right then. Let's get on with it.'

This agreement was a lot less scary to me than it could have been, for one simple reason: Eddy had been paid £30,000 for revelations about me that had appeared in a national tabloid. In a bleakly hilarious twist, there was a question as to whether I was entitled to some of this money as part of our shared assets.

The sheer betrayal of it all still took my breath away. He told some grubby reporter everything I had confided to him in the secrecy of our bed, that I confessed while we walked, hand in hand, along Grantchester Grind or through the Fens themselves; all of those deep and hidden things, which it turns out were all lies anyway, tales spun by the Red Queen out of desperation and terror, and always flight, flight, flight. Stories about the drug use, the breakdowns, the distant clashing rocks of my imaginary past.

Neither of us, however, is interested in fighting about this now. I, at least, have other priorities. As a consequence, I will keep my house, Eddy will keep his flat, and we will have no further dealings with one another.

Stephen pushed the sheaf of paper towards him. 'Mr Lewis? You first.'

Eddy signed the documents quickly, contemptuously, as though this was all beneath him, and then shoved them over the desk to me.

There was a big cross drawn next to Margot Lewis, marking where I should sign my name. My pen paused over it, as though startled. After all, who is Margot Lewis? Can she legally sign documents? Does she even *exist* in any meaningful way?

In for a penny, in for a pound. My pen scratched decisively across the paper.

And just like that, we were done.

I lingered with Stephen on the steps of his offices while he fussed with his cashmere scarf.

'Well, that was awful,' I observed.

'Yes, but better to have it over and done with.' He fastened his coat against the cold breeze. Somewhere out there the City of London was knee-deep in rush hour, but here, in the medieval parkland of the Middle Temple, all was strangely quiet, serene. 'I don't think you've been holding out for a reconciliation.'

'Absolutely not.'

'Can I walk you to the station?'

'Thanks, that's very kind, but no. I'm meeting someone in the Delaunay.'

'At least let me flag you a cab from the road,' he said.

'No really, it's fine. I'd rather walk. And I haven't spotted any reporters – though I haven't properly beaten the shrubbery around here yet, so maybe I'm jumping to conclusions.' I barked out a laugh, but he wasn't fooled and he gave me a stern glance.

'It's nothing to joke about. This is going to get worse before it gets better, Mrs Lewis,' he said, in his fussy no-nonsense lawyer voice. 'There's

Christopher Meeks to consider. The arrest is just a taster. The trial will be a trial.'

He walked me up to High Holborn and left me with a cordial goodbye near Chancery Lane before being swallowed up by the swirling crowds descending into the Underground. I pulled my coat tighter around myself and ducked out of the human current, sliding in next to the kiosk dispensing the *Evening Standard* just until I could orient myself. The air smelled of fuel exhaust and hops. It was already nearly dark and the railings for the Tube entrance were cold at my back as I pulled out my phone, about to tap out a message.

Something made me glance up – a familiar voice.

Eddy was a mere few yards away, talking urgently into his phone, his forehead furrowed. 'I don't know what you mean,' he was saying, his hand straying up to his collar to tug it as he often did when nervous. 'I never promised...'

He turned, saw me. His mouth thinned. I could see him thinking – should I turn my back to her? Pretend I haven't seen her?

In the end, to my surprise, he did neither of those things.

'Look, I'll ring you back, all right?' He swiped the phone off, dropped it into his pocket and strolled over, with a little studied nonchalance, as though it meant nothing.

'Fancy meeting you here.'

'I know,' I said. 'I had business in town.'

'Yeah,' he said, clucking his tongue. 'Me too.'

He came and stood next to me, and we both stared out at the tide of commuters flowing past, while we rested in the little harbour provided by the kiosk.

We could have been spies, meeting to pass on information.

'You know,' he said after a few moments, and his jaw was tight, 'half of the stuff they printed in that newspaper didn't come from me. I don't know where they got that from.'

I sighed. The subject was already exhausted as far as I was concerned. Part of our signed agreement was that he promised never again to sell information about me to any newspaper or media outlet – rather like shutting the stable door after the horse is gone, in my view, but Stephen was insistent.

'It doesn't matter now,' I said. It didn't.

'I know I've hardly been the ideal husband,' he murmured, 'but I really am sorry it worked out this way.'

'Yeah. Me too.' My hands were cold and I shoved them into my pockets. On the road, taxis were honking at one another over some perceived slight. The chill had brought out the roses in his cheeks.

'Can I ask a question? Since we're here?'

'Sure,' I said. 'Why not?'

'Did you really not know you were this Bethan Avery person?'

I craned up to look at him. 'Are you serious?'

He shrugged, as if to say, Well yes.

'No,' I said coldly. 'No I didn't.'

It was his turn to sigh. 'I suppose it explains a few things.'

'Like what?'

'Like why our marriage failed.' He opened his palms, as though this were a fait accompli. 'I mean, if you had no idea who you were, how was *I* supposed to know who you were?'

I stood up straight. It was time to go.

'Does it matter? The important thing has always been that you knew who *you* were. You knew who you were and what you wanted and kept me posted.'

'But...'

I wanted to tell him that our marriage failed because he left me for another woman, because he was greedy and egotistical, but instead, I simply tightened my scarf around my neck.

'Eddy, I would love to stay and chat, but I have to go.' I extended a hand. 'I'll see you around, no doubt.'

He wanted to say more, I think, but realized it would be pointless. We shook hands, like business colleagues, and within moments the human swell of commuterdom had funnelled him away into the depths of the Central Line, leaving me alone.

Martin was waiting outside the Delaunay, chafing his gloved hands together.

'How did it go?' he asked.

'Eddy,' I sighed out. Though my old rage, that furious, uncontrollable chthonic monster, has now subsided, sunk back into the depths, I am still bitterly disappointed in Eddy. However, I was not surprised. I could see past it.

I was coping better than Martin, it seemed.

'You can't stop the greedy bastard selling his story again,' he said. 'He can just turn "anony-

364

mous source", and unless we catch him red-handed, there's nothing you can do.' He ground one fist into his palm, an unconscious gesture of rage. 'Just so you know.'

I nodded. I understood.

'Are you all right?' he asked, and one of those hands now closed around my own.

'Yes, I'm fine.' I actually meant it.

'Are you ready to celebrate your divorce?'

I gazed up at the brilliantly lit windows of the restaurant, and bit my lip. It smelled good. It looked good.

'Yeah, I am...' I was tired, and not terribly publicly inclined right then, but there was no way to say this without hurting him.

'You're not so sure, are you?'

I hesitated, mortified that my feelings had been so obvious to him. This was meant to be a treat he'd planned for me, after all.

'You know,' he said, and there was a warm twinkle in his eye as he slipped my hand into his pocket, 'it's entirely possible to celebrate divorces at home too, and in equally splendid style. Which is an option we should consider.'

'But I–'

'No. Not another word. You're exhausted, I can tell. Let's get a takeaway, stay in and chill some champagne.'

I grinned at him, pleased and relieved that he got it.

'Yeah,' I said. 'Let's go home.'

I took the arm he offered, and we began the journey back to Little Wilbraham, to the house on the Fens.

'What do I call you now?' he asked me, the first time he took me back there. His voice was thick, drowsy.

I turned around in his arms. I had been sure he was asleep. I do not really sleep, myself, not yet.

'What do you call me?'

I had been dodging this question for nearly two weeks at that point. I told everybody I was too exhausted to think about it – the reporters, the police, concerned well-wishers ... the parents of the other murdered girls. Yes, I've been meeting them too. Again and again, I keep waiting for them to confront me – if Bethan, the first victim, had gone to the police instead of on some seventeen-year amnesiac bender, then so many lives might have been saved.

But none of them confront me.

Instead, they pity me.

It's much, much worse.

'Yes, you silly mare,' said Martin. 'You need a name.'

He was quite right. I must pick an identity and stick with it. Until then, I was in limbo.

'I can't decide,' I said. 'I don't want to be Bethan Avery – you know, the mad girl who was kidnapped and kept in a cellar, then forgot about it for nearly twenty years. And I'm not sure I'm legally allowed to be Margot Lewis still.'

'I can't see why you'd want to be Lewis anyway.'

Well, that much was definitely true.

They fired me in the end, once Eddy's revelations hit the papers.

366

It was bound to happen, of course. It's a different world nowadays, or so they would have you believe. What with the dissociative amnesia, identity theft, fugue states and putting a child molester's eye out – it all marks a girl's card.

To be fair to St Hilda's, I wasn't exactly fired; I was placed on leave while 'everything got sorted out', as the head said, but we both knew I would never be coming back. I was lucky nobody was pressing charges against me, and at that point it was by no means clear that they wouldn't in future.

Lily took me out to buy me exit cocktails at the Varsity Hotel rooftop bar, to take away the sting, but it was such a faff getting security to throw the reporters out that I couldn't, for the life of me, relax for the first couple of hours.

That said, once they were gone, it's impossible to stay unhappy up there, with the beautiful vista of Cambridge spread out on all sides, the frowsy towers and ivied walls, the emerald-green patches of garden, the river with its bracketing willows.

Also, they have booze.

'What will you do?' she asked me.

'Years and years of therapy,' I knocked back the remains of my white port Martini. 'Or so they tell me.'

She tried to fight through the discomfort the idea gave her, and put on a brave face. I love her for that.

'No, I mean, what will you *do?* How will you live?'

I set the glass on the table, looked to catch the waiter's eye.

'One day at a time.'

'Sweet Jesus.'

'I see what you did there. Very droll.'

She mimed a crash of cymbals, and I laughed out loud for the first time since I'd arrived.

'There's a third alternative,' murmured Martin into my hair.

'Yes?'

'You could choose a new name. People do in these situations.'

I fell silent. This had occurred to me before.

'A new name.' I relaxed into his shifting grip. I didn't say my primary thought out loud – but it feels like more running. 'What would it be?'

'Anything you like. Jane Smith. Princess Cuddlybottom. Spot...'

'Spot?!' I slapped at his hand.

'Desperate Davinia, the Most Wanted Woman in East Anglia...'

'Now you're talking...'

'Keith Bloggs. *HMS Pinafore*. Knickerbocker Glory. The Big Easy...'

I laughed, smothering it against his chest. 'The sky's the limit, I suppose.'

'I think you would have trouble fitting that on a credit card, but yeah, it could work.'

I sighed happily.

From then on, in private, he refers to me as Ms Limit.

Katie tries to sit up, perhaps moved by my sombre mood, and I can see her wince. This has been her third, and hopefully last, bout of surgery.

368

'How did the birthday go?'

'It was all right,' she says. She looks down at the bed. 'I'm sorry about your divorce.'

'Thank you.'

'Are you ... OK?' Her dark eyes are guarded, will probably always be guarded now, but there is that flicker of kindness in them.

'Yes. He's a wanker, so I'm better off not married to him.'

She nods, relieved. This is also her opinion.

Ours is a deeply strange relationship. Margot, or more properly Mrs Lewis, was her teacher, the authority figure. Bethan is her comrade-in-arms, the only other person in the world who knows what it was like, who survived the cellar. But Bethan is fractured and frequently missing. For all her youth, Katie has more mental strength than Bethan ever did. In that sense, she leads me, and not the other way around.

And in leading me, she leads herself.

'It was dreadful, what he did to you. Saying all that stuff to the papers...'

I shrug. 'You know, it doesn't make him less of an arse, but in a way I'm glad.'

She looks sharply at me, her smooth brow bent into a slight frown.

'It was exhausting, living a lie, never trusting anyone, always terrified I'd be discovered. And it gave me excuses – reasons to not examine why I didn't have a normal, joined-up life, why I never stayed in touch with anyone. I always knew something was very, very wrong with me, I just never dared look too closely at why.' I sigh. 'This way I'm forced to confront who I was. What I did to the

369

real Margot.'

She visibly double-takes. 'There was a real Margot? I don't understand. I thought it was a name you made up.'

'No,' I say. 'I didn't make her up.'

My psychiatrist is a clean-cut thirty-something called Yufeng. It was he that I was finally referred to once Katie and I were wheeled out of the Grove in that ambulance, the doctor that Greta was trying to call on that last mad day that I became Bethan Avery again.

I get the impression he's quite senior at the hospital, a hotshot with a growing international reputation, and that I'm something of a coup for him. He very kindly, after he was assigned to me, asked me if I would prefer a woman, and I told him no, I was good with this if he was. We get on – I can make him laugh from time to time despite himself – which makes me feel a lot more comfortable.

Together we embark on the course of drug-induced trances and psychotherapy my recovery requires. He tapes these sessions, and we listen to them together; I hear my own voice in the echoing acoustics of the digital recording, and don't know it. It is Bethan Avery's voice.

I was right to pick him in spite of gender empathy, as it turns out, because though the therapy has been exhausting and turbulent he has proved to be an unshakeable guide.

I told him that I am not that interested in recovering what happened with Christopher Meeks all those years ago, unless it is of material aid to the on-going police investigation.

'You're not?' asks Yufeng, his hands steepled together, his focus in action. 'Why not?'

'I have always been much less interested in Christopher Meeks than he has been in me, and I see no reason for that to change. He's going to get the full life tariff, isn't he? I mean, they found those girls buried in the garden. He's never coming out, right?'

'It's very unlikely,' said Yufeng.

I offered him a little twist of a smile. 'Well, then.'

'You don't want to know why he did those things? You're not curious?'

My eyes narrowed, and I could almost feel him retreat, as though he had taken a psychic step backward. The shadow of my old rage lay over me.

But just for a moment. Then it was gone, like clouds passing over the face of the sun.

'Yufeng,' I said. 'I already know everything about him that I'll ever need. What I want to know now is, how did I become Margot?'

Some things I do not yet remember, and I have to take on faith. I remember escaping the Grove now, but very little else has come back spontaneously or even under hypnosis, and I have been told to expect that most of it may never.

They found evidence that I tried to make a reverse charge call to my grandmother's house, and the new tenants – I'd been gone for two months by this time – told me she was dead. I do not recall this.

There was a coach journey to London Victoria. I don't know how I got the clothes or money. I don't remember losing the nightdress.

But incredibly enough, there is a record that these things happened.

It is forty seconds of CCTV footage that has survived by accident – linked to another case.

It's Victoria Coach Station in jerky black and white.

The grainy film shows a young girl, with a slightly halting, stiff gait – perhaps she's been cramped in the coach, or perhaps she's recovering from some kind of fight – certainly she's been injured. She wears a dirty dark hoodie and loose, ill-fitting pants. Despite the cold March evening she is clad in cheap flip-flops. She has no bag. She crosses the empty bus lanes with the other passengers to reach the concourse, where the camera is, in jolting stop-motion, and as she grows nearer my heart starts to hammer.

The small gaggle of pedestrians slow, as the ones with luggage mount the kerb. At the back, the girl, who has been glancing carefully all around herself, raises her head and spots the camera.

I stop breathing. I can see the dark eyes, the haunted expression. Though her nose is swollen and misshapen, badly broken, and her bottom lip is dark where it's been split, I see Bethan Avery. But for the first time, I can also see me inside her.

On the last night I am out with Angelique, I tell Yufeng in my drug-drenched trance, we are somewhere out in Canary Wharf in the ruins of Docklands. Angelique is looking for this ex of hers who owes her some money. We find him, and some manner of exchange takes place under the pillars

372

of South Quay DLR, the details of which she is very hazy about, but it involves her disappearing and leaving me alone for the best part of two hours, while I hide on a bench, partly concealed from the street by scaffolding. In fact, when she returns she is still very hazy, with that dead-eyed glaze that she wears more and more often.

I am furious and frightened because we are very likely going to miss the curfew and my bed will be given away for the night. The thought fills me with a thudding dread. What if I never get it back, and am stuck out here for ever with Angelique, in her London full of junkies and squats, unexplained favours and needle marks? This is a very real danger, as because I have no legal ID, the nuns cannot forward me on to social services as is their usual process if you stay longer than ten days. There is the real possibility that their patience will run out with me, particularly if I am regularly truant from my bed.

But I cannot tell them that I am Bethan Avery. Not now, not ever.

We need to get back before curfew, and she is making us late.

The DLR, however, is shut for repairs. We will have to walk to Canary Wharf proper. The night nips us with cold and we have no coats.

We are moving past a deserted, boarded-up house when I feel her slow.

'Come on,' I snap.

'Can't we stop for a minute?' Her eyes drift towards the house.

'No! We're going to lose our beds for the night.'

'Go on, Amy.' This is what she calls me. It's the

373

false name I gave at the shelter.

'No,' I say coldly.

She doesn't reply, instead voting with her feet, drifting off towards the semi-boarded door.

I can't leave her alone in this condition.

Oh, fuck it.

I follow her.

We pad into the house. It stinks of urine and mould, but at least it's empty. And so is Angelique, her arms slightly outset at her sides, her fingers gently waving, as though she is swimming through the fetid closeness of the old house.

I don't like this. 'Angelique,' I say. 'Why can't you wait until we get back to Flicks?'

It's a rhetorical question, and as I say it I can hear the defeat in my voice. She can't wait because she can't wait.

I try another tack, as I see her plump down on the filthy floor. 'I am not sitting in here all night.'

Also doomed, I realize, as she flaps a hand at me. 'Just a taste. It's cold out there. Just to get me home.'

I sigh. 'Just a taste.'

I watch her get her kit out – a Hello Kitty pencil case. She has about six disposable lighters in it, only one of which works at any given time. Once she has fixed herself up, she offers some to me, without enthusiasm.

'No. Absolutely not.'

Instead, I light one of her cigarettes and sit there fuming silently while her eyes roll back in her head and she makes a little coughing noise. Then she coughs again, more loudly. She slumps sideways on to her side like a wax doll in the process of melting, and I sigh, hard, realizing that I'll never get her back to Flicks while she's like this.

It takes me a little while – until I finish my cigarette – to notice that she's not breathing any more.

The ambulance seems to take for ever to come. I phoned it from the telephone box two streets away, and gave what I considered very clear directions to the derelict house, but they still stumble about for another ten minutes before I hear one shouting from within that he's found her.

I stand on the corner, with the rest of the street flotsam, watching. My grip on Angelique's little Hello Kitty bag is so tight my fingers hurt.

When I understood she was dead, there was a strange moment when I stopped swearing at her and commanding her to breathe. My conscious emotion was a kind of irritated fury, but to my surprise, I then burst into a hot white flood of fat breathless tears, squirting out with the force of bullets. I am, for some time, unable to master myself, even though in the back of my head I can hear a voice like hers screaming, 'GET UP, GET OUT, THE PLOD WILL COME YOU STUPID COW!' and I know it's right, I know it's true, but I cannot move.

The telephone box stinks of urine and is dotted with cards for prostitutes. I rub my wet red eyes with a scrap of tissue I find in her bag. The tissue is spotted with tiny drops of her blood.

I put the tissue back in the bag, and in the bottom I can see the last remaining detritus of her life. A new packet of three condoms, one missing. A half pack of mint Polos. A little bottle of Ysatis. A small roll of banknotes, perhaps as much as a hundred pounds. This astonishes me. I don't think I've ever held this much money at one time before now.

There are also a few cards in the bottom of the purse – entries into clubs, vouchers for free food at charities. But there is also one – laminated – and I turn it over under the streetlights as the wail of the ambulance dies down, examining it under the hectic red and blue lights.

It's a college ID card for West Hyrett School, which I've never heard of but is apparently in Essex and 'Encouraging Excellence'. There's a passport photo on it of someone it takes me a second to identify – a studious brunette with thick glasses and bright pink lipstick. It's Angelique, of course, in her previous life, her hair a lacklustre centre parting, but her big eyes and good skin glowing through. I don't recognize the name beneath the picture. She smiles, that crooked, secretive smile. I can feel the tears – powerful but mysterious – fighting their way back.

But I remember where I am. I drop the card back into the pencil case, drop it all in her handbag and holster it over my shoulder. The ambulance men have not come out of the house, but the police have arrived. It's time for me to go. Tilting my head down and away, I head back towards the bright lights of London Bridge and a place to spend the night.

She didn't look like a Margot.

'You took her name.' Katie's hands are laced together over her bandages as she relaxes back on the bed.

'Yes. I stole it. I stole her life.'

'Stole it?' Katie considers this. 'You sound like, I dunno, you feel guilty.'

'No,' I say. 'Not guilty. She didn't need it any more. I did. But still.' I sigh. 'It wasn't mine.'

Katie is silent. She is thinking it; what Martin is thinking, what I am thinking.

I leave her with a kiss.

When I get home, I have barely hung my coat up before the doorbell rings behind me.

It's Susannah, or more properly Detective Constable Watson, who came to my house after the letters were verified.

'Hiya, Margot.' She grins at me. I'd seen a lot of both her and Eamonn (her boss) during the trial and we'd all become quite friendly, but that was a couple of months ago.

'Hello,' I respond, surprised. 'Come in. I'll put the kettle on.'

She shakes her head. 'Thanks, but no, I can't this time. I'm really just passing by, but there was something I had to drop off to you and I thought, no time like the present.'

She holds out a small brown packet that she has taken out of her handbag.

I regard it with curiosity and a touch of reluctance.

'Take it,' she says kindly. 'It's nothing bad. We need to return this to you.'

When she's gone and I have shut the door, I open the packet with shaking fingers.

Inside there is a paper bag, secured with a

sticker marked 'EVIDENCE', some numbers and my name. I rip the seal, shaking the contents of the bag out into my palm.

The little tarnished silver cross and chain glint back at me.

I know the story of this necklace now. It came out in Christopher Meeks's confession. I stir the dull links with one finger, thinking.

After a moment I lift it up and fasten it around my neck.

Tomorrow I'll take it into the jewellers and get it cleaned.

But for now, it's fine.

'So, am I coming to yours tonight?' he asks.

I am silent, thinking, my mobile pressed to my ear.

'Margot?'

'You know what, Martin, can I come to yours instead?'

'What? Yes, of course. Is something the matter?'

I play with the cross with my free hand, gently turning the cool silver in my fingers, feeling the chain brush my neck. 'No. But there's something I need to do, and I might be back quite late.'

'Is it what you were talking about last week?' he asks.

'Yeah.'

'Do you want me to come?'

I think for a moment. That's so, so tempting.

'No,' I say finally. 'Thanks. But I need to do it alone.'

'If you're sure.'

I bite my lip. 'Yeah. I am.'

It is late when I reach my destination – nearly seven o'clock – and the sun has set. I have second thoughts about the whole endeavour, but somehow I manage to find the little road and bang the ornate knocker.

When Flora Bellamy answers and sees me, her face sets like iron.

I hold up my hands, palms outward.

'It's all right. I understand if you don't want to speak to me, and if you like, I'll go.'

There is silence as she waits for me to state my business, but I can see the thin skin on her knuckles whitening around the door.

I realize that there is no other way to do this.

'My name is Bethan Avery,' I say. 'And I knew your daughter.'

Acknowledgements

An acknowledgement is a terrifying thing to write – no book, or indeed writer, happens in isolation. If I have missed anyone out here, I apologize now. It was not intentional.

I'd like to thank everyone at Michael Joseph, in particular my editor Emad Akhtar (and his wonderful, perceptive suggestions for the text), my publicist Ellie Hughes and my copy-editor Shauna Bartlett. I'd also like to thank Claire Wachtel and Hannah Wood at HarperCollins and Sally Wofford-Girand at Union Literary in the US for believing in me.

None of this would have been remotely possible without my agent Judith Murray and her unflagging faith, encouragement, and good counsel, so all praise goes to her and to everyone at Greene and Heaton.

I could go no further without acknowledging my buds from my bookselling days – in particular Jon Atkin, Lesley Baker, Trish Beswick, Sam Hobbs, Marie Kervin, Nick Lewis, Julian Rafot and the rest of the Manchester crew. Thanks, guys.

I owe a huge debt to the T Party writing group in London, and to the following people for a fund of friendship and laughter: Jack Calverley, Peter Colley, Gary Couzens, Sarah Ellender, David

Gullen, Caroline Hooton, Julia Knight, Martin Owton, Sumit Paul-Choudhury, Tom Pollock, Rosanne Rabinowitz, Gaie Sebold, Allyson Shaw and Sara Jayne Townsend, as well as Raymond Dickey, Chuck Dreyer, Gordon Fraser, Lucia Graves and Luke Thomas. I would also like to remember Mark McCann and Denni Schnapp, who are sadly missed.

Special thanks must go to KD Grace for her unflinching encouragement, hours of writing talk, wonderful Anglo-American Christmasses and for not panicking that time I nearly drowned us on the way home from Avebury. Blame the ghost – I do.

Likewise, love is owed to the dazzlingly clever Melanie Garrett for gourmet cookery, inspired criticism, big ideas and bigger cocktails. She taught me that there is no problem in life or literature that cannot be knitted into submission. The next coffee in Cobham is on me.

I also gratefully remember Iain Banks, a generous friend and cherished correspondent who at all times and in all places showed me how to be a real writer.

Finally I'd be nothing without my friends and family. To Julie Revell, who never reads anything I write; to my brothers John and Joseph and my sister Jacqueline and to their families; and at last to my long-suffering parents, George and Ellen Callaghan – thanks. We got there in the end.

The publishers hope that this book has given you enjoyable reading. Large Print Books are especially designed to be as easy to see and hold as possible. If you wish a complete list of our books please ask at your local library or write directly to:

Magna Large Print Books
Magna House, Long Preston,
Skipton, North Yorkshire.
BD23 4ND

This Large Print Book for the partially sighted, who cannot read normal print, is published under the auspices of

THE ULVERSCROFT FOUNDATION

THE ULVERSCROFT FOUNDATION

... we hope that you have enjoyed this Large Print Book. Please think for a moment about those people who have worse eyesight problems than you ... and are unable to even read or enjoy Large Print, without great difficulty.

You can help them by sending a donation, large or small to:

**The Ulverscroft Foundation,
1, The Green, Bradgate Road,
Anstey, Leicestershire, LE7 7FU,
England.**
or request a copy of our brochure for more details.

The Foundation will use all your help to assist those people who are handicapped by various sight problems and need special attention.

Thank you very much for your help.

96.